Sing Sweet Nightingale

The Dream War Saga

Erica Cameron

Spencer Hill Press

Spencer Hill Press

Contact: Spencer Hill Press, PO Box 247, Contoocook, NH 03229, USA

Please visit our website at www.spencerhillpress.com

First Edition: March 2014
Erica Cameron
Sing Sweet Nightingale / by Erica Cameron – 1st ed.
p. cm.
Summary: Demons invade the dreams of children and create fantasy worlds in their heads and the only boy to ever escape has to show a girl that her dream is nightmare before she's trapped forever.

Cover design by Jeremy West
Interior layout by Jenny Perinovic

ISBN 978-1937053963 (paperback)
ISBN 978-1937053970 (e-book)

Printed in the United States of America

For my mom, Corey, who is always proud of my success but would love me even if I failed.

Also, for Lani. This story wouldn't have been born or found such a loving home without you.

...and hereafter she may suffer—
both in waking, from her nerves,
and in sleep, from her dreams.
Bram Stoker, Dracula

They who dream by day are
cognizant of many things
which escape those who
dream only by night.
Edgar Allan Poe

One

Hudson

Friday, May 23 – 12:34 PM

I hate this park. Wouldn't ever come here again if J.R. didn't like it so much.

My little brother is running circles around himself on the path a few feet ahead, his arms out like an airplane. My gaze jumps from him to the red oaks on either side. There are too many shadowy hiding places between those trees. I know. I've used them before.

Lifting my hand to the olive-branch wreath pendant I got from Calease, I take a deep breath, calming myself like she taught me. In four, hold four, out four. Repeat. Under my calloused thumb, I can feel the bumps and ridges of the glass leaves. I focus on the soft, white, otherworldly glow surrounding it and turn toward my brother.

I drop my pendant as soon as I look up. J.R. is nowhere in sight.

Heart pounding, I scan the path. There's no one here.

"J.R.?"

He doesn't respond. My hands clench. Despite the warm spring air, I'm chilled.

"C'mon, kid. Where'd you go?"

I'm straining for any sound. Someone running with a struggling four-year-old, or the whimper of a kid who tripped and skinned his knees. Anything. Something to lead me in the right direction. Only because I'm concentrating so hard do I hear his soft, muffled giggle.

When I zero in on a low shrub to my left, the tension drains from my body in a single flood. I catch him just as he shifts behind the plant, his shock of white-blond hair poking out from behind the evergreen leaves.

I run my hand over my own buzzed-short hair and grin. It's rare when the kid can find a good hiding spot. He's too much like me—too tall for his age and cursed with hair that practically glows in the dark.

"J.R.?" I keep looking around like I don't know where he went. Walking backward toward the bush, I check everywhere except his hiding spot.

The bush comes up to my knees. As soon as the branches poke the back of my legs, I strike. Spinning around, I reach over the bush and grab him around the waist.

"No fair! No fair!" His skin is flushed bright red. He pouts and crosses his arms when I hold him against my chest. "No fair, Hu'son. I'm too tall!" He rubs his hands over his hair, pushing down on his head like he can make himself shrink by force.

I laugh and pull his hands away. "It doesn't work, kid. Trust me, I've tried."

At four, he's as tall as some six-year-olds. I was the same way, and nothing I did kept me from topping out at six-five. From what I can tell, my kid brother's gonna end up following in my footsteps. Hopefully, he's not *too* much like me. Looks are one thing, but if he gives Mom and Dad the same problems I did, constantly getting in fights and bringing trouble home, they'll probably boot him out of the house faster than they did me. At least he won't be alone. I'll be eighteen next week. If it comes to that, he won't have to live on the streets like I did. I'll be there to take care of him.

"Ready to go home?" It's not really a question; I'm already heading in that direction.

Nose wrinkling, J.R. shakes his head and grabs my pendant, rubbing his fingers over the etched glass. He thinks it's cool because it's mine, but he can't see the glow. No one can but me.

"Aren't you hungry?" I ask.

A hesitation, but he shakes his head again. "No."

"Really? Are you *sure*? I think Mom was making pizza for lunch."

His face lights up, his pale blue eyes shining as he bounces in my arms. "Pizza! Pizza! Hu'son, can I put on the roni?"

"*Pepp*eroni," I say.

"P'roni. Peh'roni." His nose scrunches up, and he sticks out his tongue. He tries a few more times until the frustration gets to him. "Roni!" he finally shouts, giving up on trying to get it right.

I laugh. "Good enough."

J.R. chatters for a few seconds about the bird he saw chasing a squirrel away from its nest this morning until, out of nowhere, he says, "Who's that?"

"Who?" I look around, but I don't see anyone worth questioning. We've gone beyond the playground area, and this section is almost deserted. On a bench ahead of us, there's a guy asleep with oversized headphones on, and behind a row of trees a jogger is on the path, but that's it.

"No, there." J.R. puts his tiny hand on my cheek and pushes my face the other direction.

As soon as I look, my blood turns to ice. Three guys are approaching fast. The tallest one has tattoos running down his neck and covering one arm, and the shorter guy on his right is built like a linebacker but moves like a track star. I hear a blade click into place, and my eyes lock on the third. He's moving slower than the others, but the look in his dark eyes scares me more than the other two combined.

Heart pounding, my arms tighten around my brother's legs. His weight presses my glass pendant into my chest. Calease gave it to me when I made her a promise. *No more fighting,* I swore. Ever. It was part of the deal we made two years ago, after she helped me control the anger and the instincts that kept getting my ass in trouble. The same kind of trouble that's found me now.

"Hey, buddy. Do you remember the way home from here?" I'm already jogging toward the exit. Gotta get him closer to the street. It's only a few blocks to home. The last thing I want to do is send him into the city by himself, but I have to. If I run, I'll lead these guys right to my doorstep. It looks like they came prepared. There's no guarantee they don't have backup waiting outside the park. I doubt they're gonna let me go, but they might overlook J.R. He's just a kid.

J.R. nods. "I 'member. It's right and then left and then left and then—"

That'll at least get him to our neighborhood.

"Want to race?" I put him down and push him toward the street.

"Ready." His eyes widen, and he grins.

"Set." His face settles into that intense concentration only little kids seem capable of.

"Go!"

J.R. is off like a shot. As soon as he rounds the corner onto the main street, I turn toward trouble.

"Shoulda walked right by that night," the tall one growls at me.

Calease always warned me that my past would come back to bite me. Looks like she was right. I don't know who they are or what I did to them, but that doesn't matter now.

The psycho with the knife jumps in, blade plunging toward my chest. I duck and slide away, backing closer to one of the trees. I may not be allowed to fight them, but I'm not gonna stand here and let them stab me either.

I keep them in sight but look around, hoping someone comes up the path. They'll rush me as soon as I go for my phone. I'm fast, but I can't dodge them all. If I can catch someone's eye, I might have a chance of getting out alive.

Shit. Now they *all* have switchblades. The linebacker grins at me and flips his knife, catching it easily by the hilt.

"Shoulda stayed the hell outta our way," he says.

I have no clue what he's talking about. I don't have the chance to ask.

Two of them surge forward. I squeeze between them, letting their swings arc toward each other instead of me. They pull back in time to avoid slashing each other open. I try to dodge around the tall one, but he's faster than I expected. I barely duck in time. His knife catches my shoulder instead of my throat, slicing through shirt, skin, and muscle like butter.

Flexing my hand makes my eyes water. I almost scream. My arm burns like someone dumped lit propane over my skin, but it moves. Until one of them locks my arms behind me.

I break his hold on one arm. Before I can free the other, a blade slices along my ribs. This time, I can't keep from screaming.

There might be a couple seconds left before one of them lands a death blow. I could yank myself free and slam their knives into their own chests. I want to. But I catch sight of the pulsing white light surrounding Calease's pendant.

I can't do it. I *can't* do it.

I can't break my promise, but because of that promise, I'm going to die.

Jesus, I'm glad J.R. got the hell out of here.

A high-pitched shriek splits the air. All three of them cringe, looking around for cops. They think it's a siren, but I know what's coming a second before the tiny body throws itself into the mess. I heard it once. When he woke up from a nightmare.

Screaming like a banshee, my little brother flings himself into the fight and bites into the arm of my captor.

"Shit!" The guy drops his knife and shoves J.R. away. J.R. lands on the concrete with a thud, but only for a second. Before I can worry that the kid's been knocked out, he's up and launching himself back into the fray.

"Leave my Hu'son 'lone!" he shrieks.

Tough as they are, willing as they are to fillet me like a fish, all three of them hesitate when faced with a four-year-old.

I don't.

Fuck promises. I made that promise to Calease to keep my brother safe from exactly what's happening now. Not even for her will I stand by and watch him die.

Shoving my last captor away, I raise my arm to knock his head right off his neck—

And I can't move.

I can't *move.*

Why the hell can't I move?!

My head is locked down, and I'm looking straight at the pendant Calease gave me. It's always glowed with a faint white light, but the light is ten times brighter now. And it's not white anymore. It's orange.

Someone punches me in the stomach. The air pushes out of my lungs. I still can't move. It's as though I've been covered in concrete. I try to shift my weight, balance myself, strike back. There's nothing I can do to keep myself from tumbling backward.

My head cracks against the pavement. The spots in my vision clear in time for me to watch the knife arc toward my chest. I can't close my eyes.

So, I have to watch when J.R. tugs on my assailant's arm, trying to pull the knife away from me, and accidentally guides it straight into his own chest.

For the space of a single heartbeat, the world is so motionless it's as though time has stopped. All three of my would-be assassins stand over J.R., their faces masks of horror. Shock is the one thing keeping me alive. Keeping me from breaking in half.

And then the bloodstain starts growing on his pale blue shirt.

"NO!"

Something in my chest shatters, the shards shooting through my body like acid-dipped shrapnel. The orange light from my pendant pulses, and the glass is suddenly like an ice cube against my skin, but whatever was holding me paralyzed breaks.

Surging to my feet, I kick the closest body out of the way to get to J.R. I don't give a shit about them. I need to get him to a hospital.

"What the fuck did you do?" one of them screams above my head.

Sirens fade in from a distance. All three run, shoving their knives into their pockets as they tear out of the park.

"It's gonna be okay," I whisper, gently scooping him into my arms and running toward the gate.

J.R.'s eyes are wide, and his skin is pale. Too pale. He's not crying, but his breathing is getting worse. Like the air is being blocked by something. Something wet.

Before I reach the sidewalk, a cop car zooms past, directed in their chase by a lady on the other side of the street frantically pointing south. She looks up and sees me. Screaming for help, she rushes over.

She nearly screams again when her eyes lock on J.R.

"The cops are already here—an ambulance should be here any second." Her words spill together in a rush, and her dark eyes fill with tears when she sees what I already know. "Any second" may already be a second too late. I can't even try to stop the bleeding because I can't risk moving the knife. It's too close to his lungs. His heart.

The woman closes her eyes, her dark hands pressing against my arm. "Oh Lord, help us."

He's getting lighter. As though the blood dripping onto the pavement is all there is of him, and as it drains, he's actually fading out of my arms. Fading out of existence.

The hilt of the knife is sticking out of his chest, his little hands holding onto it.

"Hu'son?" He smiles a little. It's a smile I recognize—the little grin he always wears when he's going to sleep thinking about something happy. "I saved you," he says.

My knees buckle. Only the stranger's hands on my arm make it possible to sink instead of fall. The sun is shining overhead, and the sky is clear. It's a warm spring day. A few cars have stopped to see what's wrong, and a circle of strangers is slowly surrounding us. Beyond that, life is going on like nothing has happened. But J.R.'s blood is running over my hands, staining the sidewalk red and warming my skin when everything else has gone so cold.

I hear a siren different from the others—the ambulance finally arriving.

It's too late. His labored breathing has fallen silent.

Swallowing, I try to answer. To say goodbye. To say anything.

It takes a minute before I finally manage to tell him, "Yeah, kid. You saved me."

But I should've been the one who saved him.

Under Calease's guidance, I spent four years learning to dam up my anger, control it, and release it. She taught me in the name of helping me. She kept me out of trouble and made sure I earned my way back home.

Four years of work vanish the moment I feel J.R.'s life flicker out.

The one time I *really* needed help, Calease failed me. The promise I made wasn't supposed to stop me from protecting the people I loved. It *shoul*• *n't* have stopped me. But as soon as I tried to, I lost everything. *Everything.*

Only hours have passed, but it feels like years. I can't go home. There isn't one to go back to anymore. When my mom got home from the hospital, she expressed her grief by throwing all my shit onto the front lawn and trying to start a fucking bonfire. I barely got there in time to stop her.

Pacing the narrow motel room, I wait. Every night for four years, Calease has found me. No matter where I was at midnight, she could find me. I'm betting it won't be different tonight.

When the light comes, the first thing I notice is the color. It used to be white. Always white. It's not now. It's the same deep orange my pendant has been glowing since... since.

Wider and wider, the doorway opens until a solid lasso of light shoots out the center, straight for me.

I dodge, but it follows me like it's locked onto my scent. It wraps around my chest, and I tense, waiting for it to burn. Nothing happens. At least, nothing that hurts. Instead, the light sinks into my head, locks around my mind, and pulls.

It feels like peeling a huge patch of skin off a sunburn, but magnified a million times. I grit my teeth and wrench back, holding on to everything. It's been a long time since I've been awake when the doorway opens. Is *this* what she does to me every night? Rips me in half to drag me into her world?

Trying to pull free, I look down. The lasso is going straight through the pendant hanging around my neck. I yank it off, and the noose lightens. Gathering strength, I focus on what I want from her, why I'm physically stepping across the border between our worlds tonight.

J.R.'s face when the knife plunged into his chest.

His smile when he reminded me he saved my life.

The utter anguish on my mom's face as she screamed at me.

Rage, black rage I haven't felt in years, burns through my veins. It heightens the adrenaline already coursing through my body, making my muscles tremble.

I start shaking, and the lasso of energy vibrates with me. Blue lines appear in the orange rope of light like fractures in cement. Small chunks break off. Larger ones. Faster and faster until finally it shatters with a *crack*.

For the first time since the first time, I physically step into the world I visit every night in my dreams. There's a slight buzz against my skin as I pass through the glowing doorway of orange light. I shudder on the other side. It's cold. Colder than it's ever been before.

At first glance, it looks the same—evenly spaced wood pillars and reed-mat floor, the boxing ring in the distance, and the mountains as a backdrop to it all. Then I look closer. The pillars are cracking, and the floor is missing half its reeds. I was standing there just last night, but now the boxing ring looks like it's been left to rot for decades.

I catch the state of it all in a second. It's strange, but I don't give a shit. The single part of this world I want to see tonight is the woman facing me. The one who kept me from saving my brother.

Calease stands there like a warrior queen, not showing a hint of the decay surrounding her. Her curves are on display more than usual, hugged by a leather outfit straight out of *Xena,* and her white hair, normally loose and hanging down her back, is pulled tight and braided in a crown atop her head. She stares at me, her chin raised and her ice-blue eyes steady. Her eyes used to remind me of the sky on a crisp, clear autumn day.

Now the color reminds me of J.R.

"You broke your promise." Her voice, once so soft and serene, now bites. It grates more than the smirk that lifts the corner of her full lips. "Well, you tried to."

"To save my *brother's* life!"

She arches one eyebrow. "You should have run. Have I not taught you there is nothing to fear in running? Battles are not worth the fight, Hudson."

"*This* one was!" My hands clench so tight the leaves of my glass pendant bite into my skin, and the sharp edges I've never noticed before now dig in so deep I might be drawing blood.

"*No* battle is worth the price. If you value one life over another—take one to save another—you will become what you were when I found you: a dangerous child on his way to becoming a monster."

It's not the first time she's reminded me of my past, but it is the first time those words don't quite ring true. Those guys in the park knew me. Did I know them?

Something sparks in my mind, a little burst like a bolt of static electricity.

I *did* know them. I know all three, but I haven't seen them since my testimony put them in juvie for assault and battery. Those guys today, they weren't after me to avenge some wrong I did. They were after me because I'd *helped* someone—an old man who couldn't fight back when three fifteen-year-old gang wannabes attacked him late one night.

That one memory cracks the dam I didn't know existed.

More memories—thousands of moments from my own life—flood in.

Looking at the scars on my arms, I begin to remember the fights that marked my skin. Standing up for the deaf kid in third grade who didn't understand why the fifth-grader kept pushing him down. And the girl from the projects who came to school in the same dress every day—I kept her from ending up in the hospital when three girls from her neighborhood jumped her. One by one, I remember all the people I've known over the years, the reasons I couldn't keep myself out of trouble. Not because I went looking for it, but because I didn't know how to stand back and let shit happen.

The memories hit me like blows until I'm struggling for breath. My vision doubles.

"What have you done to me?" I gasp around the burning in my chest.

Her eyes begin to glow, their color shifting darker and deeper. The brighter they glow, the harder it becomes to look away.

"I saved you from a meaningless existence in service to mindless idiots. They would have used up whatever will you possessed and spat you out broken and bleeding." I'm folded over as she walks forward and runs her hand over my short hair. Her touch is icy and sends shudders through my entire body. "At least this way you will die young."

My chest aches. My lungs burn. My head pounds. Until I remembered, part of me hoped today had been some awful mistake. That something had gone wrong and Calease would help me find a way to make it right.

It wasn't. Trusting her was the mistake.

Her hand pressing against the back of my head, she bends down until she's eye level with me.

"Humans really are pathetic creatures. Shining talents trapped within worthless, weak shells." She shakes her head and frowns, but her eyes are bright. Happy. "What do I care if one more of you dies on any given day? This child was not one of mine. Humans are just talents for the taking, and I am almost done with yours."

J.R.'s face swims up before me. The burning in my chest beats back the ice of Calease's touch. I straighten, my hand shooting out to wrap around her throat.

"Give me back my brother."

She doesn't flinch at first, doesn't even blink. But when Calease realizes she can't break free, she trembles. Her blue eyes—dark and glowing—widen as she gasps for air.

"I cannot!" She grabs my wrist, digging fingernails as long as claws into my skin until blood runs down my arm.

"You *have* to!" I shake her so hard that only my hand keeps her head from snapping back. "Give me back J.R.!"

"It cannot be done!" Her face is turning red—*bright* red—and her claws dig deeper until they finally hit bone. I flinch and try to pull away.

I can't.

The olive-wreath pendant is trapped between our bodies, fusing my hand to her throat. I can move my fingers, but my palm is stuck to Calease's skin as sparks begin to fly.

"What are you doing?" I ask.

Calease's mouth moves, but all that comes out is a strangled cry.

The more I fight it, the stronger the energy shooting through my palm becomes. It zings up my arm like an electric shock, and my body locks as the current zips up my neck and jolts straight into my head.

No. *No!* I will not let her destroy me.

She cries out, and the color leaches from her skin until her face is as white as her hair. Light flashes, and her once-blue eyes are milky. In that same moment, light bursts behind my eyes. A web of lines stretches in every direction. Calease doubles, triples, quadruples—each version of her dressed differently. The world is sketched in black and white. I see everything and nothing as the colors keep flashing past.

No, no, *NO!*

I wrench my hand free. The pendant explodes.

The blast pushes me backward, knocks my feet out from under me and sends me flying through the air. My vision blurs. I slam into something that holds for a second before it tears.

I keep falling.

Falling.

Falling.

Knock, knock, knock.

The noise is persistent and pounding, each beat pulsing through my head.

"Housekeeping," a bored voice calls. Seconds later, a key slides into the lock and the door begins to open.

She sees me before I can say anything.

"Sorry. Should I come back later?"

I try to open my eyes, but the light pouring through the open door is brighter than headlights at midnight, and everything I'm seeing blurs and shifts. Lines run across my vision, reminding me of a screwed-up laptop screen. Somehow, I'm lying across the end of the bed, my head toward the door.

"Yeah. Looks like you had a night." The girl laughs and backs out of the room. "Sleep it off, dude."

The door closes, and the room plunges into darkness again. But it's not dark. Not completely. Because my hands are glowing. Like I'm a fucking nightlight.

I stare at my hands, my chest, my legs, willing the soft blue glow to go away. It doesn't.

Trying to get up isn't easy—my head spins and my knees buckle—but I manage to make it to the bathroom. I don't like what the mirror shows me. My entire goddamn body is surrounded by a blue glow.

Holy shit. I'm a Smurf.

I dig the heels of my hands into my eyes until it hurts.

"Go away, go away, go away," I mutter.

When I open my eyes again, the world almost looks normal. I'm still glowing, but it's dimmer. Almost ignorable. Taking a breath, I squint and flick on the lights so I can assess the damage.

The light washes out my vision, but it comes back into focus quickly.

I look in the mirror and blink. Again. And again. What the hell? That can't be right. I *can't* be seeing that right.

My once-pale blue eyes are solid black. Not just the irises. Both eyeballs are *solid* black. Like someone ripped my eyes out and replaced them with black marbles.

I look away from the mirror and shut my eyes tight. It's a trick of the light or something. It has to be a goddamn trick of the light. Just a trick.

The first things I notice when I force my eyes open again are the bloodstains on my shirt. The same shirt I was wearing yesterday.

My hands clench on top of the counter. I drag in a breath, and it comes in jerking gasps that stab my lungs.

Yesterday.

Less than twenty-four hours ago, I had a family and a home and a dreamworld I thought was as close to heaven as you could get without dying.

I have none of that now.

My brother is dead. My parents threw me out of the house—again—with barely enough to fill a small suitcase. And my dreamworld? I was right when I figured that, if God ever did exist, he turned his back on humanity centuries ago.

Calease wasn't an angel; she was a demon.

Breathing is getting harder. It's like the air is filled with poisonous gas.

The room starts spinning. I need to find that dark corner of my head I built when I was twelve, when my parents kicked me out the first time. The only way I'm going to survive this is by pushing away the burning in my chest and the pain eating away at my mind like acid. It's hard, nearly impossible. My head feels like it's about to bust open, and I think I'm about to black out. I force my eyes open and bite back a scream.

There are two of me.

A glowing white image is superimposed on the glowing blue version of myself. The double is me, but it isn't. It has my face and my body and those screwed-up eyes, but I'm dressed like some medieval knight. Chainmail, helmet, gauntlets, sword—the works.

What am I seeing?

The answer filters in from a different part of my mind. With it comes a whiff of honey. Before tonight, Calease's world always smelled faintly like honey.

This is what Calease saw when she looked at me. This vision filter was how she picked her victims; it showed her the children who had skills worth taking and what they would be if she gave them the right push, turned their skills into something beyond the ordinary. My skill is fighting. No one ever taught me, but I always knew when to dodge and how to throw a punch. It was instinct. Like it was instinct to throw myself into fights when I saw someone else floundering. Calease saw me as some white knight, riding in to rescue the downtrodden and the bullied. That might almost be cool if she hadn't done everything she could to rip it away from me.

When I made it out, I must've taken a lot of what she could do with me.

Fan-fucking-tastic.

I yank off my torn, bloody shirt and lift my right arm to peel off the bandage over my ribs. My body must be numb. I can't feel the wounds. Forty-six sutures and I can't feel a goddamn one of them. The tape pulls at my skin. It doesn't hurt like it should.

When it's off, I understand why.

There *is* no wound. No blood, no scar, not a *scratch.* If not for the stitches embedded in my skin, I wouldn't be able to point out where the cut had been. I rip the bandage off my left shoulder, and it's the same thing. A long line of black stitches is the only sign that I almost died yesterday.

I take a deep breath, finally slipping into the numb, detached place in my head that gives me some distance from everything.

Okay. Guess I picked up way more from Calease than I thought.

Now what the fuck am I supposed to do with it?

Calease mentioned others like her once or twice. She told me I wasn't the only human she "mentored." How many others have fallen for her lies? How many demons are out there, lulling their victims into complacency with visions of paradise and pretty promises? I can't be the only one. And J.R. can't be the only collateral damage in this war they're waging against us.

But I can try to make sure he's the last.

As all-powerful as these demons seem, they can be taken out. I'm proof of that. If I can find a way back into that world, maybe I can wage a war of my own. Or at least find a way to shut down those portals for good.

It sounds like a suicide mission, but right now I don't care. There's nothing left for me here anyway. I just have to find a way to make J.R.'s sacrifice mean something.

I have to make sure what happened to us never happens again.

THREE MONTHS LATER

Two

Mariella

Sunday, August 24 – 12:00 PM

I grip the horse's mane tight and urge her faster.

Already outpacing the wind blowing across the lake, she becomes a streak of white, her hooves cracking against the ground like thunderbolts. I rise and fall with each stride. As impossibly fast as we're flying, as hard as I'm pushing her, and as synchronized as we are tonight, it doesn't matter.

Orane is about to catch up with me.

"Is that the best you can do?" he shouts as his chestnut stallion pulls even with my white mare. Grinning, Orane kicks his steed to greater speeds, galloping slightly ahead.

Grinding my teeth, I grip my mare's sides between my knees and lean down across her neck, pressing myself against her to match her movements. I thought cutting across the lavender field would give me the edge I need, but Orane is better. And this is his world. He created it. No matter how much time I've spent here over the past ten years, I won't ever know this place like he does. And Orane never lets me win.

"Faster," I whisper into my mare's ear.

The willow tree is the finish line, and it's already in sight. My mare puts on one last valiant burst of speed, jumping a creek that feeds the lake and crushing the forget-me-nots beneath her when she lands. The sweet fragrance fills the air. I hardly notice it. My focus is locked on the first branch of the willow tree.

"Fast, Mariella. But not fast enough," Orane calls as he guides his stallion into a tight turn, tagging the branch with his hand and claiming victory with a wide grin. His violet eyes dance, and his long auburn hair flies around his face.

I slap the branch mere seconds later, but it might as well be hours. Even so, I can't keep from smiling as Orane pulls his stallion up onto its hind legs and vaults from the saddle like a circus performer.

"One of these nights, I'll find a way to beat you," I say as I slide off the back of my mare. She nuzzles my neck and whinnies, snuffling softly against my skin as she slowly vanishes.

"You almost won that time." Orane rests his hands on my shoulders and presses a kiss to my neck.

I close my eyes and lean against his chest, but the shivers running over my skin as his fingers trace patterns on my bare arms can't distract me from the blatant lie of his statement.

"It wasn't even close."

"It was closer than before." His cheek presses against mine, and I feel him smile.

He's right, but at the same time, he isn't. For ten years, we've played every game known to man and many no one on Earth has heard of. He always wins. It's usually by a slim margin, but—no. Actually, it's *always* by a slim margin. Like he's holding himself back to make me think I have a chance of beating him.

From anyone else, it'd be patronizing. From Orane?

It's a good thing I can't resist a challenge. I smile and turn in his arms, sliding my hands up and around his neck. In a loose white shirt open to the chest, black pants, and boots, he looks like a pirate. Or the hero on the cover of one of my mother's romance novels.

"If I asked you to let me win one night, would you?" I run my fingers through his hair, relishing the satin-like softness of the strands.

"You might never forgive me if I did," he says.

Smiling, I have to admit he's right; I would hate it if he stopped challenging me. "Sometimes I think you know me better than *I* know me."

"You are my favorite subject to study." Orane settles his hand on the small of my back and pulls me closer. Which I don't mind at all. He's always so careful with me, keeping a tiny bit of distance between us. My pulse picks up speed. Maybe tonight will be different.

I trace the lines of his angular jaw, his dimpled chin, the exaggerated arch of his eyebrows. Orane stands patiently under my fingers, a smile pulling up the corners of his lips.

Turning his head, he kisses the tips of my fingers, and I lean into the soft caress.

"What else would you like to do, Mariella?" he murmurs against my hand. "We have some time before you must leave."

Closing my eyes, I rest my head against him, breathing in his soft, floral scent. I hate thinking about leaving Paradise. Every night since two weeks before my eighth birthday, I've been invited into this dreamworld. And every night I have to leave again. It's the leaving I hate most.

"We haven't been to the opera hall yet," I say.

Orane grins and leans down for a kiss. His touch sends a frisson of energy down my spine, and I can barely contain the desire to slip my hands under his linen shirt and finally explore the skin that has been forbidden to me for so long. But like each time since our first kiss two years ago, he gently pulls back, planting one last, light kiss on the tip of my nose.

"I hoped you would suggest that."

He offers his arm. As I take it, the air around me shimmers, changing my riding clothes into a flowing, white lace dress, accented by a wide black belt with flowers decorating the front. I run my hand along the textured fabric and sweep my long blonde hair over my shoulder.

We walk along the shore of the lake, passing the towering willow tree and the orchard of cherry trees in full blossom, their flowers not simply the usual whites and pinks, but a wild rainbow of reds, blues, and golds. The sky above us is trapped in a perpetual twilight, never fully dark, but never quite day.

In the distance is our destination, the opera hall he created for me years ago. The cream-colored marble is carved in intricate designs, and the dark wooden doors stand open. I don't have to close my eyes to picture the interior. I helped him design it all.

Statues stand in nooks along the walls, and hundreds of seats covered in red velvet fill the auditorium. A luxuriously soft, black-velvet curtain hangs from the proscenium arch, and despite the empty orchestra pit, the finest music I've ever heard will rise into the air the moment I begin to sing.

Once we're inside, Orane tells me about the modifications he's made to the acoustics—the better to amplify my natural talent, he promises. He leads me through the door, down the aisle of the auditorium, and up to the stage. Once I'm in place, he retreats into the darkness of the orchestra seats, his face lost under the glow of the stage lights.

"What will you have tonight, monsieur?" I ask, sinking into a deep curtsey. "Opera? Jazz? Contemporary folk?"

"Sing a song about love," he calls.

"That narrows it down to about all of them." I laugh, standing straight and mentally sifting through my repertoire. "At least give me a style."

"In the style of Etta James then," he replies. "So long as you sing, nightingale, I do not care."

Etta James? Perfect. I concentrate on "At Last," my favorite of her songs, and the invisible orchestra begins to play, the opening chords rising into the air around me.

I take a deep breath, and my voice rises up, carrying the song to the farthest reaches of the theater. Pushing the boundaries of the melody, I take it higher and higher, pouring myself into the song and giving it to Orane. My performances are a gift. My gift for him. I sing for hours, flowing from R&B to pop to folk to opera to alternative. I sing until my throat burns and my hands are shaking.

As the echoes of my last song fade from the air, the house lights rise. Orane is standing in the center of the orchestra seats, applauding, but the warmth of his approval can't mask the tug under my ribs, the breathlessness that hits me and gets worse with each second. Orane approaches the stage, climbing the center steps and gliding toward me with his hands outstretched.

"Time to go already?" I ask the question, hoping the answer is no.

Orane nods and brushes my hair behind my ear, then leans forward to kiss my cheek. "It is only a day. You will be back tomorrow night."

To my right, the portal opens—a doorway of glowing white light around a darkness so black it seems solid—but I ignore it, holding onto the dreamworld as long as possible.

"Remember your promise, my sweet nightingale," he whispers.

Sighing, I roll my eyes. "*Every* night, Orane? It's been years. I remember."

Orane smiles. "Yes. Every night. Your silence is too important to take a chance. If anyone else in your world should discover this one, the consequences would be dire. The war that ravaged this land two centuries ago—"

"Killed thousands until we closed off the borders," I finish for him. It's a story I know better than the history of my own world. It's been my bedtime story for ten years. And after I almost slipped four years ago and spilled my secret to my parents, making this promise to Orane was easy. Necessary. "I would never risk your life, Orane. I know what's at stake. Talking isn't more important than protecting you."

I lift my hand to his cheek and repeat the vow I made four years ago and have fought against instinct to keep all this time. "I promise, my love. Not a word."

Cupping my face in his hands, he runs them through my hair and gently presses a kiss to my forehead. His lips are warm and soft, and his long hair brushes my cheek.

"For centuries, we've kept the borders closed in fear of war. And then I saw a little girl through a window I kept open. A lonely, sad little girl with a light inside brighter than the sun." He smiles and leans down until the tips of our noses touch. "So, I broke all the rules and brought her here to teach her what I know. Little did I know that I would discover a love I never thought I might find."

"I got lucky." Grinning, I lift up onto my toes and steal a quick kiss. "I only had to wait a few years."

Orane's smile grows, and he gives me one last kiss, soft and sweet and pure, before I turn and step through the portal.

I open my eyes, and my head spins. The ceiling fan doubles, then triples, before the images merge back into one. My gaze lands on the digital clock on my nightstand as it flicks to 12:01 AM. Hours spent in Orane's world, and one minute has passed in mine.

Clearing my throat, I wince at the rawness. A minute may be all that's passed here, but tonight I've brought the ache of my hours-long concert with me. It's usually not this bad. Years of practice have built up my stamina. Tonight, though, I challenged my range more than usual. Now, I'm paying for it. Despite the ache, I'd do it all over again for that smile on Orane's face.

I sneak out of my room and down the wooden stairs without making a sound. My parents probably wouldn't care that I felt like making myself a cup of tea in the middle of the night, but I don't want to wake them. I turn into the kitchen and nearly scream when something moves.

My mother jumps and gasps, her hand flying to her chest and half of her glass of water splashing onto the floor.

"Oh, Mari," she sighs. "You scared the bejeesus out of me."

My pulse races, and I take a deep, slow breath to calm it down.

"Are you okay?" She puts the glass down on the table and dries her hand off on her yellow terrycloth robe. "You're not getting sick, are you?"

I shake my head. I haven't been sick in…years. I can't remember the last time. I walk over to the cabinet where we keep our tea, take out the chamomile, and show it to her.

"Oh. Couldn't sleep either?" she asks.

I don't answer. She doesn't expect me to, but that's never stopped her from talking to me as though I might answer at any moment. I try to give her what responses I can, but it's not enough. And I can't even tell her *why* I can't tell her why. Protecting Orane is too important.

She refills her glass, glancing at me as I wait for my turn at the faucet. "Do you want me to make it for you?"

Shaking my head again, I hold the teapot under the running water, swallowing to ease the rawness of my throat while I wait.

"So…ten days left until you start your senior year," she says, smiling. Her hair—the same golden blond as mine—is braided, and her honey-brown eyes watch me carefully. "Are you excited?"

I nod, but only because it's the answer she's expecting. Until she mentioned it, I hadn't thought about school. Or senior year. I suppose I'm excited. In a way. Senior year means I'm almost done with high school.

"Do you need anything for school? New clothes?"

This time, I can't give her the answer she wants. I choose my wardrobe carefully. It helps me fade into the background. Giving up the hoodies and baggy jeans will attract attention I don't want. When I shake my head, her smile wilts. I look away to hide my wince and place a hand over my stomach as though the pressure can stop its churning.

She tries to understand, she really does, but how can she get it when she's missing so many pieces of the puzzle? And what choices do I have? If I explain the truth to her, I break my vow to Orane. I can't do that. Not even for my mother.

"All right." My mother sighs and shuffles closer, her slippers *shooshing* against the tile. "Clean up when you're done, Mari."

I nod, and she gently kisses my cheek as she passes.

"Good night, sweetie."

Turning, I watch her disappear while I wait for the kettle to boil.

I'm glad we've finally reached this middle ground between what she wants and what I'm willing to give her. For a while, she dragged me to a string of neurologists, behaviorists, psychologists, psychiatrists, and psychics.

None of them brought me out of my silence. They just slapped the label of "selective mutism" on my file and called me disabled.

I wanted to laugh at them.

If they knew how hard I worked, especially in that first year, to stick to my vow, they'd never dare call me disabled. Disturbed and dementedly determined, sure. Disabled, not so much.

My one concession after months of pleading from my parents—and permission from Orane—was sign language classes. My mother and I took classes together on SEE—Signing Exact English—and I agreed to use it for school and when absolutely necessary at home. There are very few moments I deem absolutely necessary. Protecting Paradise is too important to risk the smallest mistake.

The kettle's whistle is nearly ear-splitting in the midnight silence. I snatch it off the stove before the noise can wake my father.

Several minutes later, I'm curled up in bed, sipping the tea. Even sweetened with honey, it's bland and completely gross. It helps my throat, though, and that's what matters.

I know I used to like chamomile, but I used to like a lot of things that don't seem as appealing anymore. That's one of the problems with Paradise: after you've stared into the sun, the afterglow makes it difficult to see anything else.

Three

Hudson

Wednesday, August 27 – 1:31 PM

I've heard about the culture shock of moving from a big city to a small town. It's grossly underestimated.

"Have we moved into Stepford or something?" I ask Horace after the fifth casserole-bearing family drops by to introduce themselves.

Horace is a grandfather, but not mine. He's spry for a seventy-eight-year-old guy who survived a brutal beating four years ago. His blue eyes flash with quick wit and observational skills worthy of a PI, but his hair is a halo of thin white curls from his ears to the back of his head. Though he's eight inches shorter than me and looks frail as kindling, Horace is the single person I've met who can look me in the eye.

He's also the only person who knows the whole story behind J.R.'s death. No one else has stuck around long enough to listen.

I saved his life four years ago. Now he's saving mine.

"Don't you start complainin' now," he grumbles. "You said we had to move. I asked where. *You're* the one who picked this little bit of nowhere." He stands at the edge of the truck's loading ramp and huffs. "Swallow's Grove: Population three."

"Nah. At least thirty," I say as I pass him with both of our mattresses loaded on my back. "We've met half of them already."

Horace looks around, and his eyes narrow as he scratches the crown of his head. "You sure you picked the right place, Hudson?"

No. I picked this place based on a carved wooden sign in a repetitive dream. All I know for sure is that Trenton, New Jersey, wasn't giving me any answers, and staying in the city where J.R. died was slowly killing me. But the old man packed up his entire life and bought a second house just because I wanted to follow a dream. I gotta at least *pretend* I know what the hell I'm doing. "Guess we'll see."

I barely make it inside the house when darkness edges into my vision. It happens like this every time the dream hits when I'm not already asleep. I can't control it, and I can't stop it.

I'm about to sink into unconsciousness.

"Horace!"

After all the shit that went down with Calease, I hate sleeping the way some people hate airplanes. Or small, dark spaces. Or spiders. Or being on an airplane in a small, dark space filled with spiders. At least I have a reason.

In the last three months, I've started having creepy dreams that give me a glimpse of the future. Or sometimes a portal will open up in the middle of the night and something will try to kill me. There's no way to know which one I'm gonna get hit with each day. It's kinda like playing Russian roulette every night with a drunk who hates you.

I straighten and let the mattresses fall behind me, my eyes already rolling back into my head. The mattresses thump to the hardwood floor, and I follow them down.

At first, this dream is shades of green and brown light, but the light shifts and splinters until I can make out shapes. Trees. Lots of trees.

Closing my eyes, I block out the images and focus on the way the world around me feels. It's a little like standing in a really placid pond. If one of the demons is waiting for me, the energy will shift, like ripples moving through the water. I can sense it if I pay attention. But like the last five times I've had this dream, I'm alone.

Relaxing a little, I look around, cataloging each detail.

I'm walking through the same woods as before—a forest of maple, beech, and oak—when I almost trip over a low, wooden sign. Trees and little birds have been carved into the surface, the design surrounding the words "Swallow's Grove."

Yeah, I think. *Got that part already. I moved. I'm here. Show me something new.*

The dream responds.

For the first time, my feet carry me past the sign and deeper into the forest.

I keep walking until I reach a path leading to a Craftsman-style home with a wide porch and red trim. There's a girl, with golden-blonde hair so long it brushes her thighs, standing on the path. An orange ribbon is tied over her mouth. Thick lashes frame her honey-brown eyes, and the rest of her face is a mix of soft curves and stubborn lines. A button nose, round cheeks, and large doe eyes set off a strongly angled jaw and eyebrows that cut nearly straight across her forehead. Her eyes bore into mine, but it's impossible to read what she's trying to tell me. I try to speak. I can't make a sound.

She raises one arm, offering me something that glimmers. It looks like a glass bird. I reach out to pick the bird up off her palm, but when my fingers brush her skin, a shockwave shoots up my arm. I hear a crackling that reminds me of fire.

"Help her."

I turn. There's another girl a foot away from me, staring up at me with earnest blue eyes. The girl is short and curvy with brown hair that hangs past her shoulders. She's wearing a silver ID bracelet on her left wrist, and her right thumb rubs it like a good-luck charm.

"Help her, Hudson."

Tears run down the blonde's cheeks as she pulls at the orange ribbon covering her mouth. Her lips move under the fabric, and her nails dig into her skin so hard she's drawing blood. That crackling sound hasn't gone away. I look down. Flames are licking their way up her legs.

My heart jumps. I reach for her, but leap back when the fire roars higher, engulfing her to the waist.

"Help her!" the brunette screams, pushing me into the blaze.

I ignore the searing heat and wrap my hands around her arms. Lifting her off the ground, I swing us both free of the inferno. When I place her on the path again, the ground under her feet bursts into flame. I grab her, trying to get her out of reach of the fire, but the flames have climbed up her arms and the heat blisters the palms of my hands.

Gasping for breath, I sit up so fast I almost crack my head against Horace's.

"Whoa!" He jerks back and plops down on the floor, wincing when his ass hits the wood. "Damn. You all right, Hud?"

"Are *you?*"

He waves off my concern, and I examine my palms, fully expecting burns to cover the skin. There's nothing. My palms look sunburned, but touching the skin doesn't hurt. I flex my hands, but the color doesn't fade. Rubbing my palms together makes the red brighter, and the resulting heat from the friction stings like salt water on an open wound. Right. Maybe not entirely unscathed then.

"Same dream?" Horace asks.

I huff out a laugh. "Yes and no."

His bushy eyebrows pull together, but he doesn't comment. "Need help up?"

I shake my head. Those fortuneteller dreams always leave me feeling like I'm hung over. This one was a helluva lot more intense than the others I've had.

Horace waits a minute, but his curiosity wins out fast. "So…the same and not?"

I try to explain what I saw; he hands me my sketchpad so I can draw the two girls and the house.

"You don't recognize them, do you?" I ask once I've sketched them out.

"Do I look like I know many teenaged girls?"

"Your granddaughters?" Horace has one son—Horace Gregory Lawson IV, a.k.a. Greg—but that one son gave him *ten* grandchildren. And three great-grandchildren already.

"Who're all in Florida and Colorado and North Carolina," he says. "One of the younger ones—Nadette—she gets that same stubborn look on her face sometimes, but none of my girls look like either of those two."

I drop the sketchpad to the floor, and it smacks against the wood, the sound echoing off the vaulted ceiling of the mostly empty living room.

"Well, guess I didn't buy this piece of shit property for nuthin', huh?" Horace says, looking around his new house.

Horace's family has been in real estate, construction, and architecture for a few generations. When I told Horace where I needed to go, he pulled some strings with Greg. Horace took over one of Greg's deals on a house he was planning to flip, and we moved in less than a week after my first dream about that stupid sign in the middle of a forest.

Nothing I could say would convince Horace to stay the hell out of this mess.

He's looking around the room, cringing every time he notices a cracked window or a missing door handle, or the warped floorboards in the corner. His house in New Jersey was immaculate.

"You didn't have to come," I remind Horace. His eyes narrow, and I'm glad he doesn't have anything in his hands right now or he'd probably smack me upside the head with it. "It'd be safer for you back in New Jersey."

"Would've been safer for you to walk away and call the cops from a payphone four years ago. Don't mean it was the right thing to do." He grunts as he pushes himself to his feet.

I try not to remember Horace as he looked that night, all bloody and bruised and half-conscious. It was gruesome then, and time has made the image worse.

"I'd be dead if you'd picked the 'safe' choice," Horace continues. "How d'you think I'd feel if you got yourself in trouble 'cause I was playing it safe?"

"About as good as I'll feel if you get hurt for following me."

Horace snorts and shakes his head, but he doesn't really have a retort for that.

I get up and help him clear away the mess I made. Once I unload the last of the stuff from the U-Haul, I grab the keys to Horace's Camry.

"I'm going to head down to the school to get everything settled," I tell him, jingling the keys to let him know which car I'm taking.

"Boy, don't be stupid," he grumbles, holding out his hand. "Give me those."

Confused, I hand over the keys. Before I can say a word, he tosses something at me. Another set of keys. To his silver and black 1969 Camaro SS.

Horace shakes his head. "What eighteen-year-old picks a Camry over a Camaro?"

I open my mouth to argue, but he's already moving upstairs toward his bedroom. Whatever. If he doesn't mind me taking it, I don't mind *driving* it. Not in the slightest.

Scanning the streets, I look for anything I might recognize from my dream. Huge old trees are everywhere, taller than most of the houses, and the houses themselves aren't that new. There are a few Craftsmans, but none with red trim.

I wish I knew what the hell that dream meant. Am I supposed to be looking for those girls or avoiding them? Does the burning blonde need help, or is the orange fire supposed to warn me to stay away? And her friend who pushes me into the blaze—she could either be someone manipulating things the same way Calease used to, or she could be someone actually trying to help.

Guess it won't matter much until I figure out who these girls are. I haven't been getting anywhere until now.

After the fight with Calease, I've faced off with the dreamworld two more times. Neither of the attacks blasted me like Calease did, but I've been lucky so far. I finger the tiger-iron pendant under my shirt; my stone-bead bracelets clack together as they shift on my wrist. Gemstones like jet, malachite, spider jasper, and black jade have kept me safe so far, but my protections may not hold through a third attack. I need answers fast.

Catching sight of signs leading me into the school parking lot, I push those thoughts aside and concentrate on here and now.

The elementary, middle, and high schools all border a park with athletic fields, playgrounds, and open space. The high school is a mostly brick, two-story building that must have been much smaller at one point. Several wings stretch off in different directions, each one a slightly different design.

It doesn't feel like a school. Not the ones I'm used to. It looks like a mansion or some ritzy private school. I mean, hell, it's landscaped. This place is peaceful. Normal. Normal is good, though. There isn't much else in my life that qualifies.

I walk through the hall, heading for the office. The walls are lined with blue lockers and corkboards with bright flyers for different events from last year. At the end of the main hall, a black sign with thick white lettering sticks out from the wall: MAIN OFFICE.

Pushing my sunglasses up to the top of my head, I take a deep breath. Here goes nothing.

When I step inside, I hear someone humming. Underneath that, I can hear music. It's soft, though, like it's pumping through the walls from another room or coming out of headphones.

A tall, Formica-topped desk divides the center of the room, and behind it, three workstations take up the rest of the space. The carpet is dull red and threadbare in places, and the walls are covered in wood paneling that's starting to crack. It was probably nice once. When they redecorated in, like, 1975.

The humming turns into soft singing as someone shuffles papers. Leaning over the main desk, I spot a girl sitting on the floor, papers spread out around her in neatly stacked piles.

The back of my neck starts tingling, an irritating prickle that makes me twitch. It's a feeling that usually warns me when I'm close to something dangerous. I don't know why it's coming up now. She's sitting there, bobbing her head and sorting. Her brown hair is down and hides her face, but the longer I watch her, the stronger the prickle gets.

"Excuse me."

She doesn't look up, just keeps humming.

I try a little louder. "Hello?"

Nothing. Looking around, I pick up a rubber stress ball shaped like an apple and drop it.

The girl jumps and looks up. I'm staring into the blue-gray eyes of the brunette from my dream. My eyes widen, and she jumps again.

"Holy crap!" Yanking her headphones out of her ears, she leaps up, her skin flushing pink. "Wow. You—I didn't hear you come in."

She's real. Exactly the way I saw her in my dream, right down to the silver bracelet. I want to throw a thousand questions at her, but that'd probably freak her out.

"Sorry," I say. "I tried to get your attention."

In my head, two words play on repeat. She's real, she's real, she's *real.*

She's real, but I have no clue what she might know, which side she's on, or what I'm supposed to do. But I have to start somewhere.

Since I picked them up from Calease, I've learned how to control the different ways she had of looking at the world. Mostly. Shifting my vision, I search this girl for energy left over from the dreamworld. This mental filter slides over my vision easily, but it doesn't change anything. Nothing around her glows. No blue, no orange, and no white. None of the light show I'd expect on someone who's touched that hellish dreamworld.

They haven't found her yet; she's just a teenage girl in jeans and an orange T-shirt who's staring at me like she can't decide if she wants to smile or scream for help. I think she's leaning toward screaming. Every time she looks at my eyes, she jumps. It's the tiniest catch in her breath, but it's there.

"What? Oh. Right." She shifts her weight and looks away, gathering up her iPod and earbuds and dumping them on the desk. "Are you looking for someone?"

"Kind of. I need to enroll."

Her eyes pop open. "Enroll? Here? How old are you?"

"Eighteen."

She looks me up and down, her eyes narrowed and her nose scrunched like she's not sure whether to believe me. She starts gathering a bunch of papers anyway.

"What's your name?" I ask as she warily hands me the enrollment forms.

"Um, K.T."

"Katie?"

Her nose wrinkles, and she shakes her head. "No, K.T. It's short for Katalina Therese."

I can see why she shortened it. *That's* a mouthful.

"I'm Hudson." I hold my hand out over the desk, and although she hesitates, she takes it and smiles. She has to tilt her head back to look up at me.

"How tall are you?" She takes her hand back and hands me a clipboard.

"Six-five."

Her jaw drops a little. "Wow."

"Yeah. That's pretty much what everyone says."

"Guess they would." K.T. blinks and seems to shake herself out of a daze. "Um, can I have your ID so I can make a copy?"

Nodding, I hand her my license and then sit down to fill out the papers. My bracelets clack against the wood as I write. I push them up to get them out of the way, but the noise draws her gaze. As soon as she looks, her eyes pop open wide.

"What happened to your arms?"

Shit. Should've put on a long-sleeve shirt before I left the house. I look down, trying to see my skin like she does.

Underneath the soft, cerulean-blue glow, there are so many lines it looks like a roadmap. I'm so used to the ruts and puffy scars crisscrossing my arms that I forget about them sometimes. They're the legacy of the questionable talent that's kept me alive as often as it's gotten me in trouble.

The story of my life is written in the wounds on my skin. I just wish other people could read the story, too. It'd save me a lot of explaining.

Glancing at K.T., I shrug. "It's a long story."

She nods, biting her lip. I watch her for a second. When she doesn't say anything else, I go back to the papers.

"Are you wearing contacts or something?" The words burst out, and K.T. slaps her hand over her mouth. "I'm sorry. Never mind. I just—I've never seen eyes that dark."

Curiosity. Curiosity is good. Most people who notice that my eyes look like onyx marbles cross themselves and leave. Or scream curses at me. And *then* leave. Can't blame them. I would've done the same thing three months ago. It's why I've been wearing sunglasses since we arrived in Swallow's Grove. I want to delay the screaming and the pitchforks.

But she isn't screaming or leaving. And she hasn't asked about my blue glow, so I'm guessing she can't see it. Or she is *really* good at dealing with the weird. No one else has seen it yet, but I think someone else who's lived through the demons' games would.

If she hasn't ever had firsthand contact with the demons, maybe her connection to the dreamworld is through the burning blonde. This is a small town. If the blonde is anywhere near our age, K.T. probably knows her.

"They're not contacts," I tell her when I realize I never answered her question. "It's another long story."

"Oh." She starts playing with that bracelet again. "Never mind. I shouldn't have asked. You don't have to tell me. My mom always told me to stop asking so many questions."

I watch K.T. for a second, surprised when she looks straight into my eyes for more than a blink. She's the first person other than Horace to manage it.

"I don't mind telling you," I say. "I'm not sure you'd believe me if I did."

K.T. stares at me like she's expecting me to start laughing. I don't, and her expression shifts, her eyes narrowing and her head tilting to the side. "Um, it's okay. Really. It's none of my business."

She goes back to sorting papers, using the desk this time instead of the floor and leaving her iPod off. Although her eyes flick in my direction every so often, she doesn't say anything else until I finish the packet and stand up.

"Why aren't your parents doing this?" she asks as I hand over the stack.

"They're gone."

"Oh my gosh." She bites her lip, her eyes darting away. "I'm so sorry."

"No, no." I rub my hand over my face and shake my head. I really need to find a better way to explain this. "They're not dead. They're just...not around."

"Oh." K.T. blinks quickly, looking like she's trying to put the pieces together with the little bit I've given her. "I'm...um, sorry?"

My relationship with my parents was always rocky at best. The sole part of my family I cared about was J.R. Now that he's gone...well, it's hard to be sorry that I haven't seen the people who kicked me out of their house the night my little brother died.

"Told you. It's a long story."

"Yeah. I guess so." She takes my paperwork, puts it into a folder, and places the folder in the exact center of the desk. "Stop by the first day of classes, and they'll give you your schedule."

She bends down, scoops a backpack off the floor, and slips her iPod into her pocket. I guess she's done for the day.

"Why'd you move to a town like Swallow's Grove from a city like Trenton?" she asks as we walk through the halls. I wonder how she knows where I'm from for a second, but then I remember she made a copy of my license. She raises one eyebrow when I don't answer right away. "Or is that another long story?"

"All part of the same long story, actually." I hold the door to the parking lot open, and she turns with me when I walk toward the Camaro.

"Well, I know you probably have a ton going on getting settled and everything, but here."

She passes me a Post-it with a phone number written under the name K.T. Dowling. "I'm basically the one-woman high school welcoming committee." She sighs and shakes her head, but her eyes are crinkled in the corners with hidden laughter. "I don't know what they're going to do if new kids show up after I graduate."

Turning the square of yellow paper in my hand, I bite back the questions I want to ask. How the hell do you bring demons into a conversation without sounding like you escaped an institution? Better to leave it for now.

I pull out my phone, dial her number, and press *call.* Her phone starts buzzing, and she smiles as she hits *end*.

"There might be something going on this weekend," she says as we approach the edge of the lot, scanning it like she's looking for someone. "Don't know what or where, but someone will probably throw something—"

K.T. stops dead in her tracks, her eyes locked on Horace's car.

"Holy crap," she mutters, eyes wide. "Is that a '69 Camaro SS?"

I glance back at her as I unlock the door. "Yeah. You know cars?"

She shakes her head, her lips trembling. "Just this one."

Her reaction is too strong to be normal. People don't usually get choked up at the sight of a car. There's something about *this* car specifically that freaks her out.

It takes a second for her to smile, but she forces the expression onto her face. "It's my sister's favorite car."

But she doesn't look happy to see it.

"Oh." My chest aches. I don't have to ask to know something bad happened. "I'm sorry."

K.T. glances at me out of the corner of her eye, and her mouth tenses. "She didn't die." She says it like she's not sure if it's true. "She's been in a coma for four years."

"My..." I close my eyes for a second. Can I say it? I haven't said it aloud more than a handful of times. Haven't had to. Horace knew about J.R. when he came looking for me, and I've barely spoken to anyone else in the past few months. Certainly not about J.R.

Swallowing, I try again. "My little brother died a few months ago."

When I open my eyes, K.T. is watching me. Her expression is blank—the careful blankness of someone who's used to keeping people from seeing their pain—but the knowledge is in her eyes. She gets it. She knows what it's like to lose someone you love.

"Sometimes I'm not sure if that would be easier or harder," she says.

I nod as the ragged edges around the wound of J.R.'s death burn. Which *is* worse? Losing someone entirely or going years without knowing if the person you love will ever recover? Sometimes hope can cut worse than loss. But at the same time, at least you *have* hope.

A silver sedan pulls into the parking lot and honks twice. K.T. looks up and shakes herself off, her smile returning. It's forced, but it's there.

"Well, on *that* bright note, it's nice to meet you, Hudson. Maybe I'll see you this weekend."

She smiles and, waving, jogs toward the sedan.

I watch her go, trying to breathe. I remember how when I realize my hands are locked around my phone. Where I now have the number of a girl who showed up in my dream this morning.

I don't know how K.T. is connected to this mess, but she doesn't seem to be in danger or a threat right now. Guess for once I have some time to figure it out.

I hope the burning blonde is as easy to find.

Four

Mariella

Wednesday, August 27 – 5:47 PM

During the summer, days pass in a blur. I spend my mornings searching the Internet for music I haven't heard before. New singer-songwriters, old and almost-forgotten arias, hidden gems from one-hit wonders of the sixties. It's all fair game. After lunch, I listen to the songs I love until I have them memorized, creating a playlist of my favorites for my iPod and letting it play on loop while I curl up in the window seat downstairs and read. I'd rather be in my room, but the compromise with my mother means spending time in the main part of the house. Afternoons downstairs, mornings and nights upstairs.

I put my book down and rub my thumb along the cool, smooth back of my glass nightingale. The bird is about two inches long from beak to tail and fits perfectly in the curve of my fingers. Bringing it up to my eyes, I admire the way it gleams in the sunlight streaming through the window. It's not simply the way the glass reflects the light. My nightingale creates its own light—a gorgeous, pearlescent shimmer that only I can see. A light that marks it as a gift from Orane.

He's given me dozens of trinkets and figurines over the years, but this one is my favorite. I'm his nightingale, after all.

The glow gets brighter as I watch it. I smile. The gifts he leaves for me are beautiful, but what I love most is the reminder that I'm on Orane's mind as much as he's on mine. I know he's working on finding a way to let me stay. It'll happen. I have to be patient.

The front door bangs shut, and I jump. My nightingale flies from my fingers. I dive after it, catching it before it smacks against the wood floor.

Sighing, I drop my head. It's never fallen that far before. I don't know if it would shatter, but I *really* don't want to take the chance.

"Honey, it's time for—Mari, what are you doing on the floor?"

I push myself up, holding out the nightingale with one hand and signing with the other, "Dropped."

My mother's confusion clears. She nods and helps me up. "Well, be careful and come set the table."

I slip the nightingale into the pocket of my flannel pajama pants and nod. Putting my book back, I follow her into the kitchen. My father is already there, pouring two glasses of red wine. His tie is hanging loose around his neck, and his suit jacket has been tossed on a side table. Normally it takes him a little longer to unwind after work, but tonight he's grinning as my mother and I come into the room.

"Dana, remember how I told you the house on the next block might have a buyer?"

"The fixer-upper?" my mother asks as she checks the oven. "I still think you're crazy. No one would buy that place. The roof nearly caved in after that storm last winter!"

"You better believe it. I was right! It sold a couple days ago, and I found out who bought it. Makes *perfect* sense now."

My father is nearly bouncing. I haven't seen him this excited in years. Maybe ever. I glance at him as I pull the plates out of the cupboard, wondering why this is such big news. Swallow's Grove is a tiny town, but newcomers aren't *that* uncommon.

Mother's lip quirks as she watches him. "Are you going to tell me who it is or do you expect me to guess, Frank?"

"Horace Gregory Lawson III." He says the name with strong emphasis on each part. My mother blinks at him, waiting for the punch line.

"I'm sorry, honey. Should that ring a bell?" she finally asks.

My father sighs and shakes his head. "Dana, he's the father of the Lawson who rebuilt the apartments in the center of town."

She stares at him without recognition, her brown eyes steady as she sips her wine.

"He single-handedly designed the rebuild of Albany's capitol building?" my father says.

"Oh!" Her eyes brighten, and she nods. "I remember now. Are you sure it's him? His family has the money to live anywhere."

"He's on public record as the new owner. And Jen Selwyn already went over to meet him. He's *here*!"

My mother nearly drops her glass. "He moved in while the house is in *that* condition?"

They keep talking about the house, speculating on whether Mr. Lawson will do the work himself or hire out. My father throws out ideas for the redesign, the directions he'd take with restoration and furniture, and which contractors he'd hire to do the actual work. He's nearly wistful when he says, "But chances are he's going to handle the whole project himself."

"You never know," my mother says as she clears the table. "Doesn't hurt to introduce yourself."

"He's a world-renowned architect!" My father and I both pick up our plates and follow her into the kitchen. "What's he going to want with a small-town firm?"

"Well, he's moving to a small town, isn't he?" she asks. "There must be something bringing him here."

My father laughs. "Somehow I doubt it's Teagan Designs."

Mother turns and kisses him as she takes the plate from his hands. "Maybe it will be after he meets you. The worst he can say is no, Frank."

The smile that comes onto my father's face tells me it's time to escape. They're about to start cooing at each other, and they won't realize I'm gone if I go now.

At the top of the steps, I stop and sit. There's a corner where you can hear everything said downstairs because of the acoustics of the vaulted ceiling. For a while, I sit with my fingers in my ears, singing songs in my head to give them some privacy. After a few minutes I release the pressure, checking to make sure they're done.

"How was she today?" my father asks.

I know how much my silence bugs them, but it's been part of our lives for so long they rarely talk about it anymore.

My mother sighs. "She's the same. It hasn't gotten any better, but…I don't know. I guess at this point I'm glad she hasn't gotten any worse either."

"Mari always was a determined little thing," he says. "She takes after you."

"I guess we should be happy she doesn't take after your sister." My mother laughs, and I hear the scrape of her piano bench sliding against the floor. "Can you imagine raising another Jacquelyn?"

My father groans. "I'm going to forget you suggested that. I talked to Julian yesterday. The way he tells it, my sister is a model of parenthood. I can't tell if the kid is lying or delusional." There's a second of silence. "Can you believe he's going to be a sophomore?"

I barely remember my Aunt Jacquelyn—she lives in Vegas with her son Julian, and though my father goes out to see them a few times a year, they rarely come to visit us in New York. If half the stories they've told me are true, I can understand their relief. She's in her mid-thirties and still going through a rebellious teenage phase.

There's a plop and a sigh as my father settles into his armchair. "Are you going to play it again?"

"Of course." A few notes fill the air, and I breathe easier. *This* is what I've been waiting for. Closing my eyes, I lean my head against the banister and listen.

When my father renovated this house twenty years ago, he paid special attention to the acoustics because of my mother's love for music. My ears have been spoiled by the perfection of my opera hall, but the slight echo of my mother's performance space isn't a flaw. It adds a sort of ethereal quality to her songs. Especially this one.

My fingers move across my knees, mimicking hers on the ivory keys of our antique piano. This composition is deceptively simple, but there's strength in the bass line and resonance in the high notes. It is the most moving piece of music I've ever heard, and it's one I've never been able to sing for Orane. Every time I try, something stops me. This song isn't like all the others. It's not mine to share. This one belongs to my mother.

My promise to Orane has already taken too much from her. I can't take this, too.

The song fades, and my father asks, "Does it help? Playing that every night?"

"It doesn't hurt," she says, already flowing into another song. "Not more than it already does."

I push to my feet, slip into my bedroom, and close the door with a soft *click*.

Inside my room, I can barely hear the music. Here, I can pretend my silence isn't costing either of us anything.

As soon as I step into Orane's world, he pulls me from one game to another. We go rock climbing in the craggy mountains, race through the emerald-green foothills, swim in the crystalline lake, and dance across an open plain as he teaches me to tango.

"You truly love this place," he says as we start toward the opera hall.

I smile as I watch two tiny hummingbirds, their feathers a rainbow of iridescent colors, flutter past. "What's not to love?"

"Will you feel the same way when it is no longer an amusement that comes and goes?" He's smiling, but his eyebrows are low and his eyes are surrounded by deeply etched lines.

"Of course! As long as you're here, I'd—" I stop short and run his words through my head again. "Orane, did you say *when*?"

His eyes widen and his mouth opens as though he's going to deny it, but then his cheeks flush a soft shade of pink. Orane glances away and smiles sheepishly, one hand rubbing the back of his neck. "Mariella, how do you always make me ruin my surprises for you?"

"Oh, who cares about surprises?" I press closer, wrapping my arms around his neck and burying my fingers in his long hair. "Do you mean it?"

He pulls back, just far enough to stare into my eyes. "Have I ever lied to you, my nightingale?"

"Never." From the beginning, Orane has been my trusted confidant, my strongest supporter, and my best friend. He's become the standard I measure everything in the waking world against. Nothing comes close. Not even me. But staying with him has never been a possibility. If he's talking about it as a *when* instead of an *if*...

"You finally found a way to bring me here for good? How?"

Orane shakes his head, but he's smiling down at me. "I should not have told you yet. I am not certain it will work, and I hate to disappoint you."

"You could never disappoint me," I whisper against his skin, brushing kisses along the line of his jaw. "An estimate, at least? Please?"

Orane laughs, a low rumble that echoes through his chest. "All I will tell you, my impatient girl, is that I hope it will be soon."

I pull back, adrenaline shooting through my veins. "Soon? How soon?"

"No, that is all you will get from me tonight." He grins at me and touches the tip of my nose with his finger. "Not another word."

"But—"

He cuts me off in the simplest and most effective way—with a kiss.

I melt into his arms, shivers cascading up my arms and down my body. His hands run through my hair and trace patterns on my arms, and it's like my skin can no longer contain me, like I'm bursting apart at the seams. I don't come back together until he finally pulls away.

"That is better," he whispers, tucking a strand of hair behind my ear.

I blink, trying to clear my head. What were we talking about?

Orane chuckles and lifts me into his arms. My head is spinning. I lean against him for support. How can his kisses still affect me like this? Two years of kissing him, and each one feels like the first time.

Once I've caught my breath, I look up into his eyes. "You're not going to escape so easily, you know. I want to know."

Orane smiles and leans down to kiss my forehead as he carries me into my theater. "I am sure you do. But enough talking for tonight."

He walks down the aisle and places me in the center of the stage. Once he's sure I can stand on my own, he puts his hands on my shoulders and runs them down my sides. His hands create the shape of the dress, and the light follows, swirling around me until I'm clothed in a ball gown of jet-black satin with golden nightingales embroidered at the edges. The sleeves sit low on my shoulders, and the tight, corset-style bodice hugs my waist. I run my hand over the wide skirt, realizing my arms are encased in gold satin gloves. A black and gold fan hangs from my left wrist.

Smiling at his creation, Orane steps back and bows, his violet eyes never leaving mine.

I wish I had a mirror. From what I can see, this dress is the most beautiful he's ever created for me. "You've outdone yourself tonight."

"It does not compare to you." He takes my hand and lightly kisses the tips of my satin-covered fingers. "Will you sing, sweet nightingale?"

I snap the fan open and peer at him over the black lace. "I suppose. Opera, do you think? I think this dress demands an aria."

Before Orane reaches his seat, the first strains of "Habanera" from *Carmen* fill the air.

My set doesn't last long tonight, but it's stronger, the songs I pick more powerful than usual. It's not simply a performance; it's a celebration of hope.

Orane might have found a way to let me stay forever. I was content to live in silence in my world so long as I could keep visiting his, but now? Now I might be able to stay.

For the first time, when the portal opens, I barely resist the pull. Sooner rather than later, I will walk into Paradise and never leave again.

Five

Hudson

Thursday, August 28 – 11:11 AM

"What in the seven levels of hell did my son see in this place?" Horace asks.

We're standing on the street on Thursday morning, staring up at the house, after taking inventory of the place. From here, I can see five different spots where the brick needs to be repaired and pick out where shingles are missing on the sloped roof. The porch sags, and the windows are dingy. But if I let my eyes go out of focus and ignore all that, I can kinda picture what the place might look like after a little—never mind—a *lot* of TLC.

"It has good bones?" I suggest.

"It's got *old* bones," he mutters.

I smirk. "Yeah? So do you. Doesn't mean they're all bad."

He smacks my arm, but he's grinning. "Just wait till you get to be my age, and then tell me how good old bones are."

We go inside to make lunch, but since the fridge doesn't work, we're limited to food we can keep in the pantry. Which means PB&J. J.R.'s favorite, right after pizza. I have to force myself to chew the damn thing.

The dream hits me again in the middle of clearing away our lunch plates. I barely manage to set the plates down and back away from the counter before I collapse.

I come out of the dream gasping for breath. My hands sting, my entire body is flushed with heat, and each moment sends waves of nausea through my stomach. Damn it I hate this feeling.

Shuddering, I try to regain control of my body. This is the third time in twenty-four hours I've had the dream with K.T. and the burning blonde. Three times, and I've only been able to pick out three new details:

One: Even after she tears the ribbon from her skin, the burning blonde can't make a sound.

Two: The flames aren't coming from the ground; they're coming from under her skin.

And three: After I drag her out of the fire a third time, she grabs my arms, her eyes boring into mine. As soon as she touches me, her flames engulf me, too.

I can't get the images from that dream out of my head. Focusing on the blonde before the fire starts crackling at her feet helps. A little.

The determination in her eyes is compelling. She stood so calm at first, but then fought tooth and nail. Reaching up, I grab my sketchbook off the counter. It tumbles into my lap, my pencil following it down. No matter how I adjust the portrait I started yesterday, I can't capture that determined look. It doesn't feel right. I'm forgetting some crucial detail that brings her face together and makes her… her.

No matter how much I try to focus on her face, watching her scream silently as she burns alive is…Well, haunting and horrifying are both understatements.

Someone knocks on the front door as the post-dream nausea starts to pass. Horace comes from the office he's been setting up in the back of the first floor and does a double-take when he sees me sitting on the floor.

"Again?" he asks.

"Yeah." I drop the sketchbook and grab the edge of the counter to haul myself to my feet. And then fall right back on my ass when the wood cracks off in my hand. My fist automatically closes around the chunk, and I wince as splinters bite into my skin.

"Piece of *shit* house," Horace mutters, his face flushing red. "Never gonna find a profit flippin' a place in this condition."

The person at the door knocks again.

Horace huffs. "I'm comin', I'm comin'!"

I get up slowly, trying not to break anything else, and follow Horace toward the door. As I go, I pick the bits of wood out of my palm and watch the tiny slices in my skin seal themselves.

A thin man with light-brown hair and round cheeks is standing on the porch, shaking Horace's hand. Before I come into view, I knock my sunglasses off the top of my head. They drop onto my nose, and I settle them better as I step up behind Horace.

"It's a real pleasure to meet you, Mr. Lawson," the guy says. His smile is broad; he really does look thrilled to meet Horace.

"You an architect or a contractor?" Horace asks with a laugh.

I lean against the wall inside the door and watch as the guy flushes. "Well, uh, a—an architect. How did you know?"

"I've been retired too long for most people to know who I am, son. And my boy Greg's been keepin' a much lower profile than his ancestors were known to."

"Oh." There's a pause, and the guy shifts uneasily, like he isn't sure what to say. Horace never has that problem. He reaches out and pulls me closer, a huge grin on his face.

"This is Hudson, by the way," Horace says. "What was your name again?"

The man glances at me, but his attention is almost entirely on Horace. "Frank Teagan."

"Nice to meet you," I say, then I head back into the house. The guy's obviously here for Horace.

I dig Horace's laptop out of the chaos of half-unpacked boxes and plug in the wireless card he bought. I need to look for New Age stores. I find two within an hour's drive that might have raw, unworked stones. Good. I need to restock.

My recent obsession with crystals and gemstones started with a dream. As freaky as my visions of the future can be, they're also damn useful. The first one saved my life.

I dreamt I was walking through a parking lot at night when twenty wraiths appeared in the sky and attacked. Seconds before I was about to die, the entire scene froze and then played in reverse. Once I was back at the beginning, the scene repeated. This time, I held an amethyst geode the size of my fist. When the wraiths attacked, I threw my arms up and blasted them away with a beam of purple light.

When I woke up, I thought it was my fears and paranoia manifesting as a nightmare. Then, walking to the library the next day, I passed a street fair. The first stall on the row was full of crystals, and sitting on a shelf was an amethyst geode *exactly* like the one in my dream. I grabbed it, eyes locked on the clear blue sky for wraiths, and bought it. None came.

That night, a portal opened above my bed, and orange light filled the motel room. The amethyst was already glowing, creating a wall of soft light that pushed back at the dreamworld's energy. I grabbed the amethyst, and as soon as my hand closed around the stone, the wall grew brighter. Stronger. Almost solid. One of Calease's gifts let me use my own energy to reinforce the stone's power, but it wasn't until that night I realized I could do that. It was instinct.

Demons beat against my purple force field so hard the amethyst shattered, but the burst of energy released from the exploding crystal shoved them back into the portal and saved my life.

I'm pretty sure that's what happened anyway. The explosion also knocked my ass out for a few hours.

After that, I taught myself about the metaphysics of gemstones and crystals, guesstimating what might apply to the demons' dreamworld. Once I had a grasp on the subject, I spent most of the money I had left buying bracelets of malachite, black jade, and jet, and also a pendant of tiger iron. With them, I was able to hold off the demons when they tried again a few weeks later, but each attack has been stronger than the one before. I need more stones before the next one comes.

Before I decide to go shopping, my phone rings. Only Horace and K.T. have the number and Horace is downstairs, so I take a wild guess.

"Hey, K.T."

"My friend Danny is throwing a party Saturday night," she says. When I ask where, she rattles off an address. "It's west of Main, and if you go—"

"Yeah. I know where it is."

"Really? How?"

Because I stared at a map of the town until I had the damn thing memorized. I knew it'd come in handy. To K.T., I say, "I drove around a lot yesterday."

"Oh. Good memory. Guess I'll text you if anything changes?"

I can tell she's about to hang up, but I can't let this chance pass. There has to be some way for me to get the information I need about the blonde without sounding like some deranged stalker. I just have to figure out how to phrase it.

"Hey, can I pick your brain for a second?"

"That doesn't sound pleasant."

"I'll try to make it painless." There has to be some way to ask about a blonde girl I've never met. "It seemed like you know everyone..."

K.T. laughs. "It's a small town. *Everyone* knows everyone."

Then it clicks. "I was running this morning. Saw this girl and hoped you could tell me her name."

"If you've already found a girlfriend, I can promise you you've broken the hearts of about half the girls in the senior class," K.T. says.

Shit. What the hell am I supposed to say to that? The last thing I need is a girl I'll end up lying to and putting in harm's way. People I love tend to disappear, one way or another.

K.T. must pick up on the tension in the silence on my end of the line because she laughs. "I'm joking, Hudson." The knot in my stomach relaxes a little. From the tone of her voice, I can picture the grin on her face. "What does your mystery girl look like?"

It's as though the flames in the dream have burned her straight into my brain. There's no way I could forget the blonde's face, but I stare down at the sketch anyway.

"She's a little taller than you. Maybe five-seven? Long, blonde hair—like *really* long—and she lives in a house with red trim."

The line goes dead quiet. I can't even hear her breathing.

"I think you should find a different blonde," K.T. finally says.

"What? Why?"

"Mariella is..." She pauses and sighs, but that name is ringing through my head like church bells.

Mariella. Ho-ly shit. The burning blonde has a name. Mariella. It's pretty.

"You know the phrase 'hard to get'?" K.T. asks.

"Yeah."

"Forget hard to get. Chasing Mari would be like *Mission: Impossible*."

Goosebumps rise along my skin. I think I'm missing something.

"Why? Guys not her thing?"

"Umm, I don't know. The thing is...Mariella hasn't said a word in four years."

Oh. The ribbon. The orange ribbon wasn't a symbol. Or it was, but I should've taken it more literally than I did. That must've been her promise to them. Silence.

Shit. K.T. may have been right about the *Mission: Impossible* thing. How can I get answers from someone who won't *talk*? One of the librarians in Trenton helped me learn sign language years ago to communicate with this old homeless man who helped me out when I was living on the streets, but sign language only helps if Mariella knows it, too.

"Can't talk or won't?" I ask.

"Won't." K.T. says it with certainty, but then she backtracks. "I'm pretty sure it's won't. She just stopped one day."

Yeah, that sounds about right. It was probably subtler than that, a gradated slip into silence that people didn't notice until she flat-out refused to answer. That's how the demons work. Your life is there one day, and the next day it's gone. It belongs to them because of a promise you didn't understand.

"Look." There's steel in K.T.'s voice. "I'm telling you right now—don't mess with Mari."

"Why not?"

"Because I'm telling you not to." K.T. huffs and mutters something I don't quite catch.

"I don't want to mess with her." That's the last thing I want, but how do I say that to K.T.? "She…I don't know. She looked like she needed help."

Or at least a bucket of water dumped over her head.

K.T. snorts. "Don't go thinking she's some damsel in distress for you to rescue. The Mari I remember from elementary school would've kicked you for suggesting it. She could always take care of herself."

Except this time she may be up against something completely out of her league—a demon wearing an angel's mask, and a hellish nightmare hiding within a paradisiacal dreamworld.

I wonder if Mariella's been under their influence longer than I thought. K.T. talks like she hasn't seen Mariella in years. Since elementary school. When did this start for Mariella then? Middle school? That's crazy young. If she met the dream demons when she was eleven or twelve, they've had the better part of a decade to burrow inside her head. The damage to my life was bad enough after four years with Calease. I can't fathom what six or seven might've done.

"It won't kill me to try," I tell K.T. *Except, you know, it might.*

"I guess." K.T. sighs. "If you mess with her head, I'll personally hunt you down, but otherwise, good luck. If you can get her to talk, you're a freaking miracle worker. Hell, if you can get her to actually *smile,* her parents might throw you a party."

When I hang up with K.T., I realize the lie I made up for her might be true. I could actually find Mariella's house. This is a small town, and the houses in this neighborhood—with the exception of Horace's dilapidated Victorian—are all about the same size as the Craftsman in my dream. What if she's a street or two over?

I run down to the den that is serving as my bedroom—all but one of the actual bedrooms are uninhabitable—and change.

"Where you tearin' off to?" Horace calls as I jog toward the door.

"Gonna see if I can find that house."

"Don't get yourself lost. And, before I forget, we're havin' dinner at the Teagans's tomorrow night."

I look over my shoulder to the kitchen and spot the missing piece of wood that snapped off earlier.

"Uh, that's probably a good thing."

"Piece of shit house," he mutters again. "I don't want to work on the restoration, it's so bad."

I roll my eyes. Bullshit. He's already sketching out the plans in his head. Horace may have retired, but he has a hand in almost everything his family's company does. And he loves a good restoration project.

"Well, if you're going, git!" He shoos me out of the house, and I run down to the main street. I have two choices. Left or right? It's a fifty-fifty shot.

Eenie. Meenie. Miney. Left.

I turn and start running, my feet automatically finding a comfortable rhythm and my body quickly adjusting to the motion. My sneakers thud against the pavement and—especially since I'm wearing a long-sleeved shirt to cover my arms, and sunglasses to hide the oddness of my eyes—people barely give me a second glance as I pass.

For over two hours, I move south, jogging up and down every street, following the map in my head and crossing off each street as I go.

The Craftsman house with red trim isn't anywhere to be found. At least, not south of us. As I run back to Horace's, I tell myself I have time. I don't need to find her tonight.

But the itch forming along the back of my neck and across my shoulders says otherwise.

I hate this. It's like I'm racing a clock ticking down to doomsday without knowing how much time I have left.

Over takeout that night, I ask Horace if he minds lending me the money to pick up some new stones. In answer, he takes something out his wallet and slides it across the table. A credit card with my name on it.

"Since you're so damn stubborn about paying me back money I don't mind losing, it's easier to keep track this way."

Saying his family has done well is a huge understatement. Horace is far from flashy about it, but he's got so much money that buying this house outright—in cash—didn't phase him. He keeps trying to tell me that it doesn't matter to him, but it matters to me. It's his money, not mine. As soon as I can manage it, I'm paying him back for everything.

If I don't get myself killed first.

We say goodnight, and he heads up the creaky steps to his bedroom, leaving me in the darkness alone.

It was hard for him to believe at first, but I don't sleep. Not much. Before I figured out Calease was a demonic, soul-sucking, evil bitch, I spent every night for four years in her world. In my third year, I mentioned I hadn't been able to sleep for more than a couple hours a night.

"A side effect, I am afraid," she'd said. "Those who spend time here no longer require as much rest as most of your kind."

And she was right. The longer I spent in her world, the less I slept. I'm down to needing about an hour a night. If that.

One side effect she *didn't* mention—probably because she didn't expect me to live long enough for it to matter—is my memory. I remember everything. Every conversation I've ever had, every meal I've ever eaten, and everything I've ever learned, done, seen, or heard. It's like my mind has turned into a computer with infinite storage. I remember even if I wish I could forget. Like the night Calease showed up for the first time.

Everything about that night is burned into my head as indelibly as Mariella's face. It's a memory I can't keep from reliving, torturing myself wondering what might've happened if I hadn't been so desperate when she found me.

I'm fourteen and sleeping behind a long row of filing cabinets in the basement of the library. *Trying* to sleep. The zipper on the front of my leather jacket keeps scratching me, and something in my backpack is jabbing me in the neck. When I sit up to move, pain shoots across my left side.

Hissing, I ease my T-shirt up, carefully peeling it off the road rash from my latest run-in with the Bishop Kings. My shirt sticks near the top. I grit my teeth and yank. Part of the scab pulls away.

"Shit!"

Blood starts oozing from the reopened cut. I grab the gauze, take out the last packet, and tear it open with my teeth. Even though I'm working gently, pressing the gauze against the road rash makes my whole side burn. I don't even want to think about trying to reach the patches of broken skin on my upper arm. I'll need more bandages, but I don't want to steal another box. Groaning, I nudge my backpack into a better position and ease myself back down.

The Bishop Kings' idea of warning me off involved a blindfold, a plastic bag, duct tape, and shoving me naked out of a moving car. They didn't like that I'd helped put three of their inductees in juvie for almost killing Horace. I've barely left the library since.

Breathing around the ache in my ribs and the erratic twinges of pain shooting out from my side, I try to calm down. I'll lay low for a while and stay the hell out of everyone's way. If they can't find me, I'll be fine.

I almost laugh. *Fine*? Bullshit. If I have to keep stealing food to stay alive, I'm gonna get caught eventually. Unless the Bishop Kings catch up with me first. Maybe they won't have to. Last winter was colder than ever. Despite hiding in the basement of the library most nights, I barely survived. If I don't figure something out soon, I may not make it through the next winter.

I force myself to lie quietly until the pain begins to ease and my breathing evens. I'm starting to drift off to sleep—*finally*—when my vision is stained red.

My eyes shoot open, expecting a cop's flashlight, but that's not what I find.

Near my feet is a glowing archway. The light is white and shimmery, like iridescent glitter, and it's so tall the top nearly brushes the ceiling. Inside, instead of seeing the cement wall of the basement, I'm looking at evenly spaced wooden pillars and a reed-mat floor. Standing on that mat is a woman with curves that would make a *Playboy* model jealous. She's wearing a long, butter-yellow dress, and her white hair hangs down to her waist. She looks like an angel when she smiles at me, holding out her hands.

"Hudson, come with me." Her voice reminds me of the breeze rustling through the trees near the lake. Soft and subtle and calming. "Let me help you."

Did I die? Maybe the scratch on my side got infected. Maybe I've been slowly bleeding to death from internal injuries for the past week. Who knows? If this is death, if *she's* what's waiting for me on the other side, then fuck it. I'm letting go.

I push to my feet, wincing as the gauze shifts and sends little twinges of pain through my body. I was really hoping death wouldn't hurt this much.

At the edge of the portal, I hesitate. If this is a dream, it's the realest dream I've ever had. And if it's not…If it's not, I have no goddamn clue what's going on.

"Come, child," she says, beckoning me forward.

Holding my breath, I reach through the glowing arch for her hand. I jump a little when my fingers meet warm, solid flesh. And then I step into her world, and the glowing portal closes behind me, sealing me in.

I should be scared, on edge, body tingling and ready to run. But I'm not. For the first time in so long I can't remember, my muscles start to loosen. Closing my eyes, I hear birds chirping in the distance and the quiet splash of water running over rocks. There's a sweet scent on the cool breeze that reminds me of honey.

This place is impossible. Like something out of a movie or fantasy novel. I stare down into her glacier-blue eyes and ask, "Who are you?"

"My name is Calease," she says. I want to ask her more questions—like where the hell am I and how did I get here? Before I can, she takes both my hands in hers and asks, "What do you want most in the world, Hudson? If you could ask for anything, what would it be?"

Her words are like a well-placed chisel against a wall of cracking marble. One blow and everything I've been blocking out for two years busts back into my head.

Training myself not to think about the past took a long time, but what choice did I have when my parents passed me off to Social Services for being a pain in their asses?

It's not like I did it on purpose. Not once have I started a fight. Not once did I go looking for trouble. Trouble has a way of finding me, over and over and over again. I protected dozens of people who weren't willing to step up and do me the same favor. But I passed by the house not long ago and saw something that shot me through the chest. My mother was holding a baby wrapped in a blue blanket. I have a brother.

Despite everything that's happened in the past two years, there's one thing I desperately want.

My voice cracks when I whisper, "I want to go home."

"I can help you do that. If you will let me."

"Why would you help *me*?" No one helps me. The old man I saved, Horace, asked if I needed anything, but he'll forget me soon. Everyone does.

"Because you are special," she says, placing one hand on my cheek. "And because someone should."

The memory leaves me chilled. I grab a chunk of amethyst and rub my thumb along the edges of the crystal, trying to calm down. It doesn't work.

I take a shaky breath and try to ignore the burning in my eyes. I don't care that my parents kicked me out again. I *don't*. Horace has taken better care of me in the last three months than they ever did.

Remembering always dredges up too much to shove it back in a cage—too much anger, too much pain, too many of the memories that came after. So many of those memories include J.R. Body trembling, I cross the room and dig through one of my boxes until I find it.

This picture is one of the only ones I have of J.R. The kid looked a lot like me. The same white-blond hair and blue eyes. Well, we used to have the same eyes before I came back with a demon's vision and powers. He's on my shoulders, his tiny arms wrapped under my chin like a hatband to keep from falling off, and he's laughing. He was always laughing. And he could always make me laugh.

I have it because my mother threw it at me when I stopped her from lighting my shit on fire. The original frame and glass shattered when it smacked onto the pavement. The broken shards left little cuts and divots all over the picture, the worst one a long scratch that strikes straight across my chest. I screamed at her for throwing it then, but now? I probably should've thanked her. The only other picture I have of us is the one they used in the newspaper article about J.R.'s death.

Staring at that picture reminds me why I'm here. There are answers in Swallow's Grove. K.T. is connected somehow, and Mariella has to know something. Maybe she's another survivor; maybe she's a potential victim. Whatever it is, I have to find her. I have to find her before someone else gets killed because of a world most people don't know exists.

Six

Mariella

Thursday, August 28 – 12:22 PM

This aria is getting on my nerves. I've been listening to it on repeat for hours, but for some reason, the cabaletta is giving me trouble. No matter how many times I listen to it, I can't make the notes stick in my head. Giving up, I start reading a new book, letting the aria continue to loop and hoping the song will sink into my brain on its own.

The front door opens and closes, but I don't look up. My mother has students all day.

"Dana?"

The voice pulls me away from the story. I slide a bookmark into place and pull one of my earbuds out. My father is home? He's *never* home this early unless something is wrong.

I reach the doorway as he passes. He's nearly skipping. *Skipping.*

My mother comes out of the kitchen, drying her hands on a dishtowel. The concern in her expression doesn't last long. She doesn't have a chance to say hello before he wraps his arms around her waist and spins her in a circle. Squealing and laughing, she holds onto his shoulders until he puts her down and kisses her.

"You. Are. A. Genius," he says, punctuating each word with a kiss.

"Yes, I know." She laughs, her cheeks flushing. "What did I do this time, though?"

"I took your advice. Went over to introduce myself to Lawson."

"How'd it go?"

"Amazing," he says, grinning wide. "They're coming for dinner tomorrow."

"They?" My mother's head tilts a little. "Who else is with him?"

My father blinks. "Oh. Um, his name is Hudson. He's young, maybe a little older than you, Mari. I think he's Lawson's grandson."

He glances at me, so I shrug. Hudson will probably see me the same way the kids at school do—the freakish mute girl.

Lines appear around my father's eyes, and his smile dims a little. Maybe he's realizing he'll have to explain me to the man he's trying to impress? It passes, and his smile brightens again.

"We might be in luck," he says to my mother and me. "Apparently, he bought the house out from under his son at the last second. If I can come up with a proposal, I might have a shot."

My mother gasps and claps her hands. "Frank, that's fantastic!"

"Can you imagine what this could do for the company? My designs might actually be seen by the people who could put them to use!"

While my father's firm handles all kinds of projects, his personal specialty is restoration and "green" construction. He has a concept for low-cost, energy-efficient smart houses that he's been trying to get out into the world for years. If this Lawson guy really has the pull my father thinks he does, I'm starting to get why he's so excited about meeting him.

"Tomorrow?" My mother twirls the dishtowel, her lips pursed. "What to make, what to make..."

They start planning their dinner party, so I head back to my book. Before I get far, my father calls to me.

"Mari?" I glance over my shoulder, but he's standing there opening and closing his mouth like a fish. His gaze flicks to my mother before he takes a breath and lets the words rush out. "Well, do you think tomorrow you could—"

"Frank!" my mother hisses, slapping him with the dishtowel. "Don't. Just don't."

His face flushes. "I wasn't going to—"

"*Frank*!" Her eyes blaze, and my father backs down fast.

"Uh, never mind, Mari," he mumbles, swallowing hard. "Sorry."

My mother's glare sharpens, and she spins, her ponytail almost whipping my father in the face before she stalks back into the kitchen.

For a second, we both stand there staring after her, but then my father glances at me and away, his face flushing darker red.

"I *am* sorry, Mariella," he says, his voice quiet and his eyes downcast.

I wait until he looks up, then shrug before walking back to my books. It can't be an easy thing to explain to strangers why your only child refuses to say hello when she otherwise appears perfectly normal.

Settling back onto the window seat and opening my book, I make myself a promise. I will act as normal as possible for my father as long as he doesn't expect me to speak. Helping my parents out is one thing, but a famous architect and his grandson aren't worth breaking my promise to Orane.

Summer is usually one of my favorite seasons. Not because of the warm breezes or the flowers, but because I like how the days seem to melt away. It makes the time between visits to Orane's world feel shorter.

Today, I take back everything I ever said about summer days passing quickly.

Today is *dragging*.

Orane warned me not to get my hopes up, but I can't help it. I can't help the question burning through my brain—is tonight the night?

"How about it, Mari?" My mother smiles at me as we clear away the dinner dishes.

I stare at her, waiting for an explanation. I completely tuned out during the meal, so if this is a follow-up to something she said earlier, I missed it.

Her smile fades a little, but she shakes herself out of it quickly. "Scrabble, honey. It's been a little while since we played. Do you have the energy for a game tonight?"

Oh. I nod, and her smile regains its glow.

Every family has their traditions. Scrabble is one of ours. We played so often, we wore out boards and rubbed the letters off tiles. We got so good the tiles ran out too fast and the board was too small, so my father built us a custom set. Three hundred handcrafted tiles and a double-size board on a spinning base. It's dark wood and bronze accents, and it's one of my favorite things in this house. Third to my nightingale and my mother's upright piano.

The game progresses as it always does. My parents argue over spelling and meaning, constantly thumbing through a well-worn Scrabble dictionary to settle the more intense disagreements. I like listening to them, but for me, the game isn't exclusively about winning. It's about making sure some of my words have meaning. At least once every game, I play words that can serve as messages to my parents.

A few minutes into the game, I spot an opening and play my first message.

Propitiate: To appease.

Do they know I play these games for *them*? To make them feel better? To offer them something in exchange for what I've taken away?

"Oh, good one," my mother says as she tallies up the score. She doesn't see it. It's just a word on a game board to her. Frowning, I lean my chin against the coffee table.

Picking up her own tiles and placing them down on the board, she asks, "Frank, how about my curried chicken tomorrow?"

What? Why is she planning tomorrow's dinner already?

"Hmm." My father shakes his head. "Curry is tricky. What if he doesn't like spice?"

Oh. Right. I almost forgot about the dinner party. They keep talking about dinner, speculating what Horace and Hudson might like. I keep my eyes on the board, watching the growing lines of letters until I see my chance.

Two turns later, I play my next message—cherish.

"I always liked that word," my mother says as she adds up the score. "'Love' is nice, but there's something special about 'cherish.'"

"It's used less often," my father points out.

This starts a discussion about the value of rarity and whether overuse really does dilute meaning, or if one word is intrinsically more special than another. I listen, wondering how long it will take them to realize they're arguing for the same side.

Near the end of the game, I play my last message—absolve.

Watching their faces, I hope they'll see it this time.

Can they forgive me for leaving them behind? Will they *ever* be able to forgive me? If there was some way to bring them with me, I would, but it's impossible. Years ago, I asked. Orane explained most humans aren't capable of seeing his world. My parents aren't. Even if he thought it might be safe to bring them with me, they wouldn't see the doorway.

My mother sighs. "She's beating us again."

"How is that a surprise?" My father grins and runs a hand over my hair. "Mari's always been too smart for her own good."

Lot of help *that* is. I can't make them understand what I'm trying to tell them when we play these games. Even in the beginning, when my words were far more obvious, they didn't see it. Like "sorry." How could they not have recognized that one?

"Oh, all right." My mother laughs and tosses the score sheet on the table. "I can admit when I'm beat."

As my father and I clear away the game, my mother leans forward.

"This is the last weekend before school starts, Mari," she says. My father pauses, glancing at me but saying nothing.

Is it? Wow. How'd that happen so fast?

"Are you *sure* you don't want to go shopping?" she asks.

I nod. What do the clothes I wear here matter when Orane can create everything I need in his world? Plus, it would be awful to make her spend money on something I might not be using for much longer.

She sighs and dumps the rest of her tiles into the black velvet bag. "Thought I'd ask."

Her words register, but I don't really hear her.

Soon, Orane said. Soon might be a week from tonight or a year from now, but soon is so much better than never. Soon is hope, and I can live on hope this strong for a long time.

When I open my eyes in Paradise, I'm standing on the narrow cobblestone path running through the cherry orchard. I take a deep breath of the sweet cherry blossoms as the air around me ripples. My pajamas shrink and change color, transforming from black pants and a T-shirt to a Marilyn Monroe-style one-piece swimsuit in a gold cloth that shimmers in the twilight. I smile and run a hand over the soft, ruched fabric.

Apparently, we're going swimming.

I run down the path, my arms spread wide and my hair trailing behind me like a streamer. My fingers catch the low-hanging tree limbs, and a shower of petals in white, pink, red, blue, and gold rain down in my wake.

Orane is waiting for me in the distance, on the edge of the lake under the willow tree. He smiles when his violet eyes meet mine.

"Mariella."

His voice carries to me on the breeze, and I feel his lips press against my cheek despite the distance between us. Grinning, I pick up speed. Trees fly past in a blur as I cross the expanse in seconds. Time and distance mean nothing here. All that matters are dreams and whether or not you have the will to make them real.

When I'm close, I launch myself into his arms. Laughing, he catches me and spins me around.

Before my feet touch the ground, I look up into his eyes. "Is it time yet?"

Orane chuckles and kisses the tip of my nose. "Impatient little bird. I knew it was a mistake to tell you beforehand."

"So is that a yes or a no?"

"Not tonight, Mariella."

My heart drops into my stomach. Despite warning myself not to expect anything, I'd hoped. I lock my smile on my face. "I had to ask."

His hand brushes along the side of my face, and I would shiver under his touch but his eyes are holding me too tight. My smile isn't fooling him. I can tell.

"Do not despair, Nightingale," he whispers. His eyes grow brighter until they're practically glowing like bioluminescent gems. "The time grows closer every night. Soon, you will never leave this world again."

"Promise?" I hate how breathless and lost my voice sounds, but I can't help it. I can't control it.

When he speaks, the words vibrate through my entire body, like the seal of his promise is a tangible thing. "I swear it."

For a second—a minute? an hour? a year?—I'm locked in Orane's gaze and can't escape. I don't want to. The world is warm and wonderful with him this close. All these years later, he's a mystery. A challenge. Yet he's also the one person I don't mind losing to because, when I lose, I win.

His lips lock on mine, and I lose my breath. Tangling my hands in his hair, I pull him closer. It's not close enough. Our tongues dance, and his hands run across my bare arms, down my body, and play with the hem at the bottom of my suit. My pulse stalls for a moment and then catapults into speeds that would probably burst my heart if I were awake. Shivers are a thing of the past. My body is shaking, trembling, and convulsing with heat more intense than anything I thought was possible.

And then he pulls away.

Cold hits me like a wave. All that wonderful, intoxicating, mind-warping warmth vanishes. I sway on my feet, my entire body numb and my limbs leaden. Breathing is impossible. My lungs feel like they're carved out of marble.

I'm beginning to get rid of the awful emptiness when Orane smiles. He gestures toward the calm, aquamarine lake.

"Shall we?"

I shake off the last bits of the cold weight that possessed me. Smiling, I link my arm through his. "Lead the way."

We glance at each other and sprint for the water, diving under the surface as soon as we're out of the shallows. Dolphins and brightly colored fish with long, flowing fins surround us, creating a living obstacle course for us to dive under and curve around as we race from one end of the lake to the other.

In his world, the water is as breathable as air. Swimming here is what I imagine flying in the waking world might be like. We use currents in the water the way birds use currents of air, propelling ourselves at impossible speeds or floating and letting the underwater world pass around us. We play for hours until Orane takes my hand and tows me toward shore.

He stands and sweeps me into his arms, carrying me out of the water like a lifeguard rescuing a drowning girl. I suppress a smile and glare up at him.

"I can walk, you know."

"Yes, but where is the fun in that?" He wiggles his eyebrows at me, and I start laughing, my hold on my false anger disintegrating.

Within seconds, we're both perfectly dry. When he puts me down at the base of the willow tree, the air around me shifts and ripples again. Looking down, I watch my suit transform into a bright-orange, ruffled party dress.

Hmm...not one of his better choices.

"I don't know if orange is really my color," I tell him.

"No? A pity." He smiles and shrugs. "It suits you."

A snap of his fingers and the dress changes to black. Much more classic. I could do without the ruffles, but this is good.

With the appearance of a dress, I expect him to turn toward the opera hall, but instead he steps closer and picks up a handful of my hair, staring at it as he lets the golden strands fall from his fingers.

"Do you know what day it will be two weeks from tomorrow?" he asks.

I watch him playing with my hair and shrug. "A Friday?"

"Technically, yes." He tweaks the end of my nose and shakes his head. "Not quite what I meant, however."

I roll my eyes, but I can't keep the smile off my face. What's the date today? My mother mentioned that school starts on Tuesday; that makes it the beginning of September. So, approximately two weeks from the beginning of September is...

"My birthday?"

His eyes widen, and his mouth drops to an O. "So it *is*!"

I laugh and try to slap his arm, but he catches my wrist and locks it against my side, quickly doing the same with the other. His smile quivers.

"Eighteen already," he says, his voice quiet but intense. "I never imagined the sad little girl I met all those years ago would become so important."

"I didn't think you were real for a long time," I confess. "I thought you were someone I'd dreamed up."

"A dream worth reliving every night for ten years?" he asks, chuckling and slowly loosening his hold.

"For eternity," I whisper, winding my arms around his neck to keep him close.

"Good." He leans down and brushes his lips against mine. "That is exactly how long I plan on keeping you."

Seven

Hudson

Friday, August 29 – 10:45 AM

I'll probably meet Mariella when school starts next week, but I don't want to wait another five days. Plus, I had the same dream again last night—Mariella going up in flames. As disturbing as it was the first time, it's gotten worse every time since. Night after night, I've watched her burn and haven't been able to stop it once. Six times already. I'd rather not hit lucky number seven.

"Hey, I'm gonna head up to that New Age store I found," I tell Horace after breakfast.

"Take the Camaro," he says.

"I don't mind driving the Camry, Horace."

I love the Camaro—seriously, that car is a work of art—but Horace has had that car since it was built in '69. I can't make myself take it when he's got a perfectly decent Camry with a hell of a lot less sentimental value sitting around.

Horace shakes his head. "Kid, you're gonna need a car, and I'm gettin' too creaky to be driving that thing anymore. I always meant to give it to one of the grandkids, but none of them seemed to like it much." His eyebrows furrow. "Their loss, I guess."

"What? Horace, you can't just give me a car." My own parents never bought me a car. If I hadn't had driver's ed in school, I wouldn't have even gotten my license.

"Don't argue with me! I'm taking the damn Camry, so you drive the Camaro or go buy your own damn car."

He's grumping, but I can see the twinkle in his eyes and the tremor of his suppressed smile. Tossing me the keys, he waits for a second, but I am at a complete loss for words. Is he really giving me his Camaro?

"Git outta here before it gets too late to go," he calls as he heads upstairs.

I toss the keys into the air and let them fall back into my palm. The two keys on the ring are attached to an amethyst keychain I bought for Horace. Guess I'll have to buy another one for the Camry.

Tossing the keys one more time, I head out to the Camaro. *My* Camaro.

The two stores I found are in opposite directions and in different towns, but the drive is nice. When the road rises, I can see the foothills of the Adirondack Mountains in the distance. When the mountains are blocked by trees, there's the smell of pine and birch in the air and the babbling of creeks that run alongside some of the roads.

The first store I walk into is simply called "New Age," and it's what I've come to expect from this kind of store. They have a small selection of crystals; I buy most of them before getting back in the car and heading north toward a store called "A Stone's Throw From Normal."

When I walk in, I see two walls filled with bookshelves that, at a quick glance, don't appear to be organized in any particular way. Running through the center are shelves, tables, and glass cases that create a slightly hazardous maze—a fact I don't fully realize until I try turning around and almost knock a glass unicorn off its perch.

"Sorry, sorry!" a tiny girl says as she rushes out of the back room. She has short brown hair, and brown eyes behind oversized glasses. Looks like she's about ten. "I keep trying to convince Mom to let me reorganize everything, but she says it would disrupt her chi."

The girl takes the unicorn from my hands and places it inside a glass case.

"I think she's just lazy." She locks the case and turns back to me, a huge smile on her face. "Are you looking for something particular?"

I wait for her to comment on my eyes, to shy away or shriek, but she doesn't. She smiles and waits for me to explain my presence in her store.

"Um, I'm looking for amethyst geodes and maybe some raw jet, black jade, spider jasper, and malachite."

"Wow. That's quite an order." Her grin grows wider as she turns toward the one wall not filled with books. "Mom is going to be mad she missed you."

"Well, she might get a chance." I follow the girl, watching her carefully. There's something off about the way she moves. "I need a lot. I'll probably be back more than once."

She glances at me over her shoulder as she extends her arm, automatically sweeping back and forth as though clearing away cobwebs. "I can show you what we usually carry, which isn't anything larger than the palm of my hand. Except some of the amethysts."

I realize what's off. She can't see where she's going—at least, not very well. Her glasses, which are about half an inch thick, don't seem to be doing her much good, but she must know her way around the store by heart because she ends up exactly where I need to be.

"How many do you want?" She sits down and picks up a small geode from the bottom shelf, holding it so close to her face it's almost touching the tip of her nose.

"A lot."

She looks up at me from the floor. "More than we've got here?"

They have about a shelf's worth of raw amethyst, but I might need to set up protections for three different houses at some point—Horace's, K.T.'s, and Mariella's.

"Yes."

"Awesome! Here." She grins again and tosses me the geode in her hands.

I catch it, surprised by the accuracy of her aim.

"That's the best piece we have," the girl assures me, pushing herself to her feet and dusting her hands off on her jeans. "I take care of our inventory."

That's a weird arrangement if it's her mom's store. "What does your mom do?"

"Usually? Deal with customers. It's easier for her to run the register, and she's more what people expect when they come into a New Age bookstore. I'm a little too normal to fit the bill."

"Or a little too little. How old are you anyway?"

"Fourteen. And yes, I know I look like I'm ten. And yes, I know I shouldn't be left on my own, blah, blah, blah."

"I never said that." I smile. She kinda reminds me of what J.R. might have been like at this age, full of energy and humor. "I guessed you're older than you look."

She laughs and almost trips on a Buddha statue sitting in the middle of the floor.

"Oh, Goddess bless!" She sighs and straightens up, a frown on her face and her cheeks slightly pink. "I can't see very well."

"I noticed," I admit, trying not to laugh. "It seems like you do pretty well, though."

She smiles again. "Yeah. I'm legally blind, but I have days where I can almost see a foot in front of my nose. I'm Dawn, by the way." She sticks out her hand, and I shake it.

"Hudson." My hand engulfs hers entirely; it looks like her arm ends at the wrist.

"Wow." Her already-big eyes get wider as she steps closer, her head tilting back to look at me. "You actually *are* that big? I thought my eyes were playing tricks again. How tall are you?"

"Six-foot-five."

"Seriously?" She sighs. "I'll be surprised if I ever break five feet."

"Height is one of the least important things in life."

"Yeah, but that's because you have it." She tilts her head back farther and frowns. "I'm so short I could practically disappear."

With a personality like hers? "You could shrink to two feet tall and you wouldn't disappear."

She grins. "That is probably the nicest thing anyone has said to me in a long time."

Really? She must have some crappy friends. "Maybe you should get out more."

"Maybe," she says, shrugging.

I grab a basket of tumbled amethyst stones and toss everything else I plan on buying in with them. Dawn watches me with wide eyes.

"Wow. You weren't joking. That sounds like a lot."

And it might not be enough. "How soon can you get more?"

"Um, a few days at least. Especially since the weekend is, like, tomorrow."

I tell her how much I think I'll need, and her jaw drops.

"Goddess bless. And you're actually gonna *buy* all that?"

"Yeah." I load a few more chunks of black jade into the basket and stand up. "And I'll take all this today."

"Oh my Gaia!" she shrieks. "You have no idea how—I mean, this means I can get—ahhh!"

She launches herself at my stomach, wrapping her arms around my waist and hugging tight. "Thank you, thank you, thank you!"

After she lets me go, Dawn takes half of my stones and helps me carry them to the register, chatting happily about suppliers and the special computer display she can afford to buy because of how much money I'm spending.

This girl has something special, something the demons might find appealing. There's a brightness about her that can pull a good mood out of people like me.

Taking a shot in the dark, I switch to the filter that showed me as a white knight.

I knew it. Glowing with a glittering ivory light, her second self looks older, though not much taller. Her hair is still cropped to her chin, but her glasses are gone. Wider than ever, her brown eyes seem to take in everything, and her hands are held out like she's feeling ripples in the air around her.

The image is there, but I don't know what it means exactly. More importantly, it makes me worry she might become a target. Dawn is the same age I was when Calease showed up. The same age as Mariella when she stopped talking. I don't know if the demons will ever find her, but just in case…

On my way out, I say, "Dawn, this may sound crazy, but if you start having dreams about an angel-like being who promises to be your best friend, don't trust them."

"Are you serious?" She puts her free hand on her hip and rolls her eyes. "I run a New Age store. I know supernatural beings only appear to mediums, unless they've been invoked. Showing up in the dreams of someone like me? Hellooo! Major red flag."

I grin. This girl is going to be hell when she grows up. "Well, not everyone is as smart as you."

After stowing my new arsenal so the stones don't crack against each other while I drive, I head back to Swallow's Grove and aimlessly wind through town, looking for anything that might point me toward Mariella. There's nothing. At least, nothing obvious.

Giving up for the night, I stop at the grocery store before heading back to Horace's.

"Don't forget. We got dinner with the Teagans tonight," Horace calls as soon as I walk through the door.

"Yeah, I know," I shout back.

I head into the kitchen, grab every mixing bowl and pot we have, and fill them all with the sea salt I picked up on the way home. I place the stones at careful intervals in the different bowls and begin pouring the salt over them. It's a cleansing ritual I read about that helps strengthen the stones' connection to their new owner. I need any help I can get.

"If I didn't know better, I'd swear you were batshit crazy, Hud," Horace says when he walks into the kitchen and sees my bowls of salt spread all over the place. "Guess it really is a good thing someone else is cookin' tonight, huh?"

The corner of my lip twitches. "Unless you feel like eating salt soup."

After I shower and change, I find Horace peering into the bowls, shifting the salt aside with a wooden spoon.

"Don't do that." I flick the spoon away, and Horace grins.

"Is it soup yet?"

I roll my eyes and hand him one of the bowls. "Help me scoop these out."

We gather a few of the larger chunks of amethyst, malachite, and black jade, and I carry them to the car with me when we finally get ready to go. I don't know exactly when, how, or if I'm going to use them, but I'd rather have them with me. Just in case.

The Teagans are a couple streets over, but we drive anyway. The old man may pretend he's as strong as he was in his forties, but he's pushing eighty now.

Everything is fine until I turn onto the street. As soon as I do, the back of my neck starts tingling. The closer I get to their house, the more those tingles turn into pinpricks that spread down my arms and raise goosebumps on my skin. The last time I felt like this, I met K.T. The time before that, I got jumped by two idiots with knives, and one with a 9mm and a twitchy trigger finger. Without this slight warning, I would've died instead of adding a gunshot graze and two knife wounds to my collection of scars.

What's waiting for me here?

I don't have the time to guess before I see it.

There at the end of the street is the two-story Craftsman house with red trim, like it was plucked straight out of my dream and dropped into Swallow's Grove. Or, no, I've got that backward. It was plucked right out of Swallow's Grove and dropped into my dream.

I press the brake, stopping a hundred yards from the house.

"Horace."

"Is this it?" he asks, peering out the window at the house we're stopped in front of.

"Horace!" I point up the street at the house. "That's the house."

"Oh." Horace leans forward, squinting to see the house in the dying light. "Hmm. Nice work on the—"

"No, Horace. *That* is the *house*. The house from my dream."

"Ho-ly succotash. What are the chances of her father knockin' on our door the day we pull into town?" Horace's eyes get wide, and he glances between me and the house. "Every time I think I got a grip on this crazy shit going on in your head, I realize I don't know the half of it, do I?"

My eyes tracing the red trim of the house, I shake my head. "Not even close."

Horace takes a long, slow breath, whistling as he exhales. "So? What now?"

"Are you kidding?" I slowly press on the gas, and the car rolls closer to our destination. "I've been looking for her since we got here. We're going in."

"Don't do anything unnecessarily stupid, kid," he warns as I park on the street and we get out. "Whatever's goin' on with the girl, I don't think her folks have a damn clue. You scare them, and you won't be able to ask her anything."

I stop on the sidewalk, forcing myself to close my eyes and breathe. One of the most useful things Calease taught me was meditation. It's been months, but I hate admitting anything that demon taught me was useful. At the same time, I'm willing to accept help from her if it means taking down the rest of her kind.

I breathe in cycles of four until my pulse returns to normal and my hands stop trembling.

Opening my eyes, I look up at the house. In there is a blonde who has a key to the dreamworld. If I play it right, *all* the answers I need may be here.

"Should I grab my sunglasses?" I ask.

It takes a second, but then Horace shakes his head. "They're gonna have to see you without 'em sooner or later. Might as well ease them into gettin' used to you." He takes a breath. "Just don't be stupider—"

"Than I need to be," I finish for Horace. I glance at him, but his eyes are on the house. "I'll keep that in mind."

We start up the paver-stone path leading to the front porch. The daylight is disappearing faster now, but the warm yellow glow pouring from the windows lights the place up like a beacon. Horace knocks on the door, and we wait a couple of seconds before a woman opens it.

"Hello!" She smiles wide and steps aside to let us in.

In low heels, she's Horace's height. Her golden-blonde hair hangs straight past her shoulders, and her wide eyes are honey-brown. She looks exactly like the girl in my dream, just twenty years older. If she hadn't spoken, I'd think this was Mariella and I'd just underestimated her age.

"You must be Mr. Lawson." Grinning, she holds her hand out to Horace. "Frank has told me so much about you. I'm Dana."

"Horace, please," the old man says as he shakes her hand. "Never did get used to being called Mr. Lawson. This here is Hudson."

Dana looks at me—*really* looks at me—for the first time and jumps. It's a tiny hitch in her shoulders and a widening of her eyes, a catch in her breath and a slackness to her jaw, but it's there. The shock of looking at something impossible. Scarily demonic. Black eyes belong on obsidian statues and in horror movies, not on a teenage boy standing in a well-lit, comfortable entryway.

To her credit, Dana recovers fast. She smiles shakily and holds out her hand. Would she let me in her house if her husband wasn't such a fanboy of Horace's?

"Horace!" Frank's grin is as wide as when he stopped by the house. "So glad you both could join us!"

"Frank, you remember Hudson?" Dana asks. The slight tremor in her voice gives away her fear.

"Of course!" He turns to extend his hand to me and freezes mid-gesture. He flinches, swallows, and his movements slow, like he has to literally force himself to complete the motion. "It's, uh, it's good to see you again, Hudson."

"Thanks for inviting us," I say. I need to play nice. I can't do much about my eyes, but I can hope Horace's influence will make them give me a chance.

"Is Hudson your grandson?" Dana asks as her husband quickly steps away from me.

"Nah. Hudson here saved my life a few years back."

I tense and glance at Horace. What the hell? That story isn't really dinner-conversation material. But Dana's eyes widen, this time with interest.

"Really?"

As we move into the living room, Horace tells Dana and Frank all about my daring rescue four years ago. The way he tells it, I sound like some sort of superhero. It's ridiculous. Or so I think until I notice that, the more they listen, the longer Frank and Dana can look at me without wincing when they meet my eyes. Maybe the old man isn't as crazy as I thought.

"Hudson fell on hard times recently, so I basically adopted him," Horace says when he finally wraps up his exaggerated tale. "My own grandkids are scattered, so it's nice havin' someone around to help me out."

I shake my head. "You've helped me out a lot more than I help you, Horace."

The old man glances at me and winks, but otherwise he ignores me.

"That was very brave of you to do, Hudson," Dana says, smiling at me without fear or hesitation for the first time.

An alarm starts beeping somewhere, and Dana looks toward the noise. "Sounds like dinner's ready. Frank, will you go let Mari know?"

Dana leads us toward the kitchen while Frank heads upstairs. My pulse picks up. I remind myself to stay calm and breathe in cycles of four, but it doesn't help. This time I can't stop the tingling running across my skin.

Dana and Horace are talking food—not having a good kitchen in the house is bugging the hell out of Horace—but I barely hear them. I stay near the stairs to keep an eye out for Mariella.

I see the glow before I see her. The orange light is so strong it's hard to believe the house isn't on fire, but when feet appear at the top of the staircase, I can finally see that the light isn't coming from the house. It's coming from *her*.

My heart beats so fast I can't tell the pulses apart—it's one harsh thrum inside my head. If I'm a Smurf, this girl is an Oompa Loompa. No. Not even. It looks like she walked out of a horror movie. She really is on fire, burning from the inside out.

I'm staring, but I can't help it. Everyone would be staring if they could see what I see.

Horace nudges me with his elbow, and I close my eyes. The light is so bright it seeps through my eyelids until I switch filters. Opening my eyes and looking through my more normal vision, Mariella's fire is down to a soft orange shimmer surrounding her body, finally dim enough for me to see the girl underneath.

She's wearing slightly baggy jeans, black sneakers, and a shapeless, gray long-sleeved shirt. Her hair is bound in a single long braid that hangs over her shoulder and ends at the top of her thigh, and she has something in her hand she's rubbing like a worry stone.

"Mariella, this is Horace and Hudson," Dana says, beckoning her daughter closer. "This is our daughter, Mariella."

"Well, ain't you the spittin' image of your mama," Horace says, smiling at Mariella.

Dana wraps her arm around Mariella's shoulders and kisses her forehead. Mariella's lip quivers a little, but she doesn't quite smile.

"You gonna be a senior this year?" Horace asks. "Hudson here is starting his senior year up at the high school next week."

He keeps smiling, but now there's tension in the air. Dana and Frank glance at each other. Mariella tilts her head to the side, watching everything, saying nothing.

"Um, yes, Mari will be a senior this year," Dana says before the silence hits the highly awkward five-second mark. "She has a condition, though. Selective mutism. Mari hasn't spoken a word in a few years now."

Only because I'm watching so closely do I catch the tiny flare of Mariella's nostrils and the way her eyes lift to the ceiling when her mother says "condition." She seems amused by the phrase "selective mutism"—her lip tics when Dana says that. And she acts proud when her mother mentions how long it's been since she last spoke. Her shoulders pull back a bit and that tiny lift to the corner of her mouth gets a little more pronounced.

Mariella's not trapped by the demons; she's *thrilled* by their hold on her. Or she's impressed by her own silence, at the very least.

Jesus. This girl is locked into their world more than I ever was. How am I supposed to get through to someone who won't talk and probably won't listen to a damn word I have to say?

K.T. called Mariella *Mission: Impossible.* I'm starting to think she underestimated.

Mariella's eyes meet mine, and in one look, she sizes me up and completely dismisses me.

This is the girl who has the answers I need? *This* is why I moved across state lines?

Oh, yeah. This is gonna be a fucking *blast.*

Eight

Mariella

Friday, August 29 – 7:08 PM

Hudson is unlike anyone I've ever met before. The sheer size of him is *insane*. Why would anyone need to be that tall? His hands are about the size of my head. He could probably snap my neck in half without blinking.

And he won't stop staring at me. Why won't Hudson stop *staring* at me?

His eyes are the worst. Everything else, even the fact that he's built like Goliath, is normal compared to those too-large, too-black, too-glittery eyes.

My hand tightens around my nightingale, and I breathe in deep, trying to calm down.

Years ago, Orane taught me a meditative breathing cycle. It was during the first few months of my promise, when it was excruciatingly difficult to resist speaking. He taught me how to clear my head and calm my thoughts, promising that, when I held onto my nightingale and meditated, the dreamworld's light would grow, protecting me.

I do that now, but as soon as I begin, Hudson's eyes widen. He shifts forward, and my breath catches, the air locking in my throat. He freezes, then steps back until he's leaning against the wall.

What just happened? He couldn't possibly see the way the light began to spread out from the nightingale, sliding up my arms and down my legs...could he?

I try it again.

His hands clench into fists, and his entire body tenses. I keep breathing. He looks away, his jaw tense.

Who *is* this guy?

"Everyone grab a seat," my mother says, squeezing my shoulder one more time before walking toward the stove.

The dining room table is built for six, but we've rarely had more than the three of us sitting here, especially after I went silent. My father takes the head of the table, guiding me into the seat on his left. Everyone else fills in around us. I end up across from Horace and my mother. Which means...

The chair next to me glides back silently. Hudson sits, and the legs scrape against the wood as he scoots closer to the table.

I'm not used to the table being this full. It doesn't help that Hudson is so broad I'm dwarfed next to him. And it's like he's surrounded by electricity. The closer he gets, the more these static-like zaps run up and down my arm. No, it's more like my arm is waking up after restricted blood flow. That sharp pins-and-needles sensation makes it hard to sit still.

My mother scoops salad onto everyone's plate. I try to concentrate on the crunchy green food and the tangy dressing smell in the air, but it's impossible. My arm is tingling too intensely to ignore. It's only been a couple of minutes, but I'm already starting to twitch. And what is that *noise*? It sounds like someone is setting up a PA system outside and getting feedback.

Scooting my chair a little farther away from him, I grip my nightingale tighter and—

"Don't do that."

His voice is so quiet I can barely make out the words, but when I glance up, he's staring straight at me.

"The breathing? And the thing with the bird? I'd appreciate it if you didn't do that." My mouth drops open. Hudson shrugs. "The glow is giving me a headache."

My stomach clenches, and I'm breathing like I just sprinted a mile. He goes back to eating like nothing happened, but his words replay in my head. Did he say *glow*? But…he can't possibly see it. No one can see it. No one but me.

"Hudson, Horace was telling me you're an artist?" my mother asks.

Hudson tenses, looking at Horace before smiling a little and facing my mother. "It's a hobby more than anything."

"What mediums do you prefer?" she asks.

They go back and forth, discussing music and art as my father and Horace dissect my father's work on our house and a few other projects he's done around the county. In this group, I am most definitely a fifth, highly unnecessary wheel, but the longer they talk, the easier it is to convince myself I didn't hear Hudson right. There's no way he can see my nightingale's glow. He's just an overgrown boy with freaky eyes.

I sigh and push the rest of the salad around my plate with my fork. Tonight, I can't bring myself to even *pretend* to enjoy this food. Hudson shifts closer, and I barely bite back a hiss as the tingling in my arm grows sharper. I drop my fork, then clench and relax my hand, trying to get blood flow back.

The conversation pauses as my parents retreat to the kitchen to pick up the next course. They bring back a platter of chicken breasts and a bowl of vegetables and pick up their sentences exactly where they left off moments ago.

"I've taught music for years now. Mari used to play herself," my mother says, her voice heavy and thick. "But you know how it goes. I can't get her to sit down at the piano anymore."

She smiles as though she doesn't care, but she stabs the next chicken breast a little too hard. Hudson glances at me. I scoot farther away.

Hudson manages to charm both of my parents by demonstrating a decent grasp of both art and architecture, and by the end of the meal, my father is more smitten with Horace than he was at the beginning.

And the needle-sharp tingling in my arm is spreading into my chest and down into my right leg. I'm ready to crawl out of my skin.

"Of course, of course," my father says as we all carry our plates into the kitchen. "I think that's a major concern as well. Have you done much with solar power?"

Their conversation continues, but the words are lost as the needles turn into knives poking into my back. The sensation is spreading faster now, stretching out from the right side of my body and engulfing me entirely. And the feedback I thought I heard at a distance earlier climbs in volume, like the PA system is now somewhere inside the house. I wince, look around, and almost gasp.

Hudson is standing inches behind me.

Dropping my plate on the counter with a clatter, I leave. My mother's mouth moves as I pass, but I don't hear what she says.

I nearly run from the room, clutching my nightingale and trying to breathe. Even my *lungs* are prickling. Breathing makes it worse. My entire body is shaking before I reach the stairs. The feeling doesn't start to die until my foot lands on the first step.

Before I reach the second, a hand grabs my arm.

My heart stops, and I have to bite my tongue to keep from screaming. My hands come up, ready to push him away. It's Hudson. It has to be Hudson!

Then my vision focuses, and I'm looking into my mother's eyes.

"Mari? Honey, are you okay? You look pale, sweetie. Why did you run away like that?" Her hand comes up to my face like she's checking my temperature, her lips pursed. "We were going to play Scrabble. I know your father was hoping you'd play."

I take a long, slow breath, noticing that the prickles are dying down. Whatever they were. It might be stupid to consider it, but the sensation didn't start until Hudson showed up. And it's a lot worse when he's nearby. I promised my father I'd be as normal as possible, but can I sit through another couple of hours with Hudson? If my muscles keep jumping like this, my control is going to snap and I'll start screaming like a banshee.

The tingling grows worse, and I glance over my mother's shoulder. Hudson stands in the kitchen with his hands in the pockets of his khakis, watching me. His black, long-sleeved button-down is as dark as his eyes, and though he's a foot or so from the doorway, he fills the frame.

I'm about to shake my head and go upstairs, if only to get myself as far from Hudson as possible, when my focus shifts. It slides past the size, the eyes, and the scary, and I see the way his lip curls as he watches me. Like he's laughing at me. My jaw clenches, and he raises one eyebrow.

I wish I had something other than my nightingale to throw at him. It's like he knows what's happening to me and knows I can't handle it. In that one mocking lift of his eyebrow, he's challenging me to stay.

Orane may beat me, but I refuse to let some overgrown *boy* do it.

Lifting my chin, I step down from the staircase and turn toward the living room.

I hear my parents and Horace talking over the *clink* and *clang* of dishes. Because I'm listening to them, I miss

Hudson's quiet footsteps. I notice the last one a split second before the tingle returns, raising goosebumps on the back of my neck.

Gritting my teeth, I ignore him.

"That is some Scrabble board."

His voice is low, somewhere between baritone and bass. It presses against me like a weight. As he gets closer, that feedback noise gets louder. The high-pitched whine of a mic held way too close to a speaker. It sends shudders down my spine, but I force my shoulders back. He won't make me run.

I jump as his hand crosses the board, reaching for a tile. His sleeves are rolled up to his elbows now, and I stare at the bare skin, my heart pounding and the whine forgotten.

What *happened* to him? There are so many scars and discolored patches of skin on his arm I can't count them. I also can't stop staring as he shakes his wrist to untangle the bead bracelets on his arm and lifts the tile closer to his face. At least, I think he's looking at the tile. With those eyes, it's impossible to tell where he's looking.

"Good work," he says, putting the tile back in the bag. "Handmade?"

I nod and glance toward the kitchen.

"Your dad?"

I nod again.

"Cool." He sits forward, his elbows resting on his knees. I rub at my ear. It doesn't make the feedback go away.

He reaches forward again, examining a detail on my father's board, and my curiosity overwhelms caution. Eyebrows furrowed, I point to his arm and sign, "*What happened?*" It's habit to sign now, but it's probably useless in this case. I doubt he knows Signing Exact English.

Hudson stares at me. It lasts so long that I shift under the weight of his eyes, but I refuse to look away. When Hudson finally blinks, he shakes his head.

"I don't know you well enough to tell that story." He leans back in the chair and rolls his sleeves down. When he's a few feet away, the feedback fades into an aggravating background noise. The tingling doesn't lessen at all.

A minute passes, and Hudson doesn't say a word. I barely have time to hope we'll sit in silence until everyone joins us before he looks at me and says, "Your friend K.T. says hi, by the way."

What? Who is K.T.?

He's watching me again, scrutinizing me.

Hudson huffs something that might be a laugh and looks away. I push to my knees and grab some Scrabble tiles, ready to start throwing them at him. Why does it seem like everything he says to me is some kind of insult I'm too stupid to follow? It's like he's speaking another language and I can only translate half the words. And I don't like the ones I understand.

Before I release the tiles, my mother's voice gets louder.

"And he made it himself when we got tired of playing by the board's limitations," she says to Horace.

She explains our house rules, and we all pick our tiles. The game progresses quickly, and the board starts filling. They keep talking over my head, but after four years of pulling myself out of conversations, I'm so used to it I barely notice.

Hudson looks at me and puts down two letters to create a three-letter, triple-score word.

Vow.

My hand lifts to my throat as the other grips my nightingale. I watch Hudson out of the corner of my eye. He smiles and tallies the score. He's facing Horace, but I can feel his eyes on me. The tingling gets worse when he's focused on me.

Coinci•ence, I tell myself. *Just a coinci•ence.*

But it's a little *too* coincidental. First mentioning a glow, and now a vow? But he *can't* possibly know about my promise. It's impossible. Orane broke the rules to let me into Paradise. No other human has been through those portals in hundreds of years.

It's a word on a Scrabble board. I'm reading too much into it. *I'm* the one with a habit of leaving messages in this game.

Breathing in fours, I draw energy out of the nightingale and hold on to that thought. He doesn't know. He can't know.

Less than five minutes later, he plays another word that sets my head spinning.

Paradise.

I want to knock the entire board over and run upstairs.

He shouldn't know. How can he know? Orane said—

Oh, no. What if one of the others broke the rules? I've never met any of the others, but Orane isn't alone.

I want to drag Hudson into another room and demand an explanation, but I can't risk exposing information he might not have.

Wait, I tell myself. *Wait until tonight. Tell Orane, and he'll know what to do.*

The game continues, and I eventually calm down. I'm slowly adapting to the prickling running up and down my body, and the strange whine is nearly background noise now. Awful background noise, but whatever.

Then Hudson plays another word.

Songbird.

My hand locks around my nightingale to keep myself from hitting him between the eyes with it.

Something clatters to the floor next to me, and I look down as Hudson bends to scoop up a fallen O tile.

"Told you to stop playing with that bird," he mutters, his voice a quiet rumble under my parents' chatter. He's so close his breath flutters against my cheek. I flinch as the whine gets louder and the pinpricks get sharper, more insistent, pounding against my skin until it's as bad as rolling on a bed of nails. Either he doesn't notice, doesn't know, or doesn't care. He whispers across the inches, "Too much of anything isn't good for you."

I nearly scream.

I want to pound my fists against his chest and yell that he has no idea what he's talking about. I want to demand he leave my house and never come back. I want to grab him by the collar and insist he tell me everything he *thinks* he knows about Paradise.

I *want* to do all of that, but the beak of my nightingale is biting into my palm. That tangible reminder of Orane's world holds me back from the edge. Barely.

Backing away and pushing Hudson as far out of my mind as I can, I stare at the tiles in front of me, only looking up when I have to make a play. For the first time in a couple of years, I lose. By a lot. But I don't care. I survived the game and refused to let Hudson run me off with his impossibly black eyes and cryptic words. I'm still here.

I may not have won the game everyone else was playing, but I won the one that matters.

As soon as my parents get up to show Horace and Hudson out, I step away. I stay in the room, though, hovering on the edges and refusing to retreat.

"You send over that design, and we'll see if we can't get the old house livable again," Horace says as he shakes my father's hand.

My father is practically glowing. "Of course. I'll bring it over Monday."

They say goodbye, and my mother hugs Hudson. *Hugs* him! I have to press my hands against my sides to keep from pulling her away.

At last, they're gone. My parents are too busy celebrating my father's possible contract to notice me disappear.

It's not until the electric tingle fades and I'm beginning to calm down that something occurs to me.

Hudson never saw what was in my hand. I closed my fist around the nightingale as soon as I came downstairs and didn't put it down once.

I stare at the small glass nightingale perched on the palm of my hand.

Isn't it bad enough he seemed to know about Paradise? How the hell did he know this was a bird?

Nine

Hudson

Friday, August 29 – 9:53 PM

"You got your work cut out for you with that one," Horace says once we're in the car.

I drop my head onto the steering wheel and take a long breath. My hands are shaking, and my eyes are dotted with spots of orange—the afterimage of that crazy light surrounding her. Sitting up, I shake myself out, rolling my neck and flexing my hands. Jesus, I've been wanting to do that all night.

"If you keep twitchin' like that, I'm gonna think you're developing a tic."

"Standing next to her is like holding onto a live wire," I mutter as I pull away from the curb. At the end of the street, I stop. I grab a few of the amethyst geodes and malachite stones from the back, stuffing the smaller pieces into my pockets.

"Keep going. I'll meet you at the house," I tell Horace.

"You get caught, and I'm gonna have a helluva time explaining this!" he calls after me.

Yeah, I think. *Me too.*

Staying in the shadows, I head back to the Teagans's house. The heat of the day is finally dying off, and the breeze whispering through the trees is almost cool. I freeze when a dog starts barking, but it's coming from a few houses down. He's not barking at me.

Through the front window, I see Dana and Frank cleaning up the wine glasses and the Scrabble game. Mariella isn't with them. I inch around the side of the house and check the upstairs windows. All are dark but one.

Right. Okay. Great. Now what?

I need to get upstairs and hide the stones somewhere. A few won't do much, but it's a start. I want to weaken the link as much as I can before I try to talk to her.

Their yard isn't fenced, and a row of thick bushes conceals me from the neighbors' view all the way around. I reach the back without being seen and scan the house. Then I get lucky. A window's open a crack on the second floor.

I take off my button-down and create a makeshift bag for the larger chunks of amethyst, and then I use the porch rail to lift myself onto the first-story roof. Stepping carefully on the shingles, I inch toward the window and ease it open. It's a dark, empty bathroom.

In an• out, I remind myself. Getting spotted right now will ruin *everything.*

There's no way in hell I'm getting into Mariella's room tonight, so I estimate which door is hers—not hard, considering it's the sole room on this floor with the lights on—and slip into the one next to it. Through the wall, I can barely hear the music she's playing. Good. It'll mask any noise I make.

As soon as I get close to the wall her bedroom shares with this one, the electric tingle comes back. It's faint—a lot fainter than when we were a couple feet apart—but it's definitely there. Moving quickly, I hide the stones where I can—under the bed, in the space between the dresser and the wall, and behind the nightstand. I don't know what, if anything, they'll be able to do from this far away, but I can always move them next time I'm here.

Before slipping into the hall, I listen for Dana and Frank. They're downstairs.

"When are you going to show Horace the concepts?" Dana asks. Something scrapes against the floor, and piano notes echo through the hall.

"Maybe he was being polite." Frank sighs. "I don't want him to feel like I'm pushing things on him."

Perfect. I have to make sure Horace asks to see those plans. A partnership between Frank and Horace means more chances for me to see Mariella. Who knows? Maybe Frank's concept is good.

A doorknob shifts down the hall. I dive into the bathroom and out of sight just as Mariella appears. She's rubbing her ear as she creeps out of her room. When she reaches the corner closest to the stairs, she sinks down, her head tilted toward the first floor. From here, I barely make out the song Dana is playing, but Mariella can hear it perfectly. Or she already knows it by heart. Her fingers move through the air on an invisible piano, and her entire body sways with the music. When it ends, she sighs, gets up, and tiptoes into her room, closing the door behind her.

Downstairs, Dana is still playing, but I guess Mariella heard what she wanted.

Exiting the way I came, I put my shirt back on and drop to the ground. As soon as I'm down, I run, staying in the trees until I can stroll onto the next street.

Ten minutes later, I'm back at the house.

"Boy, you got yourself a pickle here if I ever saw one." Horace shakes his head. "Saw an opium addict once. The look that girl got on her face sometimes? Reminded me of that."

An addict is probably the best comparison he could make, especially in her case. She held onto that bird tightly, pulling energy out of it. The light intensified so often I don't think she realized she was doing it half the time.

If that moment on the stairs showed me anything, though, it's that she's not *completely* gone. Some part of who she used to be must be in there.

"When Frank comes over with the plans, ask him to show you whatever concepts he mentioned tonight." I need to get back into that house. Soon and often.

Horace's eyebrows pull together, but then he nods. "Right, right. He said something about an energy-efficient smart house." Shrugging, Horace flattens the little bit of hair clinging to the side of his head. "Wouldn't hurt to look at it. But I'm tellin' you now, Hud. Not even for you and this girl will I buy a crappy concept."

"Didn't ask you to buy it, old man. Only want you to look at it. Maybe over dinner?"

His eyes brighten, and he laughs. "Fair deal, kid." He looks toward our pathetically broken kitchen and raises one eyebrow. "I mean, it's not like we can cook much here, right? It's either the kindness of strangers or takeout."

Chuckling to himself, Horace heads up to bed, and I retreat to my makeshift room.

I strip off my shirts, change into pajama pants, and collapse onto the bed. Doubt I'll sleep much, but the fight for control against that damn electricity sparking off Mariella wore me out. Besides, until I come up with a plan of attack against those ten-foot-thick fortifications she's built around herself, there's not much for me to do.

Lifting my right arm, I push my bracelets out of the way and run my thumb over the tattoo there. After I stopped by the cemetery and said goodbye to J.R., I went to a tattoo parlor and got it—his initials in stark black capitals, the date I lost him, and a red line across my wrist that looks like an open wound. I can't visit him every day, but at least I can carry him with me. To remind me why I'm doing all this. To remind me why fighting Mariella's defenses is worth it.

If I can pull her out of their trap, she may be able to give me answers I don't have. And if I can't...

If I can't, maybe I can use her to find a way back in.

I don't know when I fell asleep, but I open my eyes and my pulse takes off. This is a dream, but it's not like my premonition about Mariella and it's definitely not a memory. It's not quite like the dreamworld either, but the vibe is so close it scares the hell out of me.

A long table covered with a bright orange cloth sits in the center of a grassy glade. Brightly decorated cupcakes, sparkling punch-filled crystal bowls, colorfully wrapped presents, and a five-tiered cake fill the table. It looks like something straight out of the dreams of a seven-year-old girl—or maybe the tea party scene from *Alice in Wonderland*—except it's surrounded by a shadowy forest.

I step forward, and ripples at the head of the table coalesce into Mariella. She's wearing a long, flowing, golden gown almost exactly the same shade as the tumble of curls atop her head. Unlike at dinner, she smiles at me. She looks as graceful and regal as a fairytale princess, but as I take the seat to her left, I notice several things at once.

Mariella's leg is shackled to the table with a golden chain, and the spread of food, drinks, and desserts that looked so appetizing from afar is covered with mold, fungus, and bugs. My gaze darts to the trees, where a pair of deep purple eyes watches us. I can't tell if this is a dream or if I should be preparing for an attack. Hoping for the best and preparing for the worst, I turn my chair slightly so I can watch both the eyes and Mariella.

The silence is so heavy it's a physical pressure on my eardrums. It's like I've gone deaf. Maybe I *have*. When I pick up a spoon and strike the crystal goblet in front of me, I hear nothing.

Mariella looks over and smiles, nodding toward the cake in the center of the table. Unlike everything else on the table, the cake is pristine. The blue flowers look like they might be edible, and unlit candles line each tier. Eighteen candles.

Mariella isn't smiling anymore. With solemn eyes and a determined purse to her lips, she looks down at the shackle around her ankle. I glance at the eyes in the forest. They glow brighter and brighter until their light is so strong it tints the rest of the world violet.

I want to drag her away from here, but she's locked to the table. Ducking under it, I lean closer to the leg and study the way the chain is bolted in. Above me, Mariella attacks the disgusting buffet. Out of the corner of my eyes, I see platters of cookies and trays of cupcakes flying through the air. Peering out, I realize she's destroying everything between her and the still-perfect cake.

She tugs on the tablecloth to bring the cake closer. The moth-eaten fabric comes apart in her hands, but she's persistent. Each pull brings her closer to her goal, but each second pushes me farther from mine. The bolts won't loosen, and I don't know how to break Mariella loose without risking hurting her. Before I can free her, Mariella's hand drops to my shoulder and grips hard.

Holy hell. The eyes aren't in the trees anymore. They're locked in the face of a vaguely human, wraith-like form that is moving toward us, bringing along a wall of smoke.

We're running out of time.

Mariella tugs me to my feet, pointing at the cake. With my help, we bring it within reach. She mimes lighting the candles, but I don't have a lighter. And how will that help?

Glaring, she mimes again, striking her hands together and pointing to the chain. Would that work? Gold doesn't usually spark. I grab the chain and take a step back from the table, pointing at the chair to tell Mariella to sit back down. Once she's holding onto the arms for dear life, I take a deep breath and yank.

The wood cracks as the bolts rip free and come flying toward my head. On instinct, I catch them. When I look down at the pieces in my hand, I see something black. It might be flint, but it's definitely not a piece of golden shackle.

Sound returns.

It's somewhere between a whine and a high-pitched hiss, and the pain of it is worse than flying in an airplane with a head cold.

The demon screams his wordless fury, and thunder booms and crashes as wind rips through the trees.

The pressure grows. My head feels like it might explode, but I take my cue from Mariella. The only sign she gives that she senses the pressure too is the slight twitch of the muscles in her neck.

She pulls me closer, her small hands wrapping around my wrist and sending warmth through my body. As I light each candle, her grip gets tighter and the sounds get louder. We should be running, but Mariella must know something I don't.

With each new flame, the glow pushes farther out, almost like a protective dome arching around us. When I reach the last candle on the top tier, I hold my breath.

The noise quiets, like we closed a door and shut the storm outside. The wind doesn't touch us, and when I look at Mariella, she's smiling. She touches my cheek before turning her attention to the candles.

Holding my hand tight, she studies the cake. Looking for all the world like a princess celebrating her birthday, she takes a deep breath and blows out the candles.

We both drop into darkness.

Ten

Mariella

Friday, August 29 – 10:56 PM

Maybe that feedback noise didn't have anything to do with Hudson. He's been gone for hours, and I can still hear it. It went away for about five minutes, but then it came back. Not quite soft enough to be annoyingly ignorable background noise, yet not so loud that it overwhelms everything else either.

I try to sleep, but it's not easy. Holding on to my nightingale and breathing in the light of Paradise barely ease the whine. Forget clearing my head. It's impossible tonight. Every time I try, Hudson pops up.

Where did he come from? More importantly, what, exactly, does he know about Paradise?

I step through the portal and smell lavender. I'm on the edge of the field tonight, and the scent is stronger than ever. Lavender usually calms me down, but tonight it's cloying. Too heavy. Almost suffocating. It's not the only thing off tonight.

The twilight sky doesn't make me smile, the family of bunnies racing across the field doesn't make me laugh, and the sight of Orane with a pair of snow-white unicorns barely eases the shaking in my hands.

It takes him less than a second to notice. Frowning, he walks forward, taking one step before appearing in front of me. He wraps his arms around my shoulders and pulls me against his chest, stroking my hair.

"What happened?"

I take a deep breath…and hesitate.

What if I'm overreacting? What if I'm *wrong*? Hudson didn't threaten me. He simply knew too much. I don't want to worry Orane over nothing, but if I'm right and I don't tell him…

Maybe the middle ground is the best option. If I tell Orane exactly what happened, he can make up his own mind.

"It's probably nothing." I pull away and look up. "My parents had a dinner party."

"Tell me about it," he says.

"This boy named Hudson came over with his grandfather Horace because my father admires Horace's work with…something. I can't remember what now."

Orane stiffens, but his expression is almost blank.

Starting at the beginning, I tell him the whole story, including all the moments that made me question Hudson's knowledge. The more I talk, though, the more trivial all those moments seem.

My mother might have mentioned my nightingale to Hudson, and the words he played aren't exactly uncommon. They're practically elementary-school level. His apparent ability to see the glow could be explained, too. What if his eyes are that black because there's something wrong with the pupils? It would make sense that a high sensitivity to light *might* give him the ability to see the nightingale's glow. Hudson did mention having a headache.

Orane's smile grows, and he relaxes, his fingers absently playing with the loose strands of my hair. If it weren't for his eyes, the tension around them and the way they're shifting from violet to plum, I might believe what happened tonight doesn't matter.

"You were right to tell me." His hands cup my cheeks, and he smiles. "However, he should not be an issue."

"Are you sure?" He's probably right, but it felt *so* important earlier.

"I am sure."

Before I can say another word, he wraps me up in his arms and kisses me hard, holding my face to his in a grip impossible to escape. I am a puddle in his hands, and then, suddenly, he's gone.

"To the farthest mountain and back," he shouts back to me, vaulting onto one of the waiting unicorns.

My vision is blurred and my head is heavy. I sway on my feet, almost falling, but the pounding of hooves snaps everything into focus.

"Cheater!" I yell after him.

I scramble onto the unicorn's back, grip her sides between my knees, and wrap my fingers in her mane. Without a signal, she bursts forward, running as though both of our lives depend on it.

Orane is so far ahead I can't see him.

I tell myself I don't care, that I'm used to losing to Orane and all I really want is to thunder across this world on horseback, but that is such a lie. Winning isn't the only thing that matters, but years of losing make it seem that way.

Gripping the unicorn's sides tighter, I lean across her neck. I breathe in cycles until my heart is beating in time with her hooves crashing against the ground. She instinctively avoids the pitfalls before her, jumping felled trees and small creeks without signals from me. It leaves me free to plot our route.

The turn is a huge jacaranda tree, its purple blooms nearly a match for Orane's eyes. I point the unicorn in that direction, her pearly horn like the needle of a compass directing our path, but I can't see the jacaranda yet. There's too far to go and too many trees, hills, and rocks in the way. We're riding with the wind at our back, but unless I find a course that will shave precious minutes off my time, Orane is going to win. Again.

I try to think of a path I haven't used. I need to win tonight. I can't quite figure out why, but I *need* to win tonight. I need a way through the mountains.

Wait...

I need a way *through* the mountains.

Orane doesn't look for shortcuts; he bends the world to his will. His horse races across the land so fast its hooves barely touch down. Obstacles take no time to surmount because they are all part of *his* world. He created them. He can erase them.

If I can see this place and be part of his world, can I control it too?

I better learn how, or I'll spend the rest of eternity losing at every game we play.

Pressing my hands against the unicorn's neck, I try not to think of her as a physical thing, but as the energy Orane created her from. At first, there's nothing. Nothing beyond what I can see and touch and smell. Her hair is soft and smooth against my skin; I feel her muscles bunching and stretching as she flies over the open fields and climbs into the foothills of the mountains; she smells like oats and cut grass and flowers.

Trying again, I empty my mind, pushing out what I *think* I feel and trying to feel what *is.*

Nothing happens.

The unicorn bounds across the landscape faster and faster, but it's not quick enough to match Orane, especially since he's stopped holding back tonight. I haven't seen or heard him since the race began.

I keep trying to find that energy as I use every shortcut I've ever found. My unicorn and I travel tunnels so tight she can barely pass through them and leap gorges inches away from being impossible. We're perfectly in sync, as though she's sensing my directions before I give them, and I'm making the best time I ever have.

It's not good enough. I need more.

I refuse to be some hanger-on for all eternity, dependent on Orane for everything. If I'm going to come here, I need to be able to take care of myself.

Orane always told me I was special, worth bringing into this world. If he's right, shouldn't I be able to interact with this place the same way he does? If I can be here at all, that *has* to be true. He taught me how to create music here by thinking about it, and how to breathe underwater without drowning. I have to find a way to take those skills a step further.

I breathe again, this time searching for the energy of his world the same way he taught me to find the energy within my nightingale. The same way he taught me to summon music in the opera hall when I perform.

There's a buzzing in the air—soft, like someone humming. It's there, but trying to do anything with it is like trying to paint with sound.

As we cross the last ridge before the jacaranda comes into sight, I hear a syncopated rhythm out of time with my unicorn's hooves. Less than a second later, a white blur races past me in the opposite direction. Orane. He's already made the turn and is on his way back to the willow. He's at least ten minutes ahead of me. *Somehow* he's that far ahead of me. Despite every shortcut and trick I could pull.

My teeth grind together so hard I swear I hear them crack.

No. Not this time. Tonight I am *going* to find a way to win.

As I race for the jacaranda, tag its branches, and gallop away, I keep reaching for the energy thrumming through this world. Every time, it slips through my fingers. It's like trying to hold sand. But like sand, sometimes, if you hold tight, you can keep a tiny bit.

I grab, and suddenly it's there.

Instead of running around me, a single, thin current of energy begins to run *through* me. I see the world in a way I never have before. It's more and less vibrant, as though I'm seeing it through two sets of eyes. The double vision shows me two versions of Orane's world—the bright, magical Paradise I'm used to seeing and the one underneath, the building blocks and placeholders he uses to create his universe.

A boulder is ahead, one that marks a two-mile detour around the base of the mountain. I try to push it out of the way or create a hole—anything that means I won't have to turn my unicorn away and miss the path I know lies behind it.

"Open, disappear, do *something*!" I mutter, gripping my unicorn tighter.

She whinnies and picks up speed. The energy in the air around us shifts into her, cushioning her hooves and propelling her forward faster than I thought possible. She's not turning. She's heading straight for the boulder.

Trusting her instincts, I concentrate all my thoughts on making that rock vanish.

It doesn't.

We go straight through it, just as if it had.

Laughing, I urge my unicorn faster. She moves until her legs are a blur beneath us. The wind in my face almost blows me off her back, but nothing can separate us now. We're connected through the energy of Paradise. I can almost read her mind. With her help, we push through obstacles we would'vc avoided before. Not all of them are insurmountable, but enough are. Enough to shave precious time from our race.

We pass through a valley between two mountains, and I hear hooves echoing from the upper trail. I grin as we leave them in the dust.

Faster and faster and faster we fly until I turn around that last ridge, holding my breath as I come within sight of the willow tree.

"No!"

I lost. Orane is standing there, his mount already gone, staring out over the lake as though he's been waiting for me for *hours.*

My extra speed vanishes. My will to finish vanishes with it.

The unicorn, sensing my apathy, pulls out of her gallop. When she's down to a steady walk, I slide off her back and walk beside her.

Orane hasn't noticed my approach yet. He hasn't moved at all since I spotted him.

Stroking the back of my unicorn and silently telling her to stop, I trudge up the slope alone. He still doesn't know I'm here. Hands in the pockets of his riding pants, auburn hair blowing in the breeze, and sun-kissed skin almost glowing in the twilight, Orane looks too perfect to be real. Maybe because he is. I was a fool to ever think I could keep up with him for eternity.

When I'm within reach, I bring my hand up to touch his shoulder. His entire body tenses. Orane blinks, pulling in a sharp, short breath, and looks down at me.

The tingling I felt near Hudson is nothing compared to the spark shooting through my head now. Hudson is static electricity. This is lightning. Light bursts behind my eyes, and the roar in my ears would rival a space shuttle launch. I want to scream. I can't remember how.

As quickly as they hit, the pain and the light and the sound are gone. I'm staring up into Orane's wide, violet eyes.

Despite the warmth settling over my body now, tiny aftershocks make my muscles twitch and spasm. Those tremors are the only sign that the lightning wasn't some waking nightmare.

"Mariella?" Orane reaches out to brush a hand over my hair.

I catch myself a split second before I flinch. What *was* that? It hit me the moment his eyes locked on mine—his dark purple eyes. But they're violet now, and his touch sends calming, soothing shivers through my body. His hands bring warmth and comfort, and his eyes hold love—and a touch of confusion.

"You returned faster than I expected." He's smiling, but there are lines around his eyes and a slight wrinkle on his forehead.

"Wow. Faster than you expected?" I shake my head and pull away. *Faster* than he expected? Am I really that slow?

I've always known he held back in our races. I *knew* that. Knowing it and seeing exactly how far behind him—*below* him—I really am hits me like a piano dropping on my head.

What does he see in me, other than my ability to carry a tune? Is he so entertained by music that nightly performances make it worth putting up with someone who can't challenge him on any other level? That's one of the things I love about Orane, that he pushes me to be better, faster, smarter, and *more* than I ever could've been without him.

So what does he see in me?

I thought I knew, but now I'm not so sure. I would never want to be with someone who couldn't at least keep up with me. Now I feel like I'm the remora fish and he's the whale. It costs him nothing to let me stay, but what in the name of all that's holy does he *gain*?

Clicking my tongue, I call the unicorn closer, stroking her nose when she bumps it against my chest. "How long were you there? You looked like you were waiting for a long time."

"You are upset." He walks around until he's standing next to the unicorn, frowning at me. "Nightingale, you always accuse me of holding back when we race, but this is why I do. You hate losing night after night, but you would hate losing by so much even more."

Wincing, I turn my face against the unicorn's neck.

Orane is right. I would've hated knowing exactly how hopeless victory was. But now I *do* know. So what now? What can I do to be worthy of keeping what I love so much?

The unicorn whinnies quietly.

"It's not your fault," I try to tell her, stroking her neck. "You did everything I asked of you. I didn't know how to ask for more."

"Mariella?" His hand traces the line of my braid. "Nightingale, look at me, please."

He phrases it like a request, but it's not. Orane can be as stubborn as me when he wants to be. Too bad that, right now, I'm feeling especially stubborn.

I grip the unicorn tighter. My eyes burn, my chest aches, and my muscles are jumping from the effects of that bolt of lightning. Or whatever it was. The weight pressing down on me is heavy, almost like grief. I've lost something, and I don't know what it is.

"Mariella," Orane sighs. His hand presses against the unicorn's neck. Maybe because of how hard I worked to find the energy tonight, I sense the pulse he sends through her. It's a command. He's sending the unicorn away.

For the first time in the ten years I've known Orane, something in his world doesn't listen to him. She shifts her weight and her dark eyes lock on Orane, but my unicorn is still here, solid and real under my hands.

Orane is standing so close I feel his tension. He commands her to leave again, sending a stronger pulse through her body, one that makes her muscles jerk.

My unicorn whinnies and brings her head around to rest on my shoulder. Almost as though she's asking me for permission to obey.

"Go ahead," I try to tell her. "And thank you."

She rubs her cheek against mine before fading from sight.

I should've named her, I think as she disappears. *She was so sweet.*

Orane sighs and places his hands on my shoulders, turning me to face him. Despite how much I want to duck my head and look away, I won't. I can't let myself. Staring into his eyes, I look for an answer, some hope that keeping up with Orane might be possible.

I have to make a decision for both of us. Right now. Is it even possible to make myself stronger? Should I struggle to make myself able to keep up with him, or is it better to step away before the pain of leaving Orane gets worse?

I almost laugh. Worse? There's no such thing. No matter when it happens, leaving Orane will leave a gaping void in my life.

Guess that makes my decision for me.

Soon, Orane said. Soon may be a few weeks or a few months, but it's not tonight.

Keep fighting, I decide. I will keep trying to control this world the same way Orane does. When the time comes for me to leave my waking life behind, I'll know what my decision should be. If I've made significant progress, if I can believe that keeping up with him—*really* keeping up with him—will be possible eventually, I'll stay and throw myself into learning everything he has to teach me.

If I can't? If no significant changes happen between now and whenever his "soon" comes to pass…

Well, that will be the night I have to figure out how to live with a broken heart. Leaving him behind won't just shatter it; it'll disintegrate it until the few pieces left are small enough to pass through the eye of a needle.

"Can you forgive me?" he asks, his fingers brushing down the side of my face and his violet eyes locked on mine. "I did not mean to upset you so."

Decision made, I shake my head and wrap my arms around his neck. "There's nothing to forgive."

"Are you sure?" Orane kisses my forehead.

"I'm positive." I breathe in his beautifully floral scent and, for the first time since I stepped into Paradise tonight, relax.

"There isn't much time left," he whispers after a minute. "Will you sing tonight?"

I pull back and smile at him. "Have I ever not?"

At this point, it really is all I can give him. I swallow the lump in my throat and try to think of something special to sing for him tonight. Something worthy of him.

"Well, then, the star needs a gown." With a sweep of his hands, he pulls on the front of my linen riding shirt. The material rips away and disappears with a poof.

The dress he leaves behind is magnificent.

The large skirt is made of hundreds of pieces of chiffon and crinoline in shades of purple. Hugging my chest is a black corset top decorated with dozens of glittering stones in the same shades of purple as the folds of the skirt. My hair is piled on top of my head in an elaborate pattern of braids and curls.

I love this dress. It comes second to my recent nightingale gown, but this one matches Orane's eyes. It's a *very* close second.

As we stroll toward the opera hall, choosing the songs I should perform tonight, my determination grows. With each step I take, I renew my promise to myself. I will make myself Orane's equal, someone worth his time and attention and devotion. And I will succeed. Or I will die trying.

Eleven

Hudson

Saturday, August 30 – 12:00 AM

Lying in bed and breathing slowly to ease my nausea, I try to dissect that weird-ass tea party dream.

Some of it is obvious. Mariella is stuck in a fantasy world, trapped by the wraith. By her demon. But what'd the cake-throwing mean? And the eighteen candles? They could represent her birthday or the number of months I have to figure this out or something else I haven't thought of. And the light coming off the candles and the storm—what am I supposed to do with *any* of that? The last dream was pretty literal, but assuming this one will be the same might get me in trouble. I have to figure out how to talk to a girl who won't say a word.

Glancing at the time on my phone, I cringe. Midnight. The witching hour.

This was when Calease always came for me.

I hate midnight.

Rubbing my hands over my face, I breathe in cycles and clear the worthless thoughts away. I'll know what to do when I run into it. I hope. I mean, I could always—

Crack!

Orange light floods the room, and I dive to the side as a single spear of energy hits inches away from my head.

"Hudson Vincent…"

My own name hisses through my head in a strange, echoing voice that sends tremors of pain, like electric shocks, through my body. What I felt around Mariella was nothing compared to this. Needles next to a broadsword.

"You do not belong here. Do not think you can defeat me as easily as you did the other."

I smell something burning. All I know is it's not me.

The stones are already glowing, pulsing out their protection and shielding me from the worst of the energy, but it's not strong enough yet to keep me safe. I grab a handful and throw myself into the corner where I left the largest amethyst geodes. The orange light pulses again, and the lightning running across my skin starts to feel more like fast-burning acid. I bite the inside of my lip to keep from screaming. I taste blood.

The stones pulse brighter, reacting to the energy coming from the dreamworld. As soon as I touch them, using one of Calease's stolen talents and pouring my own energy into the stones, they burn brighter. The searing burn across my body recedes. It only takes a couple of seconds to reach a manageable level, but those seconds are endless. Agonizing.

Keeping my hand on the largest amethyst, I arrange the other stones in a circle around me. The orange light pulses again. This time, the acid burn across my skin barely worsens. There's a momentary flinch in the light surrounding me, but the shield holds. It shimmers, and the quiet chime I usually hear when I focus on the stones turns into a powerful ringing in the air. The harder the orange light pushes, the louder that chime gets.

Taking a breath, I try to figure out what I can use to close that damn portal. The light is so bright I can't tell where it's originating from, but that doesn't matter. The light means a demon, and the demon needs to go away. Before it makes *me* go away.

The energy fills the room until it's pressing down on my small, protected space. The chiming gets louder, stronger, until it's vibrating against my ears. The louder it gets, the more the orange light fluctuates. If I can push it harder, I might be able to push the demon right back where it came from.

I focus on the piece of tiger iron hanging around my neck and pull strength from it. Putting my hands on the wall of purple energy in front of me, I push it outward.

Nudging the stones anchoring the protective shield to move with me, I edge closer to a group of smaller stones. Barely more than chips, with some maybe as big as my fingertips, I might be able to use these as ammo.

The more I move, the more energy I channel into the stones surrounding me. It's like becoming a conduit is sapping the life out of me, sucking me dry quicker and quicker.

My legs are trembling by the time I reach the stone chips, but my shield holds. It's buckling as orange streaks appear in the wall of purple and green light, but it's holding.

Grabbing a handful of the chips, I toss them one after the other straight at the brightest concentration of the demon's light. I haven't seen the demon, but I didn't the other two times either. They don't like appearing in our world. Or they can't.

Doesn't matter. I keep throwing.

The stones zip out of my hands like I shot them from a BB gun. Every time they hit the open portal, the light flickers for a second. It's not enough. They're not big enough. I'm not strong enough. And the longer I keep throwing, the less I have left, the more my arms are starting to shake, and the sooner I'm going to collapse.

The light gets stronger, so strong it warps my shield and knocks me to the floor.

I try to get up. My elbows buckle, and I slip back to the floor, my head striking the wood with a *crack*.

One more time I try. One more time I fall.

The light gets brighter. I hear something shatter, and the air sparks as energy rolls across the room. Was that one of the stones exploding? I think so, but I can't lift my head to look.

That's it. It's over. So much for payback. If they're *this* strong, I never stood a chance.

I hold my breath, waiting for it to stop.

"Mariella?" I hear the demon say.

The light shifts, beginning to fade. With the pressure easing, I manage to shift my elbows under my chest and lift my head. In the afterglow, I catch a glimpse of a world at twilight, one with a field of trees in a rainbow of colors, a stone building, and the largest willow I've ever seen. I smell lavender and hear a horse's whinny, but it all disappears as the light, the image, and everything else folds in until the portal collapses with a quiet pop.

With no outside energy to keep it active, my force field vanishes. My arms give out, and I barely catch myself before my head smacks against the wood floor again.

I feel like I ran a marathon. Every muscle in my body is trembling, and my lungs burn. Sweat drips off my skin into tiny pools on the floor. The blue glow that always surrounds me is so dim it's barely visible. Or maybe that's my vision fading away.

As I fall asleep, I know I'll need to find a reason to go to Mariella's in the morning. I hope she's there when the sun rises.

I doubt she realizes it, but I think she saved my life.

I jerk awake all at once, my heart pounding and my mouth bone-dry. My vision doubles but clears quickly.

It's over. I survived. And Horace is staring down at me with worry in his eyes.

"Boy, what in the hell did you do to your mattress last night?"

Looking over, I see what's left of my half-burned mattress on the other side of the room.

I try to explain, but the air running through my dry throat makes me cough. Swallowing doesn't help. Just makes it worse. Makes my throat burn.

Horace hurries out of the room as I lean against the wall. The exhaustion of what happened last night lingers. My muscles ache and randomly convulse, which makes them ache more. But I'm alive. I can deal with pain. Relief almost makes it feel good.

Horace returns with a glass of water, but it takes a few minutes before I can talk. Explaining what happened doesn't make the worry on his face clear. His wrinkles get deeper.

"You have all the stones I gave you, right?"

He pulls a silver chain out from under his shirt to show me the two stone pendants hanging there and then pats his pocket, the *clack* of stone against stone assuring me the rest are in place.

It's not enough. It's not anywhere *close* to enough.

"Take it we're heading back to the New Age stores?" Horace asks, eyeing the amethysts around me. The shattering I heard was one of the smaller amethysts breaking into tiny shards.

"Hell yes." I don't care what it takes. I am fortifying this house out the ass. Mariella's, too.

Pulling out my dog-eared copy of *The Book of Stones*, I check out some new options before I call Dawn. Once I'm sure I know what I want, I reach for my phone and stare at the screen. It doesn't come on. Opening the back of the case and taking out the battery, I huff when I see the blackened circuitry under the casing. Well, shit.

"Can I use yours, Horace?" I ask, showing him the casualty.

"Damn," he mutters, passing me his phone as he peers into the casing of mine.

I dial the number of Stone's Throw from memory and wait as it rings.

"A Stone's Throw From Normal," an airy voice says on the other end. Definitely not Dawn.

"Is Dawn there?"

"Oh, I'm sure she is," she says, laughing. "We're all *there*, my dear."

I have absolutely no idea what she's talking about, and I don't have the patience to try figuring it out. "Can I talk to her?"

"So direct. Be direct and sure of the path you tread, but not so sure that you pass the paths better suited to your feet, brother."

I blink and look at the screen. Did I misdial?

"Dawn Breeze? Dawnie, you've a caller," I hear the airy woman call. There's a clatter and some shuffling, and then a voice I recognize comes on the other end.

"Hello?" Dawn sighs.

"Dawn, it's Hudson. I came in the other day and bought—"

"Your weight in crystals," she says, her voice brightening. "You're not someone I'll forget in a couple of days, Hudson. Not after a purchase like that. Is anything wrong with the stones? I haven't gotten in that other order yet."

"No, nothing's wrong. I need more."

"More." She repeats the word, and then her voice rises to a squeak. "*More*? Like, more-than-I-already-have-ordered more?"

"Yes."

"Goddess bless," she breathes.

"And I need different stones, too." Everything I have right now is concentrated on protection. But if protection doesn't work, I'll need something to fight back with. If such a thing exists. Everything I've read about these stones so far tells me their natural inclinations are for positive energy and healing. Trying to use them to kick a demon's ass might not work so great.

"Different. On *top* of the more you're already planning on ordering?"

"Yes."

I can almost hear her grinning. "Awesome!"

It takes a minute to give her the list—quartz, lazulite, bloodstone, sugilite, scapolite, rhodizite, spinel, red jasper, and obsidian—and tell her to rush everything.

"It won't be cheap, but I'll get you as much as I can," Dawn says.

"Quick is better than cheap."

When I hang up, Horace is still examining the burned-up insides of my cell phone.

"If this is what they can do to a phone, I hate to think what they would've done to your head," he mutters, tossing the broken phone onto my smoldering mattress. "Guess I don't have to ask where you're goin' today?"

"You *did* want those concept plans, right?"

I ignore the way my legs tremble as I push myself to my feet. Unlike the last two times a demon tried to kill me, this time I know it was Mariella's demon. I hope he didn't take his failure to kill or capture me out on Mariella. I hope she's alive when I get to her house.

The exhaustion of last night's battle knocked me out until after nine, so as soon as I clean myself up—hard to do when most of my clothes smell like smoke—I head over to the Teagans's.

The stones I couldn't sneak into Mariella's house last night are sitting in the backseat. How do I get them inside? One of the amethysts is about the size of a football. Sneaking it in isn't going to be easy.

So I won't sneak it. Amethyst is beautiful. A lot of people have geodes on display in their houses. After being invited over for dinner, a thank-you gift is a very nice gesture.

I hope Dana agrees. It's the best idea I have.

When I pull up in front of the house, I stuff as many of the smaller stones in my pocket as I can, and pick up the largest amethyst geode and a black jade statue for Mariella before walking up to the house.

A couple of kids are playing hockey down the street, and a bluebird chirps as he swoops a few feet over my head. It's a peaceful summer day, bright and warm. No one on this street knows what it's like to live fearing that, at any moment, you could die in a burst of light. Or vanish completely.

I don't know what would happen if they got to me. All I know is I don't want to find out. And I don't want Mariella to find out either.

"Good morning, Hudson!" Dana grins at me and steps aside to let me in. "You just missed Frank. He left about twenty minutes ago. Had some things to work on at the office."

"Oh, I can come back later." I'm glad he's not here. It gives me a solid excuse to be here this evening. "I wanted to bring you this."

I hold out the geode, and she stares at it for a second before reaching out to take it.

"Horace and I collect crystals. We wanted to give you this to say thanks for having us over for dinner last night."

Dana's cheeks turn a little rosy. "You really didn't have to do that. It was a pleasure to have you both."

"Amethysts are supposed to be good for clearing away negative energy," I tell her. Dana raises her eyebrows, and I nearly wince. Damn. There has to be something more positive to say. "And, uh, they bring luck."

"Well, thank you, Hudson. It's very thoughtful," she says, carrying it into the dining room and placing it in the center of the table. "Purple is my favorite color."

I peek into the living room and the kitchen, but I don't see Mariella. There's a faint pulse of bass coming from somewhere in the house, so I guess she's upstairs. Maybe she only comes downstairs for dinner? If that's the case, I need to get invited to dinner again.

"Yeah, um, we owe you a favor. We've burned through most of the restaurants in town already. And, anyway, even good takeout can get old fast." Dana glances at me, and I smile. "Until the renovations on the kitchen are done, we're pretty much stuck with it, though. Home-cooked food was a nice break."

Dana puts her hands on her hips and watches me for a second. Then she smiles and says, "We'll have to have you over more often until that kitchen gets done."

It starts soft but builds quickly—the static sparks I felt when Mariella was around last night. Without moving my head, I look toward the stairs. Because of the vaulted ceiling, I can see the edge of her legs poking around the corner. It's the same spot where she sat to listen to her mother's performance last night. I don't know if she can hear what we're saying, but it's probably a safe bet that she knows I'm here.

"We don't want to impose," I tell Dana, keeping most of my attention on Mariella.

"Oh, no imposition! We're more than happy to have you."

"Thanks. I'll let Horace know. He'll be thrilled." I turn to go, but then stop like I remembered something. "Um, Horace said something about concept plans? That's what I needed to see Frank about. Horace wanted a copy of some concept Frank mentioned last night."

Dana's cheeks get pinker as she stammers, "The c-concept?" She swallows and starts nodding like a bobblehead doll. "Of course! Frank would be happy to show them. We both—I mean, they're Frank's designs, of course, but he's more than happy to share them!"

I smile. "You don't happen to have a copy here, do you?"

"Yes!" Her eyes widen, but then her lips purse and her eyebrows furrow. "I mean, I think so. Let me check."

She runs off, and a door crashes open. Rummaging of paper and drawers opening and closing, and then, "Hudson, let me call Frank. Make yourself at home, okay?"

The door closes, and I'm left alone with my watcher at the top of the stairs.

"Spying isn't polite, Mariella," I call softly, turning in her direction.

A gasp and a soft *thump*, and then there she is, standing at the top of the stairs in red plaid pajama pants and a baggy gray shirt, her long hair unbound and spilling over her shoulders. She's running her thumb along that glass bird in her hand, and the orange light surrounding her is crazy bright. I wonder if she knows what she kept from happening last night.

"Brought you something." I pull a statue as tall as my hand out of my pocket and hold it out. Being near her sets off sparks along my skin, but next to the lightning of last night, this is as painful as a puppy licking my face.

Her eyes narrow, and she stares down at the statue like it might attack her. It's a rearing horse, its hooves raised to pound someone into the ground. I wiggle it a little like it's dancing.

"It's carved from black jade. Thought you might like it."

Her eyes widen, and she takes a couple of steps down. And then stops. I move forward about a foot and offer the statue again. Mariella walks down three more steps.

Jesus. This is like coaxing out a terrified stray dog.

I step closer, and she flinches, her head twitching to the side and her empty hand coming up to rub at her ear.

That last step intensified the static sting. Mariella rubbed her ear at the same moment. I don't hear anything, but she's jumpy. Does she feel the static when she gets too close? Is that why she practically *ran* from me last night?

I look down at the blue light surrounding me. The edges of it are dancing like waves on a rough sea. I look at the edges of the orange light around Mariella. It's doing the same thing.

Our energies are reacting to each other, like two chemicals that don't want to mix, and they're trying to keep us apart. Maybe it's some kind of warning system. *Stay away,* it's trying to tell me. This girl is tied to something dangerous.

Too bad that's exactly why I want to stick around.

Inching forward, I place the statue on the bottom step and back away.

Twelve

Mariella

Saturday, August 30 – 10:39 AM

Hudson eases away from the bottom step, moving like he thinks I might bite him.

I'd almost gotten used to the feedback, but now it's worse. More intense. And the tingling is back, too. The noise may not have anything to do with Hudson, but this pins-and-needles thing only happens when he's around.

I shudder and wish I could go back to when it was contained to one arm. It's everywhere now, moving in waves across my body like a rolling pin covered in electrodes.

Clenching my teeth and tightening my grip on my nightingale to help ignore the pain, I take another step down. Instead of looking at Hudson, I stare at the statue he's set on the step.

He brought me a horse. How strange is that? Not the horse itself—I suppose it's normal for someone to like horses—but for him to bring me one *today*? After losing the race last night, I'm not sure I want to see anything equine.

Is the universe mocking me?

Taking another few steps down and shuddering when the pinpricks pick up intensity, I consider the statue sitting in the center of the step.

It's carved out of black stone, but the detail is incredible. The horse's mane looks like it's flowing in a breeze, and its mouth is open in a silent cry.

The longer I look at it, the more I think it isn't mocking me. This is a reminder of the progress I made last night. I lost, but I surprised Orane with how fast I finished and I surprised myself when I figured out how to sense the energy that controls and shapes his world. Crouching down, I wrap my hand around the cool stone.

The feedback ratchets up about fifty decibels, going from dial tone to rock concert in a split second.

I jump and let the statue go.

The whining, grating noise quiets again.

What the hell was *that*? It's a rock. Isn't it? There's not some speaker hidden in there that plays things straight into your head, right? Can't be. That doesn't exist, or I would've heard about it. I would own one.

It's a rock. Just a rock.

Unless it's not.

Is this some kind of trick?

I look up at Hudson, prepared to pick up the statue and chuck it at his head if he's laughing at me. He's not. Hudson is frowning and watching me carefully, his black eyes narrowed and deep lines etched in the skin surrounding them. He looks worried. Genuinely concerned.

So, not a trick then. Maybe.

Taking a deep breath, I try again.

The feedback gets louder as soon as my hand closes around the horse's body, but the intensity is less. I can bear it. Standing up, I examine the workmanship on the statue. I'm so focused on the horse that it takes a second for me to notice the change.

There's another sound underneath the feedback. The longer I hold the horse, the more both sounds start to warp, one overtaking the other. It's hard to place, but I'd say it's like the ring of a glockenspiel or maybe a pure note from a violin. Even the pinprick tingles have quieted—not gone, but almost bearable.

I glance at my other hand and see my nightingale. The glow coming off my tiny glass bird is so strong I have to blink to clear my vision; it leaves sunspots across my eyes.

Smiling, I stroke my thumb along the bird's back and grip the statue tighter. It's not the statue changing the noise; it's Orane.

It's so nice to listen to a chime instead of that stupid feedback noise that it doesn't bother me that Hudson is silently watching me. He can stay here all day; I don't care.

"Do you boys like curry?" my mother asks as she comes out of my father's office carrying a roll of papers. She blinks when she sees me standing on the stairs. "Oh. Mari, honey, you're down early. Are you hungry? I wasn't going to start making lunch for a while yet."

I shake my head, and she glances between Hudson and me, speculation in her eyes. Hudson smiles and holds out his hand for the papers my mother is carrying.

"Horace and I eat pretty much everything," he says, answering her question. "I'm gonna go drop these off with Horace, but do you need help with anything today?"

"What do you mean?" My mother's forehead wrinkles. I know my face is mirroring hers. What *does* he mean?

"Until school starts, I'm at loose ends." Hudson shrugs, the action rippling muscles most people don't know exist. Who needs that many muscles? "And I don't really know anyone in town yet, so I figured I might as well see if you needed help with anything around here."

My mother's eyes widen, but she smiles and shakes her head. "That's very sweet, but you don't have to do that."

"I don't mind. I like being busy." He smiles, and a second later my mother caves.

"Actually..." She bites her lip and glances toward the back of the house. "I've wanted to rip some bushes out of the backyard for a few months now, but I haven't gotten around to it. It's kind of a big project, but—"

"No, that's perfect." Hudson says it like he's afraid she'll change her mind.

Wow. Be careful what you wish for, I guess. I wasn't serious when I thought he could stick around. Neither of them asks for my opinion.

Hudson leaves to drop off my father's concept and change clothes, and my mother calls Teagan Designs to relay exactly what happened to my father.

I walk upstairs with my new statue, but when I turn into my room, I have to squint.

All of the gifts Orane has given me over the years, glass figures and trinkets like my nightingale, are spread out along the top of my dresser, my nightstand, and my desk. They always glitter with a pearly, iridescent glow, but now every single figure is burning like a star about to go supernova. And the chime is swallowed by that obnoxious whine again.

I wince and drop Hudson's statue onto my bed. As soon as the stone leaves my hand, the light from Orane's gifts dims. It's a lot brighter than normal, but it's better. Or maybe I got used to it. The volume on the feedback gets turned down, too.

Testing a theory, I wrap my hand around the statue again.

The glass gifts pulse and explode with color, blazing so bright that closing my eyes and looking away doesn't help—an image of my bedroom sketched in light and shadow is burned onto my retinas. The rise in volume is a split second behind the change, but the chime doesn't return. Only the feedback.

Shuddering and letting go of the horse, I open my eyes, peeking through squinted lids to make sure it's safe. The light is too bright, but it's not as powerful. I think. My vision is so washed out, it's hard to tell.

Plopping down onto my bed, I stare at the horse. The detail on the carving is exquisite, but it's just a stone statue. It doesn't glow like the gifts from Orane's world, and it doesn't seem to be anything except what Hudson told me it is—a hunk of rock.

I'd rather not take chances. Squinting, I pick up the horse and hide it in the top drawer of my dresser. The intensity of the glow and feedback dims but doesn't disappear. This is ridiculous. I'm going to have to get rid of that statue or whatever it is. Later. After Hudson leaves.

I hear a thud from the backyard and walk over to look out the window.

Hudson is there in shorts and a white T-shirt, pounding at the ground around the boxwood shrubs my mother has decided she hates. Under the shirt, I can see the muscles in his back shift and stretch each time he swings the pickax at the ground. It's nice of him to offer to do this for my mother, but it's hard to forget the way those black eyes bored into me.

Orane is so sure Hudson doesn't know anything about Paradise, that he has no connection to it, but none of these weird noises and bursts of light started until he showed up. If he doesn't have anything to do with Paradise, there has to be something else going on with him.

Orane may not see it, but it *has* to be there.

Thirteen

Hudson

Saturday, August 30 – 11:14 AM

I fall into a rhythm. Swing, *thud*, lift. Swing, *thud*, lift. The repetitive motion leaves my mind free to wander, but it doesn't wander far. Only up to Mariella's bedroom on the second floor.

The light show when she picked up the statue was insane. Blue cracks spread from her hand, up her arm, and across her entire body in less than a second. When she dropped it, I thought maybe she'd seen what was happening and would leave the statue alone. Or throw it at me—it kinda seemed like she wanted to throw it at me for a second.

But then she looked at me—actually looked at *me* for a second and didn't fixate on my eyes—and changed her mind. That determined, pursed-lipped, narrow-eyed expression came over her face, and she gripped that statue like she was strangling it.

The light show started again, the blue cracks spreading thicker and faster than before. The fire coming off her nightingale brightened so much I could barely see Mariella under its glow. Blue fought from one side, orange from the other, and Mariella was lost underneath it all. When I shifted my filters, switching to one that shows me the world the way everyone else sees it, I could watch as Mariella stood there staring at the horse, shifting it this way and that to look at the detail of the carving. Just a girl admiring a horse.

I wanted to tell her I understood what she was going through and where she went at night, but seeing as she didn't exactly react well when I mentioned her glass bird, I'm thinking she wouldn't take the news kindly. Calease made me believe I was one of a very select few chosen to be brought into their world. If Mariella's demon did the same thing, meeting someone else who's been "chosen" might be more than she can handle. Yet curiosity drove her to ask about my arms, and stubbornness made her stick around when she obviously wanted to run, so there might be a way to make her figure it out on her own. Maybe. I hope.

"Wow. You work fast."

My rhythm falters, and I miss the spot I was aiming for, slamming the end of the pickax into the grass instead of the roots of the boxwood shrubs. Turning, I see K.T. watching me from a few feet away.

"What are you doing here?"

She raises one eyebrow. "I was coming to invite Mari to Danny's party and saw your car out front. What are *you* doing? Did they hire you as a gardener?"

"I didn't know when I talked to you yesterday, but Mariella's dad kind of knows my…uh, the guy I'm staying with. Horace. I offered to help out around here."

"Talk about fate." K.T. grins, and her blue eyes light up. "Maybe you won't need my help."

"What kind of help?" Especially after last night, I'm not sure I have a shot at winning this fight. Turning away any level of support might be suicide.

"That's why I was going to invite Mari tonight. It was a test to see if you were serious about helping her." K.T. shrugs. "*If* she'll agree to come. She hasn't come to a party since middle school. I was going to call you tonight if she said yes."

"I wouldn't have gotten the message." I picture the burned-out circuits of my phone and try not to shudder. "My phone broke last night."

"Oh. Guess it's lucky I ran into you then." She glances over her shoulder at the house and shrugs. "Here goes nothing."

She turns to go, and I realize she's going up to Mariella's room. I can't ask her to pass along all the stones in my car without offering some really strange explanation, but maybe I can convince her to give Mariella one more piece. Even if I sneak in again tonight, I won't be able to put anything *inside* Mariella's bedroom. K.T. can.

"Hey, hold up!" I drop the pickax to the ground and jog after K.T. I pull a roundish piece of amethyst about half the size of my palm out of my pocket and hold it out. "Would you give this to her?"

K.T. tilts her head to the side as she takes the stone and examines it. "Pretty. Is it amethyst?"

"Yeah."

"Why don't you give it to her yourself?"

I shove my hands in my pockets and shrug. There's no answer I can give that wouldn't either sound crazy or be an outright lie. K.T. smiles and slips the stone into her pocket.

"All right, Romeo. I'll go see if I can get Juliet to come to the ball tonight."

K.T. winks and walks around to the front of the house. I watch her until she turns the corner, and then look up just as Mariella steps up to the window.

For a flash, the Mariella from my dreams superimposes on top of her. Her orange glow becomes fire eating away at her, and she's standing there calmly trying to dig an orange ribbon off her face.

My hands clench when the light around her gets brighter and she pulls back from the window, retreating into her room.

K.T. thinks I'm chasing Mariella to get her to go out with me, but it doesn't matter what she thinks as long as she's willing to help. I pick up the pickax and slam it into the roots of the next boxwood.

Mariella is buried so deep in the clutches of the dream demons I'm gonna need all the help I can get to free her.

Fourteen

Mariella

Saturday, August 30 – 11:26 AM

Someone knocks at my door, and I pull away from the window. Glancing at the clock, I realize five minutes passed while I was staring out at the backyard.

"Honey, K.T. is here to see you," my mother says as she opens the door.

K.T.? The name rings a bell. Didn't Hudson mention her last night?

A girl with round cheeks and blue eyes comes in behind my mother, playing with a lock of her straight brown hair.

"Look who dropped by! It's been a while since K.T.'s been here, hasn't it, Mari?" She watches my face, waiting for an answer.

I stare at the girl. She feels familiar. Looking at her is like hearing a song I haven't heard in years.

Then I get a flash. A memory? K.T. is younger, elementary-school-aged maybe, and she laughs as she grabs my hand, towing me across the playground toward the swings.

The light from my gifts pulse. Energy rolls across the room, hitting me like a blast of warm air. The feedback noise subsides, and my vision goes black—like a head rush when you stand up too fast. I blink, trying to refocus.

My mother is standing in the doorway with a girl I don't recognize. When did they come in here? Did they knock?

"All right, well, let me know if you need anything, K.T.," my mother says to the stranger.

"Thanks, Mrs. Teagan," K.T. says as my mother leaves, pulling the door shut behind her.

Once we're alone, K.T. turns to me.

"Hey, Mari." She shifts, brushing her brown hair over one shoulder. "Do you remember me? We've been in the same classes since elementary school."

K.T.'s gaze lingers on the figurines sitting on my dresser, but she doesn't look long enough to make me think she notices something strange about them. Like the fact that they're glowing.

K.T. looks back at me like she's waiting for a response. I don't really know what to do. I don't remember her. She says she's been in my classes since *elementary* school, though. Why don't I remember her?

Sighing quietly, K.T. smiles and shakes her head. "It doesn't matter." She runs her hand over her hair again and then tosses it back over her shoulder. "That's not what I came here to talk to you about, anyway."

The thudding from the backyard stops, and a chainsaw roars to life.

Stepping toward the window, I look out as Hudson saws one of the boxwoods in half. I watch him for a moment as he picks up a huge section of sawed-off boxwood and tosses it twenty feet. Show-off.

"I wanted to see if you could come to a party tonight. Pretty much the entire senior class is going to be there. Hudson is coming, too," K.T. says.

She's standing near my nightstand now. Wasn't she on the other side of the room a second ago? And did she say something about a party? I blink and try to focus, but my head is fuzzy.

"I didn't know you'd met Hudson already." Walking across the room, she stands at the other side of the window and looks out. "Do you like him?"

Like him? Hudson isn't the kind of person I'd really describe as *likable.* Overgrown, strange, surprisingly thoughtful… Well, he's not exactly *un*likable, either.

I shrug to answer K.T.'s question, and we watch Hudson demolish another boxwood bush. Sweat has made his thin white shirt almost see-through, and it's sticking to his skin, accentuating the lines of his muscles and the ridges of some of the scars crisscrossing his torso. What *happened* to him? Whatever it was, I'm surprised he survived it.

"School starts on Tuesday," K.T. says. "We're having a party at Danny's."

I don't know who Danny is, but she says the name like it should have meaning. Is he another person from *elementary* school I've somehow forgotten?

"So? You coming?" K.T. leans against the windowsill, her arms crossed over her chest.

Do I want to spend the evening with an incredibly strange stranger and a houseful of people I don't really know? Or stay locked in my room with that irritating feedback and the too-bright glow of Orane's gifts? Neither one sounds especially inviting. Is there a third option?

"Oh, come on." K.T. laughs and shakes her head. "How is this a choice?" She holds out her hands like she's weighing the two options on a scale. "Go to a party and hang out with the hot new guy, or stay home on a Saturday night? Hot new guy or home alone? Hmmm."

As she hums, her right hand—the Hudson hand—rises and rises until she's holding it straight up over her head. She glances up, then looks at me.

"Seems like no contest to me." Her hands drop, and she looks out at Hudson. He's already worked his way through a quarter of the boxwood bushes; their shattered carcasses are piled at the side of the yard.

"Plus, you already know him," K.T. says. "So you won't have to explain the whole no-talking thing."

Yeah, but the "no-talking thing" won't exactly make "hanging out" with him very easy. Especially since I doubt he understands enough sign language to hold a conversation. There's always notes and written messages, but that's a lot more effort than I usually put into communicating with strangers.

At the same time, I really wouldn't mind getting away from the stupid feedback noise. Leaving for a few hours sounds like a good idea. I glance out the window and then back at my room.

Sighing, I nod. K.T. grins and bounces up to me, wrapping her arms around my shoulders. The action is so unexpected I don't know what to do except pat her on the back and wait for her to let go. I wish I could remember this girl. She's sweet.

"Awesome! I'll talk to your mom and let Hudson know, okay? He can probably drive you over tonight. And here." She holds out a palm-sized purple stone. "Hudson wanted me to give this to you."

What is it with Hudson and rocks? I wonder as I reach for the stone. Amethyst maybe? Like the black statue, this boosts the volume on the grating whine. It's soft, but I can make out a musical chime underneath it. The noise sucks, but the stone is pretty, shading from deep purple on one end to pale lavender on the other. It reminds me of Orane's eyes.

"Great!" K.T.'s grinning like she won the lottery and bouncing on the tips of her toes. "So, um, see you tonight, okay?"

With a quick, jittery wave, K.T. turns and practically runs out of the room, leaving the door wide open. I can hear her feet pound down the stairs as she calls out, "Hey, Mrs. Teagan?"

I walk to the hall and listen as K.T. tells my mother about the party.

"Well, I don't know. I should ask Mari," my mother says.

"Oh, I did!" K.T. says. "She said yes. And Hudson is coming, too, so he could bring her if you don't want to drive her over."

"What?" My mother sounds a little breathless. "It's not far, so I don't mind driving, but—she really said she'd go?"

"Definitely. You don't mind if she comes, right?"

"No, of course not. I guess Hudson can take her after dinner if he's going, too."

"Okay! I'll go tell him."

Before my mother can say another word, the back door opens and shuts. Turning the piece of amethyst over in my hand, I move toward the window again, watching K.T. run to Hudson. She's bouncy and makes wide gestures as she talks. He watches her intently, his head tilting toward my window more than once. I don't bother hiding. She seems to know him well. She reaches out and grabs his hand before nearly skipping out of my yard. And Hudson is smiling as he watches her go.

Good, I tell myself. They must have something going on. I don't know why K.T. would want me to spend time with Hudson if *she's* interested in him, but at least I won't have to worry about Hudson misreading things.

Staring out at Hudson, I rub my thumb over the smooth sides of the purple stone, trying to figure it out. There's something about these rocks that reacts to Orane's gifts, but I don't understand why. It's stone. Just stone. A rock should only be able to hurt something if you throw it. The stones Hudson's given me defy the laws of physics or something. I want to know why.

Everything I learn about Hudson further convinces me he knows things that should be impossible. Secrets I took a vow of silence to protect.

"Hudson!" I hear my mother call a little while later. "Take a break. Want some lunch?"

He nods and sets his tools down. And I realize I'm still standing at the window, watching him work.

My cheeks heat up, and I pull back before he notices me. I wasn't watching *him;* I was thinking and happened to be staring in his direction. He's not handsome compared to Orane. He's scarred and way too tall and just…strange.

I know my mother will come to collect me for lunch soon, so I head downstairs, slipping my new amethyst into the pocket of my pajama pants. I should leave it behind, keep my distance, but I have to figure this out. Plus, the color reminds me of Orane.

Hudson is coming in from the backyard as I reach the bottom of the stairs. My nightingale is in my hand, and as he looks at it, the small smile on his face disappears.

"You know the funny thing about dreams?" he asks. My heart stops, and I stare up at him. He waits a beat, his black eyes locked on me. "It's amazing how fast one that seems like paradise can turn into a nightmare."

There's that word again. Paradise. It's normal on its own, but coming twice from the same person? And now he's talking about dreams? Out of nowhere and without any lead-in. He throws it out there the way someone might comment on the weather.

Without another word, he turns and heads into the downstairs bathroom.

"Oh, good! You're down." My mother smiles and nods toward the dining room. "Can you set the table, Mari?"

She heads into the kitchen, but I'm locked on the bottom step, my heart racing and my hands trembling. Maybe I didn't explain all these oddities about Hudson to

Orane right. Last night's conversation is fuzzy, but I think I told him everything. Obviously, I need to tell him again. Why would Hudson say something like that if he hasn't seen Paradise?

I sit through lunch, letting the conversation wash over me, but I watch Hudson out of the corner of my eye. If he's seen Paradise and doesn't know to keep it secret, he may be putting everything I love in danger. But how can I convince him to keep his silence without breaking my own promise to Orane?

When I shove the tasteless sandwich in my mouth as fast as possible and clear my plate away, Hudson's gaze follows me across the room. I want to talk to him—or at least pass him a list of questions and wait until he answers every single one of them—but I can't. Not until I talk to Orane. And I can't do that until I go to this party I agreed to attend.

Maybe it was a mistake to agree to go. What do I know about this guy? And I'm going to let him drive me to a party filled with people I don't like well enough to remember? What was I thinking?

It seemed like a good idea when K.T. asked, to leave the feedback behind and figure out what Hudson might know. Now?

I glance at Hudson as he looks my way, those dark eyes watching me closely.

Now, I'm not so sure.

Fifteen

Hudson

Saturday, August 30 – 8:54 PM

Dinner at Mariella's was an exercise in invisibility.

She wouldn't acknowledge my presence. I kept kicking myself for that idiotic line about dreams turning into nightmares, but I couldn't help it when I saw that stupid bird in her hand. It's too strongly linked in my head to the image of her combusting into a fireball, her screams heard by no one. I've never touched the thing, and I still hate it. I want to grab it out of her hand and shatter it against the wall.

I want to, but I think that'd piss her off more than a little.

Mariella heads upstairs after dinner, and Dana watches her go. "Um, let me make sure she still wants to go, okay?"

Dana barely glances at me as she follows her daughter up the stairs. After a second, Frank excuses himself, too.

"Why do I get the feelin' it's your fault that girl was in a mood?" Horace mutters.

"Because you're a pessimist."

"You're tellin' me." He huffs, and the corner of his lips twitch. "Went over to that store you told me about and bought the place out."

"Thought I did that yesterday." Dawn only had a few small stones by the time I left.

"Didn't say I got anything *useful,*" he grumbles, rubbing the crown of his head. "But after what happened last night, I'd rather have a house of expensive, useless rocks than wakc up and find you dead."

And the last thing I want is to head upstairs and find out the demon switched targets. Guess I can't fault him for caution.

When Dana comes back down, she's got a bemused smile on her face.

"She's getting ready. Give her a couple of minutes?"

I make small talk until I hear Mariella's feet on the stairs. It's warm outside, but she's dressed for autumn. Her jeans might have fit at one point, but they hang loose on her thin frame, and the rest of her is nearly lost in an oversized black hoodie. The one spot of bright color is the braid of golden hair hanging over her shoulder.

The weirdest part is, it doesn't matter. Even dressed like she's trying to disappear under her clothes, the girl is gorgeous.

Don't be stupi•er than you nee• to be, I remind myself. *Remember Calease? The last glowing girl you talke• to trie• to kill you.*

"Ready to go?"

Mariella shrugs and steps toward the door. I wonder how K.T. got her to agree to come. She doesn't look thrilled to be going anywhere with me.

"Have her home by eleven?" Dana asks as we leave.

"No problem." I don't want to be out in the open at midnight. And as much as I want to keep her away from the dreamworld, I'm not ready to try.

Mariella slides into the tiny backseat of the Camaro until we drop Horace off. When he gets out, he pulls the seat forward and reaches in to help Mariella into the front.

She hesitates, but I shake my head and crook my finger at her.

"C'mon. I won't bite, and I don't like playing chauffeur."

Sighing, she takes Horace's hand and switches seats, plopping into the passenger side and buckling herself in.

"Have fun," Horace says as he closes her door. The way he says it makes it sound a lot more like "good luck."

On the way to Danny's, I try to find something to say to break the silence. The best I can come up with is, "These people aren't insane or anything, right?"

She glances at me, her forehead wrinkled.

"You grew up here, didn't you?"

Mariella nods, but she doesn't look any less confused.

"So you know these kids. You gotta warn me if any of them are crazy or something."

The creases in her forehead deepen, and she looks away. The glass bird is locked in her left hand, but her right comes up to her mouth and she starts nibbling on the ends of her nails.

What is going through her head? It's like she doesn't know the people she must've gone to school with since she was five. Calease stole a whole bunch of my memories, but they were bits and pieces centered on the skill she was trying to take. She took the memories of my fights and replaced them with fakes that made me believe her when she told me I used to be a monster. Calease did her work so well I didn't realize anything was missing until it all flooded back into my head. It seems like all Mariella has left is a void. How much more has this demon stolen from her?

The party is in full swing by the time we get there, and the street is so packed we have to park down the block. Music spills out from the house and people sit on the lawn. A few of them are smoking.

As soon as we're spotted, the whispers start. I'm the stranger, so at first, all the stares are focused on me, but then someone recognizes Mariella.

"Holy shit! Isn't that the mute girl?"

"What the hell is she doing here?"

Mariella tenses, but her face is completely blank. Pretending she can't hear them.

Why do people assume one deficiency comes with another? Just because she's mute doesn't mean she's *deaf*. People are morons. I step closer to her and glare at the whisperers, not caring when they jump at the sight of my eyes.

We barely make it into the house before K.T. appears in front of us, a huge grin on her face.

"You made it!" She pulls Mariella into a hug; I'm surprised by how easily Mariella gives in to the gesture. K.T. glances at me and waves before her attention goes back to Mariella.

"Are you hungry? Do you want a drink or anything?" K.T. takes Mariella's arm and guides her deeper into the house.

Mariella shakes her head, her eyes wide as she looks around. The party is loud but tame. There's a group of guys playing Ping-Pong on the back porch, some girls wiggling in a way that might be dancing in the hallway, and a mixed group playing *Mario Kart* in the living room. I try to see it the way Mariella must see it after spending so much time alone.

She's gotta be overloading—and we just walked in.

"Want to go out to the backyard?" I ask her.

She jumps a little but nods quickly, her eyes wide.

Yeah, this is going great. She's so freaked there's no way I'll be able to get anything out of her tonight.

K.T. sighs and lets go of Mariella's arm before she bolts for the back door. Mariella nearly knocks one of the Ping-

Pong players over as she rushes past. They hurl protests at her and immediately return to the game as she runs down the steps, through the crowded backyard, and keeps going.

I follow as close as I can without looking like I'm chasing her but stop past the last of the folding picnic tables set up behind the porch. K.T. comes up next to me, and together we watch Mariella reach a corner of the yard, sink down to the grass, and pull her legs into her chest. She surveys the house with her chin resting on her knees, but the expression on her face is so strange. It's like she can't figure out what she's seeing or why anyone is acting the way they are. She's like an alien who's been plopped down on our planet with minimal knowledge of human behavior and she can't quite grasp any of it.

"Do you believe in faeries and demons?" K.T. asks.

I glance at her, but her face doesn't tell me anything. That question comes out of nowhere and is way too close to something *I* would like to ask *her*. And she's playing with the bracelet again, the same one she had in my dream.

Looking back at Mariella, I nod. "Yes."

"Magic?"

"Yeah."

"Curses?"

"Depends on how you mean. Most stories about curses sound like someone used them as an excuse for failing epically at something."

We're both watching when Mariella reaches into the front pocket of her hoodie and takes out the amethyst I gave her, but only I can see the blue sparks that shoot up her arm as soon as her hand closes around it.

"Why'd you give her an amethyst?"

"Because it's supposed to help clear away negative energy."

"Like a curse?"

"I don't know…just negative energy."

Her mouth lifts as she looks at me out of the corner of her eye. "You don't trust people easily, do you?"

"And you never stop asking questions, do you?"

She smiles. "Not really."

"Well, same answer." The single reason I have to trust K.T. is because she showed up in a dream, and that's not enough. The demons show up in my dreams every so often, too—doesn't mean I'm going to trust them. Horace is the sole person who's never let me down. Trust doesn't come easily.

"You want to know why I decided to help you spend time with Mari?"

I nod.

"Because of how you said it. You didn't ask because she's pretty or because she looked lonely or any of that. You thought she needed *help*. Before you knew she was mute, you thought she needed help."

"That's it?"

K.T. falls silent, her gaze locked across the dimly lit yard where Mariella is watching us with the same confused frustration with which we're watching her.

"You know what most people in this town see when they look at Mariella?" K.T. barely pauses before she shakes her head. "Nothing. They see right through her like she doesn't exist. When I told Danny she was coming, he couldn't remember who she was."

"I'm not sure Mariella remembers anyone else either," I say after a few seconds.

"She doesn't." K.T. crosses her arms over her chest, but it looks less defensive and more like she's trying to give herself a hug. "I've reintroduced myself every time I've seen her for the past four years. Even during the school year when we saw each other every day."

"That's... Wow. Really?" I can't imagine that. I can remember everyone I've seen on a daily basis. How does

Mariella function? Is she passing her classes in school if she can barely remember going? But then I realize something. "She remembered me from last night."

K.T.'s head whips toward me, her eyes wide. "Seriously?"

"Yeah." Mariella is lying on her back now, her hood pulled up over her hair. I don't know if she's sleeping or staring at the sky, but she's obviously lost interest in the house. "She wasn't exactly thrilled to see me, but she knew who I was."

"Hmm." She glances at Mariella, then up at the dark sky, chewing on her bottom lip. Muttering something I don't catch, she covers her face with her hands. I wait. K.T. knows something. All these questions about magic and demons and curses? She *has* to know.

Then she takes a deep breath, and I tense, waiting for whatever she has to say.

"One morning, my sister Emily told me there's another world only a few people can see."

My breath catches in my throat, my hands clench, and my pulse pounds faster. Her *sister*? That's the association? But her sister is in a coma. How does she connect?

K.T. watches me as though she's judging my reaction to see if she should tell me anything else. Whatever she sees keeps her talking.

"I told my parents about that when she dropped into a coma on her eighteenth birthday. They told me to stop making up stories."

She knows what it's like; that's what she's trying to tell me. K.T. understands what it's like to have this piece of information in your head no one else will believe.

Wait...*on* her eighteenth birthday?

Another memory of Calease's surfaces, carrying with it the whiff of honey.

It's *always* eighteen. Or, no, that's not true. It's always the age of majority in whatever culture the kid lives in.

Fifteen in certain Latin American countries. Thirteen for Jewish kids. Eighteen for us. Whenever you're seen as an adult in your culture, that's when they hit. That's what Calease was waiting for.

I was a week away from that deadline.

I have to clear my throat twice before I can speak. "I believe you."

K.T.'s shoulders drop a little. She takes a deep, slow breath and shifts her weight, looking out over the backyard. "I was pretty young. I thought we were playing make-believe. Emily never talked about it again, even when I tried to bring it up, but I could see it in her eyes after that—she looked at everything around her as if it had lost its color."

Everything *does* lose its color. They wrap you in their sickening light, and you can't see the world for what it is anymore. It's like an addiction, and only they have the drugs to keep you floating. Calease did everything she could to make sure I needed her more desperately than I needed my next breath. And she was very, very good at what she did.

Calease convinced me she could make me better, turn me into something extraordinary. She was trying to help, she promised. The thing is, Calease *did* help me. I never felt in control of my anger until she taught me how to manage it, lock it down, and make sense of it. I was never able to stay out of trouble until she showed me how. By the time my eighteenth birthday approached, I was firmly caught in her game.

K.T. rubs her hands on her jeans and fidgets with her bracelet again. "At first, I wasn't sure anything was wrong, but then I left for summer camp. I was gone for a month, and when I came back..." K.T. clenches her fists and starts trembling. "When I came back, my sister looked at me like I was a complete stranger. She had no idea who I was anymore. It took two weeks before she remembered my name without me reminding her."

I look out to where Mari is crouched next to a small garden, examining the labeled rows of herbs. "Why do you think the same thing is happening to Mariella?"

"She faded away the same way Em did. Mari's been pulling away for years, but then she stopped talking in eighth grade."

It's hard to believe. Four years is a long time to lock your voice away. Staying out of fights was hard. How do you stop doing something as instinctive as *talking*?

"Mari knew who I was, though. Until we came back to school freshman year. Then it didn't matter how often I reminded her who I was; it was like something erased me out of her head every night." K.T. shudders, closing her eyes and hugging herself tighter. "I've already watched someone disappear once, Hudson. I *don't* want to watch it happen again."

Noise spills out from the house, and we both turn in time to watch a shrieking, giggling girl run out of the back door being chased by a guy with a handful of ice. I touch K.T.'s elbow and nod further out into the yard. This isn't a conversation I planned on having somewhere this public. I may not be ready to dig in, but K.T. is. I don't know if I can trust her, but I don't think I have much of a choice. Even if she's not tied directly to the demons, she's tied to Mari. She might be able to help.

"Do you still want to know why I moved here?"

K.T. nods. Damn. I almost hoped she'd say no.

Swallowing the lump growing in my throat, I try to keep my voice steady as I tell her my story.

"The world your sister talked about? It's controlled by demons. They make you think they're your friend, but they take away the things that are most important to you. Whatever you're really good at. For me, it was surviving. Fighting. It's an instinct I've always had."

"Art." K.T.'s voice is so hoarse the word comes out as a croak. "Emily was an artist."

"The demon made me promise to stop fighting. I did, but one day I had to choose between breaking my promise to her and risking my brother's life." I rub my hands over my face and head. My hands are shaking, and the burn in my lungs is back. Thinking about this is painful. Talking about it? Ten thousand times worse.

"You picked your brother?" K.T. asks.

Dropping my hands, I nod. "For all the goddamn good it did."

K.T. is frozen—I can't tell if she's breathing. As hard as I try to control it, my voice is trembling so bad I barely sound like myself. I suck in a breath, ignoring the acid-like burn in my chest. I can still hear him screaming for them to stop.

"He tried to protect me. He caught a switchblade that was meant for me."

"Oh my God!" K.T. sways on her feet. I reach out to steady her before she sinks. There are tears in her eyes, and her voice is quiet and shaky when she asks, "How did you get out?"

How? I lived through it and I don't know. Instinct, I guess. Instinct and unadulterated rage. I try to explain, telling her what Calease said, and how I was pushed out of the dreamworld by the explosion that broke my pendant to pieces.

K.T. wipes her eyes and looks up, her lips trembling. "Did you kill her?"

The way she asks it, I can tell she's hoping the answer is yes.

"I think. Maybe. As much as one of them can die anyway." I exhale slowly, finally getting my voice under control. A little. "Everything with them is mental. I pulled everything she stole out of my head back, but I took too much."

To give myself a second, I check on Mariella. She's sitting in the grass studying her two presents—that ugly glass bird and the amethyst I gave her this afternoon. To me, it's like she's holding neon bulbs in her hands, one blue and one orange. I wonder what it looks like to her.

"You asked what happened to my eyes the day we met."

K.T. nods when I look back in her direction.

"They used to be blue. Lighter than yours. They've been like this since that night."

"But you can see?"

"Yeah. Everything you can and a ton more." And now, to see how much weird she can take... "It isn't exactly a coincidence I moved here."

She opens her mouth and closes it, her eyes narrowed. "What do you mean?"

"I had a dream. About this town." Her eyes widen. "And then, when I got here, I had another one. About you and Mariella."

She looks away, her jaw set. It takes a minute for her to say anything, but when she does speak, the words aren't what I expected.

"Why didn't you tell me before?"

I almost laugh. *Is she serious?*

"The same reason you didn't tell me more about what happened to your sister. I wasn't sure if you'd believe me, and I wasn't sure I could trust you."

K.T. glances at me, then out at Mariella. Her face is partially lost in shadow, but she seems to be turning over my words, trying to decide whether or not to believe me. When her right hand comes down to the bracelet on her left wrist again, I follow the motion. It must have some significance to her. Before I can ask, a voice cuts through the air.

"Hey, K!"

We both turn. A redheaded guy is jogging toward us, a tight grin on his face.

"I've been looking all over for you," he says when he comes up. His gaze softens when he looks at K.T., getting a little hopeful when he says, "We're going to pick up the pizza. You coming?"

She looks at the redhead and blushes. "Uh, yeah. I guess. Danny, did you meet Hudson? He's starting school with us on Tuesday."

Danny glances at me and flinches when he meets my eyes, swallowing a startled gasp. He recovers fast, his smile so tight I'm not sure if it can still be called a smile. "'Sup?"

I nod a greeting, trying not to laugh at how he's puffing up. He's tall by most standards, though he's still about five inches shorter than me. He's not muscle-bound, but not a weakling either. I could probably knock him out in one hit, but I guess none of that matters. This guy shifts closer to K.T. and seems ready to take me if I give him a reason to. Like he's trying to protect her from me.

"I'll meet you out at the car, okay?" K.T. says.

Danny's smile drops a little, but he nods. "Yeah, sure."

As soon as he's out of earshot—leaving with a couple of backward glances—K.T. looks up at me.

"You meant it, right? That you wanted to help Mari?"

"I meant it."

She sighs, her shoulders dropping as she runs her hands through her hair. "Let me know if you can figure out how. Nothing I've tried has worked." K.T. bites her lip and glances out at Mariella. "And we don't have a lot of time left."

"What?" My heart drops like a brick into my stomach. "When's her birthday?"

K.T. barely meets my eyes as she turns to follow Danny. "Two weeks from yesterday."

Even in the warm summer night, I'm cold.

Two *weeks*?

Time is slipping away faster than I could've guessed, and I don't have the first damn clue how to loosen the noose around her neck.

I walk toward Mari and have to concentrate to keep my hands from locking into fists. I want to punch something, but there's nothing around except Mari.

She hides the amethyst in her pocket as I approach. Pointing at the party, she signs, "Sorry I ran."

The knot in my chest loosens a little, and I smile.

"No problem," I tell her as I settle next to her on the grass.

She may be an addict, but she's not lost yet. I have twelve days and thirteen nights to make sure she survives. And I have help, someone who knows Mari and might be able to dig her out of her shell. We'll need a plan and a lot of luck, but at least now I know what I'm up against.

Sixteen

Mariella

Saturday, August 30 – 11:15 PM

Back home, the feedback comes and goes at random intervals, switching between an almost-pleasant chime and an atrocious whining so fast it jolts me out of the few moments of peace I manage to find. Falling asleep is going to be so much harder than usual with the noise and the growing ache in my head.

Going to the party was a bad idea, but it wasn't that awful after I escaped the heat and the noise and the stares of the crowded house. The quiet backyard was kind of nice, even after Hudson joined me.

He was much better behaved, not saying a word that hinted he knew things he shouldn't, but he didn't do anything to convince me he *didn't* know either. He talked about inconsequential things like the constellations and the stories attached to them. I listened, but part of my mind was busy dissecting everything he'd said this afternoon. And last night. Worrying about what Hudson may or may not know gave me a migraine.

By the time I step into Paradise, my head is killing me. The piercing pain behind my eyes makes it hard to handle the light coming off my glass trinkets, tinting them a pale orange. The twilight of Orane's world is soft, but it hurts my eyes. When the portal closes behind me, Orane is waiting. For the first time, he's not smiling.

"Mariella." He breathes my name out like a sigh, and his expression relaxes. Orane pulls me into his arms. I close my eyes; his lavender scent eases the ache in my head, and I take comfort in his warmth. Orane strokes my hair. Each touch erases more of the pain. "I worried I would not see you tonight."

"What do you mean?" All I want to do is stay pressed against his chest, but I force my eyes open and look up at him. "Have I *ever* missed a chance to see you?"

"That is not what I meant." The lines are back around his eyes. He places his hands on my cheeks. "Tonight something tried to keep you away from here."

"What?" I've never truly understood how I can visit Orane's world; trying to figure out what could keep me away is like an unsolvable puzzle.

"I struggled so much harder to bring you to me tonight." He takes my hand in his and leads me to a red brocade chaise that appears under the willow tree. "Why was it so hard?"

"I don't know." I spent time outside of the house today, which is unusual for summer, but I leave the house all the time during the school year and he's never had a problem bringing me through the portal. The one *unusual* thing about today was Hudson.

As we sit, I ask, "Do you remember the boy I told you about last night? Hudson?"

Orane stiffens. It's a tiny motion, but I've known him too long not to notice when his mood shifts. Orane's eyes narrow and darken, shifting closer to plum. "He was at your house again?"

I pull back farther and stare at him. "How did you know that?"

"A guess, Mariella." He smiles and tucks my hair behind my ear. "Why else would you bring him up?"

"Oh." I guess that makes sense. "I know you said I was overreacting, but I really think someone else in your world is bringing people here."

Orane leans down and presses a kiss to my forehead. "Why would you think that?"

He's tense. Waiting to hear what I'm going to say.

"He said something today when he saw me holding my nightingale. He said, 'It's amazing how fast something that seems like paradise can turn into a nightmare.'"

The hesitation is slight—less than a breath—but it's there. A moment between when he should have said something and when he finally answers.

"If someone else has broken through the barrier, we must be more careful than ever," he says, rubbing his hands along my arms. "Hudson may be a danger to everything we have been working for. You must avoid him if you can."

Is he serious? I tell Orane someone might have *breached* the safety of his entire world, and his answer is "stay away from him"?

Why didn't he immediately discount the possibility? The last time we talked about humans being capable of crossing between worlds, he said the number was nearly insignificant. Like the chances of snow in Bali. What are the odds of meeting someone who can survive the crossing? Not only someone who *can*, but someone who *has.*

More than Orane stressed the impossibility of others surviving—like my parents, who I'd hoped to bring with me to Paradise when I was younger—he swore no other of his kind would be capable of creating the portal.

That was what he told me years ago—that he had found a weakness in the border because he'd long been the most powerful of his people and that the weakness recurred every twenty-four hours in my world. Every 480 days in his. So small no one else would be able to find it or be strong enough to use it.

Swallowing, I make myself say it. "You said no one else could bring people here."

"Perhaps I underestimated my kin." He shakes his head and tries to smile, but he's still too tense.

I take his hand and hold it tight. "Orane, if Hudson... Shouldn't I try to get him to realize he's putting this world in danger by hinting about it like that? It doesn't seem like he knows."

"Has he spoken of being here?" Orane's eyes blaze for a second, lighting up like neon bulbs. "Or *told* you he knows this place?"

Remembering Hudson's exact words... "Well, no. Not *exactly*, but—"

"Then leave it to me to sort out," he says, stroking his hand over my hair. His eyes return to normal. The motion is soothing, and my eyes close more with each touch. When Orane speaks, his voice is more dulcet than usual. "This boy is dangerous, and I do not want you to come to harm."

Hudson? Dangerous? I thought so at first, but he's been nothing but nice. Weird and a little prescient, but nice. I shake my head and the motion of Orane's hand halts.

"I don't think he's dangerous, just lost." I force my eyes open, fighting against the heaviness falling over me. "I think he needs help, Orane. Can't we bring him here so you can explain things to him?"

Orane's eyes darken. Not as deep as last night, but the soft violet dips closer to the color of the twilight sky above us.

"Mariella, why are you so concerned about this boy?"

"Why are you *not* worried about him?" I can't understand how he's taking this so calmly. "What if he's told other people, Orane? What if someone else knows about this place? What if they tell the wrong person, someone who remembers the old stories? How can you *not* be worried?"

He strokes my hair again, his eyes deepening until they're almost black. I try to blink, to move my head, to breathe. I can't. I'm locked where I am, held in his gaze as though he wrapped his arms around me and held me here.

"I will take care of everything." His voice echoes inside my head, and each word gets louder until it drowns out my ability to think. "You do not need to worry about a thing."

His words become a weighted yoke draped over my shoulders, pressing me to obey. The more I resist, the heavier the order becomes.

Why is this happening? My vision blurs and my chest burns as a vibrating energy passes through my head. More than a vibration. A chime.

Holding onto the note, I grasp the thread of energy I found last night. The tighter I grip that energy, the louder the chime gets until finally—*finally*—light bursts in front of my eyes.

Colors sway and swirl. I take a breath as my eyes slowly close. Shaking my head and forcing my eyes open, I try to talk, but the words won't come. What was I about to say? We were talking about Hudson and he said not to worry… Oh!

"Telling me not to worry doesn't mean there's nothing to worry about." Orane's eyes narrow and I know he's going to argue with me, so I cut him off before he can. "I'm not saying Hudson is dangerous, but he might lead to trouble if we're not careful. He could—"

Orane's hands tighten on my back and my head, and then his lips lock against mine.

This doesn't feel like a kiss. There's none of the warmth or the comfort. This is like being smothered, trapped against a rock and unable to move. His arms, always so supportive, are now restraints. Trying to fight makes his grip tighter. I'm being crushed, and even though I'm searching for help, for an escape, all I can see are his eyes. His eyes are the same deep purple as storm clouds at midnight.

"Do not worry, Mariella. Let it all fade away. I will take care of everything."

I grasp for anything that might help me escape. For a second, I feel a thin thread of energy. I hear a chime. But then it slips through my fingers and all I have is silence and darkness.

I fall and fall and keep going until I can't remember anything but the darkness and the purple eyes glowing far above me.

Seventeen

Hudson

Saturday, August 30 – 11:20 PM

When I get back to the house, Horace shows me where the stones he bought earlier are soaking in bowls of salt. Dawn put each type of stone in a separate bag and labeled them all. Horace ripped the labels off and laid them on top of the salt.

I shake my head. "I can't believe I didn't notice this before." The bowls are everywhere, spread out across the entire kitchen.

"You weren't exactly lingering when you burst in earlier."

True. I'd stayed at Mariella's as long as I could. That project with the boxwoods took most of the afternoon, and afterward I'd talked to Dana for a while about what she wanted to use to replace them. I barely had time to shower and change before we were due at the Teagans's for dinner. And I was too busy planning a way to sneak more stones upstairs to check out Horace's kitchen.

After we brush the salt crystals off the stones and lay them out on the cracked countertop, we try to figure out where to put them all.

"Probably would be best all in one place after what happened last night," Horace says as we stand back and stare at the rainbow of stones laid out in front of us.

"I'm not leaving you unprotected, Horace."

Horace snorts. "I'm not trying to be all noble. I ain't a saint, kid. I'm talkin' about putting them all somewhere we're *both* spending the night."

I think I like the idea of Horace left open and vulnerable better. At least alone, there's a chance that the demons might pass him by. In the same room as me? The chances of passing the night without a visitor are low. Like winning-the-lottery-and-getting-struck-by-lightning-on-the-*same-day* low.

"I don't know." I rub my thumb over one of the scars on my palm and try to think of some other solution.

"Boy, I wasn't really giving you a choice," Horace says. I look at him and know I'm toast as soon as I see the steely glint in his eyes. "You need protection, and this is what we got. You either pile it all in my room with that mattress I bought you today, or you dismantle my bed and bring it down here. I ain't sleeping if I'm gonna be worrying about the house burning to cinders around me 'cause of one of your friends visiting in the middle of the night."

He picks up some of the stones and carries them upstairs. I don't bother arguing. He already knows he's won.

With what he bought and the few extras I have stored in my car—the ones waiting to find their way into Mariella's room—it *might* be enough. I hope it is. It won't only be my life on the line tonight. It'll be Horace's, too.

My mattress barely fits on the floor after we pull his entire bed away from the wall. Every stone and crystal in the house is set up in a circle around us, one touching the next all the way around.

Horace is asleep on his bed, but I'm sitting on my mattress with my back against his footboard, waiting. The seconds tick past like a countdown, each one thudding through the house with the metronomic rhythm of a grandfather clock. Slowly, midnight approaches. It's a little like being tied to train tracks and watching an express train barrel toward you, knowing you can't escape. And that it won't stop.

The stroke of twelve gets closer.

And closer.

I tense, my gaze darting across the room for the first sign of the portal.

There's a few seconds left.

My phone beeps—my midnight alarm.

Every muscle in my body contracts, and my hand locks around the closest amethyst.

Nothing happens.

12:00:15

I watch the seconds pass on my new phone.

12:00:30

Where are they?

12:00:45

This isn't right.

12:01:00

They're not coming?

I should be relieved. I slowly exhale the breath I've been holding, but the tension in my body doesn't ease. This is wrong. Something is very, *very* wrong.

Why wouldn't they try again? Mari's demon knows where I am now. And I can't imagine Mariella didn't tell him I visited her again. She might have even mentioned the amethyst I gave her, or the black jade horse. If she did, the demon will know exactly what I'm trying to do. Why would he let it slide? He definitely didn't pull any punches last night.

Unless...maybe my fortifications kept him out. I look around the room, mentally tracing the protective ring around our beds. Is this what it takes? Is this how many stones I'll have to sneak into Mariella's room to keep the demon from getting at her?

I do a quick estimate. There's about 150 or so stones of various sizes here. Right now there's sixteen in Mariella's house. How the hell am I gonna smuggle over a hundred stones into her house? And not just into her house, into her *bedroom*. Maybe now that K.T. knows, she'll help. Dana is going to be a lot more likely to let K.T. up there than me.

I pick up my phone and check the time. 12:08 AM.

I roll my shoulders and relax. The witching hour—or the witching *minute,* I guess—is over. Guess Mari's demon had more important things than me to take care of tonight.

Crack!

Orange light floods the bedroom, and I grip the amethyst geode so tight the edges cut into my skin. The stones pulse with energy of their own, glowing in shades of purple, green, and the white light that emanates from the jet and black jade. Almost as though they've become bioluminescent. Like last time, a bolt of bright orange energy shoots out of the wall like lightning and straight at the center of my chest.

I dive to the side, but the bolt never reaches me. As soon as it hits the ring of stones, the pulsing light rises up out of the stones and creates a domed arch over our beds. Because the stones make a complete circle, I only have to touch one to control the flow of power. They'd work well on their own, but I can reinforce them and strengthen the protection in the spots that need it most.

The energy I'm pulling in from the real world races through my body like an electrical current, but it doesn't burn like the dreamworld. Although it's draining my own energy, the ache is bearable. And the chiming tone that rings through the air buzzes through my body on its own frequency, spurring me on and keeping me balanced.

The bolts of orange light crack against the shield, warping it but not breaking through. Wherever the two clash, a burst of blue fireworks explodes. Each bolt is like a cinder landing on my chest, but compared to the agony of the acid-like burning last night, this is nothing.

I haven't heard a peep from Horace. God, I hope the old man's okay. I want to check on him, but I can't take my attention off the shield.

The chime changes pitch, and the sound grates against my ears, building in volume and pressure until something bursts behind me. Shards of crystal slice into my arm, a shockwave of sparking energy rolls over me, and I wince as a section of the shield above my head begins to fade. The orange bolts strike faster.

No!

Gritting my teeth, I breathe in, pulling energy from the world around me, energy most people never feel. I'm almost grinning from the strain. What would Calease think if she saw me using her power to protect myself from the rest of the demons? I pull it through my body, pouring more of my own energy into the shield. Another stone shatters. And another. Each explosion sends out a blast of power that pushes the orange light back, but whoever is attacking me tonight is a lot stronger than the demons I've faced before. They push right back.

The constant pressure and pounding energy are too much for these smaller stones to take. They're buckling under the assault. And so am I.

Another stone shatters. The light of the shield fades further, faster and faster with every second. The shield is disappearing, but the bolts have stopped as well.

As the orange light folds in on itself, crawling across the ceiling and the walls like fog, a voice hisses inside my head. The same one I heard last night.

"You will not take what is mine, boy," he says. "Run now, or I will turn my full attention on you."

The light vanishes. The shield drops. With a final pulse, the light fades from the crystals.

I collapse onto my mattress as the world fades to black.

What is that buzzing?

"Answer it, Hud," Horace grumbles from the bed.

It's dark, but my phone is lit up, K.T.'s name flashing on the screen below the time: 12:45 AM. I fumble with it for a second, my fingers about as nimble as bricks. Somehow, I catch the call before it goes to voicemail. She wouldn't be calling at this hour unless something bad had happened.

"What's wrong?" My voice is scratchy and lower than usual.

"I'm sorry." K.T. sounds breathless, and her voice is thick, like she's been crying or trying not to cry. "I didn't want to wake you up, but I—"

Her voice cracks, and I hear her sniffle.

"K.T., what happened?"

Horace's face appears over the footboard, his bushy eyebrows furrowed.

"Maybe it's nothing. I almost didn't call because, you know, maybe I imagined it after everything you told me. But then I started thinking...you know, what if I *didn't* imagine it?"

"Imagine *what*?"

She takes a deep, shaky breath and finally says, "I had this weird dream, Hudson. This door opened in my wall and there was this library, and this guy with auburn hair and violet eyes tried to get me to come with him."

My heart stops, and I jerk upright, ignoring the twinges of pain from my body.

"You didn't, did you? K.T., tell me you didn't follow him." My heart thumps faster and faster. Above me, Horace's eyes widen.

"N-no, but when I refused he said I had two choices. Follow him willingly, or he'll take what he wants anyway." The tears must start falling then because her voice gets heavier and rises about an octave. "Can they do that, Hudson? Can they take what they want like that?"

"I don't know."

But wait...that's not true. I taste honey before the memory surfaces. Calease was impatient once with a boy who asked too many questions. She ripped what she wanted out of his head, and the boy died. She wasn't entirely satisfied because the talent was incomplete, but obviously they *are* capable of it.

"Wait. Yes, they can."

She starts crying harder. "I don't know what they want! What can I possibly have that they want?"

"It doesn't matter. The important part is not letting them get it."

But how the hell can I do that? She needs a collection at least as big as the one I have here, and I bought out both New Age stores within decent driving distance.

"You're gonna have to spend tomorrow night at my place. And maybe Monday."

"What? I can't! There's no way my parents are going to let me do that."

"So lie. I can keep the demons away from you, but you have to be here." At least until all the extra stones I ordered come in and I can send her home with her own arsenal.

She's quiet, but eventually she swallows. "Yeah. Okay. I'll figure something out."

"Call me if anything else happens. Anything weird at all. Whatever time it is."

"Yeah, sure. Um, thanks, Hudson."

I say goodbye and hang up, dropping the phone to the mattress.

"Guess I missed the party," Horace says, holding up the broken pieces of stone.

Nodding, I take a broken piece of amethyst and pinch it between my thumb and forefinger. It used to be a deep purple color. It's almost gray now, like the color has been leached out of the stone. Before I've exerted much pressure, the crystal shatters. A few big chunks break off, and the rest crumbles into pieces so small they're practically dust. Not a good sign.

No one delivers on Sunday, so what we have has to last at least another day. I hope the new shipment comes in before everything else shatters and leaves me with more wounds than I can heal.

Eighteen

Mariella

Sunday, August 31 – 12:12 PM

I open my eyes and try to sit up, but as soon as I move, my stomach tries to jump into my throat. Collapsing onto my pillow, I put one hand on my stomach and one on my head. Why do I feel like someone closed my head in a grand piano? Maybe because someone in the house can't get the tuning right on a set of speakers. Did my parents get a new system or something? That feedback is ridiculously aggravating.

My head throbs, each heartbeat thudding through my body like a bass drum. I can't open my eyes because there's too much light in the room. It burns and makes the throbbing worse.

Someone knocks on my door. "Honey, did you want—"

The voice cuts off as the door opens.

"You're still in bed? Mari, are you okay?" My mother walks over to the bed and presses her hand to my cheek. "You're a little chilled. Do you want some soup? Or some tea?"

Thinking about food makes nausea climb up my throat. I lift my hand and sign "no." The feedback changes pitch, getting an octave higher. Wincing, I sign, "What is that noise?"

"Noise?" Her head tilts to the side, and she listens. "What noise, honey? I'm not sure what I'm listening for."

I close my eyes and bite back a groan. She can't hear it. Great. So either my headache is so bad it's making me hear things or…I don't know what.

"Do you feel sick?"

Yes. Awfully sick. But I don't want to see a doctor. Moving my head hurts too much, so I sign "no" and add "tired." I try opening my eyes again—slowly—and this time the burning isn't quite so bad. I can see why it seemed so bright at first. In addition to the gleaming light from Orane's gifts, sunshine is streaming through my thin curtains. What time is it?

I try to move my head toward the clock, but the slight motion sends the room spinning. I close my eyes and sign "time?" instead.

"It's noon," my mother says.

My eyes pop open. *Noon*? I've slept since midnight? I always wake up after leaving Paradise. I haven't slept more than an hour in *years*. And suddenly I sleep for *twelve*?

"Didn't mean to oversleep?" My mother smiles at me, but there are creases around her eyes. The sudden change worries her. I haven't overslept since middle school.

"I'll give you some time to wake up and we'll do a late lunch, okay?"

I lift my hand and sign "yes." Hopefully my stomach calms down by then. She brushes my bangs off my face and kisses my forehead before heading for the door, then stops with her hand on the doorknob.

"Last chance to change your mind about new school clothes," she says with a tight smile. "If we don't hit the mall before tomorrow, it'll be too late."

What? I have at least two weeks before I have to go back to school…don't I?

I sign "no, thank you," and my mother shrugs, playing off her disappointment.

"All right. Lunch in an hour, okay?"

As soon as she's gone, I grab my phone from the nightstand and check the date.

August 31.

What?

Ignoring the lingering uncertainty in my stomach and breathing through the way my head starts spinning, I lurch off the bed and stumble to my computer to double-check. My phone *has* to be wrong.

My computer says the same thing. Sunday, August 31.

Staring at the calendar, I try to backtrack over the past two weeks.

Focusing on the entire period brings up bits and pieces—dinners with my parents, Scrabble games, books I've read—but no matter how hard I try, I can't fit them into an actual order. The moments are jumbled in my head like puzzle pieces in a box. Except none of them fit. There are gaps that don't make sense and time I can't account for.

My pulse picks up, each beat surging through my body like a spark of fire.

Calm down, I tell myself. *Start with last night.*

I think back to my time with Orane, waiting for the familiar wash of lavender and rush of longing—

And get nothing.

It's like I'm looking through a blizzard at night or a thick, soupy fog. I can almost make out shapes and shadows in the distance, but when I get closer, they vanish into the mist.

My breathing gets shallow and fast, and the throbbing in my head gets worse, going from bass drum to jackhammer.

Fine. Don't start with recent memories. Go back to the last thing you remember for certain, I decide. *Go back to the last moment you can pinpoint for certain on the calendar.*

Day by day I go back, staring at the box on the calendar until I'm absolutely sure all I see is fog. Finally, when I reach the seventeenth, a memory filters up. We had pizza that night, my parents were talking about Julian and Aunt Jacquelyn, and my father challenged me to a game of chess after dinner. I let him think he might win.

I thought finding a moment I could pinpoint might help figure this out, but it doesn't. It makes me realize that the last two weeks—*exactly* two weeks—are gone. Lost in the fog that's settled into my head.

My eyes burn, tears fighting to leak out and roll down my cheeks.

I fold over my legs, my hair creating a curtain around my face and filtering out some of the light.

What is happening to me? Did I fall? Is that why my head hurts so much? But then my mother would have said something. She wouldn't be surprised to see me in bed, and she would have checked on me earlier. Right?

Unless she doesn't know. Maybe it happened last night. Or maybe something went wrong when I came back from Paradise. But in the decade I've been visiting Orane's world, nothing like this has ever happened. I think.

It doesn't make sense!

Pushing my hair out of the way, I dry my eyes and sit up. As I do, my gaze locks on something sitting on my nightstand that I don't recognize at all—a purple stone about the size of my palm.

Where the hell did that come from? It's not glittering with the light of Paradise, so I know it's not from Orane.

I stare at it, trying to remember. Nothing comes. Almost nothing.

For some reason, I keep wanting to glance at my dresser. There's nothing out of place there, but I stare at it, trying to figure out what's pulling my attention. Finally, I get up and open the top drawer. There, half-buried in a pile of socks, is a black statue of a rearing horse, slightly taller than the length of my hand.

Where did this come from? And what the *hell* is it doing in my sock drawer? And why did I almost remember putting it there when everything else about the past two weeks is gone?

Carefully, I reach forward and untangle it from a few stray socks. As soon as my hand closes around the statue, the feedback I've been hearing since I woke up shifts. Louder, higher-pitched, more insistent. I wince. Before I can drop the horse back where I found it, the sound changes again, the feedback slowly replaced with a much more pleasant sound. It's almost like the long ring of a small bell, or maybe a high note on a cello.

Something shimmers in the too-bright light coming from Orane's gifts. For a moment, I see a face. It's blurry, almost impossible to make out, but I get the sense of overwhelming size and a comforting smile. Surrounding the vague form, all I see is darkness. There's a voice whispering in the black, but I can't make out the words or remember why darkness would feel warm and safe.

Keeping hold of the statue, I move toward my dresser and pick up the purple stone—I think it's an amethyst. The noise shifts again, the feedback fading further into the background as the soothing chime takes over. Bringing the stone closer to my eyes, I look at the way the color shades from deep purple at one end to pale lavender at the other. It's pretty. It reminds me of Orane's eyes.

It's not until I pull my gaze away from the stone that I realize my head doesn't hurt quite so much. I take a deep breath; my nausea has begun to recede. *Finally.*

Rubbing my thumb over the cool, smooth surface of the amethyst, I try to shake off the lingering unease crawling like ants along the lining of my stomach.

Does it matter if I can't remember the last two weeks? Probably not. It's summer, and nothing much happens in the summer. It'll be fine. Orane will help me figure it out as soon as I get back to his world tonight.

At least, I hope he can help me.

Nineteen

Hudson

Sunday, August 31 – 7:02 PM

As soon as I walk in the door, I know something is wrong. Mariella is staring at me with wide eyes, her entire body trembling.

My stomach clenches. Fear. That's flat-out fear in her eyes.

What the hell did her demon say to her last night? I thought we'd gotten past this. I thought we'd reached some sort of weird middle ground where we could be civil, if not friendly. I'd started to believe I could tell her my story and try to change her mind about the dreamworld.

"Come on in," Dana says. "Everything should be ready in a minute."

Mariella's eyes shift to her mother, and creases line her forehead. She looks at me again and flinches when she meets my eyes, but not as much as the first time. I try to tell myself I don't care, but I do. More than I thought I would.

At least now confusion seems to be overtaking the fear. Kind of.

"Mari?" Dana calls as she heads back to the kitchen. "Can you and Hudson finish setting the table? He should remember where everything is."

Only because I'm watching so closely do I see the split-second slackening of her jaw and the way her nostrils flare. Surprise and then confusion. The lines around her eyes deepen, and then it's all gone. Her face is a blank mask wearing a fake smile.

Mari waits for me to go first and watches me once I step into the kitchen. Does she want to see if her mother is right? What is this—a test?

Grinding my teeth, I head straight for the cabinet with the plates, open the door, and glance back at Mari. The creases are back, but the confusion has morphed into frustration.

Her lips thin as I ask her, "Do you want to carry the plates or the bowls?"

It takes a second, but she cups her hands together and moves them out. Bowls it is, then.

As soon as I get close to her, the tingling is back, the pin-prickly sensations that being around Mariella always causes. The same moment I feel it, Mariella jumps, her hands clenching as she looks around. Trying to figure out what's happening? Yeah. Me too.

The tingling is as strong as it was before, but she relaxes around me faster than she did the night we met. Mariella has the amethyst I gave her in her pocket, but when she takes it out and looks at it, she stares at it with this intense concentration it really doesn't warrant.

I lean closer and whisper, "I gave that to you yesterday."

Mari jumps, and the amethyst flies out of her hand. I grab it in midair and hand it back.

"Didn't mean to startle you, but it's true. The black horse, too."

A quick, sharp gasp is all the response I get before the mask and the smile are back.

"I know," she signs.

I shake my head and turn back to my plate. "Don't lie, Mari. You're not good at it."

For the rest of the meal, she glances at me every few seconds, sometimes long enough for me to catch her. Her reactions when our eyes meet are strange, running the entire range from flinching to blushing.

I can't get a read on what she's thinking. The longer I watch her, the more I think I'm not the only thing missing from her memory. Maybe I'm just the first thing to pop up out of her forgotten past. Glancing at the amethyst in her hand, I shrug. At least, the first thing that *talks.*

How strange does this have to be for her? Calease took memories from me, but I never realized it until the night I saw through her lies for the first time. Until the last day, I was never faced with living proof something was missing from my mind. "Disorienting" doesn't begin to cover it. Finding one hole would make me start questioning the rest of my memory, too, poking through it and trying to find more. How far back would I have to go before I was satisfied nothing else was missing? And what the hell do you do if you figure out more *is*?

Reminding myself that this is harder for her than it is for me, I let her adjust and leave her alone. At least until she leaves the table after dinner and I can have a moment without her parents overhearing what I have to ask her.

"How much time are you missing, Mari?"

She looks up at me, frozen instead of trembling.

"A few days? Do you remember what happened Friday?"

A deep breath and a shudder. Mari shakes her head.

"A week?"

Mari brings her arms up and hugs herself. She won't look at me.

"I know you don't remember me, but you can trust me."

She doesn't move her head, but she glances at me, her warm brown eyes meeting mine for an instant. I don't know how I should play this. Hint at what I know like I did before, or lay it all out? I might scare her off if I tell her straight up. She'll probably tell her demon everything, and I'll get another visit. But a little scare might get me the information I need. And if her demon wiped her memory for what little interaction I've had with her, she probably won't remember what I'm about to say tomorrow.

What the hell—here goes nothing.

"I know where you go at night, Mariella," I whisper.

Mari gasps and backs away, her eyes doubling in size and the tremor reappearing.

"You visit a dreamworld no one else knows about, and there's someone waiting for you every night, someone who made you promise to never speak about what happens there."

She looks around like she's about to run. There's nowhere to go.

"They're lying, Mari. If they're so benevolent, why are you missing more than a week of your life? Why can't you remember meeting me or where we went last night?"

Her eyes narrow, and she signs, "Where?"

"Your friend K.T. invited us to a party. The entire senior class was there, and you didn't remember any of them. People you've gone to school with since kindergarten, Mari."

Palms facing up, she slaps the back of one hand down on the palm of the other. Proof. She's asking for proof.

I take out my phone and show her a picture I took a few minutes before we left the party. We'd moved closer to the house, and she was standing in a pool of light, looking up at the sky. The lights from the house made her hair more golden, and with her face turned toward the moon, she looked like a star trapped in human form, longing to return to the sky. It was an impulsive moment when I snapped that picture, but now I'm glad I did.

In the background, you can see the other kids and the party, proving we weren't alone. And we weren't in her backyard.

Mari takes my phone and stares at the screen, examining the picture like she's determined to figure out how I faked it. The longer she stares, the less she shakes. Her expression is shifting so fast I almost can't keep up, but I can guess what she's thinking. Wondering how much she can trust me and what else I might know. Wondering what her demon might be lying about. Wondering what the hell else she's forgotten.

I'm amazed at how calmly she's taking this. She must've known time was missing before I got here, but she had it under control. Most girls—hell, most *people*—would be on the edge of losing their minds already, but not Mari. She seems determined to figure this out, to solve the problem and do it herself if she has to.

I've been avoiding examining Mariella with the filter that showed me as a white knight—the one that shows me people's inner selves or their souls or...something. I should've done it the first time we met, but it was hard enough to concentrate around the electric sparks running across my skin. And I couldn't know what I would see. I've already seen her burning alive and chained to a table. What if this is worse?

Doesn't matter. I can't put it off any longer. While she's occupied, I bring up the filter. I look at Mari and have to lock my jaw to keep it from dropping open.

She looks like a goddess. Literally. Mariella is bathed in golden light and dressed up like Athena in a golden robe with one hand clutching a spear, the other a scroll, and what looks like a lyre strapped to her back.

The image reminds me of statues kings and emperors would commission of themselves, but on her, it's somehow not as pretentiously overblown as those things always were. This is who she is—benevolent and decisive, a leader people would follow to the ends of the earth. One with a talent for music, I guess.

That shining beauty only lasts a second before the image shimmers and shifts, going from what she *should* look like to…

Her golden light is wrapped up in chains that look like they've been heated in a forge. The metal glows like hot cinders and sears her skin wherever it touches. Her dress is ragged and torn, her arms are trapped across her chest, and she's screaming silently while tears stream down her face.

Physical strength is one thing—I have that, and it's rarely done me much good—but Mariella has been fighting against the demon's hold for years. That takes willpower and a level of perseverance I've never seen. That strength, the kind of strength Mariella has? That will last a lifetime. It's the kind of strength that will earn people's respect and help her weather all the storms life will throw at her.

As long as she can make it past her eighteenth birthday.

I blink and shudder, taking a deep breath and wishing I could unmake that last decision. Jesus. That was like walking into a room to see someone you know being tortured. My stomach turns and my fists clench. I want to grab Mariella and run for it, anything to get her out of the reach of the monster that's doing that to her. How could anyone do that to her? To anyone?

I try to shake the image out of my head, but I know I'll never be able to forget what I saw. Fucking demons and their side effects. I *can't* forget. Even the things I wish I could.

Something pokes me in the arm, and I look down. Mari is handing me back my phone.

I take it, knowing I should say something, but my throat is closed and the words won't come. I want to hug her, to hold her and try to make her see that I understand what she's going through, but right now she wouldn't thank me for it.

Swallowing, I force out something I hope is coherent.

"How much time are you missing, Mari?" My voice is as soft as I can make it. I stuff my hands in my pockets and concentrate on what I need to know. "A week?"

Her eyes flick up to meet mine, and she shakes her head, holding up two fingers.

"*Two* weeks?"

That doesn't make sense. Why would he take that much time away from her in one fell swoop? Did he think she wouldn't notice? Did he think I wouldn't come back and poke at her memory to see if I could stir anything up?

When she goes back tonight, he'll be pissed. Especially if I warn her what he's up to. But if I don't try now, I might lose my one shot at getting through to her.

"Mari, I don't know what whoever you meet in that world has told you, but you can't trust it." Her face flushes red, but I press on, leaning closer to her to make sure my voice doesn't carry. "You have to get out and stay out or it's going to take a lot more than your memory. It—"

Her hand moves so fast I hear the *smack* before I see or feel it. She's not strong enough to do damage, but I can tell she tried to put more than a little power behind that slap.

Yep. Should've been expecting that.

Before I can react, her hands are flying, the gestures so angry I can almost feel the heat of the emotion rolling off her in waves.

"Liar! You don't know anything. It's not possible. You wouldn't be allowed inside!" her hands tell me.

The tirade lasts a few seconds before she shoves me backward, turns, and runs upstairs.

I watch Mariella disappear, and my heart clenches. She's going to run straight to her demon and tell him everything. And he's going to wipe her slate clean again. And unless I come up with a plan quick, there's nothing I can do to stop it from happening over and over again until she goes to sleep on her eighteenth birthday—eleven days from now—and never wakes up again.

When Horace and I get home, K.T. is sitting on the porch waiting for us.

"Sorry," I say as I run up to unlock the door. "Have you been here long? Are you okay?"

K.T. picks up a backpack and shrugs as she follows me inside.

"I've definitely had better days." She looks around, and her eyes widen. "So has this house. Wow."

"It's a work in progress," Horace mutters as he passes. "Piece of shit property."

K.T. giggles—a surprised little laugh—and relaxes as we show her around. Given what happened last night, all three of us will be spending the evening in Horace's room where the stones are set up.

"And these will really keep us safe?" she asks, her eyebrows raised.

"Hey, don't knock it. They've already saved my life four times."

"This was almost his head." Horace tosses the burned-out cell phone at K.T., and she squeaks when she sees the fried circuitry inside.

"Where do your parents think you are?" I ask while she pokes at the insides of my phone.

"I don't know. I told them I was going to stay over at a friend's house. They actually didn't ask. Might not be as easy on a school night, but I'm fine for now."

That's good, I guess. "What about your boyfriend?"

"What?" Her eyebrows furrow, but she doesn't look up. "Don't have one."

"Oh. Sorry. I thought Danny was..." I trail off, trying not to shove my foot any deeper down my throat.

K.T. flushes a little and shakes her head. "No, we're just friends."

After a few seconds of awkward silence, I tell her, "I saw Mariella tonight."

That finally pulls her attention away from the phone.

"Is she okay? I worried after she left last night that it might've been too much for her."

I laugh, but it sounds more like choking. "Oh, no. She's fine. She doesn't remember going. Or you. Or ever meeting me before tonight."

K.T. flinches but doesn't look surprised. "Welcome to my life."

"That's not all."

I tell K.T. and Horace everything I learned and saw tonight—everything except for the image of Mariella wrapped in burning chains as she screamed in agony. I don't think anyone else needs to be burdened with that picture.

K.T. is quiet when I finish, but she's biting her lip, and her eyes dart back and forth like she's reading something in the air in front of her.

"She reacted to the picture, right? Did she remember anything?"

"She seemed to believe what I said, but I don't know if she remembered anything."

K.T. purses her lips and falls into silence again, twirling a lock of her dark brown hair around her index finger. "Maybe it wasn't a night she had any attachment to. What if we pulled from further back? Before she met this creep?"

"Don't know. It might work, but I don't know anything about her childhood."

"I do. And I can talk to her mom."

K.T. keeps talking, and we outline a plan. We'll create a scrapbook of pictures. If we pull in enough missing moments, we might be able to convince Mari we're telling the truth.

"But what do we do after that?" K.T. asks.

I groan and rub my hand over my hair, letting my head *thunk* back against Horace's footboard. "I don't have a goddamn clue."

Horace's soft snores are the only sound in the room after a while. K.T. tries to stay awake, but exhaustion wins eventually and she drifts off to sleep. She collapses into a ball, curling around her pillow and clutching it tight.

Midnight passes. Twelve-thirty passes. One o'clock. It's quiet, and I'm the only one awake. I can't get K.T.'s question out of my head. It echoes back and forth. It creates a great soundtrack to the memory of Mariella wrapped in those burning chains.

Even if K.T. and I can get her to listen, what then? How can I fight against a demon who wipes her mind every night? How can I fight someone I can't *get* to?

Two-thirty and I haven't come up with an answer. I'm starting to drift off, ready to let myself get the little bit of rest I need each night, when the orange light floods the room.

"Leave now or I will see you wiped from the face of this planet, you worthless creature," the demon says.

K.T. jerks in her sleep, her face scrunched up. When the first bolt strikes the shield over our heads, she sits up, her eyes wide and her mouth hanging open.

"Oh my God! *What?*" she shrieks.

I shake my head and keep my hand on the closest amethyst. Explaining will split my concentration too much.

The demon sends a barrage of energy against us. Bolts hit fast as machine-gun fire, and I grit my teeth, shoring up the stones with my own energy as much as I can.

When the shield begins to warp, a surge of strength enters the ring.

I glance up. K.T. is kneeling on the other side, her hands on a chunk of malachite and her eyes closed. With her hands on the stones, I'm able to use her energy, too, pulling from her as much as she can give. We only lose three stones before the attack finally ends and we both collapse.

"How did you do that by yourself before?" She's panting for breath and pale, but we're both alive. Right now, that's all that matters.

"I don't know. How did you know to touch the stones?"

"Didn't. I copied you."

I nod and drop my head back to the mattress. It was a smart move. Brave, too. A lot of people would've screamed and cowered until it was over. Because of her help, I can keep my eyes open after one of their attacks for the first time.

K.T. swallows and turns her head to look at me. "Do you really think we can save Mari?"

I glance at her but can't meet her eyes for more than a second.

More than anything, I want to be able to tell her yes and mean it. Really mean it. Maybe it's that stupid "white knight" thing rearing its head, but it bugs the hell out of me to think I might fail at this. That I won't be able to come up with a way to save Mariella.

It's not about what happened to J.R. right now. For the first time, I'm not thinking about him when I think about getting into the dreamworld. I'm thinking about Mariella wrapped in those chains, and the trust in K.T.'s eyes when she asks me that question. Even so, the best I can do is tell her the truth.

"I don't know."

Twenty

Mariella

Monday, September 1 – 9:18 AM

I almost think I could handle *two weeks* of my life disappearing if I could figure out why I'm hallucinating noises! And of all the noises to have jumping through my head, did it have to switch between glockenspiel tones and microphone feedback?

On top of that, Orane's gifts are all glowing exponentially brighter than I've ever seen before, so bright it's giving me a headache. It makes the bedroom seem too small, like the light is taking up space or the walls are creeping closer each second. I've been jumpy and jittery since I woke up at eight this morning—*eight!* I haven't slept that late in years!

I have to get out of here.

I run downstairs and out to the backyard. I take a deep breath, savoring the scent of cut grass on the warm breeze and—

Wait...what happened to the boxwood bushes? Tiny plants now line the side of the yard once cut off by thick boxwood bushes. And they look fresh.

Grinding my teeth, I look away. One more thing I don't remember.

As I turn away, I see a huge pile of branches and leaves. The missing boxwoods. A memory flashes—blond hair and

The light from my pendant pulses and the fog grows thicker, almost drowning out the tiny golden lights entirely. Energy rolls off my necklace and the nightingale in my pocket, sinking under my skin like the crackling heat that rolls off a fire. My vision goes black as my head starts spinning.

I blink and shake my head, trying to clear it.

Wait…I was in the car. How did I get to school so fast? And why is a girl in a bright red shirt staring at me?

The feedback noise I thought I left at home rears up, and the muscles in my neck convulse as I fight the urge to cover my ears.

Oh, that can go away at *any* time. I'd totally be okay with it. Promise.

"My name is K.T." The girl shifts, lifting the strap of her purse higher on her shoulder. It makes noises like marbles striking against each other. What does she have in there? She runs her hand over her hair, then tosses it back over her shoulder. "I came to talk to you about Hudson."

Hudson? That name sends a spark of energy through my chest and pulls a recent memory out of the fog.

Hudson. The towering giant with the onyx-black eyes and unusually sweet smile. Mother knew him—and she expected me to know him, too—but I've never seen him before. Or this girl who seems to know me. I'm a stranger in a school I've been attending for *years.*

K.T. shrugs. "Hudson is new this year and in the honors program with us. You've been assigned to be his mentor."

I've been *what*?

I wait for her to laugh. This has to be some screwed-up joke on the mute girl. Part of the benefit of being called "disabled" is getting out of stupid crap like playing tour guide to a new kid. Especially one as strangely appalling and appealing as Hudson.

dark eyes and a smile that sneaks out when he thinks no one is looking. I saw that face earlier, too, when I touched the purple stone sitting on my nightstand. It doesn't make sense. I don't know anyone that tall…do I?

Digging my hands into my hair, I bite my tongue to keep from screaming.

I don't know the answer to that question.

Do I know him? I didn't two weeks ago, but did I meet him since then?

My eyes burn, but I refuse to cry. What the hell kind of good will crying do?

Dropping my hands, I breathe in fours like Orane taught me. It's stress or something. Stress over *what,* I don't know, but something. It has to be. The memories will come back. Orane will help me figure everything out.

I head toward the hammock my parents set up during the summer, but something sparkly catches my eye before I reach it.

Walking closer to a tree, I see a golden chain with a tiny nightingale pendant, a miniature of the nightingale sitting on my nightstand upstairs.

I smile as I reach out for it, tension easing out of my body. How does Orane always know when I need him? He's never left anything for me outside my bedroom before, but he must have known I would come out here today. Or maybe it's been out here waiting for me.

As soon as I touch the chain to lift it free of the tree, Orane's voice fills my head.

"For you, my nightingale. Wear this and think of me, as I will be thinking of you."

I can smell the lavender of his world and feel his lips brush against my cheek. I bring the nightingale closer to my face to get a better look.

Unlike my other gifts, this one is not empty. Inside the glass is a softly swirling silver mist, and bobbing along in the current are dozens—maybe hundreds—of tiny golden pinpricks of light. Some are brighter than others, but they all swirl in and out of the fog. It's like watching fireflies dance on a foggy night.

I unclasp the necklace and clip it in place. The pendant is cool against my skin at first but it warms up quickly, and I can't help smiling when I place my hand over the charm.

Warmth washes over me. My lungs burn slightly, as though I've been holding my breath for too long. Blinking, I shudder and the warmth begins to recede.

Looking around, I try to remember why I came out here. It's a pretty day, but I need to find some new music. Something special to thank Orane for such a perfect gift.

Inside, I hear voices coming from the living room. One of them is my mother, but I don't recognize the second.

"A memory book *and* a slideshow? You always were ambitious, K.T.," my mother says. "I'm sure I can find something."

"Thanks, Mrs. Teagan. I don't know where most of my pictures went."

I peek into the living room as my mother hands a book to a curvaceous girl with brown hair.

"Here. You look through that one, and I'll check this one." My mother sits down and starts flipping through another book. A photo album, I think.

Not wanting to get sucked into whatever project they're working on, I slip upstairs and into my room. It's already after eleven. I don't have much time if I want to prepare something special for Orane tonight.

I smile and gently stroke my fingers along the nightingale around my neck. A gift of love that I can carry with me everywhere. It's perfect. He's perfect. And I have to find a way to say thank you.

Twenty-One

Hudson

Monday, September 1 – 8:44 PM

Without an official invitation to dinner, Horace forces me to stay home Monday night.

"Make yourself a nuisance and they won't let you in the door," he said. As much as I hate staying away, I know he's right.

This will be the first time since we've met that I go an entire day without seeing Mari. Not seeing her for a day shouldn't bug me this much. But it does. About the same amount as worrying about what her demon has done to her in the meantime.

It's on my mind all afternoon. As K.T., Horace, and I sit there eating takeout, my thoughts are a couple blocks away, wondering what Mariella is doing. And how she's doing. And if she would remember me if I walked into her house right now.

"I had an idea."

Staring at K.T., I wait, but she doesn't say anything else. "Are you going to tell me, or do I have to guess?"

"We have this mentor program at school." K.T. picks through her lo mein. "New students are paired with someone in a few of their classes to give them a guide for their first week. You're in honors with Mari and me, so I pulled some strings and made myself your mentor. I want to trick Mari into doing it."

Horace and I raise our eyebrows at the same time, but he says it first. "Seems like that ain't something she's gonna agree to easily."

"Who says I'll give her a choice?" K.T.'s lips curve into a smile I'd almost call diabolical. "I plan on telling her that refusing means doing a thirty-hour community service project and a five-page paper. She wouldn't care about the paper, but I don't see her wanting to go out into the world and be civic-minded."

It's a decent plan, but it's not without flaws. "What if she opts out?"

"We come up with something else." K.T. shrugs and runs a hand through her brown hair. "I didn't say it was a *perfect* plan. Just a plan."

"What if she forgets she's agreed?"

Before K.T. can consider an answer, Horace says, "Have her sign a contract."

K.T. and I both stare at Horace. He glances between the two of us, his forehead creased.

"What? It's obvious to me. Show someone their own signature on a contract and the fight tends to go out of 'em quick." He grins, and his eyes light up. "Trust me. It's a trick I've used a time or two in my life."

"A contract," K.T. says. It takes a few seconds, but that diabolical smile slowly spreads across her face. "I can write a contract. I can even print it on letterhead from the office."

Horace grins at me. "I like the way this one thinks."

I nod and let out a slow breath. Yeah, I do, too. I just hope it's enough.

To keep people from asking questions—like the *not*-boyfriend Danny—or spreading stories that might get back to her parents, Horace drives K.T. to school in the Camry and I drive the Camaro. If anyone asks, K.T. can say he's a friend of her family. We both doubt anyone will ask.

"Today is going to *suck*," K.T. mutters, sipping at the coffee she picked up on the way to school. There are circles under her eyes, and I know the lack of sleep from last night is hurting her today but it could be worse. They could have attacked last night.

I don't want to scare her, but they still could.

I *thought* the doorways only opened at midnight, but that was obviously what Calease wanted me to think. That danger is why I dumped a bunch of stones and crystals into K.T.'s purse before she left the house and why there are a bunch more in my backpack. Horace has the rest.

If we don't get more stones today, I don't know what I'm going to do. K.T. was barely able to convince her parents to let her sleep over at her "friend's" house last night. She's not going to be able to pull it off a third night in a row. She has to go home, and I'll have to send her off with at least half of the stones I collected. Half isn't going to protect either of us.

We're standing near the entrance, waiting for Mariella. We got here early so K.T. could print out our "contract" and make sure we don't miss Mari's arrival. Now, we're wasting time as kids straggle onto campus. Ten minutes before the bell, Dana's black SUV pulls up.

"Showtime," I say, nudging K.T. to make sure she's awake.

She nods, taking another sip of coffee and hanging back as I jog over to say hi to Mrs. Teagan. Dana grins when she sees me and rolls down her window.

"Morning, Hudson! How did you and Horace fare for dinner last night?"

"Fine. Takeout Chinese."

Dana cringes. "Can't have been better than 'fine,' then. We don't really have a decent Chinese place in this town."

"It was all right." It was awful, but that's not what I want to talk to her about. I glance at Mariella, who is watching me through narrow eyes, and smile. "Hey, Mari."

She flinches when her eyes meet mine, but when her mother glances over at her, she picks up one hand and jerks a wave at me. Dana's eyebrows pull together and her mouth opens, but I cut her off.

"Dana?" When she looks at me, I give her the good news. "Horace really liked the plans, and he wants to get started on the restoration as soon as possible. Could you let Frank know?"

"Oh! Really? Well, that's wonderful!" Dana beams and pats my hand where it's resting on the door. "Do you both want to come for dinner again tonight? We can celebrate over my famous lasagna."

I'm watching Mari, so I notice her reaction when her mother invites us for dinner *again.* Her eyes widen and her nostrils flare.

She's been wiped clean. Mari doesn't remember me, or Horace, or any of it.

Seeing that blank fear and confusion in her eyes makes my fists clench. I want to break through the barriers and wrap my hands around her demon's throat for taking so much of her life away from her. For taking *me* away from her.

Taking a breath, I remind myself that this might be a good thing. At least this once. If she doesn't remember me, it means she doesn't remember slapping me Sunday either.

Over the roof of the car, I signal to K.T., forming a zero with my hand.

I talk to Dana for another minute before jogging back toward the school. I know I need to give K.T. time to work, but some crazy part of my brain wants to grab Mariella, carry her back to Horace's, and watch over her for the next ten days—until she's survived her eighteenth birthday.

Like I said. Crazy.

Twenty-Two

Mariella

Tuesday, September 2 – 7:49 AM

I stare at each person I pass, waiting for one to look familiar. They all do a little, but more in the way a celebrity looks familiar. Not because you know them, but because you've seen them before. It's highly unlikely that I wouldn't know *any* of these people, isn't it? Maybe I've lost more than the past couple of weeks. How much of my life is missing, and how in the world am I supposed to answer that question?

How do you remember what you've forgotten when you don't know what you forgot?

"Hey, Mari! Wait up!"

I turn and see a short girl in a bright red shirt hurrying toward me, her dark ponytail swinging behind her as she moves. Do I know this girl? I stare at her, waiting for something to click into place.

Then I get a flash. A memory? She's much younger and sitting on my bed with tears running down her face.

"Mari, if Danny asks Jen out I'll just—I'll just *die*!" She covers her face and flops backward onto my bed.

K.T.'s not laughing. She's not even smiling. But…I mean, she can't be *serious*, can she?

"You'll do it, right? It's easier than the community service project."

What community service project? I shake my head, my eyebrows furrowed.

"If you haven't served as a mentor by the end of your senior year, you have to do this extra community service project." K.T.'s lip twitches. "It's about thirty hours of volunteer work. And then a five-page paper about why service is so important."

Her blue-gray eyes watch me carefully, but I'm trying to process what she said.

Thirty hours? The paper I don't care about. As a replacement for my participation grades in class, I've been doing extra papers since eighth grade. A five-page paper is nothing, but how many service-hour opportunities are there going to be that won't expect me to talk? I've never looked into it, but I'm guessing not many.

"So?" K.T. asks, her patience obviously at an end. "Which one would you rather do?"

Squire an incredibly strange stranger around school for a week or track down a service project that won't require speaking? Neither one of them will be easy. Or inviting.

K.T. laughs, but it's not the harsh laugh of someone poking fun at me. "You already know him, so you won't have to explain your silence. And he speaks sign language."

Really? Huh. I guess that makes it easier. And I have to admit that she's right, in a way. Communicating with Hudson will be a lot easier than the service project.

"Plus, he's really cute." She wiggles her eyebrows at me and I almost agree, remembering his smile. It doesn't matter, though. "Cute" doesn't cut it when I have Orane to compare everyone to. Next to my love, Hudson is no more than passable.

So, I have a choice between Hudson and community service. Given the options, Hudson is definitely the lesser of two evils.

Sighing, I nod, and K.T.'s grin spreads across her face, her eyes lighting up.

"Great! One last thing." She pulls a piece of paper from her purse and hands it to me. "I need you to fill this out and sign the bottom. It's the mentor contract."

They have a *contract*? They take this way too seriously. But K.T. is standing there with a smile on her face, waiting for me to take it. Fine. Whatever. It's a piece of paper.

I take the sheet and the pen she's holding, lean against the closest locker, and fill in my name and the dates I agree to mentor Hudson at the top. A week, K.T. said. Tuesday to Tuesday. At the bottom, I sign with my wide, loopy signature and pass the paper back to K.T.

"Thanks, Mari!" She raises her eyebrows. "Guess we should go find Hudson, huh?"

I gesture for her to lead the way. It doesn't take very long for me to notice there's not much "finding" involved. She heads straight for the corner of the school where Hudson is waiting like she's tracking a homing beacon.

"Hey, Hudson! Mari is going to show you around this week, all right?" She glances up at Hudson, and it's like she's trying to tell him something without talking.

Standing between the two of them, the feedback shifts, getting higher-pitched and transforming into something a lot more pleasant. It sounds like high C on Mother's piano.

Then K.T. spins around and skips off down the hallway. "See you guys in class!"

The farther away she gets, the more the piano fades and the feedback takes over. Guess it was too good to last for long.

Looking up at his face, I flinch when I meet his coal-black eyes. I try not to, but even expecting it, those eyes are a shock. Steeling myself, I look again. I hate when people talk about me like I can't hear them or treat me like a moron because I choose not to speak. If I can help it, I'm not going to do the same thing to this guy simply because his eyes are...strange.

I open my backpack and reach for the notebook I usually pretend to take notes in. Hudson stops me before I pull it from the bag, his hand hot and heavy on mine.

As soon as he touches me, a tremor of energy runs up my arm, like a breeze carrying an electrical current. Though my body is warming under his steady stare, I shiver. Staring up into his eyes, it's like I'm looking into the night sky. I can almost see stars and hear someone whispering stories in the dark.

But then he blinks and the image is gone. The electricity isn't, though—that subtle warmth and quiet tingle that wasn't there before.

"Forgot already?" His lips tilt into what may be a frown. "I understand sign language."

I flush and look away.

"Right," I sign. Glancing up at him, I add, "Sorry."

"It's fine." He shrugs and picks up the backpack sitting on the ground at his feet. Like K.T.'s purse, it clacks like it's full of rocks. "I'm getting used to the fact that you find me incredibly forgettable."

He makes it sound like I've forgotten him more than once. My stomach rolls, and I hug myself tight. How many times have we met? I want to ask him. I *want* to, but I don't. Missing time is awful. Finding out it's happened more than once? That would be *so* much worse.

I wrap my hand around my pendant and take a deep breath. It doesn't matter. Orane promised we would figure out what happened and fix it. He's never broken a promise.

"That's new. Where'd you get it?"

Hudson is staring at my pendant, his eyes squinted like he's trying to look straight into the sun. Without letting go of the nightingale, I fingerspell, "Gift."

He snorts. "Uh, yeah. Kinda figured that. You're not exactly a shopper, Mari. I meant who gave it to you? It matches that other bird you always carry around."

My grip on my pendant tightens. He knows about my other nightingale?

I let go of my pendant long enough to sign, "Not important."

Hudson's expression tightens, his forehead creasing and highlighting the scar along his left temple, but then the wrinkles disappear. "All right. Whatever. How'd you sleep?"

Almost in unison, we turn toward our first class. K.T. mentioned that Hudson was in the honors program, so I know he'll be in all of my core classes. Maybe *all* of my classes. As we walk through the crowded hall, he watches me, waiting for an answer. As though the answer matters.

"Fine," I sign.

There's a slight pause before he says, "Oh, I brought the stone you asked for."

He reaches into his pocket and brings out a green stone with black spots and whorls. It's small in his hand, but about the size of my fist. When I don't immediately take it, he shifts closer and holds it out again. The feedback noise gets louder, but it's different, layered with a higher-pitched sound. Softer. Something closer to the high C I heard earlier. Similar to the chime I heard this morning when I touched the black horse statue in my room.

"To go with the amethyst I gave you last week," he says.

My entire body tenses. The amethyst? That purple stone in my room is an amethyst? And *Hudson* gave it to me?

"Gave you the black jade horse, too." I don't answer right away, and he sighs. "Here, I'll put it in your backpack."

He steps behind me and opens one of the pockets on my backpack, dropping the stone inside. The feedback is in the background, but the chime is more prominent. I don't understand how, but it's such a relief I'm not sure I care.

Did I ask him for the green stone? I don't even know what it is. Did I ask him for the other two sitting on my nightstand, or were those gifts? If I ask, he might get upset. I know I'd be a little peeved if someone didn't remember I'd given them a present.

Biting my lip, I sign, "Thank you," when he reappears at my side.

His eyes are so dark it's hard to tell where he's looking, but I think he glances at me as he says, "No problem, Mari."

When we reach our first classroom, he holds the door open for me, claims the desk next to mine by dropping a notebook onto the seat with a *thwap,* and walks up to the teacher with a piece of paper. The teacher checks some paperwork and signs a few pages while Hudson waits. Everyone else in the room is eyeing Hudson like he's a sideshow attraction.

It's obvious when they catch a glimpse of those glossy, black eyes. More than one person gasps, and then the whispers start. The girl in front of me is nearly shaking as she gasps, "What is *wrong* with his eyes? I thought Danny was exaggerating, but *Jesus*!"

If he hears it—and how could he *not*?—it doesn't show on his face.

Standing up there, a good half a foot taller than the teacher, he doesn't look like he should be in high school. Hudson glances down, and the man flinches before handing back the paperwork and waving Hudson toward his seat. Even a *teacher* can't treat Hudson like a normal person?

Watching him walk through the aisle, while the idiot children pull away from him like he's about to reach out and strangle them, I try to figure out what to do. I promised myself I wouldn't treat Hudson like the others treat me. Guess I should start by actually communicating with him. What do people usually ask new students?

"Where are you from?" I sign, hoping I haven't asked this question already.

"Trenton," he fingerspells out of the teacher's line of sight. "New Jersey."

"Why move here?"

He looks at me, and I concentrate on meeting his gaze. It's hard not to fidget under the weight of those eyes. After a second, he looks away, reaches into his pocket, and pulls out his wallet. I don't understand until he unfolds a newspaper clipping and hands it to me. It's a slightly crumpled and well-creased article.

LOCAL BOY DIES IN GANG-
RELATED INCIDENT

Oh my God. I skim it quickly, trying to figure out what happened.

According to the article, Hudson helped the police apprehend three street thugs, putting them in juvie for nearly killing a man named Horace Lawson. Over four years later, Jackson Ryan "J.R." Vincent died in a retaliatory attack against Hudson. It was revenge for something that happened before J.R. was born.

Under the title is a picture of Hudson and a grinning little boy. I can't keep from staring at Hudson. Not the one sitting next to me, but the Hudson in the picture with the happy smile and the bright eyes. The bright and very normal eyes. If this glowing teenager became the black-eyed, glowering giant in front of me, something in him—some core part of him—must have died.

With shaking hands, I pass the article back, but I can't meet his eyes as I do.

Trying to look anywhere else, I see K.T. across the room. She's not looking at me. She's watching Hudson with a concerned furrow in her brow. K.T. might be the only one who isn't scared of Hudson. Maybe I can do something to get them together. Everyone needs someone to rely on, someone they can confide in and trust as much as I trust Orane. Maybe I can help Hudson find that here.

Taking a slow breath, I glance at Hudson. "Sorry," I sign.

"Thank you," he signs back.

I can't imagine losing someone that close to me. As much as I hope to one day step into Paradise and never leave, the thought of never seeing my parents again, never listening to my mother play piano or my father talk about his latest design project, never playing Scrabble with them after dinner—it's heartbreaking.

It takes a certain kind of strength to keep going after a loss like Hudson's. When I look at him now, I can almost see it, see the iron will that keeps him going after the devastation he's suffered.

And, the longer I look at him, the more I see that K.T. is more right than I want to admit.

He *is* cute.

"Ahh, Mariella," Orane sighs as he folds his arms around me. "What is wrong?"

He knows me too well. I don't bother pretending he's wrong, but I'm hoping *I* am. Orane has told me before that I have an overactive imagination. I really want that to be the case this time, too.

Hudson and I were sitting outside with K.T. during lunch when I started breathing the way Orane taught me, expanding the pearlescent light and letting its soothing warmth relax me. Before the light had gotten more than halfway up my arm, Hudson glanced at me, flinched, and covered his eyes with his hand, like the light coming off the pendant was too bright for him to bear. Like he could actually see the glow from Orane's world.

It had to be because the sun was reflecting off the glass pendant. He couldn't have seen the actual glow. Orane always told me the number of humans capable of perceiving his world was exceedingly small. As likely as snow in Bali.

Taking a deep breath, I try to explain it to Orane. "There's this new guy in school named Hudson and I think—well, I mean, it kind of seemed like he could see the light from my pendant, and he—"

I gasp as Orane's hand tightens around mine so hard my bones grind together.

"That boy is becoming an aggravation," Orane growls.

"What do you mean he's—"

His eyes darken, and his grip gets tighter until I feel my bones might crack. I cry out, my knees buckling as tears stream down my face. My breath comes in pants that don't hold any oxygen, and my chest burns. I want to scream and pull away, but I can't move. I can't think. My vision fades until all I see are Orane's glowing eyes.

"It appears I must keep a much closer eye on you, Mariella."

His voice echoes in my head like it's being projected from speakers in a concert hall.

I gasp for air as the blackness takes over completely.

Twenty-Three

Hudson

Tuesday, September 2 – 3:36 PM

Because Dawn is a girl of her word, K.T. and I are able to go over to Stone's Throw after school on Tuesday and pick up about half of what Dawn's ordered so far. It'll shore up the defenses at Horace's, and I can send K.T. home without worrying I won't see her in the morning. The stones Dawn ordered are larger, too, so they should be able to hold up against the demon's attacks better, I think. I hope.

I managed to sneak a few more stones into Mari's house when Horace and I went over for dinner. Not enough, though. I knew I wasn't ready to storm the gates, so I kept quiet about the dreamworld and her annoying habit of sucking energy out of her glass birds. It was bad enough when Mari just had the one she kept in her pocket. Her addiction seems to have gotten worse since she got that nightingale pendant.

Through dinner and the Scrabble game afterward, Mari kept telling me how nice K.T. is and suggesting I spend time with her. At first it was hard to keep from glaring at her each time she brought it up—I felt like I was being fobbed off—but she was working too hard at it. In the last few days, whenever she didn't want to deal with me, she was pretty straightforward about it.

It took me a few minutes to realize she was trying to play matchmaker. That made me smile. I didn't think Danny would like it much if I hit on K.T., but for some reason, Mari decided she liked me enough to set me up with her only friend. Either that, or she felt sorry for me because of what happened to J.R.

Usually I like pity about as much as I like watching people flinch when they look into my eyes, but in this case, I think I'll take it.

Tonight, I don't know if it's because the new stones keep the demon out or if he's planning to attack when I'm off-guard, but her demon is a no-show. Whatever the reason, I get to school on Wednesday after another demon-free night. I even managed to get an hour or so of sleep.

But the little bit of hope I have that this might be a good day evaporates when I watch Mari get out of Dana's car and look around like she has no clue where she is.

Shit. Again? I rub the back of my neck, kneading at the knots locked there.

Fuck this guy. Seriously.

But did I really expect anything else? Of *course* he wiped her again.

Never thought this was going to be easy.

So much for progress. Pity won't matter if she can't remember feeling it. At least the light show around her is in flux. Less than half of the glow surrounding her is blue, but every so often it flares stronger, gaining ground against the orange light of the dreamworld. Some part of her unconscious mind is fighting. Now I have to find a way to help that part of her win.

K.T. comes up next to me with a wide grin as she holds up a thick scrapbook. "Got it!"

"Good." I grind my teeth and jerk my head toward Mari. "Look."

Mariella passes K.T. and me without a blink or any sign of recognition.

"Ugh. Good thing Horace suggested this," K.T. mutters, opening the scrapbook and pulling out the contract Mariella signed yesterday.

I tell her to hold onto the contract as a last resort. After three minutes, we're ready to fall back on it.

As Mari reads the contract, I wonder how she's keeping Dana and Frank from noticing her memory loss. If a couple of weeks is all she's missing, it might be easy to fool her parents. People she met during that missing period—like me—are the ones who'd pick up on the loss.

"Before you go looking for a notebook, I know how to sign," I tell her.

Mariella looks up and blinks, blushing as she signs, "Sorry."

Something is off about the way she's signing. Wait...she used her left hand instead of her right. And she's wearing gloves. In summer.

Mari holds out the contract to K.T., wincing and dropping the paper when she has to move her hand.

Narrowing my eyes, I stare at her right hand. Each motion is careful and slow, like she's trying not to jar an injury. I know what that looks like. I've done it.

"What happened to your hand?"

Her eyes widen, the honey-brown irises catching the early-morning sunlight and turning almost a golden color. She shakes her head and steps back. K.T. glances between Mari and me, lines appearing around her eyes. She hadn't noticed yet, I guess. But then, she's not watching Mariella as closely as I am.

"Nothing," Mari signs.

"It's not nothing. We should go see the nurse if you're hurt."

Mariella shakes her head again and tries to put her hand in the pocket of her hoodie. Her pinkie finger doesn't bend in, catching the edge of the fabric. Mari gasps and folds over herself, her skin going pale.

"Let me see."

She shakes her head again.

"Mari, let me see, or I'll call Dana and tell her to take you to the doctor."

Her mouth drops open. "You know my mother?" she signs.

"Yeah. I had dinner at your house last night." She stares at me, still too pale. "And Sunday night. And Saturday night. *And* Friday night."

Mariella stands frozen in front of me, but I know I have to see her hand. I reach out, gently holding her forearm and lifting her hand higher. After waiting to make sure she's not going to freak out on me, I carefully pull off the oversized glove.

And as soon as I do, I wish I hadn't.

Bruises so deep they're black circle the center of her hand. Her pinkie finger looks swollen and distorted, like it's broken or at least dislocated. Redness and inflammation spread from the bruise down past her wrist and up to the tips of her fingers.

I'm too shocked to move.

If this had been an accident, she wouldn't be at school right now. Dana would have taken her to the doctor, and Mari would have a splint or a cast or at least a fucking Ace Bandage.

She doesn't have any of that, which means she probably woke up with her hand in this condition, freaked out because she couldn't remember what happened, and couldn't bring herself to worry her mom.

It means her demon did this to her.

I already wanted to kill him for what his kind did to J.R., but now I don't want to just kill him. I want to fucking obliterate him.

What did she say to make him this mad? Why would he hurt her like this and risk pissing me off? Unless...

Unless this was *meant* for me. A warning that he can get to her faster than I can save her. That he can hurt her and she'll trust him anyway because she won't remember a goddamn thing in the morning.

I will *kill* him. I will kill him myself. Tear him limb from limb and smile while doing it.

"Come on, Mari." K.T. guides Mariella toward the building. "I think I can get you an ice pack or something."

I see them glance over their shoulders at me, but I refuse to let myself move. Not until they're inside. As soon as they disappear, I sprint toward the far side of the building where the forest surrounding the town butts up against the school.

The air against my skin is warm, but I'm so cold the contrast makes me shudder. My hands are shaking, and my vision is blurry. The forest is a natural obstacle course, so I have to channel all my concentration on keeping up my speed without crashing into low-hanging limbs or tripping on roots. I force my mind to empty while I run, and slowly the blind rage eases into focused anger. I push harder, sweat dripping down my face and into my eyes. I welcome the sting. It's more of a distraction, and the blurring of my vision makes it trickier to avoid pitfalls. The shuddering chills get worse, but my head starts to clear.

The problem is, there's nothing in my head I want to hear right now.

The image of that bruise comes up again and I scream, sliding to a stop and slamming my fist into the closest tree.

Chunks of bark fly off the trunk, and sparks of pain shoot up my arm. The skin over my knuckles breaks and blood drips from the wounds, but within seconds, the pain begins to fade as the skin heals. I watch it happen and wish this stupid power let me do more than heal my own injuries. I can't help anyone else heal, and I can't injure my own hand. At least, not for long enough to help me keep my mind off how bad Mari's must be hurting her.

I laugh, the sound nearly hysterical, especially when it echoes through the empty forest.

Jesus. I am a goddamn master of getting myself in over my head, aren't I? All these years and all the damage I've caused, and I still can't keep myself out of other people's fights.

Despite all that, I'm not going anywhere. I can't. Mari needs my help. Even if she doesn't see it yet.

I start a meditative breathing cycle and turn back toward school. Four in. Hold four. Four out. Hold four. Repeat. I block memories of the weeks Calease spent teaching me how to empty my mind and channel my energy. Where this skill came from doesn't matter. What matters is using it to undo some of the harm the demons have caused.

Bit by bit, I regain control.

I can't do anything about what's done. I can only change what's coming.

But I can't stop the thoughts racing through my head.

Right now, Mariella's strength is working against her. She's a druggie raised to think addiction is a good, healthy thing. Or someone with Stockholm syndrome, convinced the person keeping them locked in the basement is really a kindhearted soul. Mariella has adapted to the way things are so much that convincing her to see the world another way feels nearly Sisyphean.

But I either have to find a way to get through to her or leave her to fight alone. And *that* I'm definitely not capable of doing.

I have Horace call me in late and slip into second hour with a pass. K.T.'s shoulders drop when she sees me. Mariella looks confused.

"Where did you go?" she signs. With her left hand. Her right is tucked away.

"Running," I sign back. The teacher already glared at me when I came in late. Talking in the back of the class will probably make him want to kick me out of the room.

Her head tilts, and she stares at me. After a few seconds, she fingerspells, "Running?"

"Yes. R-U-N-N-I-N-G." I fingerspell it back and emphasize each letter.

"Okay." She signs it, but she keeps watching me as though trying to figure out where I *actually* went. As long as she keeps that hand out of sight, she can stare all she wants. It's hard enough to keep my calm without looking at the reason I lost it in the first place.

At lunch, we have to try to teach Mariella about her own life. As much as we can. If he's willing to hurt her like that, we don't have a lot of time left.

"Are you sure about this?" K.T. whispers as we guide Mariella through the lunch line. "He keeps wiping her mind. If we push him too far, she might not wake up tomorrow."

"If we don't do anything, he wins anyway." I wish I had something more comforting to tell her. "We've got nine days. What else are we supposed to do?"

K.T. takes a deep breath and glances at Mariella. "Pray?"

"Yeah, okay." I pay and grab the tray of food for Mariella and me. "Do that and let me know how it works out."

We don't get a chance to talk to Mari. We don't get a chance to *try*. As soon as we open the scrapbook and step within three feet of her, the light around her flashes, a pulse so bright that the entire world is tinted orange to my eyes. The air is so cold I could convince myself I'm standing next to a glacier.

When it all clears, Mariella is swaying on her feet and looking around like she's trying to remember what she came into the room for.

"Did her necklace…light up?" K.T. asks.

"You saw that?" I want to look down at her, but taking my eyes off Mari might be a bad idea. Same goes for getting any closer to her right now. Despite the stones in my backpack, touching that light is asking for trouble. I'm not scared—much—but I'm not stupid either.

"It was only for a second, but I swear I saw it glow orange." K.T. closes the scrapbook and steps closer to Mariella, progressing slowly.

"Yeah. A reminder from her friend that he can get to her when she's not sleeping."

I put a hand on K.T.'s arm to slow her down. Probably better if Mariella sees us before we pop up in front of her. And I want time to run in case her demon reaches through again.

Mariella's eyes meet mine, and she flinches. Yep. She's forgotten who I am.

I should be getting used to it by now, but it was like the first flinch shoved a pike through my chest and every flinch afterward has driven it deeper. It shouldn't bother me—I know it's not her fault—but I don't want to be forgettable. Not to her.

"Introductions?" I mutter to K.T. as we approach.

She shakes her head at me and smiles. "We can sit here if you want." K.T. says it like she's continuing a conversation.

"It's a little closer to the center than you usually pick, Mari, but that's okay."

For a second, Mariella hesitates and looks like she's about to bolt.

"Time to ice your hand again," K.T. says. Mari freezes, not coming any closer but not disappearing either. "Don't want it swelling more."

After setting down her tray, K.T. lifts the bag of ice she talked out of the kitchen staff. Smiling, K.T. pats Mari's right elbow.

Her eyes wide and uncertain, Mariella lets K.T. guide her into the seat and gently place the bag of ice on her hand. On top of the glove. I can't see it, but I have no problem remembering what the injury looks like. My heart is ten times heavier than usual, and I grip my tray so hard I hear the plastic crack.

"Here, Mari." I set the tray down between us and turn it to the side so the sandwich she picked out is closer to her. "Chicken salad sandwich, right?"

She stares at me before she nods and picks the sandwich up with her left hand.

"My name is Hudson." I sign to her while I talk to remind her that I can. Her eyes bug out of her head. "In case you forgot."

"I didn't forget," she signs as soon as she drops the sandwich to the tray. "I know."

The blush on her cheeks calls her a liar.

I point at K.T. and introduce her, too. I'm getting tired of doing this. Gotta hand it to K.T. for being willing to go through introductions after years of being forgotten. Each time, it grates on my nerves. I usually don't mind it when people wipe me out of their heads—it's happened to me more than once. But with Mariella? It bugs the goddamn hell out of me.

Mari's twitchy, but she manages to choke down half of her sandwich before she drops the rest to the tray and signs, "Excuse me. Restroom."

Climbing off the bench—and taking the bag of ice with her—she heads toward a set of doors. The wrong set of doors. Those lead out to the track. The ones to the rest of the school and the bathrooms are on the other side of the room.

"Mari?"

She turns. I keep my eyes locked with hers as I sign, "wrong way," and point to the other doors. Better to sign than say it and embarrass her.

Mari closes her eyes and turns, striding out of the cafeteria and toward the bathrooms.

As soon as she's gone, K.T. runs her hands over her hair and sighs. "She's getting worse."

"And we're running out of time."

K.T. bites her lip. "Look, I think we have to strike before he can," she whispers, leaning closer so her voice won't carry to the rest of the table.

"Meaning...?" She might be on the same train as me, but I need to make sure.

"It's like he knows what's going on here, right? Her... whatever?"

She glances around the table, and I know she has trouble saying "demon" where it might be overheard. I nod when she looks at me. He knew exactly when we were about to approach. How is he watching her that closely?

One of my broken memories surfaces, the ones that come with a whiff of honey.

The pendant she's wearing is the final gift before the victim's eighteenth birthday. The last days are so crucial to the process that the demons always worry something will go wrong. They start spying on your waking moments as well as your sleeping ones, monitoring your conversations and your actions to make sure you don't come within a mile of breaking whatever promises you made. The pendant is a convenient place for a bug. A spy.

"Her nightingale necklace," I mutter. "He can hear and see everything happening around her when she has that damn thing on."

"What are you guys talking about?" a girl sitting nearby asks, her eyebrows pulling together.

My mind blanks, and my tongue locks to the roof of my mouth. K.T. doesn't even blink when she looks at the girl and says, "Developmental neurology, cognitive disorders, and the rise of mental instability in children."

"Oh." She doesn't look any less confused. "Sure. Okay."

She turns away, and I raise my eyebrows at K.T. "Do you know what that means?"

"Yes. Guarantee she doesn't, though."

K.T. picks up her tray and stands. Just as Danny, her *not*-boyfriend, steps up behind her.

She doesn't see him, I don't warn her soon enough, and he can't get out of the way. When she bumps into him, her drink tips off the tray. I grab the scrapbook off the table before it gets covered in soda. The impact knocks her backpack off her shoulder. Danny catches it before it hits the floor, but not before the strap hits the crook of her arm and makes her drop her tray.

"You've got to be kidding me!" Her face is red, and her jeans are splashed with catsup and soda.

"Oh, shit. K, I'm so sorry!"

Danny's face is as red as his hair as he grabs napkins off someone else's tray to give to K.T. Her eyes pop open when the napkins are pressed into her hand, but she sighs and sags back when she sees me holding the scrapbook.

"I was coming over to sit down and suddenly you were getting up and—"

"It's fine, Danny." She shrugs. "I was on my way to the bathroom anyway."

Danny tries to pick up her backpack to hand it to her and almost drops it, his face going from tomato to rice paper in a flash. "Whoa. What do you have in here—rocks?"

"Actually, yes. I'm starting a collection." She unzips the top and shows him the amethyst geodes and other stones we carefully packed inside yesterday. "Do you mind cleaning this stuff up? I have to go before I get all sticky."

Without waiting for him to answer, she turns to me. "I'll bring her back here if I can."

And then she's jogging out of the cafeteria, her backpack swinging from one hand.

Danny watches her go until I start to clean up the mess K.T. left behind.

"I got it," he mutters, his face flushing red again.

I try to help, but he grabs everything up like he doesn't want me touching it. Backing off, I drum my fingers on the scrapbook, waiting for Mariella to reappear. I never thought I'd wish for co-ed bathrooms, but now they seem like a *really* good idea.

Danny piles the last of the sopping wet napkins onto K.T.'s tray and turns toward the trash. Before he gets more than a step away, he spins around, his blue eyes overly bright. My attention is on the doors K.T. disappeared through, so for a second, I think he's staring at the girl a couple seats down from me.

"If you hurt her, I'll make you wish you hadn't."

I blink and turn toward him. My eyes are a little wider than usual, and I don't think he's really seen them before. He twitches, his hands shaking so bad one of the pieces of plastic on the tray flutters off the side and onto the floor.

"Who?" I ask, pretending I don't know what he's talking about. "Mari?"

"*Who?*" He blinks. Is he that shocked by my eyes that he forgot what he asked, or does he honestly not remember Mariella's name? "Oh, no. What?"

Jesus. He barely remembers her existence. They've probably been in the same school since kindergarten, and he doesn't remember her. Gripping the scrapbook to keep myself from punching him, I turn my attention toward the door.

"Oh, you mean K.T.?"

"Of course I mean K." He says it as though there is no one else, no other option anyone could find remotely interesting. I grip the scrapbook tighter. And then realize it'd make a nice, solid projectile.

"Don't worry, dude. She's playing matchmaker."

Mariella walks into the room, K.T. a step behind her, and a little of my tension eases away. Mari's looking at K.T. as K.T. whispers something into her ear. She smiles a little.

"A tip?" I say as Danny starts to turn. His expression is hesitant and wary, but he stops. "Stop treating K.T. like she's a toy you're afraid to lose and you might stand a better chance."

He stalks off as K.T. and Mari make it back to the table. K.T.'s eyes follow him, but she sits down next to Mari.

"She has a headache," K.T. says. "But a little more food should help, right?"

"Yep." I offer Mari the rest of her sandwich—luckily it didn't get soaked by the soda spill—and Mari's smile grows.

"Thank you," she signs.

K.T. and I make small talk for the rest of lunch, but my hand stays locked around the scrapbook. We have to counteract that necklace, or nothing I can say or do will matter.

My phone buzzes, and I take it out to see a missed call from Dawn. Finally, I smile for real. I think Mariella's crystal collection is going to grow tomorrow.

Twenty-Four

Mariella

Thursday, September 4 – 11:23 AM

I stare at the pages of pictures and fight against the burning in my eyes and the bell-like ringing in my ears. In my hands are pictures of people I don't recognize and moments I don't remember. This must be what going mad feels like.

It was horrible to get shoved into a school day unprepared, but being faced with people I don't remember meeting, a contract I don't remember signing, and a life I don't remember living?

Hudson and K.T. crowd in on either side of me, their bodies and three heavy bags holding me in place. Too much has hit me today. I'm an empty shell. I have nothing left.

My *alarm* woke me up. I slept for seven hours, and my eyes want to droop shut. I don't even remember my time with Orane last night...if I had time with Orane last night.

The tears burning my eyes spill over, running down my cheeks.

Why didn't he come to get me? Or do I not remember?

Taking a single deep breath is impossible. It's like something is wrapped around my lungs, keeping them from filling up and clearing the woozy, foggy feeling that's plagued me since this morning. I bite my lip, and my hands tighten on the scrapbook, the edges digging into my palms. My blurry eyes are locked on a picture of my eight-year-old self on stage dressed as Santa Claus.

I'm missing such a huge chunk of time. More than I realized this morning. An entire *life*. If Mother finds out, she'll take me back to the neurologists and psychologists and they'll poke and prod at me like a science experiment and I'll be—

"Mari?"

The sound pulls my eyes up, but as soon as I glance into the solid black eyes of the boy who introduced himself as Hudson, I flinch. He towers over me, and scars run down both of his arms and mar the edges of his face. He's over-muscled and intrusive and convinced we know each other, but he's not in this scrapbook and I've never seen him before.

Right?

I look up again and make myself hold his gaze. The longer I stare, the more the rest of the world fades until something glimmers on the edge of my thoughts.

"Do you know that constellation?" Hudson smiles and leans back against the grass, taking my hand and pointing my finger toward the stars. I shake my head, and he looks up at the sky again.

"It's called Lyra, the lyre. Do you know the story of Orpheus?" He glances at me, his eyes blacker than the sky above us but warmer. My heart skips a beat and I don't know why. I don't know why I shake my head "no" either. My mother is a musician. Of *course* I know the story of Orpheus. But there's something soothing about Hudson's low voice in the darkness. Something almost familiar. And after the barrage of noise and strangeness in the party we walked through, familiar is nice.

Hudson raises an eyebrow like he knows I'm lying, but he tells me the story anyway.

"Orpheus was a musician—the best. When he played on his lyre, wars would stop and animals would pause to listen. So he had to be pretty damn good."

His full lips curl into a half-smile. I smile back, looking up at the sky and letting his voice wash over me.

"He fell in love with a nymph named Eurydice because, you know, it happens."

My smile grows, and I roll my eyes. "It happens" is all he has to say about a love as strong as Orpheus's and Eurydice's?

"He loved her so much that he went down into the underworld to face Hades and Persephone when Eurydice died. He played until they told him to just shut up and take her."

I bite my tongue to keep from laughing and toss a pebble at Hudson's chest.

"Wanted to make sure you were paying attention," he says, grinning at me.

The smile brings a brightness to his face I haven't seen before. He should smile more often.

Why do I care that he doesn't?

I look up at the stars, tracing the invisible line that connects them into Orpheus's lyre. After a moment, Hudson keeps talking.

"He got Hades to agree to let Eurydice come back to Earth, but Hades made him promise not to look back until they reached the land of the living. On the way out, he screwed up." He takes a deep breath. I'm not looking at his face, but it's like I can hear his smile disappear. "He looked too early. And he lost her."

An almost tangible weight settles over me. I want to look at him, to see if I can do something to lift the cloud, but I know there's nothing I can do. I don't know what's wrong.

"The guy didn't handle losing her twice very well, especially when it was his fault the second time. Guilt can be a bitch."

This time, I can't keep myself from looking. He says it like he knows.

His eyes are closed, his entire face tight. I want to reach over and trace the lines his thoughts have carved into his face, but I stop myself before I can do anything that stupid.

Hudson's eyes open, and he catches me watching him. My lungs contract and my heart starts pounding, but he doesn't say anything. Not about that. He picks up the story exactly where he left off.

"He swore off women—started spending time with young boys. Which, honestly, he'd probably get arrested for today."

My breath slowly releases, but I can't get my heart rate to return to normal. I run my thumb along the curves of the amethyst Hudson gave me—it's warm from how long I've been holding on to it—and wait for the end.

"Envy can be as debilitating as guilt, and the women of Greece are very good at envy. When Orpheus wouldn't pick a new wife, they stoned him and dismembered him one night when they were all drunk out of their minds."

I cringe. Of all the ways to go. What had to have been going through the minds of those women, though? What would it take to feel that kind of possession over something that was never yours to begin with? How self-righteous and egotistical do you have to be to assume you have the right to control someone else's life and how they live it?

"The gods buried Orpheus and put his lyre in the sky so they could remember his music." Hudson turns his head toward me, one eyebrow cocked. "Weird, considering they didn't think it was worth the trouble of saving him from the psychos."

He's close, so close his breath stirs the blades of grass near my cheek. The longer he stares at me, the warmer it gets, hotter and hotter until I'm burning up. My body is on fire, but my hands are trembling. He shifts, moving closer, and I jump to my feet.

"It's late. I need to go home," I sign quickly.

I expect him to argue, to remind me it's early and try to persuade me to stay, but Hudson exhales heavily and stands up.

"C'mon," he says quietly, his hand on my lower back directing me toward the side yard. So I won't have to face going through the house again. "I'll take you home."

Light swamps my vision, white light so bright it leaves orange and blue spots behind. Warm energy rushes up my body, making my head spin.

"Mari? Mari! Hold onto this!"

The book disappears, replaced by something heavy and cool. I almost scream as ear-shattering feedback shoots through my head.

My vision clears. There's a huge amethyst geode in my hands. I glance at it for a second before my entire body freezes, my heart jumpstarting to impossible speeds.

I'm orange. My entire body is encased in an orange glow with the brightest points centered on my two nightingales—the pendant that appeared around my neck this morning and the slightly larger bird in my pocket. The light writhes and swirls like waves in a storm as bolts of cerulean-blue light pulse out from my hands. From the contact points with the amethyst.

Not since my first month of silence have I been this close to breaking my promise to Orane. I bite back the scream before it leaves my lips, and I drop the amethyst. Stumbling to my feet, I run.

"Shit! Mari!"

"Mari, wait!" K.T. calls.

Light flares again, brighter and hotter and faster than before. I trip, my palms scraping against something rough.

Agony shoots up my already-injured right hand. The light gets brighter until it washes out everything, and then I fall straight from pure white into pitch darkness.

Twenty-Five

Hudson

Thursday, September 4 – 11:26 AM

Mari slumps over, unconscious. Her hands hit the sidewalk, but a stroke of pure luck makes her head land in the grass.

I had known this reaction was a possibility, so K.T. and I had brought her out to the side of the school where we'd be less likely to fall under someone's eyes. Instinct is screaming at me to help her, but I can't. Every time I try to touch her, the chill rolling off her burns my hands, numbing them to the point of frostbite in milliseconds.

She wasn't this cold when I first met her, but ever since her demon has been wiping her mind, it's like her body temperature has permanently dropped. I can feel it in her house from downstairs now; the chill emanating from her room is strong.

"Is she *glowing*?" K.T. asks, her eyes wide.

"Yeah. And I can't touch her until she stops."

I swallow, struggling to keep my voice from giving away how much it terrifies me to watch this happening and how much I hate having no way to stop it. The one thing I could do is surround her in stones until she wakes up, but interrupting whatever is going on in her head might do more harm than good.

K.T. bites her lip, her eyes filling up with tears. "What happened? It was like she started to remember and then..."

And then she flipped her shit.

"Did you see the colors?" I ask K.T.

"I thought the light looked orange and blue for a second, but then it was gone. That wasn't the sun?"

"No. I think she saw that, too, and it freaked her out."

K.T. shudders, her arms wrapping around herself. "It'd freak *me* out." Swallowing, she looks at me. "Can we take them away? Her necklace and her other bird? If we took them now, would she know they were missing?"

"Maybe, but I don't know what that would do to her." I wish I could, though. I wish I could grab them and shatter them both against the pavement. "Those things are tied right into her head. Trying to take them from her might hurt her more than it helps."

The light finally dies, and I gently lift Mari off the ground and carry her back to our bags.

"Is she okay?" K.T. asks.

"Check her hands for me?"

K.T. shifts her arms to look at Mari's palms and hisses through her teeth. "Broken skin on both hands. And, seriously, she might need to go in for an X-ray on her right hand."

Shit. I was worried about that. But Mari doesn't know how she hurt it. How would she explain an injury like that to Dana? And what would Dana do when the explanation is "I don't know what happened"?

Mariella stirs, her slow blinks coming faster and her movements becoming more purposeful. Her eyes pop open, and for an instant, she's staring up into mine.

She doesn't flinch. For a moment, she relaxes, almost like she's relieved to see me, but then her eyes widen and she tries to roll out of my arms.

"Careful, Mari." I shift her so her feet are angled toward the ground and slowly stand her up. She sways, her right hand coming up to her head until she bumps it against me and sucks in a sharp breath, her face going pale.

"You fell. I tried to catch you. Do you remember?"

She swallows hard a couple of times, but her face is too pale. Looking at her hands and her grass-stained knees, she shakes her head. Biting her lip, she mimes writing.

"I sign, Mari," I remind her. Again.

K.T. and I slowly explain who we are and where she is and what happened—well, we *kind of* explain that last part. She's trembling when K.T. takes her to the office so she can call Dana to come get Mari.

I doubt anyone is going to buy that this injury just happened, but someone needs to look at it. With the way that bruise has gotten darker and the swelling has picked up, it needs to be X-rayed. K.T. promises she'll go with Mari to the doctor if Dana will let her, and I have to watch them walk into the school, knowing I don't have the right to follow.

K.T. has known Mari since kindergarten, so Dana has no reason to question her concern. Me? I'm practically a stranger. I could walk away right now and lose nothing. Mariella has never technically spoken to me. It'd be easy for Dana, for anyone, to think that I have no reason to care what happens to Mari or if she's hurt or if she falls asleep eight days from now and never wakes up again.

But I do. I care.

It's not about ridding the world of the demons anymore. Or not *just* about that. It's about seeing Mari come out of this haze she's in. Watching her wake up from this half-life she's living. Being there when she morphs from this silent, hidden girl into the glowing Grecian goddess she's supposed to be.

But, as I catch Mariella glancing over her shoulder at me before the door closes behind them, I finally admit to myself that it's also because I think she might be able to save me, too.

I'm sitting on my mattress, leaning against the footboard of Horace's bed with the scrapbook spread open on my lap. Flipping through the pages, I look through Mariella's life as it was before the demons stole it.

She was always in bright colors—turquoise cowboy boots, hot-pink ruffled dresses, sunshine-yellow pants—and always surrounded by people. Mari was on stage constantly, doing anything and everything to be in the limelight. Her face in the pictures her parents snapped of her performing? She's nearly sublime. I didn't know kids could be this happy. I sure as hell wasn't when I was little.

Someone knocks on the front door, and I grab my backpack of stones, swinging it over my shoulder before I head downstairs. I don't go anywhere without it anymore. Not with the constant threat of the demons hanging over my head like Damocles's sword.

"Hud, Kate's here to see ya!" Horace calls.

"K.*T.*," I hear her correct him as I reach the front door.

Horace's eyebrows pull together. "'S what I said."

"What happened?" I ask K.T. before she can correct him again.

She sighs and runs a hand through her hair, pushing it out of her face. "No breaks, luckily. Two sprained fingers, though. Index and pinky."

That's good news. I guess. Still want to barge through the barrier between our world and theirs and break her demon's face, but she's going to be okay. That's what matters for now.

"Oh, good." K.T.'s shoulders drop, and she smiles a little. "I really hoped I hadn't left that sitting on the grass."

She gestures toward my hand, and I look down. I'd barely noticed I brought the scrapbook down with me.

"You stayin' for dinner, K.*T.*?" Horace asks.

After a slight hesitation, she agrees, and we all order food while Horace grumbles about kitchens that don't work. As we wait, I flip through the scrapbook again. I can't help wondering what Mari would be like now if the demons hadn't derailed her childhood.

In the pictures, as Mari gets older, it's like I can watch her pull away from the world.

It starts small—her wide grin turning into a smile that hides secrets—but then she literally starts pulling away from people, showing up at the edges of pictures instead of the center. She stops looking into the camera. Instead she stares off in another direction, like her mind is somewhere else. Her clothes change, getting darker and baggier, and her hair keeps getting longer. The pictures stop before her freshman year. Like she disappeared completely.

Exhaling slowly, I flip back to the beginning and start over. There has to be something here that will spark Mari's forgotten memories, crack the bonds her demon has tied her down with. I just don't know what.

K.T. snorts. "Oh, wow! How did I miss this the first time around?"

She pulls the book out of my hands, leaning over a picture of Mariella standing on the top bar of one of those domed jungle gyms, an impish smile on her face.

"I dared her to do that. Never thought she would, but she climbed right up there and balanced on that thing like a tightrope walker. She was fearless. With everything." K.T. places her hand over the picture, like she's trying to press it into her skin. "I remember this one day—there used to be this kid named Johnny Dodd. He moved out when we were ten."

She flips until she finds a picture and points to a tall, angry-looking kid at the edge of a group.

"Johnny was probably the biggest ass to ever live in Swallow's Grove, even at seven. He'd been picking on this girl because she'd gotten braces, and Mari overheard. She's, like, half his size, but she walks right up and kicks him in the shin so hard he starts bleeding." K.T. smiles. "She was wearing her turquoise, metal-toed cowboy boots that day."

The smile doesn't last more than a moment. As soon as she starts flipping through the book again, looking at all the moments she remembers and her one-time best friend doesn't, it disappears. She pauses on the picture of Mari dressed up like Santa.

"What about this?" I ask. "There *has* to be a story attached to this one."

Her smile starts to come back. "We were about nine. It was for Christmas, and most of us were ornaments and trees and reindeer, but Mari decided she *had* to be Santa Claus."

"The boys didn't fight her on that one?" Horace asks, leaning over the page.

"Most of them didn't dare—not after the thing with Johnny—but Seth fought her for it." She bites her lip, but she can't keep from grinning. "The day of the audition she told him that, if he lost on purpose, she'd give him a bunch of kisses."

What? That doesn't sound right at all. Or is that me thinking I know a person I've barely met? What do I know about Mariella really? Maybe she's exactly the type to bribe guys with kisses. At nine. I try to wrap my mind around it, but it feels wrong.

K.T. laughs. "I was with her when she told him. He got *so* excited. He flubbed the audition, and the next day she brought him a whole bag of Hershey's Kisses. He was furious, but he couldn't say a thing because she never said she'd kiss him—she just said she'd *give him* kisses."

I smile. *That* makes sense. "Who played Mrs. Claus? Seth?"

"Nope. Me." K.T. points to another picture, and though K.T.'s face has changed more than Mari's, once she points it out I can see the resemblance. They're standing in the center of the stage, their hands clasped together and their faces pressed cheek to cheek as they stare out into the audience with wide eyes.

Glancing at K.T. now, I notice the shadows around her eyes. She stares at the pictures in front of us, and the longer she stares, the bleaker her expression gets. I try to close the book, to hide the pictures of the friend she's watched disappear in front of her eyes, but she holds it in place.

"Do you really think we can save her?" K.T.'s words are whispered, and she doesn't look at me.

I want to nod, but I can't. I'm *not* sure we can save her, but I am sure of something.

"I'm gonna try."

For a second, everything is frozen. Then K.T. exhales a long, slow breath and the color starts to come back to her cheeks.

"I guess that's all we can do. Try."

Twenty-Six

Mariella

Friday, September 4 – 12:00 AM

Before I can say a word to Orane, he sweeps me onto the back of a black horse and races across the lavender field. The thudding hoofbeats make my headache worse. For a second, I forget the sprains in my hand and try to grip the horse's mane to steady myself. Pain rockets up my arm, and I gasp, my vision blurring.

Warmth spreads through my body, starting at the spot where Orane's hand rests on my arm and spreading down to my hand.

"You should be more careful," Orane whispers in my ear.

The intense sparks of pain shift to a dull throb. Dark and deep, the bruises are as bad as ever, but by the time the heat fades, the pains in my hand and in my head are almost gone. Sighing, I lean into Orane's embrace and smile, letting myself enjoy the wild ride.

After the agony and the strangeness of today, it's so nice to let go of the questions that have been spinning in my head as relentlessly as a hyper hamster trapped in an exercise wheel. Like I've suddenly shed twenty pounds of dead weight. The worries aren't gone, but for now they drift somewhere behind us as Orane's steed runs so fast it's almost like flying.

Too soon—*far* too soon—the black stallion slows, and Orane helps me slide from his back. My bare feet settle into the grass, and the breeze plays against my skin. I close my eyes and breathe in the comfort of the lavender. I take a deep breath and…it's not there. Breathing again, I wait for the scent to hit me, but it doesn't. Nothing does. I smell nothing.

I open my eyes to make sure I can see lavender in the distance. It's there. Purple lavender and blue forget-me-nots and lilacs. But I can't smell any of it. I can't smell anything.

Orane steps in front of me and runs his fingertip along the creases that have dug into my forehead.

"What troubles you so, Mariella?"

His violet eyes meet mine, and I start pouring out everything that happened today. I'm still so confused. It's lucky K.T. and Hudson were there to help me when I came out of whatever fog I spent the morning in. The more I tell Orane, the thicker the lines around his eyes get and the deeper his frown becomes.

When my words run dry, he pulls me against his chest, kisses the top of my head, and strokes my hair. "I wish I could have been there to help you through such a day."

I hold him tight, breathing deep and smelling nothing. Before I can tell Orane, he pulls back and smiles.

"I had not planned on telling you so soon, but I think you need good news today."

His eyes are sparkling, and he looks so excited I can't help smiling back. "Good news? What kind of good news?"

"The kind I have been waiting for years of your time to be able to share with you." His voice is soft but intense, and his hands are warm when he brings them up to my cheeks. "Mariella, I may have found a way to bring you here for good."

My heart stops, and tremors run through my entire body, a spasm that feels like my muscles are trying to tear themselves away from the bone. I almost scream in pain, but his lips descend on mine and then the pain doesn't matter anymore because Orane is kissing me.

His long fingers tangle in my hair, and he holds me like he's afraid I'm going to disappear. Blazing heat spreads across my skin, the kind that turns my thoughts to dust and makes my knees buckle. This kiss goes deeper than any other we've shared. He kisses me with a passion I thought was reserved for movies, with a consuming intensity I thought was impossible.

He kisses me like he's saying goodbye.

The longer the kiss lasts, the less I care about memories or injuries or missing out on the lavender scent of his world. What does any of it matter when I have him?

Twenty-Seven

Hudson

Friday, September 5 – 7:40 AM

K.T. slides to a stop in front of me as I wait for Mariella to arrive Friday morning.

"Have you ever heard of Dr. Lucas Carroll?" she asks before I can say hello.

"No. Unless you mean the guy who wrote *Alice in Wonderland?*"

K.T. rolls her eyes. "No, that was *Lewis* Carroll."

"I know. So, no, then. Who is he?"

"A *neurologist*!" K.T. grins, but I can't see why she's so excited about neurology all of a sudden. "I found an article he wrote online about sudden-onset comas."

Okay, *now* I'm a little more interested.

"He theorizes certain coma cases are related, caused by a phenomenon unlike anything science has seen."

Her eyebrows go up and mine follow. But maybe not for the same reason.

Cases? *Plural*? How many has he found? And how many of them are victims of the same demons that got Emily? That almost got me?

My chest aches. While I'm in the middle of nowhere trying to save Mariella, how many other kids are about to fall into their trap?

K.T.'s smile gets wider. "He talks about energy and brain waves that shoot off the charts for no apparent reason, and he insists there's a *paranormal* aspect to the cases."

"He might know something. You think he can help us get through to Mari?" I ask, not quite sure where she's going with this.

The smile fades a little. "Maybe?" She hesitates, and her cheeks heat up. "Um, no. I *was* researching for ways to help Mari, but when I found Carroll, I thought he could maybe help Emily."

My instinct is to remind her that Mariella is on a deadline, while Emily has been in the exact same condition for four years. She can probably wait another few weeks. I *want* to say that, but I don't. Because if I were her, I'd hate to hear someone say that.

Dana's black SUV pulls into the drop-off circle, and I take a step toward the car.

"Call him if you think he can help," I tell her, "but I have to focus on one fight at a time." She glances over her shoulder at Mari. When she meets my eyes again, I add, "If I survive Mari's eighteenth, I'll do whatever I can to help you with Emily, all right?"

Dana is starting to pull away, so I run toward her, flagging her down to get her to stop.

"Morning, Hudson." She smiles, but she looks tired. The circles around her eyes are too dark to be completely hidden by her makeup, and her blinks are slow.

"Sorry. I, uh, I wanted to catch you before you left. We have this history project we have to do in groups, and Mari is in a group with K.T. and me."

Dana's eyes widen. "A *group* project? Mari doesn't usually—"

"Well, she volunteered," I lie. There isn't a project, but K.T. and I need *some* excuse to spend a ton of time at Mari's house, and this was the best we could come up with last night. "And I think she's getting used to us."

Dana looks toward Mari in time to watch K.T. give her a hug and start talking to her about something. I can't hear it from here, but I hope it's the "project" we need to start working on. A sniffle from Dana pulls my eyes away from their conversation, and I realize there are tears running down her cheeks.

"Oh, I'm sorry." Dana laughs and wipes her eyes, but then she looks up at me and gives up, letting the tears fall as she smiles. "Hudson, maybe this is crazy, but she's changed so much since she met you. She's been leaving the house and spending time with friends and she smiles more often when she's with the two of you. You and K.T. are practically bringing her back to life, and it's—"

She covers her mouth with her hand, her other hand patting my arm. I force a smile onto my face and cover her hand with my own, waiting the moment out.

Dana's gratitude is like a choke chain around my throat. Each heartfelt tear pulls it tighter until it gets hard to breathe. She's thanking me. She's *thanking* me for bringing Mari back to life when, a week from tonight, Mari might fall out of it completely.

"You're welcome to come over whenever you want," Dana says when she regains the ability to speak. "You have a standing invitation at our house. Project or not."

I force my smile wider and nod. "Thanks, Dana. I can bring Mari home after school if you want."

We arrange the details, and Dana promises to call Horace and invite him for dinner before she drives off. Grinning. Like I need more pressure to succeed.

I don't have to introduce myself to Mariella this morning, but K.T. and I don't push our luck. After we fill Mari in on the "project" she missed yesterday, we talk about inconsequential things—homework assignments, sports, clothes. K.T. and I are careful to not let Mari out of our sight or say anything to piss off the demon listening through her brightly lit nightingale pendant.

The rest of the stones I ordered from Dawn have finally arrived, so after school, K.T. and I take Mariella down to Stone's Throw. K.T. has been down there to pick up some books on stones, but from the way Mari's head tilts as she examines the storefront, I don't think she knew it existed. If she's been here before, she definitely doesn't remember it.

The wind chimes tied to the door tinkle as we walk in, but the store looks empty. Until Dawn's head pops up from behind a low shelf like a meerkat peeking out of her burrow.

"Is that you, Hudson? Of course it is. I don't know anyone else so big." Dawn scrambles over a low bookcase and stops short in front of me, a huge smile on her face. "You, sir, have been very good for business."

"I'm going to be even better for business before I leave today."

"*C'est magnifique*!" She dances in a quick circle and then dashes off to the counter. "Let me show you what we got in today. I have some new jewelry pieces, too."

I trail behind her, checking the shelves I pass for anything that might prove useful. "I know I've said this before, but you really don't act like you're fourteen."

Dawn ducks behind the counter and starts gently placing geodes and statues on top. "Yeah, well, neither do you."

"I'm *not* fourteen."

"And I am. Your point?"

"I don't know," I admit, my head spinning a little. "I seem to have lost it. What's *your* point?"

"What's age got to do with it?"

I smile and step closer to look over everything. "Nothing, I guess. Just like height."

She places the last of the stones on the counter and grins at me. "See? I knew you had brains in there somewhere."

Mariella is following K.T. around with wide eyes. I can't be sure, but I think the single thing keeping her demon from reaching out and wiping her mind again is the fact that she's been surrounded by crystals and gemstones all day. And there are more here. If I can keep her memory intact long enough to convince her to listen to me...

So far, so good, but I don't want to get my hopes too high. If I've learned anything from dealing with this demon of hers, it's that half the things I thought I knew about them and half the rules I thought they had to follow are wrong. Underestimating him now might be deadly.

I shake my head and focus more on the stones in front of me, touching them one by one. They respond well. Usually I don't sense a thing from new stones. When I place a hand on these, I can hear their energy ringing in my head—a low, soft chime in the background.

"Did you cleanse everything already?" I ask Dawn.

She cocks her head to the side and smiles, her short brown hair swinging. "Thought you might notice that. You're not an average collector. They sell better if they're not already tuned to someone. Even the ones you don't take will find better homes this way."

I continue my inspection, picking up each stone. Dawn has good taste. Or her suppliers do. These are all high-quality pieces.

"What's up with your friend?" Dawn asks after a few minutes. I doubt she's asking about K.T. I follow Dawn's stare and wonder how much she can see from this far away.

Mari is standing in front of the store's nearly empty stone display and listening as K.T. points out the different types of stone.

"Her name is Mariella."

"I don't usually get a read on people unless they're giving off some pretty strong vibes, but wow. That girl needs an aura cleansing *fast.*"

"Yeah. I know." I look away from Mari, forcing myself to focus on the selection Dawn has laid out in front of me. "It's a work in progress. There are extenuating circumstances."

Dawn switches her penetrating brown eyes to me. "Like demon fairies visiting her dreams?"

I freeze with my hand on a pair of amethyst earrings. Almost forgot I told Dawn about the demons. After what happened to K.T., I don't think I did Dawn any favors by letting her in on that little secret. It's like knowing they exist makes you more of a target.

"I shouldn't have told you about them. They're not anyone you ever want to meet, Dawn."

"But the gemstones protect you, right? That's why you're stockpiling?"

Nodding slowly, I keep my eyes locked on her face to make sure she's taking this seriously. Dawn seems to take every word to heart.

"Our house is attached to the back of the store." She points to a door I thought led to a storage closet. "I'll load myself up with crystals before I go to sleep every night."

"Make sure you do." I look back over the collection on the counter and make a decision. "I'll take all of it."

Dawn's jaw drops, but only for a second. She starts packing the stones up, shaking her head as she does. "One of these days, you're going to walk in here and announce you're buying the store itself."

I laugh. Horace would *love* to add a New Age store to his list of properties, I'm sure.

"Almost ready?" K.T. asks, coming up to the counter.

Mariella steps up next to her and leans over the counter, staring at the stones. Her eyes lock on a piece of tumbled amethyst, oddly shaped but smooth, and shifting through at least eight shades of purple. It's a pretty rock, but there are others on the counter that are prettier. What is pulling her toward this one?

When she picks it up, I finally notice something I've missed all day.

She's using her right hand.

It's bruised as hell—in fact, it looks worse than before—but she's using it like there's nothing wrong. Like it doesn't hurt and the bruises aren't there.

Mari takes the amethyst and walks away, practically claiming it for her own.

As I pay, I can't help wondering what kind of game her demon is playing. Does he know what we're trying to do? Who am I kidding? Of course he does.

So I guess the real question is, what is he planning to do about it? And do I stand a snowball's chance of surviving it?

Mariella opens her bedroom door, and I almost scream. The light pouring out of that room is blinding, burning. It's like staring through the gates of Hell, but the air coming out of the room is so cold I could convince myself I've walked into Antarctica without a jacket.

K.T. steps inside without a thought, but I can't. Pulling a filter over my eyes to block out the worst of the glow barely helps. My hands are shaking, and my heart is beating so fast I can't feel it anymore.

"Coming?" K.T. asks, her forehead creased as she looks back at me.

"It's, uh...it's really nice outside. Can we work out there?" I step into the room, take Mari's hand, and pull her back out again. This close to the epicenter of her demon's influence, the chill hits me harder, and I shudder. It reminds me of walking into Calease's world that last night. Worse, actually. It's already colder than that. I'm so cold I barely notice how icy Mari's skin is against mine.

"You don't mind, right?" I ask as I pull her out of the room.

"Computer?" she signs, glancing over her shoulder at her room.

"We're planning tonight," K.T. says as she brings up the rear. "We'll be fine."

I should probably let go of Mari's hand now, but instead I hold it a little tighter. She doesn't pull away, but she doesn't tighten her grip either. She trusts me because I've proven I know her and I've helped her fill in some of the blanks in her memory, but I don't think that trust goes very far. If I push it, she won't listen to a thing I say.

When I look at Mari now, it's like I see her in layers—the burning blonde with the ribbon over her mouth, the princess tearing apart a screwed-up tea party, the goddess wrapped in burning chains, and the girl who is somehow all those things yet isn't aware of it. Who doesn't even see the cliff she's running toward at full speed.

I just hope I can keep her from going over the edge.

Twenty-Eight

Mariella

Friday, September 5 – 4:14 PM

For a project that seemed crucial at school, K.T. and Hudson aren't too concerned about it now. We've barely made any progress this afternoon—reminding me why I hate group projects so much—but then they stayed for dinner, too. It's like now they've gotten into my house, neither is inclined to leave.

After dinner, my parents and Hudson's grandfather, Horace, retreat into my father's office to finalize contracts and a schedule for inspections on some restoration project they're working on. K.T., Hudson, and I head upstairs. Like earlier, Hudson stops short at the door to my bedroom and shudders, his eyes closing and his entire face tightening.

K.T. notices, but she bites her lip and takes his hand, pulling him across the threshold. "It'll be fine."

"You don't know that," Hudson grumbles, shuddering again when he steps inside. The convulsions are so sharp, it looks like someone is poking him with a high-powered stun gun. He was fine before. There's nothing in this room that would do this to him. I mean, the light from Orane's gifts is brighter than usual—a *lot* brighter, almost blinding—but that doesn't have anything to do with Hudson. He shouldn't be able to see it, let alone feel it. *I* can't feel it.

As he steps into the room, the annoying feedback noise that's plagued me since...well, at least since yesterday, changes tone. It shifts higher and is more solid, less vibrational. It sounds like someone struck a piece of crystal, and the chime doesn't fade. It gets stronger and higher. It should be annoying, but it's not. It's musical. Beautiful.

"How can you stand how cold it is in here?" Hudson rubs his arms and adjusts the straps of his backpack.

Cold? This is always the warmest room in the house.

"Hudson."

That's all K.T. says, just his name, but it's like there's a whole message in that one word. Hudson stops moving and looks at her. K.T. stares right back, her dark eyebrows raised, until Hudson grunts and looks away.

He can't stop fidgeting, pacing back and forth across my room, his footsteps surprisingly quiet on the wood floor. The movement is so ceaseless and nervous I'm surprised by how calm his voice sounds when he asks, "Mari, do you remember anything from the past three weeks? Anything before yesterday at school?"

The words register, and I stop breathing. The first moments after "waking up" at school yesterday are fuzzy. I remember K.T. and Hudson being there, but did I tell them how much time was missing?

"How did you know that?" I sign.

Hudson starts to translate for K.T., but she shakes her head. "I know what she said."

"Since when?" Hudson asks.

K.T. rolls her eyes. "She stopped speaking *four years* ago. How else was I supposed to understand the few things she said?" Then she turns to me and asks, "What's the last thing you remember?"

I bite my lip and look away. Why is Hudson so twitchy? It seems out of character. And they know more about what's happened to me than I like. More than makes sense.

But what if they can help me fill in the blanks? They told me I've spent time with them the past few weeks. Maybe they know some of the things that are missing.

Exhaling heavily, I rub my hands over my face before answering K.T.'s question.

"Three weeks ago, my parents were talking about a trip to Las Vegas to see Aunt Jacquelyn and my cousin Julian," I sign. "We had pizza for dinner."

"Did you have that necklace three weeks ago?" Hudson asks.

I put a hand over the glass bird, and my heart rate picks up.

As I shake my head, they exchange a glance. I hold my breath, waiting for whatever is going to come next. Hoping it's some bit of my life they can fill in.

Hudson finally sits down on my desk chair and rolls closer to the bed. Leaning forward, his eyes lock on mine. "Do you know where you got it?"

Oh, hell. How in the world do I answer *that*? I don't know *when* I got it, but I know Orane must have given it to me. Memory loss or not, I can't give them that detail.

Sitting up straighter, I shake my head.

K.T. looks at Hudson, but his eyes never leave mine.

"I've told you before not to lie, Mari." He leans forward an inch. "You're not good at it."

He's told me before? I fight the urge to shrink away as I sign, "I'm not lying."

They exchange another one of those speaking looks, the ones that show me there are a couple dozen layers to this conversation I can't see or understand.

His dark eyes glint in the light from my lamps, the reflections like tiny flames dancing inside his eyes. Or stars. Pinpricks of light against a pitch-black background. He takes a deep breath and lets it out slowly, those glittering eyes watching me carefully.

"If you won't tell us what you know, how about I tell you what *we* know?"

Hudson stills, but only for a moment.

"We know where you go every night." Hudson's voice is quiet, but I can hear every word as clearly as if he was screaming. "We know there's a guy, probably with reddish hair and purple eyes, and we know he's told you that he can help you."

When I was younger, when I slept more than an hour a night, nightmares plagued me. After Orane told me about the wars, I had weeks of nightmares about moments like this, where people would somehow know all the secrets I protected. Now it's happening and I don't know what to do. My palms sweat and tingle as my heart pushes adrenaline through my body so fast my head feels like it's lifting off my shoulders.

"We know he gave you all those glass baubles on your dresser. And that pendant."

How does Hudson know any of this? Orane said that all the others who knew the secret of opening a doorway between the worlds had died in the war. But maybe not all the human participants were wiped out. Maybe a few survived to pass down the stories to their children.

But how did they find me? And what do they want?

I hold myself motionless, not daring to move until I know exactly where this is going. If they think they're going to use me to get back into Paradise and start another war, they underestimate what I'm willing to do to protect Orane. I'll die before I let them hurt the man I love and the world he's trying to protect.

"And we know what happened to your memory, Mari." Hudson takes a deep breath. "But I don't think you're going to like it."

With barely more than a second's pause, Hudson launches into a story that makes no sense and is all too familiar. A doorway made of light, an angelic being who promised friendship and aid, a promise, a talent—it's like my own life. And it should all be impossible.

Each word Hudson utters is like an expertly wielded fillet knife peeling away the layers of protection I've constructed between the waking world and Paradise. My heartbeat becomes erratic and unreliable as Hudson tells me a story too awful to comprehend. One that ends with a newspaper article about the murder of a four-year-old boy named J.R. Hudson's little brother.

If it *is* true, that makes it more likely that Hudson is on the wrong side of everything Orane has tried to protect for centuries. I don't need to be holding this article to keep the memory of J.R.'s bright, innocent smile. If that had been *my* brother, I'd want revenge, too. But understanding why he's looking for revenge doesn't mean I'm going to be the one who gives Hudson the key. Hudson doesn't know the whole story, and I *will not* let him unravel Paradise.

I shove the paper back into Hudson's hands, cringing when it crumples between our palms. My hands are quivering so much that signing is nearly impossible, but I finally manage to tell him, "This is crazy. You're making it up."

"It's as crazy as glass birds that glow like floodlights," Hudson mutters, closing his eyes and rubbing them with the heels of his hands.

Cringing, I try not to glance at my birds. He's right—they're brighter now.

"You don't remember, but it happened to my sister, too," K.T. says.

She tells her own tale of woe and reveals her family's tragedy—her sister Emily's inexplicable, four-year-long coma. When she reaches the present, K.T. shifts, taking my hand in hers before I can pull it away. Her blue eyes bore into mine.

"Mari, I watched her fade away the same way you've been fading for years. If you don't listen to us, to what Hudson is trying to tell you, the same thing is going to happen to you."

I yank my hand away, but I can't run. Hudson has moved closer, and the two of them have literally backed me into a corner. They shift forward as the chime in the background turns into a whine, closer to the feedback noise I heard earlier. K.T. doesn't seem to notice, but Hudson stiffens and looks around, his jaw tight.

"Mariella, we've known each other since preschool, yet you can't name a single time we've spoken before yesterday," K.T. says. I think. Her voice sounds far away. All I can hear is the whine.

Hudson's lips move, and he bolts out of the room. K.T.'s eyes follow him, but she doesn't move. Locked in place—and keeping me trapped—she keeps talking.

"Don't you think that's strange?"

I can't think about *anything* with that noise! My head jerks to the side, and the muscles in my face twitch. The louder that noise gets, the harder it is to keep from shoving K.T. out of the way and running from the room like Hudson did. He had the right idea, but it's like K.T. doesn't even hear it. *What* is happening?

Oblivious, K.T. passes me a thick book open to a page of pictures. My hands are shaking so hard I can't hold on to the scrapbook, and it takes a second for my brain to make sense of what I'm seeing. It's almost as though I'm looking at pictures of...me.

Hudson bursts back into the room with another bag and a large amethyst geode. My nightingale pendant pulses, the glass warming up so fast it burns my chest. I bite back a scream. Hudson shoves the geode into my hands and dumps a bunch of rocks onto the bed with me. The lights in the room pulse brighter, and the sound changes, the harsh whining feedback fading and the high-pitched chime taking over again. K.T., caught up in his mania, jumps up and opens her backpack, pulling more rocks out and adding them to the growing pile.

The light pulsing from Orane's gifts is no longer the glittering iridescent glow I've seen for the past ten years. It's become an orange so vibrant it looks like my room is on fire. Everything is washed out except for the sparks of blue shooting up my arms from the contact with the geode, and the multi-colored energy emanating from the rocks on my bed. Whenever the orange glow meets any other color, light explodes and sparks fly.

I can't move. I can't breathe. I can't even blink. My eyes are wide open and locked on Hudson's as this tornado of colors and energy swirls around us.

Body screaming in pain, I try to shove the amethyst away. Hudson's hands close over mine, and he won't let me move. Making my eyes as wide as possible, I silently plead with him. His face is the only thing I can make out in the room—maybe because he's touching my skin.

Please, let me go, I try to beg. *Don't do this.*

"Hold on, Mari." His voice is a whisper, but I hear each word clearly. "Just hold on."

From the moment Hudson's hands cover mine, locking me to the amethyst, the edge disappears from the energy. It's like I've become a spectator instead of a participant, watching the light show instead of suffering as the energy whips through me like lightning. I don't feel it, but Hudson is convulsing like he did when he first stepped into the room. Like he's become a buffer between me and the swirling lights.

Then, as suddenly as it started, the light pulses one last time and begins to disappear, pulling back into Orane's gifts like a genie being sucked into a lamp.

Within seconds, the light is back to how it was before. Almost. Orane's gifts still glow orange, but the light is far less intense. Like someone turned the brightness down.

Hudson's head drops so low he almost smacks his forehead against the amethyst.

"Jesus. The day I don't have to do *that* anymore…" He rolls his shoulders and shudders before his head lifts. His hands never loosen their hold on mine.

Without looking away from me, he tells K.T. to go into the guest room next door and find twenty-six stones hidden along the wall. My eyes widen. She disappears without a blink or a question.

"I'll let go of you," he says as soon as she leaves. "I'll let go *if* you promise to sit exactly where you are, with that amethyst in your lap, and listen—really *listen*—to what I have to say."

I want to spit in his face and slam this amethyst into his head for thinking he can control me like this, but I'm not that stupid. He's fast and doesn't hesitate to use his strength to his advantage. But he's also willing to tell me what he knows. Letting him talk might give me information to take to Orane. Assuming every word out of Hudson's mouth isn't a complete lie.

As soon as I nod my agreement, he slides his hands off mine, his fingertips trailing along my wrists, the backs of my hands, my fingers. Sizzling warmth spreads up my arms until it buzzes in my chest like a kaleidoscope of butterflies has taken residence there. I suppress a shiver and close my eyes to block him out. That shivery sensation in my chest is something I've never felt under Orane's touch, but it wasn't disgust. It felt…nice. Good, even.

I don't like it.

Hudson paces the room, hands clenching like he's on the verge of punching something. Or someone. It never crosses my mind he might hit me. It never occurs to me to be scared. Angry, yes, but never scared.

When he speaks, his voice is lower than before. Rougher.

"If we'd let that light hit you, you wouldn't have remembered who we are. That demon of yours would've wiped your slate clean again."

I tense, and my hands tighten on the geode, itching to chuck it at his chest.

How *dare* he? Demon? *Demon?!* Orane is so far from a demon he makes angels look demonic. He's kind and good and giving and—

"Don't look at me like that, Mari." Hudson has stopped moving. "I know you want to throw that thing at my head, but don't. Not yet."

Actually, I think now is a perfect time.

Gripping it tighter, I lift the geode off my lap. His lip twitches, and in one step he's back in front of me, sitting on the desk chair and pressing his hands down on mine.

"You stopped listening. I know you did. And you promised you'd listen." He raises one eyebrow, and his thumbs run along my index fingers. I have to suppress another shiver. "You also promised you would keep this in your lap."

Before I can figure out how to respond, K.T. comes back into the room holding a blanket like a basket. Inside I see about a dozen stones larger than her hands and a couple handfuls of smaller ones. All that was in the guestroom? When did Hudson do *that*? K.T. looks between us, her eyebrows pulling together.

"Trouble?" she asks as she kicks the door shut.

"Nope. Not that kind anyway."

"Oh." Her expression relaxes, and she nods as though his answer makes perfect sense. Maybe it does to her.

"I think it's your turn, K.T.," Hudson says.

K.T. adds the new stones to the pile on the bed before clearing a space next to me. Picking up the book of pictures she shoved into my hands earlier, she flips through the pages and offers it to me. I try to pull my hands out from under Hudson's, but he refuses to move. Finally looking at him, I narrow my eyes.

"I'm not sure I trust you to keep your promise yet, Mari." Hudson's lip curls into a crooked smile when I scowl at him. He doesn't move his hands.

Glancing up, I take a deep breath and remind myself why I agreed to Hudson's terms. They know too much. I need to find out exactly how much so I can pass the warning on to Orane.

I give K.T. my attention, shifting position slightly with Hudson's approval.

Less than a minute later, I wish I'd ignored her.

The pressure of Hudson's hands is all that's keeping mine from shaking. Each breath burns, and I can't remember how to blink.

The longer she talks and the more pictures she flips through, the more my mind whirls. It's like I'm stuck on a spinning amusement-park ride that's been amped up past its full speed.

K.T. is holding an entire life in her hands. *My* life. And I don't remember a goddamn second of it.

When did I ever dress up like Santa Claus? And I thought I was terrified of that domed jungle gym in elementary school. Then again, I barely remember elementary school. I thought that was normal, but K.T. knows the stories attached to every single image in this scrapbook and the name of every person the camera captured with us.

Not one person looks familiar to me. I hardly recognize myself.

Chills radiate through my body from the center of my chest, leaving shudders in their wake. My eyes burn and my chest aches, but I can't look away from those pictures.

It doesn't make *sense*. Why don't I remember?

"What about the party Saturday night?" Hudson releases my hands and pulls his cell phone out of his pocket, bringing up a picture and showing me the screen.

It's me. A much more recent picture of me than the ones K.T. has.

I'm standing in near-darkness staring up at the sky; in the background is a house, and a bunch of people I don't recognize. I start to shake my head to tell them I don't remember this either, but something tickles at the back of my mind, an itch more mental than physical. Leaning closer, I zoom the picture in on my face.

Flashes. Sounds and images and emotions jumbled together in a nearly incomprehensible mess. Heat, closeness, and claustrophobia, and then cool breezes and open space. Blasts of noise, and then Hudson's voice telling stories in the darkness. People staring and whispering, and then the comfort of observing from a distance.

Bit by bit, Saturday evening filters back into my head. The longer I stare at that picture, the more I remember. Hudson was so kind that night, and it was so nice lying on the grass, listening to him whisper Orpheus's tale.

Like a crack in a dam, remembering that one night brings others in its wake.

It starts with a trickle, but soon the memories are rushing into my head, battering against me like rough waves. I gasp and curl over the amethyst, my hands digging into my hair like they might be able to keep my head from exploding. The weeks slam back into my mind in an instant, and I'm left gasping for oxygen in a suddenly airless room, trembling under the weight of things I never should have forgotten.

I remember all the times K.T. and Hudson reintroduced themselves. I remember the dinners with Hudson and Horace and the strange hints Hudson kept dropping—hints that all make sense now. I remember watching Hudson tear up the boxwood bushes in the backyard, and I remember K.T. inviting us to that party. I remember everything. Except my nights with Orane.

"Are you okay?" Hudson whispers.

Swallowing, I nod. I can hear Hudson's voice, but my vision is too blurred for me to make out his expression.

Every day of the last three weeks is back, but I don't have the nights. I don't have a single memory from Paradise.

I focus solely on my nights with Orane. I get a whiff of lavender, but it doesn't smell right. There's a tinge to the scent like it's burning. All I see is swirling fog filled with bursts of light and swaths of shadow. Tiny shocks run across my skin like a thousand little lashes. It's nothing like Orane's world.

Fear makes my already-pounding heart skip beats, but I can't tell where the fear is coming from. I want to convince myself it stems from Hudson, from his presence in my room or some instinct that this is all a trick he's playing on me, but when my vision clears and I look into Hudson's dark eyes, the fear starts to fade. As much as I want to tell myself I'm scared of Hudson, I'm not. It's thinking of Paradise that frightens me.

Why does thinking of Paradise scare me?

Because you can't remember it, I tell myself. It's not Paradise that's terrifying; it's the missing pieces of my memory. Orane would never scare me.

But what happened to my memory? I remember being constantly lonely and scared of everything. Why is K.T. holding a scrapbook that shows a life of friendships and fearlessness?

"Do you believe me, Mari?" Hudson asks.

Do I? It's a loaded question. Do I believe that Hudson's story is true? Yes. Do I believe it is *the* truth? No. It can't be. I *can't* have been that wrong about Orane. I must be missing some piece of the puzzle that will force this all to make sense.

Taking a deep, steadying breath, I sign, "Truth is relative."

Hudson huffs out a sound halfway between a groan and a laugh. "Truth is relative? That is such a bullshit answer. You said you remember the last three weeks and you *still* don't see what that guy is doing to you?"

Should I admit this? It might give Hudson another opening, another piece of "evidence" to throw on the scale against Orane, but I don't know what else to say.

"I only remember the days," I sign.

This time, Hudson *does* groan. "Of course you do." He pushes to his feet, running one hand over his white-blond hair, his jaw clenching spasmodically. K.T. watches him as though she's not sure if she should try to comfort him or stay the hell out of his way.

"What do I have to show you to get you to consider the possibility this guy isn't who you think he is?" Hudson's voice is louder. K.T. and I glance at the door at the same time. "They're not angels, Mariella; they're demons. They suck out pieces of your soul and leave the rest of you behind like garbage when they're done. You're like a talking cow to them—they may think it's amusing to keep you for a while, but that's not going to stop them from slitting your throat and turning you into dinner when they get hungry."

Heat burns through my body, and the last lingering tremors of fear are scoured away by anger. Gaps in my memory or not, I refuse to let him call Orane a *demon.*

I lift my hands to sign, and Hudson freezes, his eyes locked on mine.

"If you love someone," I sign to him, "you should have faith in them."

Hudson is silent for a long time. Or maybe it only feels like a long time.

"Love? You *love* him?" Hudson's face flushes red. "Do you really think he loves you? Love isn't taking away what makes you special and hiding it so no one else can see it. True love would accept you the way you are or help you become the person you're supposed to be."

Before I can clear my mind and form some kind of response, Hudson sucks in a breath and kneels in front of me, laying his hands over mine and peering up into my eyes. His skin is so warm it almost burns. I want to pull away, to tear my hands out from under his, but his stare locks me in place.

"Give us one night. Let me come with you. If this guy can answer all the questions and make sense of all the gaps in your memory, maybe we're wrong. But if he doesn't, then maybe we're telling the truth, and you're a week away from ending up like Emily."

He takes a breath, and his hands tremble on top of mine.

"Mariella, please. Let us help you."

I glance at the photos of my forgotten, happy childhood. I look at K.T., the friend who persisted despite my apparent indifference. And then I stare at Hudson, the stranger who thinks he's jumping into a riptide to save someone who's drowning.

I hate to contemplate it, but I have to. There are too many questions and too much proof for me to deny the possibility completely.

Swallowing the bile rising in my throat, I nod. I already think I'm going to regret this, but after everything that's happened, I have to know for sure. I have to know if Hudson is right.

Hopefully Orane can forgive me if I'm wrong.

Twenty-Nine

Hudson

Friday, September 5 – 9:56 PM

I explain the plan to Horace on the drive home, but I can't stop worrying K.T. won't be able to keep Mariella from changing her mind. Especially since I can't head back until eleven. At the earliest.

We reach Horace's at ten. For an hour, I have nothing to do but pick this awful plan to pieces and try to put it back into a shape that makes sense. No matter how I try to create some sort of battle plan, it all comes down to predicting the moves of an enemy I've never seen and a girl I barely know.

"This house already has too many holes in it," Horace grumbles. "You keep pacing like that and the boards are gonna give out right under you."

I lock my feet to the floor and close my eyes.

Get a grip, I tell myself. *Get a go••amn grip, or you're going to give yourself a heart attack before mi•night comes.*

Despite the variability of the attacks on *me,* I can't imagine the demon would risk changing anything on Mariella now. Especially not when he didn't manage to wipe her memory.

"Are you listening to me, boy?"

My eyes pop open. Horace is standing in front of me, his hands on his hips and his blue eyes gleaming.

"No." Was he talking? I didn't hear a word. "What?"

Horace pokes me in the chest with one of his bony fingers and glares. "I said that if you get yourself killed tonight, I'll find a way to bring you back to life so I can kill you again!"

"Dying isn't exactly Plan A, old man, but it's not like I can make any promises."

His lips purse, and he stares at me for a moment before shaking his head.

"So many things in the world I could've helped you out with. Could've gotten you into any college you wanted. Internships, travel—could've done any of that for you and taken care of it all. But you go and jump headfirst into something I can't do a damn thing to help you with."

I open my mouth, but what can I say to that?

Before I can try to think of words, Horace pushes me toward the door.

"Get going before you start tearing the floorboards up again," he says. "If you're gonna pace, might as well do it on the Teagans's grass."

After Horace promises to stay within reach of the stones and crystals I'm leaving behind for him, I head out into the balmy night, keeping to the shadows until I can resume my pacing and planning within sight of the light spilling from Mariella's window.

Unlike the last time I snuck into Mariella's house, this time I have to do it knowing everyone is upstairs, quietly waiting to fall asleep. I have to do it knowing the wrong sound will bring Frank and Dana out of their room, wondering if someone is trying to break in. The problem is, they wouldn't be wrong.

Despite the danger, I make it back to Mari's room without getting caught and find her pacing as anxiously as I was a few minutes ago.

K.T. and Mari both turn when I slip in. K.T.'s shoulders drop as soon as she sees me. "Mari said—"

K.T. doesn't have to tell me what Mari said because Mariella's hands are already flying.

"You have to leave. Now. I don't want you here." Her hands are trembling so much it's hard to be sure I'm reading her signs right.

"Why?" I sign back. My voice carries, and the last thing I want is for Dana to hear it.

"I'm sorry about what happened to you, but you need to leave. Now."

I glance at the clock. 11:03 PM.

"I'll leave at 12:01," I sign.

Mariella bites her lip and digs her fingers into her hair, dislodging locks so they stick out at all angles. I don't think she cares.

"If you don't leave, I'll wake my mother," she threatens.

"Why?" I sign. "Give me one good reason *why* you want me to go, and I might listen to you."

She flushes red, her cheeks solid globes of color. It takes her a few seconds to come up with a suitably vague response, though. "Because you're crazy. And because faith means never asking for proof."

Frustration grinds my stomach like an overheating engine, and I have to look away to keep from grabbing her shoulders and shaking her until she sees sense. Why is she denying *all* the evidence we've piled up in front of her? *How* is she denying it?

Exhaling slowly, I turn back to Mari and mutter, "There's a fine line between faith and gullibility. You're standing on it."

Her mouth tightens and her hands clench. She's probably offended—I mean, who likes being called gullible?—but that doesn't mean it's not true.

Antagonizing her isn't going to help, I remind myself. I take a deep breath and try another tactic.

"Look, I've spent the past week learning everything I could about your life. Right now, I know you better than you know yourself. Living under this guy's thumb has left you a shell of the person you should be."

Her hands come up to yell at me in sign again. I catch them and press hers between mine. They're so small they disappear completely, and they're so cold. Not surprising with the chill in the air of her room, but I hold on a little tighter, trying to pass my warmth to her as I whisper, "You're a shell, Mari, but you could be so much more. And I want to meet the real you because I think she'd be pretty damn spectacular."

For a moment, she stares at me, her eyes wide and her cheeks now just tinged with pink. Her lips twitch, and I think she might be hiding a smile.

"Flattery will get you nowhere," she mouths.

I relax a little and let myself smile. "No, but the truth will get me everywhere."

Thirty

Mariella

Friday, September 5 – 11:43 PM

Nothing I said made Hudson or K.T. leave. The more insistent I got, the more over-the-top Hudson's flattery and flirting became. I mean, he's barely known me for a week. There's no way he can think I'm that spectacular in less than a week. Right?

It doesn't matter. What matters is he refuses to leave, I haven't fallen asleep, my room is full of crystals and gemstones, it's almost midnight, and Orane is going to be *so* disappointed.

Or I'm about to find out that Hudson is right and then...I don't know what I'll do then.

Technically, I haven't broken my promise; though K.T. and Hudson have talked about their "dreamworld" for hours, nothing I've said has really confirmed I know what they're talking about. But what will that matter when they watch a portal open on the stroke of midnight? If they're wrong, vague answers won't save me when they follow me into Paradise. *If* they can follow me into Paradise.

Hudson and K.T. made me change into a pair of cargo pants cinched tight with a belt. The belt is a necessity because every pocket on these baggy pants is filled with stones. I fought them on it, but they reminded me that

I agreed to try things their way for one night. That's stretching the truth—I agreed to *listen*—but they didn't care about semantics.

They tried to make me take off Orane's nightingale pendant, but I refused and Hudson wouldn't touch it. He acted like it might burn him or bite him. They "let" me keep it, but Hudson looked physically ill when he relented. Each time he looks at me now, his gaze locks on the nightingale hidden under my shirt. The closer it gets to midnight, the more often his eyes drop to my chest. And his skin gets closer to gray every time.

My face might look the same way.

It's almost midnight. I watch my phone tick down the seconds, my heart pounding with each lost chance to get rid of them.

"Don't let the energy touch you," Hudson whispers.

I don't have the chance to glance at him before time runs out.

Orane's gifts all go supernova, burning bright orange as a portal opens in front of us. In my dreams, it always looks like a doorway made of glowing white light. Now, the gateway to Paradise is ringed in flames that lick the walls and ceiling.

The night I met Orane, he stood on the edge of his world and held out a hand, inviting me to come play. Tonight, though I see him in the distance, he doesn't reach for me. Instead, a tendril of orange fire shoots out from the portal aimed directly at my chest.

On instinct, I duck. The tendril follows. Heart pounding, I cringe as it reaches for me—and cringe again when it slams against a purple, pink, white, and green force field.

Oh my God! What is this?

The orange fire lashes like a whip against the surface of the protective barrier, each strike sparking and crashing like blue lightning. I have to bite my lip to keep from screaming. Ducking away does nothing—it's like it has some sort of heat-seeker built in—but I still end up crouched on the floor with my hands over my head trying to get away.

An arm drapes over my back, and Hudson leans close, his lips nearly brushing against my ear. Despite the fear burning through me, his closeness makes me shiver.

"It's your pendant, Mari. It's connecting him to you. I *told* you to take it off."

My body is screaming at me to dive under my bed and hide, but I force myself to look up at him. The lines etched into Hudson's skin aren't anger—they're concern. Worry. Fear.

Testing his theory, I unclasp the necklace and toss it to the side. I don't have to wait more than the blink of an eye to see that Hudson was right. The light follows the pendant like a guided missile. But he wasn't *completely* right. A second vein of light splits off, this one smacking against the protective shield surrounding me.

I glare at Hudson and sign, "Now what?"

Before he can answer, both tendrils freeze midair. Their twisting shapes look like the light left over from the twirl of a sparkler on the Fourth of July. Then, both trails retreat, pulling back until they disappear into the flames surrounding the portal.

"Did a lasso of light just try to grab Mari?" K.T. asks, her voice shaky.

Hudson doesn't look back at her, and his voice is hoarse when he says, "Yes."

"Okay. Just checking."

I take a breath and stand up, glancing over my shoulder. K.T. adjusts her grip on the largest stones, using their energy to hold the portal open. With rocks. I didn't think it'd work, but I didn't think crystals could create force fields either.

"Ready?" Hudson asks, looking at K.T. and me.

K.T. nods, the motion jerky and forced. I don't answer. It's getting harder to deny something strange is happening within Paradise, but I don't want to believe it has anything to do with Orane. If I'm wrong, Orane is going to be *so angry* with me. Keeping my promise not to *tell* anyone about Paradise means nothing if I let them trail me there.

Even if what's happening has nothing to do with Orane, he has to be told what's going on in his world, how the others are putting him and everything he's worked to protect in danger by taking revenge on humans. He thought no one else has ever been capable of opening a portal to Earth, but at least two have managed it in the last eight years of my life.

I take a step forward and shudder as a blast of cold air hits me. Paradise has always been a perfect seventy-six degrees, but tonight it's closer to taking a walk through the middle of a lake-effect blizzard. Wrapping my arms tight around myself, I force my feet to keep moving.

My hands are shaking so hard. I try to tell myself it's because of what I'm bringing with me—the bad news and the visitors—but the closer I get to Paradise, the worse the shaking is. It's getting harder to convince myself there isn't something *in there* that scares me. I just can't remember what it is.

I take that last step, and my bare feet land on lush grass instead of wooden floorboards.

Everything looks the same—the lake, the mountains, the willow tree, the opera hall—but it feels different. The feedback that's plagued my bedroom for so long has transferred here, but it's less of a noise and more like a vibration in the air, like something is fluttering against my skin and my eardrums. It makes me twitch. Especially without the usual lavender scent to soothe me.

Did Hudson follow me? So many times, Orane has told me how few people could survive the crossing between worlds. But Hudson and K.T. know what Orane looks like. Hudson is here now, standing beside me in a world no other human is supposed to know exists.

My chest clenches, and something dark and solid and dangerous takes residence in the pit of my stomach. It coils like a snake and burns like dragon's breath. I close my eyes as the foundation of everything I believe in trembles under the heavy stare of one relentless boy.

"I have had such faith in you for so long, Mariella. What have you done?" Orane's voice is like a sigh, laden with sadness and disappointment. He's so far away I can barely see the expression on his face, but his voice is as clear as if he was standing right next to me.

Most nights, this is the one place I can speak, but tonight is different. Hudson is here, and I'm not sure which rules apply—the ones I follow in my world or the ones I follow in Orane's. Holding on to hope, I decide it's better to play it safe for now. Just in case.

I walk faster to close the distance between us. Hudson is close behind me, and his presence blocks some of the buzzing energy hitting me from every other side.

Hudson's hands close around my upper arms a split second before I was about to stop anyway, leaving a few feet between us and Orane. I want to run into Orane's arms, but there are too many questions I need answered. And the answers to those questions are far too important.

Keeping my gaze locked on Orane's glowing, violet eyes, I pull my arms away from Hudson and sign, "I told him nothing. He knew about Paradise, and his story scared me."

Orane's eyes narrow as he looks between us. The buzzing gets stronger, like an extra pulse of energy rolling through the air, but the stones in my pockets pulse right back. Their power sounds like a chime. The louder the chime gets, the more the buzz fades. And the easier it is to breathe. The less chilled I feel.

"You are not welcome here," Orane says to Hudson, his eyes glowing brighter. "This place is not for you."

Hudson snorts. "No shit. Didn't exactly think you'd be happy to see me, considering she thinks no one else knows about this place."

"No one is supposed to." Orane's eyes narrow further, and he looks at me, immeasurable sadness in his face. "I have not wanted to worry you, Mariella, but for some time I have known that the others are fighting a centuries-old war. They do unspeakable things in the name of retribution, and my orders have not stopped them from leaving a path of destruction in the human world."

The knot in my chest loosens a little. It makes sense, but there are other questions I need to ask. Too many things I don't understand.

"Why did you tell me humans can't survive the crossing?" I sign.

"Because it is true. Most cannot." Orane's eyes flick to Hudson, and his lips thin. "The odds of being a passenger on a crashing airplane are extraordinarily low, but that does not make it impossible."

Hudson is shifting and muttering. I can tell he's on the edge of calling bullshit and saying something stupid. Reaching back, I touch his arm to tell him to calm down. I don't expect it to work, but it does. The instant my fingers brush Hudson's arm, he settles. The muttering stops.

"Though it was unlikely for you to meet another human who could survive—" The slight sneer to Orane's smile becomes a little more pronounced. "—let alone one who *has*—the prospect was never impossible."

His answer nags me. *Like snow in Bali,* he'd said. So unlikely as to be nearly impossible. *Impossible.* But now that

I've met two people who've survived the crossing—seen two days of snow in Bali—he's changing his song.

There are too many changes to Orane's story, too many holes in the rules he's drilled into my head since I was a child. Too many holes in *my* head.

"The life I remember doesn't match the one they showed me," I sign. Orane's eyes widen, and his entire body goes tense. "I don't remember people I went to school with for ten years. I don't remember my own friends. It's like I don't remember the right childhood."

I step forward, and my hand forms the most important question yet.

"Why?"

There's a hesitation. It's brief, but it's there. Enough to put me on guard when Orane finally opens his mouth.

"Some things, some moments in life, are better forgotten, Nightingale. There were so many nights you came to me in tears, and I did what I could to take away your pain. You would have done the same in my place. Anyone with a heart not carved from stone would have."

I want to believe it, but there's something in his eyes, a calculating light like he's trying to gauge my response so he knows what to say next. Piled on top of the evidence Hudson and K.T. provided, and the holes Orane's poked in his own stories tonight, the scales tip.

I take a breath and speak.

"You're lying."

Hudson stiffens, his head whipping around to look at me. I barely spare him a glance. My attention is too focused on Orane.

His purple eyes darken, but the glow is brighter, stronger. The chime gets louder as the energy swirling around us tries to break through the defenses the stones have woven. The energy of Orane's world is attacking us, and if I've learned anything over the years, it's that everything in this world obeys Orane's commands. He is God of his own little universe, which means one thing.

Orane is attacking me. *Orane*, the man I thought *loved* me, has not only been lying to me for years. Now, he's actually *attacking* me?

My arms hang like dead weights by my side, and my lungs feel like they're made of stone, making each breath a struggle. The world in front of me blurs, and for a second I see it for what it is—an incredibly beautiful but fake dream Orane constructed to keep me enthralled. Underneath the surface, there's nothing. Endless darkness. The mountains are like a painted set, and with the slightest push, they could all come tumbling down.

I can see it all, and the more I see, the more I remember.

I remember the last twenty-one nights in Paradise. I remember telling Orane about Hudson's first visit and the lightning that struck me from his eyes when I found him standing under the willow tree. I remember the kiss he gave me that felt more like a claiming, that dropped me into the blackness underneath the façade of this world. The way his eyes changed color and trapped me where I stood. Each memory is another weight dropped like an anvil onto my shoulders until it's all I can do to stay standing as I stare at the face of someone I don't recognize.

The tremor starts in my chest as my heart shatters. The shockwaves make my knees buckle, but Hudson catches me before I hit the ground. I shake him off as soon as I'm back on my feet. The last thing I want right now is someone—*any*one—touching me. My skin flushes and cools in a cycle so quick I can't adjust. I think shock is all that's keeping me from sobbing harder than I've ever cried for anything in my life.

"I was trying to protect you, Mariella," Orane whispers, his eyes wide and his voice low. "It was for the best."

His words slam into me like a heat wave, burning away my desperate, heartbroken agony and leaving raw fury behind.

"Protect me? From *what?*" My voice sounds harsh, foreign to my own ears. "Parents who love me? They've never been anything but kind, even when I suddenly wouldn't *speak* to them anymore."

Each word that falls from my mouth is like a knife slicing through my heart. The man I loved has been using me.

"I have a friend who's introduced herself so many times she's lost count. There are pictures of a childhood most people would *envy*. And you're trying to tell me my life was secretly hellish? That it's for the *best* I don't remember my own *childhood?*"

By the end, I'm nearly screaming, the words burning my throat and my hands clenched into fists.

"I never asked for *protection*." I shudder and rub my hands over my face, cringing when I notice how icy my skin has become. Something Hudson said earlier runs through my head and I laugh, a laugh that sounds more like I'm choking. "Hudson was right."

I look into Orane's eyes in time to watch his eyes darken. "About what?"

"Someone who—" My throat closes completely. I have to force the words out, practically throwing them across the few feet that divide us. "Someone who loves me wouldn't ask me to give up my life, give up the things that make me happy."

Orane's entire body is as rigid and silent as the cherry tree he's standing next to. He doesn't protest or explain or agree. He simply stands there, waiting. And the last little flame of hope I'd kept buried deep in the center of my chest dies.

"I'm done, Orane. I'm not—"

My mouth keeps moving, but the rest of the words are lost. Hudson looks at me, waiting for what I was trying to say, but no matter how many times I try, the words won't come. My chest contracts, and panic knocks my thoughts into disarray faster than a tornado.

For years, I was silent by choice. Now, choking and straining and silently screaming, I actually know what it's like to be silenced.

Across from me, Orane begins to smile.

This smile isn't like any I've ever seen on his face before. It spreads across his face like a shadow, darkening his eyes and revealing the malice barely hidden below the surface.

"Give it back," Hudson growls, stepping forward. "Whatever you did, undo it."

"Or what? You will throw more pebbles at me?" Orane laughs, and the sound intensifies the buzzing against my skin, sending shocks through my chest. "You were smart to come here so heavily guarded—smarter still to leave the door open behind you—but you know nothing about this war. You have no chance of winning, boy."

"I already took out one of you." Hudson stands strong, his voice steady, but he reaches behind himself and nudges me backward. Toward the portal. "I can do it again."

Orane grins and spreads his arms open wide. "You are more than welcome to try. Which of us do you think will prevail first? Are you quick enough and strong enough to protect Mariella while confronting me? You could never touch me."

"Maybe not. But she can."

Orane's smile freezes on his face.

"Mariella could tear your world apart if she wanted to, couldn't she? And you just gave her every reason to try."

Without warning, Orane lunges, his hands extended to rip out Hudson's throat. I scream silently and try to pull Hudson out of the way, but he tears out of my hold, his fist slamming into Orane's chest and sending Orane flying backward like he was blasted with a cannon.

Before I can process anything, Hudson's arm wraps around my waist and I'm lifted into the air as he hurtles toward the door.

"Faster, faster, faster," he mutters to himself.

The ground rumbles, and the buzz of Orane's energy turns into the roar of a freight train. I grit my teeth against the pressure. The crystals' chime makes it bearable, but I have to lock my hands around Hudson to keep from jumping down and running on my own. It would be stupid to try. I'd slow both of us down.

"Hurry up!" K.T. screams.

I close my eyes and hold my breath, trying to pretend we're running from a monster. Not the angel I gave my heart to so many years ago.

There's a jolt and Hudson shouts, "Close it!"

Cracks and crashes and shudders. I don't know what any of it means or where we are. With my eyes shut tight, I concentrate on the chime hanging in the air, the way Hudson is cradling me against his chest like something precious and fragile, anything else that will keep thoughts of what is *really* happening at bay for a few more moments.

"Is it over?" K.T. gasps. Her words are close to my head, but I can't open my eyes to look at her. Not yet. "Is she okay? Why isn't she moving?"

"Mari?" Hudson shakes me gently, and the mattress gives beneath us as he sits. "Mari, breathe, at least. You're starting to scare me."

Have I been holding my breath this whole time? As soon as I think about it, I realize my chest is burning, and it's not just from the ache of Orane's betrayal. I release my breath and gasp for another one, but breathing hurts more than I can bear. The tears I've been trying so hard to hold back break free, and I scream. I scream and scream and don't make a sound.

Over my head, Hudson is giving K.T. instructions that make no sense. Something about a drawer and tumbled stones and glass.

Across my closed eyelids, the last week replays in bits and pieces in my head, jumping from one moment to another in no order that makes sense. Each one is more painful than the last.

I wanted Hudson to be wrong. I wanted him to be a liar or the enemy or anything that meant Orane was right all along. Instead, Orane reached into my chest with claws dipped in venom and tore out my heart. And took my voice with him, just for the hell of it. Or maybe Hudson was right, and that's what he wanted all along. If Hudson was right about this much, why wouldn't he be right about everything?

Each breath I take escapes out of a gaping hole in my chest. The deeper I breathe, the more it hurts. I try to grab on to something that will keep me from falling down a bottomless pit, and my mind latches on to the memory of Orane's smile the moment I fell silent. That triumphant smile, and the fear in his eyes when Hudson said I had the power to tear his world apart.

It takes a moment to gather my energy, but I haul myself out of Hudson's arms and prop myself against the headboard, my knees tucked into my chest and my eyes squeezed shut so tight it hurts. It takes a good deal longer to stop the tears running down my cheeks. It takes even more time before I can think about opening my eyes to face the people sitting on the other end of my bed. I can feel them watching me, waiting to see how far off the deep end I've fallen.

"You with us, Mari?" K.T. asks. Her voice is soft and gentle, but it makes me jump when it breaks the silence.

She sighs and shifts, the bedframe creaking as she moves. "Sorry."

My face hidden and my eyes shut, I try to ask them what happens next. I try to whisper the words and scream them. My throat aches the more I try, but the only sound I make is the rush of air leaving my lungs.

Without looking up, I lift my hands and sign, "Why can't I talk?"

"Because you switched sides. You broke your promise, or you were going to." Hudson moves closer, so close I feel the heat rolling off his body, but he doesn't touch me. "Remember what I told you earlier? As soon as I decided to fight, I couldn't. Calease locked that ability away, and I was left paralyzed. It's the same thing now with your voice."

Guilt nibbles at the lining of my stomach like a rodent, sharp and biting. I'm agonizing over not being able to speak when Hudson had to watch his baby brother bleed to death.

I try to sink into detachment. Maybe if I find an empty place in my head, I won't have to deal with the pain. I don't think I'm strong enough to survive it. But if I can't face that, what can I possibly do against a being so powerful he can create entire worlds? How do I defeat someone who's known me for ten years, who I spilled every single secret to?

Hudson thinks I can do it. He has faith in me for some reason. He's been right about everything so far, but I'm not so sure he's right about me.

Thirty-One

Hudson

Saturday, September 6 – 12:03 AM

I glance at K.T., and she mouths, "What else can I do?"

Looking around, I shrug.

She's already hidden all of Mariella's glass trinkets—cleared out the bottom drawer of Mari's dresser, lined it with stones, and dumped every single figurine inside. The crystals and stones should keep her demon—Orane, I guess his name is—from reaching through and doing…anything. Whatever he's planning on doing to us.

At least, I hope they will. It's already helped Mari.

The orange light surrounding her is there, but it's been nearly overtaken by the same cobalt-blue glow that surrounds me. Every so often, the energy surges higher, sparking around her like a fireworks show. I'm not sure if she can see it or not.

Mariella has been sobbing, her shoulders shaking and her hands locked into fists so tight her nails must be digging into her skin, but all I hear is her gasping breaths. Each time I've tried to comfort her, she pulls away, but the tears are finally slowing. Her breathing is evening out, and she's shifting her weight like she's ready to sit up and face us.

I'm already so close to Mari it's hard to keep from bumping into her, but I shift a little closer anyway. To be there to comfort her or maybe to keep her from bolting, I'm not sure which. All I know is being close to her feels better. Safer. Especially now that she's not wearing that stupid pendant.

She must have felt me move because when she brushes her hands over her hair and slowly lifts her head, her eyes instantly find mine. And she doesn't look surprised to find me less than two feet from her face.

Mari blinks and leans closer, her eyes narrowing as she signs, "Why are you blue?"

I look down at myself. "You can see that now?"

When I glance at her, she nods, biting her lip. "It's a side effect of surviving. When you make it through next week, you'll be blue, too."

"You're *blue*?" K.T. whispers.

"It's a good thing you can't see it," I mutter. "Be glad."

"But Mari's not blue?"

I shake my head. "Only half-blue."

Mari looks down at herself and jumps. Holding her hands out in front of her, she stares at the light show I've been watching shift and change for a week. She's more blue than orange now, but it's an ever-changing balance between the two.

Exhaling heavily, Mariella drops her hands to her sides.

"Anything else you want to know?" I whisper. Locking my fingers around the comforter on her bed keeps me from reaching out and stroking her hair like I want to.

"How did you find me?"

Signing as much of it as I can, I tell her more about what happened after I fought Calease—the different ways I can see the world, the Wolverine-like healing power, and, most importantly, the dreams.

I try to make it sound as non-creepy or stalkerish as possible, but I don't know if there is a non-creepy way to tell someone you moved across state lines because of a sign in a dream and then spent days scouring that town for them. No matter how I phrase it, I sound psycho.

Mariella barely reacts. Her forehead creases a little and her head tilts, but then she nods. Almost like this was the answer she was expecting. Or maybe I've already told her so much crazy shit this news doesn't even register on the scale of one to weird.

"Do my parents know? About the dreamworld?" she signs, fingerspelling "dreamworld" and creating a new sign for it—the sign for "world" with her hands making a D instead of W.

Her face is too composed for me to guess if she's hoping the answer is yes or no. I lock my hands around the fabric of the comforter again. The longer she sits there pretending she's not on the verge of drowning, the harder it is to keep myself from taking her hand to remind her someone else is here with her.

"No, they don't know," I finally sign back.

"Do you want them to?" K.T. signs.

Mariella considers the question for a second before she shakes her head. "Only if..."

Her hands freeze, and her entire face crumples. A few tears fall from her eyes, and this time I can't stop myself from touching her. My thumb wipes away the tears on her cheeks, and my fingers brush her hair behind her ear. Her skin is too cold, but it's warmer than before she faced down Orane.

She doesn't react to my hand at first. It's almost like she doesn't feel it at all. But then her eyes open, and she stares at me with more pain than a lot of people our age know exists in the world. For less than a breath, I wonder what might have happened if she hadn't been targeted by the demons. If we'd met by chance instead of design. If I'd found her before she'd had her heart squeezed into pulp. What would we have been then?

I let myself imagine what the world might be like if I had a one-in-a-million shot at a girl like Mariella. Someone who wouldn't see me as damaged or broken or freakish. Someone who'd fight *with* me instead of waiting for me to fix everything. Someone so gorgeous I could stare at her for days and never get tired of the sight—that part doesn't hurt either.

But then she pulls away, and the moment is gone. Even if I don't die pulling her through this, what are the chances she'll want anything to do with me? I'm the person who pulled the weak stone out of the foundation of her life and brought her carefully constructed, fake love crashing down. Why would she want to stay around a reminder of one of the most painful nights of her life?

"Tell my parents the truth if I don't make it past my birthday," she signs.

"You're going to be fine." I don't remember to sign. The words are out before I can lift my hands.

She looks at me, but I can tell she doesn't believe me, doesn't quite believe in herself. There are pieces of this picture missing, and I need to change the subject, so I sign, "What did you do, Mari? I mean, what did he want? Do you know?"

I watch her face, trying to decipher what it means when the lines around her eyes and across her forehead shift like that. After a couple seconds, she sighs and raises her hands, but when she signs, "I sing," she doesn't seem convinced that's the right answer.

Because it isn't.

"Not only that," I sign. Slowly—reluctantly—pulling away, I search her room until I come up with what I need—a pencil and a blank piece of paper.

As I sketch, I explain how this ability works. I end up tripping over my own words, making the explanation hellishly convoluted, but I think Mari gets it.

"You see the reason they..." She pauses for a second before signing, "Target us?"

She understands. Warmth spreads through my chest, and I almost smile. "Yes. Exactly."

Not wanting to freak her out more than necessary, I draw Mari's second self as she should be, not as I saw her. I leave off the horrified expression and the burning chains. I soften the way her arms are folded and set the lyre at her feet instead of strapped to her back.

When I show the sketch to them, K.T. glances at it and smiles, nodding as though the symbolism makes perfect sense to her. Maybe it does. She knew Mari before Orane sunk his claws into her mind. Mariella, though, grabs the page and stares at it like I drew her as a clown or an alien or something. Her lips move slightly, like she's muttering to herself, but when she looks up at me, she simply signs, "What?"

"You were always the best singer, Mari." Mari and I both look at K.T. "It's true. I mean, you'd give shows on the playground and people would stop a game of kickball to listen to you, but that wasn't the only thing."

Mari rubs her eyes and leans forward, setting her chin on her knees and watching K.T.

"It was like you were a magnet. People wanted to be around you, and you could always get people to follow your orders." K.T.'s eyes widen, and she shakes her head. "Not that you were, like, ordering everyone around. Just...you had this way of getting people to listen to you. You were always the mediator when people fought and the judge when there was some stupid contest or game. People trusted you. If...Well, if you hadn't met this demon, you probably would've been class president all four years. Whether you put yourself on the ballot or not."

"You're a leader," I whisper. "That's what he wanted. He wanted that magnetism that makes..." I stop, wondering if it's too soon to say this. "That quality that makes people adore you."

Even people like me, who so rarely find a reason to see the rest of humanity as more than tolerable. But did she pick up on that part? She's sitting with her chin resting on her knees and her eyes closed, so I don't think so. And I can't tell if I'm relieved or disappointed.

"Will he come back?" Mari signs, her eyes still closed.

"I don't know." I keep my voice low. "He's attacked me more than once, but he has to be careful with you. You're awake, which means he doesn't quite have what he wants yet. I think he was about to take it when I pulled you away. I think the stones are all that's keeping him from taking it now." I force a smile and try to make this less awful. "You're about to become a very avid collector of semi-precious gemstones, Mari."

She opens her eyes but doesn't smile back. Looking at her nightstand, she reaches out and trails her fingers along the mane of the black jade horse I gave her last week. For a second, it almost looks like she's about to smile, but it never appears. Mari draws her hand back and runs it over her hair, smoothing the bits pulled out of her braid. Then she sighs and lifts her hands.

"Tell me what to do," she signs. "I'll do it."

I wish I could see anger or frustration or pain in her face, but there's nothing. Nothing but the circles forming around her eyes and the way her head hangs. It's a resignation and a weariness that makes me wish I could let her sleep and take care of this myself, but I can't. Orane knows she has a chance of taking him down. It has to be her fight.

I have a week to make sure she's ready for it. And to prepare myself to do whatever it takes to get her out alive.

Mariella leans forward when we pull up in front of Stone's Throw, her eyes jumping from the hand-painted sign to the window display of books, crystal balls, wind chimes, and dream catchers.

It's earlier than when the store is usually open, but I called ahead and warned Dawn we'd be coming. She's already unlocking the door and grinning at us from the entrance.

"Before you ask, the business is *not* for sale," she calls.

"Good. Wouldn't know what to do with it anyway." I grab my backpack full of crystals and pass Mariella hers while K.T. brings up the rear with two more. The store probably has plenty of crystals to keep us safe, but we're not taking any chances. When Dawn sees the bags, her eyes widen, magnified by her thick lenses.

"Are you moving in?"

"No. I'm being overcautious." Before she can ask, I open the bag and show her what's inside. She leans so close her nose almost brushes the top of the bag, but then she flinches and pulls away fast.

"Wow. I have *never* felt that kind of energy rolling off a bag of crystals. What did you do? Electrify them?"

Mariella brushes past us into the store, her lips pressed tight, but I keep my attention on Dawn. "Something like that."

"Hmm. Well, if you want more, I've restocked. Have more than I carried before."

"We'll take it."

Dawn shakes her head. "Without looking at it?"

"You pick good stuff, and I need more. Why waste the time?"

"All right, big spender," K.T. says as she passes, smiling.

Dawn's attention has already wandered. Her eyes follow Mari around the store. She's already standing in front of the glass shelves of stones and grabbing as many as she can carry.

"Mariella is...different," Dawn says without looking away. "What happened?"

"A lot. And not enough."

Dawn nods like my answer actually meant something. "She still needs a cleansing."

"Yeah, that's one of the reasons we came."

Smirking, Dawn finally turns back to me. "Not just to clean me out again?"

"Nope. Wanted to pick your brain, too."

Her smile widens. At least until I start explaining exactly what I need. What's happening. What we're up against.

"You really know how to pick your fights, don't you?"

I huff out a laugh and rub one of my hands over my hair. "Yeah. It's, uh, kind of a talent of mine."

Dawn looks up at me, her eyebrows pulled together. "Yeah, I know. That's why I said it." Then, with a roll of her eyes and a quick turn, she's off to the bookcases and pulling down seemingly random titles.

"Your best bet to link everything together is silver," she says, beckoning me into the back room of the store. She drops the stack of books on a neatly organized desk and sits. Grabbing one, she flips through the pages and then slides it under a camera on a movable arm. With the press of a couple of buttons, the text from the book appears on her oversized monitor, but it's fuzzy.

"Thanks for this, by the way." She grins as she adjusts the settings on the projection. "You bought all those stones, and I bought this."

"Glad to help." I look up at the screen as the page comes into focus. It's the entry on silver from *The Book of Stones*—the main book I used to teach myself about the crystals.

"Its power is heightened by the moon, and since these demon-y things like to hit at night, silver will help you out. Expensive, but useful."

I finger the tiger-iron pendant hidden beneath my shirt. "Okay. Any ideas on what to do with it?"

Dawn is already flipping through another book, her nose pressed close to the pages until she finds what she's looking for, then places it under the camera. She points at a choker of silver and stones.

"This was found near where the Oracle of Delphi supposedly lived. Archeologists think the arrangement of the stones was meant to protect her from evil spirits." Before I can comment, she switches the book again. "This is a belt that was made from a description of one once worn by Merlin."

"The wizard? Like King Arthur and Merlin?"

Dawn grins. "The very same."

She shows me a few more, bracelets and anklets and designs supposed to enhance the stone's powers and connection to the wearer. Even if they don't work, I figure they can't hurt. Plus, it'll be easier than being forced to carry around a backpack of crystals for the rest of my life. I mark all the pages and pile up the books to take with me.

"You don't happen to carry silver wire, do you?" I ask as we move toward the counter where K.T. and Mari are waiting.

"Sorry. I can order some, though. Rush, of course. Even ship it straight to you."

"Perfect. I'll take as much as you can find."

It takes Dawn a little while to ring everything up, but soon we're headed to the car with a few new bags of stones and a stack of books.

"Good luck," Dawn calls after us. "Come see me again when it's over."

"Of course." *If I'm alive,* I add in my head.

Before we head back to Mariella's house, I swing by Horace's to pick up a few things. He must've seen us coming because he opens the door before we reach it.

K.T.'s phone rings as soon as she steps onto the sagging porch. She checks the screen, biting her lip as she glances at me, and answers the call.

"Hey. Can I call you back in a minute?" A short pause and then the call is over.

"Who was that?" I ask.

"Um, do you remember that neurologist I said might be able to help Emily? Dr. Carroll?" She smiles, but it's a little too bright. Forced-bright. "He's kind of here."

"You really brought him here?" She's putting a lot of trust in someone she found online. Horace opens the front door and steps out as I ask, "What do you know about this guy?"

"Hudson, I'm not an idiot." K.T. tenses and glares at me. "When I told him I might have information, I said I'd only work with him if he could prove he was who he said he was. He signed a release to let me do a background check. He has no criminal record, and his medical degrees are legit."

I raise an eyebrow, and Horace laughs. "Well, that's somethin' at least."

K.T. takes a breath. "I'm not asking you to help, Hudson. I just wanted to let you know that he's here." She pauses, her lips pursed. "If he can connect the dots, I'll tell him what happened with Emily."

I know how important this is to her, so despite my desire to warn her off a probable dead-end, I nod. "All right."

K.T. relaxes, turning around and heading into the front yard as her fingers move over the screen of her phone.

"Think the doc'll help?" Horace asks.

"Who knows," I mutter as we step inside.

Mariella hasn't been here before. She looks around like she can't quite believe someone could live here. Considering her house is practically an architectural showpiece, it's not surprising she's a little skeptical.

Work on the restoration has already started, but at this point it looks worse. There are huge holes in the wall where they had to get at wiring and plumbing, and the kitchen has been completely gutted.

"This place is a mess," she signs when she catches me watching her.

"It's a work in progress," I explain. "If your dad's plans work out, it should be pretty nice when it's done."

She bites her lip and looks around. Then she exhales quickly, her eyes flick up to the ceiling, and, without looking at me, she signs, "You should ask my parents if you can stay with us while your house is in ruins."

My heart stops and I stare at her, but she won't look at me. Apparently the crown molding is worth an in-depth analysis. Move in? She's asking me to move in?

"What'd she say?" Horace asks.

I tell him and expect him to laugh, but his lips purse. Holy hell. Is he actually taking the idea seriously?

"Her birthday's next Friday, ain't it?" he asks after a few seconds. I nod. "Probably best to wait, right? That's the night you'll want to be there."

My voice has completely dried up. All I can do is nod. Yes, that's the most important night, but I can't leave her alone every night before then. What if her demon comes back?

Mariella finally meets my eyes and shrugs. "You'll have to sneak in until then."

I hold my breath and nod, wondering if I should tell her I was going to do that anyway.

Thirty-Two

Mariella

Sunday, September 7 – 12:15 PM

I stand in front of my closet and realize I hate every piece of clothing I own. All of it. I have to go back to school tomorrow, and I don't want to wear any of this. It's all awful and doesn't fit and why did I think it was such a good idea to own so much black?

"Mari? Are you listening?"

I sign "No," over my shoulder at Hudson and start pulling things off hangers and shelves. Everything in this closet is because of *him.* I hid myself away because it helped me vanish in plain sight. It was easier to stay silent if no one wanted to talk to me, so I drowned myself in fabric.

My eyes burn, but I don't notice I'm crying until Hudson pulls me away from the closet and wipes my cheek dry with his thumb. I grab a tissue from my desk and wipe my eyes, ducking my head to hide the way my cheeks heated up as soon as he touched me. Even after I scrub at my face with my dry half of the tissue, I can feel the exact path his thumb took across my face. The warmth of it was such a nice change from the chills I've been fighting off all weekend.

He's standing so close I hear the soft sigh before he asks, "What do you want me to do with all this?"

I open my eyes to see him gathering up the clothes I tossed out, folding them in neat piles of shirts and pants and jackets. He's avoiding my eyes, so he doesn't notice when I sign for him to stop. But it's probably better if *he* does it. Once they're out of my closet, I don't want to touch them anyway. And Hudson's folding is a lot neater than mine would've been.

Going back to the closet, I keep pulling clothes out, biting my lip to keep the tears from rolling again. But I can't keep my hands from shaking or ignore the way the air burns my lungs when I breathe.

Ten years. Ten years of accumulated lies. Ten years of my life, gone.

I was in love with Orane for a long time, before I even knew what I was feeling. I started dropping hints when I was fourteen, and I thought he was being chivalrous or dense when he didn't pick up on the hints for two years. *Two years.*

I kneel down, my fingers digging deeper, yanking out shoes and winter coats and everything else stuffed inside. My cheeks burn hotter as I dig into the forgotten corners of my closet until there's nothing left.

Orane took so much more than he should have. I saw the look on Hudson's face when I told him I loved Orane. He was angry and disgusted, but that showed up *after* the shock. Even in the memories he stole from Calease, Hudson told me he's never heard of a demon making their victims *love* them. But he's also never heard of someone getting stalked from the age of eight.

If the dreamworld is all someone knows, is it any wonder they fall in love with it?

But my real life disintegrated because of it. My friendships vanished. My memories are gone. And it's no wonder none of my damn clothes fit. I weighed myself on the scale in Mom's bathroom, and I'm so underweight it's gross.

"What do you guys want for lunch?"

I freeze at the sound of Mom's voice. It's too late to hide the chaos. She's already here.

"I was thinking—"

Her eyes widen when she sees the mess, but it doesn't look like she's upset. A flush spreads over her cheeks, and her eyes get a little watery as she takes everything in.

"Well, um, fall cleaning, sweetie?" she asks, laughing a little through the words.

"She wants to donate all of this," Hudson says before I can answer.

No, actually. I want to burn it all, but I guess that's a little selfish. Someone might as well benefit from this disaster.

"Okay, sure." Mom's nodding like a bobblehead. She always does that when she gets excited about something. "But you're not keeping *any* of it, Mari? What are you going to wear?"

My eyes burn. I rub my face to make sure the tears aren't back and then sweep my hands back, pushing my hair over my shoulders. I can't keep the grimace off my face as I sign, "Can we go shopping? Please?"

Shopping is the last thing I want to do right now, but it's either that or get arrested for indecent exposure next time I leave the house. I am *not* wearing any of this crap again.

Mom starts fluttering and twitching, her face getting even redder.

"Oh! I mean—just, um—I'll be right back!"

I glance at Hudson, but he looks as confused as I am. He meets my eyes and shrugs.

"Don't ask me," he says as he goes back to folding my discarded clothes.

I return to the last drawer and go back to work. As I finish, Mom comes back with about ten huge shopping bags.

"I bought some of this a long time ago," she explains as Hudson takes a couple bags off her hands. Her voice is an octave higher than usual, and every few seconds a tear escapes her eyes and runs unheeded down her cheeks, but her smile makes her entire face glow. "Some of it is probably out of style by now, but we should be able to find something for you."

Once the old stuff is out of the way, Mom and Hudson dump the bags into a pile on the floor and we all start sorting. There's everything from tank tops to long-sleeved shirts, skirts to slacks, thin sweaters to down-filled winter jackets. When I look at Mom, she smiles and shrugs.

"I got it all just in case," she says. "You might have gotten tired of black, you know."

I pick up a long-sleeved shirt in deep blue. Blue is a good color right now. Hudson glows with a blue light similar to this, and the glow surrounding me gets closer to blue every day. It grows stronger the further I pull away from Orane. If Hudson is right, I'll be glowing blue for the rest of my life, so I should get used to wearing it. My heart drops into my stomach, and I clutch the shirt tighter. If I survive, anyway.

"Here." Mom hands me a white tank top. "That shirt dips kind of low. I think you'll probably want to wear this underneath it."

She starts saying something about jeans, but then her head tilts to the side.

"Honey, where'd all these stones come from?"

Breath catching in my throat, I try to keep my expression calm even as my heart pounds. What the sun-dappled hell am I supposed to tell her about my new gemstone collection?

"Oh, those are mine," Hudson says. "With all the renovations, I wanted a safe place to keep my collection. Mari offered to hold on to it for me."

Dana grins. "That's nice of you, Mari. Hudson, if you or Horace need to keep anything else safe while the work is going on, you let me know, all right?"

Hudson's attention shifts to me. What started as painful pinpricks when I first met him has become a warm tingle of awareness whenever he's nearby, whenever he's focused on me. He's most likely thinking about what I suggested yesterday, that he and Horace ask Mom if they can stay here for a while. But Horace wanted to wait, so neither of us is going to bring it up now.

"Thanks, Dana." Hudson's voice is hoarser than a moment before. "I'll let him know."

Heading to the bathroom to change into clothes that, thankfully, have *nothing* to do with Orane, I leave Mom humming as she hangs up summer dresses and dress shirts in my closet. Hudson offered to arrange everything that goes in the dresser, probably to keep Mom from discovering the strange new storage place for my once-precious glass figurines. I wonder if she'd even care. She never really noticed them before.

The best I can say about the clothes is they fit better than my old ones, but I'm so skinny that the jeans sag in all the wrong places and the shirt—which I think is supposed to be fitted—hangs like a peasant blouse. Gritting my teeth, I promise myself I'll go find a bowl of ice cream or something. Out of its braid, my thick hair flows loose down my back—it's probably the lone part of me that's escaped Orane in decent condition.

By the time I come back into the room, the new clothes are put away and Mom is talking lunch options with Hudson. The conversation stops mid-sentence when I step into the room. Mom clasps her hands in front of her face, and I can tell she's trying not to cry. It's harder to read Hudson's expression, but his eyes are a lot wider than usual.

"Very nice," Mom finally chokes out, a huge grin on her face. "I'll let you know when lunch is ready, okay? Something special, I think."

Stopping to kiss my cheek, Mom skips from the room. I'm left alone facing Hudson.

His cheeks flush, just a touch of pink, and he smiles. "Blue's a good color on you."

"Good," I sign, a little bit of the pain locked in my chest trickling away. Enough to let me smile back. "I'll be wearing it a lot after this week."

Hudson's smile transforms into a grin, and his entire face lights up. "'Atta girl."

This time, the expression doesn't last very long. His attention keeps shifting between the drawer where my glass trinkets are hidden and my open bedroom door. When he finally tells me what's on his mind, he switches to sign.

"Do you remember the story about my fight with Calease?"

I wish I could forget the images his story burned into my head. I nod, though. Considering my recent history, I know why he asked if I remember, but unless Orane literally rips those memories out of my head, I don't think I'll ever forget.

"My pendant was what helped me win," he signs. "I think yours might be the key."

This time, my eyes drift toward the drawer, too. We haven't opened it since Friday night when K.T. shut everything inside. Contemplating opening it now is like considering sticking my hand in a cage of hungry rattlesnakes after playing with a rat. It's asking for trouble.

But that doesn't mean I can say no.

"What do you want to do?" I sign.

He turns around, adjusting a few of the stones before taking a deep breath and crouching down next to the bottom drawer. With his hands on the wood face, he pauses, muttering something I can't quite hear. Then, in a flash, he yanks the drawer open, reaches in, grabs the necklace from a glass box in the center of the drawer, and slams it shut again.

The pendant pulses with a strong orange light; tendrils of it reach out for Hudson and me like tiny snakes. The soft chime of the gemstones' energy that's been a constant presence all day grows louder. Hudson is wearing all the gemstone jewelry he's had for months, but...I pat my pockets. Oh, no. My stones are in my pajama pants!

Gasping, I grab an amethyst off the top of the dresser and hold it tight against my chest.

"What are you—?" Hudson's jaw goes slack. "Damnit, Mariella! You took off *all* the stones? I gave you those for a reason!"

Heart pounding, I lunge across the room and pull the stones out of my old sweatpants. I stuff my new pockets with the stones he gave me earlier, slip the too-big, stone-bead bracelet on, and—turning my back on Hudson—even slip a few smaller ones into my bra. Just to be safe.

Behind me, Hudson is fuming. "Do you not get it? One second—that's all it would take, Mari. *One* second. If you step out from under this shield at the wrong time—"

My face burning and my eyes watering, I have to take a few deep breaths before I can turn around to face him. I was so busy looking at the way my shirt fit and petting my own hair that I forgot—completely forgot—to switch the stones. Stupid. Careless. Idiotic. All the work Hudson has done to keep me safe from my own stupid decisions, and I put myself at risk like that?

"I'm sorry," I sign as soon as he looks up at me. The pendant is on the floor in a circle of stones; I glance between that and Hudson's face. Hudson's tight lips and narrow eyes. He's angry, and I can't blame him. I'd be angry, too. I *am* angry. I'm mad at myself for being that shallow and stupid.

"Don't apologize. I shouldn't have yelled at you."

His voice is muffled and rough. I have to look. He has his face covered by his hands, and the muscles in his neck are standing out like corded wire. I want to reach out and run a hand over his close-cropped hair or pat his back to let him know I'm here, but then he shakes himself off and sits up, a flush on his cheeks and a forced smile on his face.

"You've got plenty to deal with without me making it worse. Just..."

The smile fades, and he stares up into my eyes from his seat on the floor. In this moment, I get an inkling of how alone he feels, trying to keep everything together when none of us know what we're doing. Abandoned by his family and mistrusted by everyone he meets because of the scars on his arms and the impossibility of his eyes, Hudson has every reason to tell the world to go screw itself, but he's here. Putting himself in danger to make sure what happened to him and J.R. doesn't happen again. That's what he told me his reason for doing this is, anyway. But with the way he's looking at me right now, I have to wonder if that's all it is. And what I'll do if there really is more.

Hudson clears his throat and looks away, adjusting the stones to keep the bursts of energy coming off the nightingale pendant at bay. "Try not to forget again, okay?"

I pull a couple more stones off the dresser and sit across from him. Waiting until his head finally tilts toward me, I sign, "Promise."

He stares at me, his hand shifting like he's going to reach out and touch me, but he doesn't. Exhaling a long, slow breath, Hudson looks down at the pendant.

"What do you see?" His voice is even and calm—inflectionless, almost.

I wish I had Hudson's talent for sketching, but if I tried to draw, it'd look like a lump of nothing. How do I describe what I'm seeing in sign, then?

"Orange energy moving around it like snakes," I finally sign.

He nods. "What did you see before? Before you woke up."

I try to explain the glittering light and the silver mist inside the bird. "It was beautiful."

"Yeah. It's supposed to be beautiful. They use them to spy on you, so they don't want you taking it off. Ever."

"It worked," I sign, my nose wrinkling when I look at the pendant again. How had I been so blind?

"Worked on me, too." He shifts closer to the pendant, his eyes narrowed like a general surveying a battle. "Okay, well, what I think we might be able to do is—"

As he speaks, he reaches into the circle of stones and pulls out the necklace, but when the nightingale clears the top of the stones, the power flares, lashing out and reaching straight for me. I scream, even though it makes no sound, and push away. The stones I'm wearing warm against my skin, but Hudson is already in motion. He pulls the drawer open, drops the necklace back into the glass box, and closes it.

"What we might need to do is come up with a different plan," he mutters, breathing as hard as I am. "Part one of the new plan—don't touch anything in that drawer until I figure out how the hell to neutralize it."

I nod, my left hand pressed to my chest as though that will keep my heart from beating its way out through my ribs. "Should we get rid of them?"

He opens his mouth, then closes it again. Sighing, he shakes his head. "No. We need the pendant until Friday and I don't want anyone else finding the other shit."

Fair enough. "What's part two of the new plan, then?"

Hudson takes another deep breath and collapses to the floor. Looking up at me, he shakes his head. "No goddamn clue. I'll let you know when I come up with one."

I almost want to go back in time. *Almost.* One thing I can say about living under Orane's thumb is that it was a lot less confusing.

How long does it take a broken heart to heal? A year? Six months? Two months? However long, I'm sure almost everyone would agree that a few days is far too soon.

My heart is in pieces, pieces barely able to continue beating as a single unit. Each beat is painful, like a tiny heart attack, but it keeps me alive.

Somehow, though, Hudson has touched all the pieces of my broken heart. Even if he can't put it back together again, the pain isn't quite as bad when he's around.

And he's been around a lot.

For the week in between the worst night of my life and my birthday, Hudson and K.T. walk me through my own life. We pull out home videos and more pictures than I knew existed. Some of it comes back to me. Most of it doesn't.

Hudson and K.T. never give up. They keep digging, asking everyone in the senior class to bring in elementary and middle-school mementos. As an explanation, K.T. volunteered to make a massive slideshow project for the graduation party at the end of the year. It works. Pictures and memorabilia and video clips uploaded from home collections pour in. It all helps, but at the end of the week, we estimate I've reclaimed less than a third of the memories I *should* have.

After Dawn got us the promised silver wire, Hudson spent every spare minute piecing together chokers, pendants, charm bracelets, anklets, rings, and belts of stone and silver. For a guy with scars all over his body and hands the size of a gorilla's, his work is beautiful. Surprisingly delicate yet strong, the intricate twists and bends in the wire reinforce the grip on the pieces of stone they're designed to hold. If I didn't know why he was making it, I'd want to wear them all. As it is, I wish I didn't have to.

Friday morning, we walk out of the house after breakfast. Hudson and Horace brought enough to stay for a week when they came over for dinner last night. It shouldn't have changed anything for me, since Hudson has already been in my house every night for the past week, but it did. It isn't a secret anymore. We had breakfast together with my parents and Horace, and now he's smiling at me over the hood of his Camaro. My pulse picks up. I'm not sure if it's from apprehension or excitement. When we slide into the car and I feel that increasingly familiar shiver I get when we're close, I realize it's a little of both.

It's ridiculous. Even before Hudson "moved in" yesterday, we spent nearly twenty-four hours a day together. He and Horace were over for dinner every night and Hudson would leave for a couple hours before sneaking back into my room and sitting on the floor, making jewelry and formulating plans B through Z while we waited to see if Orane would attack. He hasn't yet.

I thought I'd be glad of the reprieve, but instead, the silence makes me nervous. It makes me think Orane knows something we don't. That he's so sure of his victory that playing with us like this is a way of punishing us. Letting us grow hope.

Hope hasn't bloomed very much, but something else has. Something centered on Hudson. He makes me nervous in a way Orane never did. He's a puzzle—a challenge—but

I know he expects these powerful, impossible things from me. He expects me to be that goddess-like creature he drew, and I don't know if I can do it. Even wearing the jewelry he's been giving me all week, I don't believe I'm that girl right now.

"Happy birthday, Mariella." His voice is lower than usual, closer to bass, and the words rumble through the car.

Hands trembling slightly, I force a smile and nod my thanks. No one mentioned it this morning, and I'm glad. Honestly, my birthday is the last thing I want to think about right now. My birthday is the deadline. Tonight is the war.

Yeah. Happy freaking eighteenth to me.

"Horace convinced your parents to let us skip school today."

My eyes nearly pop out of my head. What?

Hudson smiles. "There's nothing else we can do to prepare. Whatever is going to happen is going to happen at this point."

Yeah, I guess, but what does that have to do with skipping school?

"I thought it might be a good idea to pretend you're actually happy it's your birthday. We should spend the day forgetting what's coming."

He watches me and his expression is light, almost carefree, but his hands are gripping the steering wheel too tight and the tension in his shoulders is too much. He wants me to think this doesn't matter, but it does. He's planned it all out, and if I don't want to play along, it will matter a lot to him.

"What d'ya say? You in?"

My heart starts pounding, and part of me wants to say no. Falling in love has only hurt me so far. Letting myself get closer to Hudson can't be a good idea. Not with what we're about to face. But then I remember everything he's done to help me without asking for anything in return and the stories about his life Horace has told me those few times we've spent any time alone, and I can't make myself say no to his plans. Bad idea or not, he deserves this as much as I do. More, probably. I smile and sign, "Okay."

He tries to hide his grin, biting the inside of his lip to keep it at bay, but he can't hide the way his eyes light up. Without a word, he shifts the car into drive and pulls away from the curb.

I want to ask where we're going, but he's driving. He won't see it if I sign. And does it really matter? I'm not at school. For now, that's enough.

Thirty-Three

Hudson

Friday, September 12 – 7:36 AM

Mariella doesn't ask any questions, just curls up in the seat and stares out the window—or pretends not to stare at me. The first time she questions anything is when we pass the huge sign warning us that we're approaching the Canadian border.

"Are we running away?" she signs when I glance at her. "I don't have my passport."

I laugh. It occurs to her that I'm trying to run off with her, and she starts worrying she won't be able to come with me? That's awesome. And a huge relief.

"Don't worry. I planned ahead." I reach into the door pocket and pull out both of our passports. "But we're not running away. I don't think borders matter much in the dreamworld."

Mariella shrugs but looks confused, cute little wrinkles covering the bridge of her nose and hovering around her eyes. We get through the border crossing without a problem, but Mari pays more attention after that. Watching the signs, she guesses our destination pretty quick.

"Why are we going to Ottawa?"

"Because it's the closest city less than two hours away." It's a lot easier to plan a full day of activities in a city with actual tourist draw.

Before long, we pull into the underground parking lot near the National Gallery. It's Canada's largest art museum, and it's a work of art in itself. Cream stone pillars separate walls of glass along the front of the building, and a multifaceted glass structure rises from the center. It takes up at least a square city block; we should be able to spend most of the day wandering around inside without seeing the same thing twice.

Though the cashier gives me a funny look for wearing sunglasses indoors, everything is fine until we get to the end of the admissions process.

"And if you step over to the cloakroom, they can check your bags for you."

My heart stops, and Mari tenses beside me. "Um, we'd rather keep them with us."

Translation: You're not touching the damn bags. Out of the corner of my eye, I see Mari tighten her grip on the straps of her bag.

The cashier shakes her head and points to the small print on a sign posted off to the side: "Backpacks must be checked."

Goddamn stupid bureaucratic bullshit!

Gritting my teeth so hard they creak, I slide the tickets back along the counter. "Never mind, then."

There goes my plan for the day.

I get my money back, and Mariella and I head outside. My hands clench and release, and I want to take one of the stones out of my backpack and throw it through one of their oversized windows. As soon as we're away from the building, I exhale and look down at Mari.

"Sorry." I rub the back of my neck. "Next time I'll read the fine print."

"It's okay," Mari signs, stepping closer. "It was cold in there anyway."

"Yeah?" My lip twitches, but it can't break into a full smile. All that work to plan out a day of events to keep her mind off tonight, and I strike out on step one. How messed up is that?

"Well, umm, we'll find something else to do." I pull out my phone and open up the browser, but then Mariella's smile stretches into a grin. Her hands come up and she signs, "How crazy would they think we are if we tried to argue two bags full of rocks past security?"

This time, it's only a second before I smile back. "Pretty damn insane."

Mari starts giggling, and it bubbles out of her soundlessly. Within seconds, she's laughing so hard her face is red, and I'm laughing nearly as hard. It's not that funny, but finding anything at all to laugh about, today of all days, makes the release of hysterics that much better.

When we can see where we're going again, we walk across the street and down a trail to a small grassy space overlooking the locks that separate the Rideau Canal from the Ottawa River. Grinning, we walk along the edge of the water, watching the boats pass below us. Just after the canal widens, Mari puts her hand on my arm.

My skin instantly heats up. She still avoids physical contact with everyone except her mom and K.T., so when she touches me—when *she* reaches out and touches me instead of the other way around—it's like an electric shock. The good kind. The kind that leaves you energized and buzzing with warmth and heat and happy thoughts. It's so strong this time that I have to blink to clear my vision and make sure I'm actually paying attention.

"What's up, Mari?"

"Can we do that?" she signs, pointing down to the river.

I follow her finger. "What? Go out on a boat?"

"A canoe," she fingerspells. "It's a nice day."

When I look again, I notice the smaller boats moving along the edges of the canal. I smile. "You're the birthday girl. If you want a canoe, we'll get a canoe."

I offer my hand, holding my breath until she takes it. She smiles at me—a light, free smile—and my heart beats harder. Whatever happens when the time runs out and the clock strikes twelve, at least I gave her today. At least she had this moment where the sun was shining, her eighteenth birthday was hers to do with as she wanted, and she could pretend her whole life was laid out before her.

And at least I got to spend it with her.

We spend *hours* in that damn canoe. Nearly capsize it once when Mari stands up too fast to try to pet a duck that's paddling past the boat. Water splashed over the side, drenching our pants. Luckily, that happened *after* we had lunch in the five-star waterfront restaurant Mari picked. I don't think they would have let us in smelling like canal water.

Later, we walk through the little shops near the edge of the water, and I buy anything Mari looks at for more than a minute. By the end of the day, all the extra pockets of our backpacks are stuffed with souvenirs, and Mariella can't stop smiling.

After we change clothes, I guide us downtown. We're walking close together but not touching. At least, not until Mari gently links her arm through mine and rests her head against me.

I don't know if my heart is pounding or if it's stopped altogether. I don't know if I'm breathing or holding my breath. Are there people surrounding us on the streets or have they all vanished? I don't know. I don't care.

All of my awareness has shrunk down to the points of contact between Mariella and me—her hand pressing against my forearm through the fabric of my shirt, her shoulder bumping into my elbow, her forehead resting against my tricep. I want to slide my arm around her shoulders and pull her closer, but I'm afraid to move, afraid to ask for too much and ruin the moment or scare her off. I hold my breath and keep walking as if I have all the time in the world, as if we aren't ignoring a deadline that's looming closer every second.

When we reach the restaurant—our second five-star stop of the day—her parents, Horace, and K.T. are there with a pile of presents and huge grins. As soon as she sees them, Mari straightens, pulling away from me. I have to remind myself not to be stupider than I need to be to keep myself from pulling her back.

"Happy birthday, Mariella!" everyone shouts, grabbing the attention of everyone at the nearby tables. Strangers grin and call out birthday greetings, adding their wishes to her family's.

The rest of the night passes in a blur of food and jokes and music. We have an early dinner and then head to a concert at a small venue featuring one of Mariella's new favorite artists. I already know all the songs because Mari's had them playing in the background on near-repeat all week.

Even halfway through the day, I wasn't convinced this birthday trip was a good idea. Was she playing along or actually enjoying herself? Did this feel like a celebration or a last supper on death row? Then, during the concert, Mari looks at me, her eyes lighter than I've ever seen them and her smile even brighter than it was this morning, and signs, "Thank you."

It should prove she's enjoying this, that today took her mind off what's coming a few hours from now. It should make me feel better.

It doesn't.

All it does is introduce me to a glimpse of the girl Mariella should be, show me what it might be like if she survives this night and walks away in one piece.

If she survives.

Watching her sway to the music, mouthing the words even if she can't sing along, I know she'll survive. Even if I have to trade my life to make sure it happens, Orane is not taking her out of the world. Even if I'm not here to see her transform into what I know she will be, that bastard is not allowed to have her.

I won't let it happen.

Because as stupid and impossible and ridiculous as it is, I love her, and I'm not letting someone else I love disappear if I can do something to stop it.

Thirty-Four

Mariella

Friday, September 12 – 11:51 PM

We left the concert early to get home before midnight—K.T. begging my parents for permission to spend the night while we drive home—but we gave ourselves too much time. Now all we have left is the waiting.

I hate waiting. I *really* hate waiting. Especially when it's not for something pleasant, like a present or a concert. Hudson's trick of taking me out of town, away from the reminders of what was coming, was brilliant, but the last hour has been like knowing I'm about to get a root canal without any anesthesia. Or maybe more like preparing to walk into a sentencing with a fifty-fifty shot of a death-row verdict.

However, now that midnight is minutes away, I wish I could go back and wait some more. Anything to not be standing in the middle of my bedroom on my eighteenth birthday wearing silver and chunks of semi-precious stones like armor, about to head into a battle against a man I once thought was an angel.

"Remember to hold it by the chain," Hudson says as he hands me the nightingale pendant. He constructed a cage for the little bird, a contraption made of silver wire and bits of gemstones that's barely strong enough to keep the energy swirling inside from reaching me.

I glance at K.T., but she's sitting with her back against the wall, her eyes closed. Unlike Hudson and me, K.T. actually needs full nights of sleep, and she hasn't been getting them. She's held together well, but part of me is glad she'll get to go back to something close to a normal life tomorrow. One way or the other, this has to end tonight.

"With the stones blocking him, he shouldn't be able to get into your head as well," Hudson explains for the fifteenth time. "But he's known you for so long he's going to have a strong hold on you. Once you're in there, K.T. will hold the door open, and I'll be right behind you. You need to concentrate on—"

I raise my hand and place it over his mouth to get him to stop talking. His lips keep moving even though he doesn't make a sound. He kisses my fingers. Warmth spreads down my hand and up my arm, and I suppress a shiver, shoving it to the side. Whatever this may be between us, now isn't the time to do anything about it.

Pulling my hand away and shaking it to get rid of the tingling scattered across my palm, I quickly sign, "Calm down. I'm already nervous."

Simultaneously, we glance at the clock on my nightstand. 11:58.

Hudson closes his eyes for a second before crouching down in front of K.T. to make sure she's with us. By the time all three of us gather in the middle of the room, eyes wide and waiting for the first sign of the portal, time is almost up. One minute before midnight, K.T. wraps her arms around my waist and pulls me tight.

"Good luck," she whispers. When she pulls back to look at me, her blue eyes are nearly drowned in unshed tears. "Hurry back, okay?"

I bite my lip and nod, but then we all flinch.

Bright orange light floods the room, and with it comes an icy wind that bites into my bones. Hudson steps closer, his attention locked on the portal and the tendrils of light beating against the shield created by the gemstones. We can't carry enough with us to keep it up. We have to go in with what we're wearing. Without turning toward me, Hudson's hand finds mine. Holding each other tight, we both take a breath and jump into Hell.

Orane's world is in chaos. The opera hall is crumbling and the cherry trees are bare, but the willow tree is triple its usual size. The once-lush ground is a desert, and the crystalline lake has become a roiling black mass.

Hudson told me that Calease's world started decaying as soon as he fought her control. Maybe I've been doing the same thing. Maybe I've managed to weaken him. Then again, "weak" is a relative word. Orane can create buildings in the blink of an eye and has the ability to probe into my mind for my darkest fears and worst faults. An overgrown tree and a cracking façade are nothing to gloat over. I need to face down the man himself.

"Happy birthday, my sweet nightingale," Orane coos. He's standing at the edge of the cobblestone path, between the cherry orchard and the willow tree, but his voice seems to come from everywhere at once. It echoes across his world and inside my head. "You do not look like yourself tonight. The last human who came to face me protected by those designs lasted all of a minute."

He's taunting me, knowing I can't answer. He's already taken away that ability. In his mind, he's already won. This entire meeting is for my benefit. A punishment.

The energy around the nightingale flares, tendrils escaping the confines of the silver cage and reaching out for me. My legs tremble, and my throat goes dry. I have to force myself to keep walking. He's trying to use my own fear against me, make it overwhelm everything else until I cower at his feet and surrender.

If Orane succeeds, I'll never see my parents, K.T., or Hudson again. I'm risking everything for the chance to live a life I willingly turned my back on before. The irony is not lost on me.

"Even now you cling to the tokens I sent you." Orane laughs and moves closer, his voice echoing inside my head and his step sending ripples through the ground under our feet. "It is endearing. Though your taste in champions is poor."

Hudson stiffens but doesn't say anything. He slides closer and presses his hand against my lower back, energy pulsing into my body. He's like a conduit, passing power directly to me. It helps, grounding me and giving me the extra bit of strength I need.

Using the stones and Hudson as an anchor, I close my eyes and reach down into the core of the dreamworld. I touched it before, the power that makes everything I see and hear and touch in this place possible, but that was just a glimpse. That was playing in a puddle compared to jumping into the ocean.

On the back of the unicorn, the energy buzzed. Guided by the power in the stones I'm wearing, there isn't a buzz; the power is pure music. It's every instrument I've ever heard, from the bell-like tones of a glockenspiel to the bass thunder of tympani. The melody is impossible to capture, but within that gorgeous chaos, something pulls at my chest, making my heart ache and my eyes burn.

I'm aware of everything around me, even with my eyes closed. I feel the way Orane is directing the power under the surface of what we see, pulling energy away from the façade of the world and using it to supercharge his own abilities.

But Hudson is doing the same thing, channeling the dreamworld's energy, sucking it out of the air and pushing it into the stones we're wearing. Compared to the two of them, the area around me is nearly a void, a calm spot in a struggle between opposing currents. The deeper I reach into the magic of this world, the further the stillness spreads.

Slowly moving closer, Orane laughs.

"And your plan is to do what now? Nothing? Is this a surrender?"

Hell no, this isn't surren•er.

The ground ripples, and Hudson wraps his arm around my waist, steadying me. I picture a marble wall and build it high, encasing my mind and pushing Orane out. With each foot of marble that appears, the music shifts, growing louder as the melody changes, becoming less dense, less complex. Higher and higher the walls climb until they meet at the top like a marble igloo. The moment those walls close off, I open my eyes and gasp.

Okay. That works. I actually built a wall.

Hudson spins, his hands on the smooth white stone, searching for a way out.

"What the hell? What good does this do? He—"

I grab his arm and sign, "I built it."

"*You* did? But—"

The world trembles and shakes, the ground below us rolling like waves on the ocean. My stone igloo absorbs the energy, more supple than any stone should be, but it's not immune to the pressure. Tiny fractures appear. This protection won't last forever.

Hudson didn't regain his memories until he was back in the dreamworld. I have to keep Orane at bay long enough to find mine.

"Am I suddenly so frightening?" Orane's voice echoes in time with the quaking ground. I use my grip on the energy of his world to keep our little section stable, but it won't last for long. "How many times have you begged to stay with me forever? Why does it scare you to know that was exactly what I planned?"

I pull harder on the energy below my feet, and the music shifts again, the myriad of instruments dropping away until all that's left is a piano. Mom's upright piano.

It's the song she plays every night before she goes to sleep, the one I would sneak out to the landing to listen to without her knowing. The one I could never sing for Orane. I thought it was because the song belonged to Mom, but it doesn't.

The song isn't hers.

It's *mine.*

I wrote that song in elementary school. My first and only composition. Mom gave me the knowledge to write it, but the melody was mine. That's why she plays it every night, hoping against hope that one night I will come back down and play it with her.

Tears stream from my eyes in rivers as my own life hits me like an avalanche, ten years of forgotten moments streaming into my head until the weight of it all pushes me to my knees.

Sensation disappears. It's as though I'm floating in the center of a crystal globe, watching my own life play across the surface like a movie. It's peaceful here. Emotions, sounds, and colors are all muted, their edges dulled, but the closer the moments flashing before my eyes come to the present, the faster they stream. The louder the music plays. The brighter everything becomes.

The crystal globe shatters into multicolored smoke, a rainbow of color and light swirling around me faster and faster, closer and closer, until it seeps under my skin, memories reunited with the person they were stolen from.

My eyes open slowly when the tremors get worse. I'm thrown against the wall, my shoulder slamming into solid stone. Orane's voice echoes across the world, but this time it's barely audible inside my head.

"You are trying to steal what does not belong to you anymore. That, I will not abide. I will give you one last chance, child. Give me what I want, and I will give you your life."

For less than a hundredth of a second, I consider it. Can I really get Hudson and myself out in one piece by giving up something I've lived without for years?

A part of me wants to cave in, the same part that was fooled into believing he loved me. But with each piece of my mind I restore, each piece of myself I reclaim, it's easier to look back at the last ten years and see every moment he lied to me.

All I have to do is listen to his voice. I remember every false promise and every description of what our lives would be like if I could join him here forever. Every single lie. He sounded like this every time he told me he loved me. Every time, his voice was sweet and apologetic with the tiniest hint of laughter.

Looking back on all the waste—the time and energy and friendships I will never get back—fury rises within me, giving me strength and burning away my fear. I grab Hudson's hand and shove his palm against the stone, trying to make him understand what I want him to do. The marble around us is cracking. I need him to pour his energy into the wall and stabilize it. I need more time. Just a little more time.

"You cannot defeat me, and you cannot hide. I could find you anywhere, Mariella."

Hudson reinforces the walls, but it doesn't stop new cracks from forming. His grip on the dreamworld's energy is too weak. He barely buys me the time I need to adjust my hold on the nightingale pendant and get ready for the only endgame I have.

Orane's scream makes the world shudder. The wall shatters into dust, and Orane is there waiting, his hand outstretched and his fingers spread like claws reaching for my throat.

I hold up my nightingale pendant, dodging his strike and letting his hand close around the silver birdcage. He hisses, smoke rising as the stones burn his skin. I yank on the chain and the birdcage breaks open like Hudson designed it to. I catch the nightingale as it swings out of Orane's hand. Orane growls and reaches for me again, but my hand is already flying for his cheek.

The physical power behind the strike is nothing. I'm exhausted and weak and human. But that doesn't matter. I'm pressing the nightingale pendant against his skin. It ties me to him. It contains a tiny piece of my soul—and my voice—but it also contains a tiny piece of him.

A door opens between our minds. For less than a second, I'm staring into an expanse so vast I can't comprehend how one person can contain it.

"Give it back." I grip the first thread of energy I can catch from the other side of the doorway, and I give it a powerful yank.

It's like unraveling a tornado.

Orane screams. I scream with him, and for the first time in over a week, I hear my own voice. Lightning shoots up my arm, sparking and burning and freezing all at once. It slams into my mind, and my head snaps back. Thousands of people are screaming for help. The voices of every child Orane ever hunted. Bits of all of them are here.

All I want is what he took from me, but once the flow starts, I don't know how to make it stop. Everything Orane kept locked away—his memories and the pieces of others he stole over the centuries—rushes into my head in a burning stream of light and color. I'm screaming my throat raw, but no matter how hard I try to pull away, the connection won't break.

My mind hisses and crackles like a piece of wood about to split in a fire. Before the pressure and the pain and the fear and the sorrow pouring in can shatter me, the connection breaks. Like the door slammed shut from the other side.

I drop, something solid barely catching me on the way down.

Thirty-Five

Hudson

Saturday, September 13 – 12:00 AM

Her scream is like a siren's call. It's beautiful and terrifying, sending jolts through my body. It's also a signal. A pulse blasts through the world like the first shockwave after a nuclear explosion.

It hits me square in the chest and knocks me off my feet. I barely lift my arms in time to catch Mari when she drops.

Her eyes flutter open and shut, but all I see is white.

I duck, covering Mari as something goes flying low over our heads. Holy shit. Was that an entire cherry tree?

It was.

The shockwave shattered Orane's control over this world. The black lake has become a cyclone, tearing limbs off the willow and bricks out of the opera hall. The sky is a mass of storm clouds in impossible shades of dark green and red, lit up by large strikes of violet lightning.

I have to get us the hell out of here. Mariella hasn't moved.

"Mari!" I lean over her, chest pounding so hard it's like all of my organs are pulsing in time with my heart. "Get *up*! Mariella!"

Mari shifts, lids fluttering faster, each blink lasting longer. Her eyes—the same honey-brown she came here with, thankfully—open, and she gasps.

Before I can say a word, her hand grabs the collar of my shirt and tugs me out of the way as a huge willow branch flies by where my head would've been.

Time to go.

Swinging Mari into my arms, I scramble to my feet and run for the portal. Dodging flying debris and jumping trenches that open under my feet, I keep running. Holding Mari tight against my chest, I run. I try not to worry that she's barely moved. I try not to worry that the portal seems to be getting farther away and the space between more impassable. There has to be a way to make it through the end of a world alive.

Thirty-Six

Mariella

Saturday, September 13 – 12:00 AM

The knowledge and the abilities I pulled from Orane all activate at once.

I can see the path we traveled falling into a black void, and the world in front of us is collapsing too fast. Hudson won't make it out before this world disappears unless I can ease the way.

Fear forces me to think clearly, and I grasp a thread of power I didn't have before. My nightingale pendant is still in one hand. I grip it tight. Acting on an instinct I barely understand, I breathe out.

Everything in our path tumbles out of the way.

I bring up one hand. The ground in front of us levels.

We're almost to the portal, but that might not matter. The air is pulling us backward. It's the suction of a world collapsing. I put my hand on Hudson's chest, silently urging him forward, close my eyes, and pray.

Hudson loses his step. He recovers, but not enough. Diving, Hudson throws me forward as far as he can.

No! I will not lose him, not after everything.

Moving faster than I thought was possible, I twist and use my last bit of strength to grab his hand and pull him with me. The momentum Hudson gave me isn't enough.

Using every ounce of what I drew from Orane's mind, I propel us forward and yank him through the door. He groans in relief as we both land on my bedroom floor.

"Are you guys okay?" K.T. whispers. She places her hands on my cheeks and peers into my eyes. "Mari?"

Hudson leans over me. "Mariella? You with me?"

My lips move, but the words don't come. All I get is a slight curve that feels like a smile.

"Thank God."

I barely hear him. There are so many voices and so many images flashing through my head. Emotions that aren't mine send my pulse flying and plummeting as chills crawl through my body. I'm drowning under the weight of everything I stole from Orane. It's all a jumbled mess in my mind. Without some idea how to control it, I'm losing ground fast.

Hudson rests his hand against my shoulder and stares down at me with something wonderful in his deep black eyes.

I've been silently begging for help, but neither of them has seen it. Neither of them has heard. Hudson finally notices something. His eyes narrow.

"Mari? What is it? What's wrong?"

K.T. pops up, the color draining from her face. I manage to open my mouth, but images of people I've never seen and places I've never been swarm my vision. I can't separate them, and I don't know what's going on. Fear swamps me, buzzing through my veins like a swarm of locusts, but so many other emotions hit me that all of them cease to mean anything. They are pure energy, my body is an overloaded circuit, and I can't keep my mind from taking the only course left and shutting down.

I give in to the blackness as Hudson calls my name.

Thirty-Seven

Hudson

Saturday, September 13 – 12:01 AM

"Mari?" I almost shout, but I catch myself at the last second. Even so, I hear a door open down the hall and know I have to get the hell out of here.

My chest aches and my hands shake when I pull away from Mariella and dive for the open window. I'm barely out of sight when her door opens and I hear Dana's voice.

"Girls, I thought I heard—oh my God! Mari?"

Forcing myself to keep moving along the eaves of the house, I climb in the next window and slide into the guest bedroom. Horace is awake and waiting for me.

"What happened?" he demands as soon as I appear.

"Don't know."

The voices in the next room get louder, and Dana starts crying. I take a deep breath to ease the trembling ball of fear in my chest, open the door, and hurry into the next room.

"What happened? Is everything all right?" I hear myself asking the questions, but it doesn't sound like me.

K.T. rattles off Mari's address to someone on the phone. Shit. They're calling 911. Of course they are, but I'd bet Horace's entire fortune that the hospital isn't going to be able to do shit. They won't even be able to tell us what's wrong.

Everything was fine until the end. There was an explosion of white light, and then Mari dropped, her eyes rolling back and her body going limp except for her fist locked around her nightingale pendant. I thought it was shock, but what if it's not? What if I didn't act fast enough to save her from a danger I never even saw?

My entire body goes cold, and numbness crawls out from the center of my chest. Sooner than I expected, paramedics shove me aside as they rush into the room. From that moment, everything seems to happen in fast-forward. They check her vitals, ask a series of rapid-fire questions—most of which K.T. answers—and then strap a brace around her neck, lift her onto a stretcher, and carry her out of the room.

K.T. follows the stretcher, but I grab her arm, holding her back until everyone else is out of earshot. The last thing I want is to drag someone else into this, but if Mari is going to the hospital, I need an inside man. Someone who knows what's going on. I came back with the ability to heal in seconds. Who knows what Mari picked up?

"Call Dr. Carroll," I whisper. "Tell him what happened, and tell him to get his ass to the hospital."

K.T.'s eyes widen, and she dials as we head downstairs. We jump into the Camaro with Horace, following the ambulance's blindingly bright lights across town.

After that, it's a waiting game. For the second time tonight.

We're not family, so we're relegated to the outer waiting room. Carroll stops in to see us when he arrives, so that he can get the full story.

He's not what I expected. Tall and lanky, he's all arms and legs and can't have hit thirty yet. His sandy-brown hair is messy, but his expression is tight and serious. I answer his questions as best as I can before he runs in through the doors we're not allowed to pass.

Minutes tick by. Hours. We're still here. And Mariella is still in there.

The numbness sinks deeper until all I feel is my heart pounding ten times faster and harder than normal.

My mind goes through what happened in the dreamworld over and over again. Was there *anything* else I could have done? I'm not sure it matters now.

I don't know what happened or what's wrong or what they're doing to her or if we'll ever get her out of here. All I know is she *has* to wake up because I can't handle losing her now.

Carroll eventually comes to collect us, shuffling us toward the room they've placed Mariella in.

"They've admitted her," he says.

I cringe. That *can't* be a good sign.

"They're letting me consult," Carroll tells us as we hurry through the halls. "Without her parents actually switching me onto the case as her primary, that's the most I can do."

We walk into the room, and I can't tear my eyes away from Mariella. She looks green, and she's convulsing continuously, having tiny seizures that must be causing her a lot of pain if the grimace on her face is any indication.

The numbness that's kept me together for the past few hours thaws a little, replaced by a thousand tiny knives stabbing me in the chest. I was so sure if we could make it past her birthday, everything would go back to normal. What *happened*?

The doctor—a tired-looking woman holding a clipboard—is talking to Dana and Frank when we walk in. "The convulsions started after we undressed her for the exam, and they haven't abated. The movement makes getting scans or X-rays difficult, but from what I can tell the convulsions are not related to a seizure disorder. At least, not one I've ever encountered before."

"Seizure disorder?" Dana asks, horror infusing her breathless voice.

The doctor shakes her head, but her eyebrows are pinched. "With most states of persistent unconsciousness and comas, this type of movement is highly abnormal."

"Coma?" Frank repeats as Dana leans heavily against him.

The seizures started *after* they undressed her? Where's the nightingale? She was clutching that thing like a lifeline when she collapsed. I look around, but there's no telltale glow and no gleam of silver.

"Now, given what you told me about her previous speech issues, it's possible that—"

"Where did they take her things? Her clothes and jewelry?"

Everyone stares at me, even K.T. and Carroll. I don't look at anyone but Dana. She's the one I have to convince.

"I wouldn't ask if it wasn't important, Dana."

She stares at me, her red-rimmed eyes narrow and her lips tight, but she nods and glances at the doctor.

"If you go to the nurse's station and tell them Dr. Leventhall authorized you to collect them, they'll get everything for you."

I'm out the door before she's finished talking. A few minutes later, I jog back to Mari's room, searching through the bag as I go. The necklace is at the bottom of the pile. I hit the door with my shoulder to open it as I unclasp the nightingale pendant's silver chain, adding on an amber charm.

Something about the pendant catches my eye, and I pause inside the door. Something's different.

Inspect it later, I tell myself. *Test the theory now.*

"It'll be okay," I whisper, bending over Mari and wrapping the chain around her wrist. The pendants fall into her right hand, and she curls her fist tight around them.

For a second, her heart rate spikes and every muscle in her body seizes. My body tenses in response, my pulse jumping as high as hers.

"What's happening?!" Dana screeches.

Dr. Leventhall shoves me out of the way with an angry glare. But then Mari sucks in a huge breath and heaves a long sigh of relief.

The doctor checks her vitals and the readouts from a few of the machines, but my eyes stay on Mari's face.

She's at rest. Her face is relaxed. The only tension in her body is in her fist locked tight around her pendants. If not for the doctor hovering over her and the various wires and tubes stuck in her arms, I'd believe she was sleeping.

Holy hell. It worked.

Everyone is staring at me, but my mind has gone completely blank, emptied by shock and relief. Luckily, I don't have to think of an explanation for Mari's sudden stillness. Carroll does it for me.

"Odd as it sounds, I've seen stranger things happen." Everyone looks at him like he told us a pink elephant might know the answer, but Carroll smiles. "We doctors want our patients to believe we can solve every problem and answer every question, but there's a lot to the world, to human beings in particular and the human *brain* even more so, that we don't understand yet."

Leventhall doesn't seem to agree, but she takes advantage of the situation anyway, wheeling Mari away to run as many tests as they can. When they leave, all I can think is that Carroll better stay on his toes. He's gonna have to come up with a plausible explanation for anything unusual that turns up on those tests. This hospital has no idea what they're actually dealing with.

"The tests were all inconclusive," Dr. Leventhall says later, her nose scrunched. "I've never seen activity patterns like this."

"But what—I mean, is there damage?" Frank asks.

"Not that I can see," the doctor hedges. "There's actually an unusually *high* level of activity. In fact, these levels would be considered high even if she were conscious."

Leventhall rambles on about cortexes, but my mind is racing.

What would *my* brain look like in a scan? More importantly, what would my scans have looked like hours after I escaped Calease? I walk over to Carroll and tug him out of the room, whispering my theories.

"We need to get her out of here," I insist. "If she wakes up with the ability to turn invisible or something, we don't want the doctors turning her into an experiment."

Carroll's eyes bug out. "Is that a possibility?"

"I don't *know*! That's not the point!"

"Right. Right. Sorry." Carroll flushes and looks away. After a deep breath, he nods. "There's always home care, but we'd have to convince her parents it's the better option. Which might not be easy."

"I think you need to tell them the truth, kid."

Carroll and I turn toward Horace's voice, but I can't quite believe what he's telling me.

"They've got the right to know, 'specially now."

Jesus. He's serious. My hands go cold when I think about sitting down in front of Dana and Frank and spilling out a story like mine. They live in a world of music lessons and PTA meetings and green construction and civic pride. What would they do with a story about demons and parallel universes and magic?

"They're not gonna believe me! Why would they?"

One of Horace's bushy white eyebrows climbs up. "Besides the fact that you got three people backing up your story? Plus Emily's case, and that little vanishing-wounds trick."

"Vanishing wounds?" Carroll asks.

"It's the only way they're going to let you get her out of here in time," Horace says.

There are no gray areas here. I have to make a decision. One of them is the right choice, one of them isn't, and I have no goddamn clue which is which.

If I don't tell Frank and Dana, Mariella stays here and we'll have a hell of a time getting her out if she wakes up. *When* she wakes up.

If I tell them and they don't believe me, they'll lock me out. Or lock me *up*.

But if I tell them and they *do* believe me, we actually have a chance of getting her out before anyone discovers *exactly* how weird the things going on inside her head are.

Horace is right. As much as it sucks, I have to take the chance.

"This isn't funny, Hudson." Dana's voice snaps like a whip, and her hands clench like she wants to hit me. "I don't know if you're being purposefully cruel or if this is some misguided attempt to comfort us, but you can't expect me to believe—"

"He's tellin' you the truth, Dana."

Dana's mouth gapes as she stares at Horace, her skin flushed. "Don't be ridiculous."

Horace glances at me. "Show her your magic trick."

Exhaling heavily, I pull my pocketknife out and flick it open. Horace grabs a bunch of paper towels from the connected bathroom and holds them under my hand. Across from us, Dana pulls in a shaky breath.

"What are you doing?"

"I'm not making this up, Dana. I wouldn't do that to you."

Before I can reconsider, I slide the blade across the palm of my hand. I barely feel it when the skin parts and blood starts flowing; I'm too focused on Dana's face. She looks a little green, but when I hold up my palm, her eyes are locked on the open cut. I'm exhausted, drained from everything that happened tonight, but it starts to heal eventually. After a minute, the blood stops flowing. After two, the scar is completely gone.

I wipe my hand off with one of the towels Horace hands me and show her my clean, wound-free hand. Carroll is bouncing and biting his lip as his face flushes bright red. His eyes bug out, and he looks like he's a few seconds away from bursting.

"Oh." Dana sways and almost falls.

"And you're saying these demons are why Mari stopped talking?" Frank asks, his eyes bright. "And why she ended up here?"

I have to swallow hard before my voice is steady enough to be heard. "Yes."

"You *believe* them?" Dana stares at her husband, mouth still hanging open.

Frank takes her face in his hands and kisses her hard. She gasps, but he leans back before she can react.

"Dana, it explains *everything*," he says. "We saw how different Mariella was once Hudson showed up. It explains why she changed, and it explains why she's here. They're telling us they can help her wake up. All the doctors want to do is run more tests and inject her with more drugs to see what happens. If there's a chance Hudson is right, are you going to give up on that?"

He's nearly breathless by the time he's done, but I think it worked. In the middle of that rant, the color started rising in Dana's cheeks. By the end, her lips are trembling as they curl into something almost like a smile.

"You always were a little crazy," she whispers.

The words jumpstart my heart. I don't even have a chance to ask her if that means she'll let Carroll take over before she takes Frank's hands off her cheeks, squeezes them tight, and then looks at me.

"What do you need us to do?"

Thirty-Eight

Hudson

Saturday, September 20 – 9:21 AM

It took the doctors a week to admit they had no clue what was going on. We were lucky none of them were in the room when Mari's body heated up so fast steam started rising from her skin. It was gone as quickly as it happened, but it made me fight harder to get her the hell out of there.

As soon as they could, Dana and Frank switched Mariella to Carroll's care and ordered a medical transport van to bring her to the mini-hospital room Carroll set up in the den downstairs. With substantial financial and legal help from Horace.

I try not to pace as Frank signs a stack of forms to release Mari against medical recommendation. Leventhall makes them jump through a lot of red tape before she lets anyone shift Mari to the transport stretcher. I hate that Mari hasn't woken up, but I'll breathe a little easier when she's out of this place. It smells like Lysol and death.

On the way out, Horace's phone rings. He checks the screen, and his eyebrows pull together.

"She never calls me," he mutters as he picks up. "Afternoon, Gracie. How're you—"

His mouth is open, frozen in the middle of his greeting, and his skin leaches of all color.

"What in the name of all seven sins did she do that for?"

Another pause, and this time his eyes nearly bug out of his head. "Pushed him down the *stairs*? Nadette? *My* Nadette?"

Horace walks away, moving fast until he's halfway across the parking lot. Dana glances at me, but I shrug. He called the woman Gracie. If I remember right, that's his daughter-in-law.

He's back before our little cavalcade even makes it to the medical transport.

"Hate to leave right now, but I've got a bit of a family crisis. My sixteen-year-old granddaughter got it in her head to run away." He says it like it doesn't matter, but his eyes are tense and he's fidgeting with his keys. "Apparently she's already been gone a day."

"You've done plenty, Horace." Dana hugs him and kisses his cheeks, bestowing a warm but wobbly smile. "I hope everything turns out well with your granddaughter."

"Never woulda expected it of Nadette," he mutters as he pats me on the shoulder. "Her sister Jessica, sure. That girl'd take flight like a dandelion seed. But Nadette was always a rational little thing."

"Be careful, okay?" I grip his shoulder and make sure he stops to look at me, pays attention to what I'm saying. "Make sure you take those stones with you."

"Kid, I ain't messin' with these demons of yours if I don't have to." He starts walking off, but then stops and scuttles back. "Dana, you mind lookin' after the kid while I'm gone?"

"Of course." But then Dana glances at me and smirks. "Though I doubt we would've gotten rid of him even if I said no."

Pretty much. As much as I hate it, I've become crazy good at sneaking into their house.

I help Carroll get Mariella set up on the bed in the den, then pull a chair up to her bedside. I stay long after everyone else has gone to sleep, exhausted.

Holding her hand, I run my thumb along her fingers.

Wake up, Mari. Wake up, wake up, wake up, I chant in my head. *Please wake up.*

The door opens, and I look up as Dana comes into the room. "How is she?"

"The same." I whisper like Mariella is sleeping and we're trying not to wake her.

Dana leans over the bed, her expression tight as she reaches out and traces the line of Mariella's face with her fingertips. This has to be hard for her. She's trusting me with something precious, and right now all we can do is wait.

"You're really sure she'll wake up?" Dana whispers.

"I'd stake my life on it. I just don't know when."

It takes a moment, but Dana slowly pulls back and nods. Resting her hand on my shoulder, she leans down and presses a kiss to my head. It takes every bit of concentration I possess to not tense up and jump away. Even on her good days, Mom wasn't exactly affectionate. Despite everything, Dana seems to have accepted me into her family on some level. And I'm terrified of letting her down.

"Take care of her, Hudson," Dana whispers before she turns and walks back upstairs.

Once she's gone, I take a deep breath—one that's too shaky for my liking—and focus on Mari.

I hear a crackling sound as the energy in the air spikes. Everything in the room rattles and shifts, tilting toward Mariella. I tense, ready to deflect anything that goes flying toward her, but it doesn't move. I watch the lamp on her nightstand wobble in a circle like an off-balance top before finally settling down.

I collapse against the chair and rub my hands over my face. Whatever is going on in her head is so much bigger than what I went through. I *want* to take care of her, but all I can do is wait. Wait for her eyes to open and wait for her to decide what happens after that.

Even if I want to take care of Mariella, there is no guarantee she's going to let me.

Thirty-Nine

Hudson

Monday, September 29 – 5:18 PM

The first two weeks of my life in Swallow's Grove blew past me with the speed and force of a bullet train running on rocket fuel. The past two have dragged, each second seeming to move slower than a sleeping sloth.

Mari has been home from the hospital for just over a week, but I'm going fucking stir-crazy.

There's nothing to fight. And if I try to put any more stones in this room, the floor might collapse into the basement under the weight. All the flat surfaces are filled with protective stones and others that exude health and positive energy—tourmaline in green, pink, red, gold, and brown; quartz; transparent pink and green calcite; chlorite phantom crystals; bixbite; pyromorphite; blue aventurine; astrophyllite; zoisite; and amber. Dawn is right. I could start my own store if I wanted to, but all the stones in the world won't give me a goddamn clue where to go from here.

I've done everything I can for Mari, so…what now?

Pacing the length of the room, I run my nails along my scalp. The answers I'm looking for are out there somewhere. How do I open a portal from this side? Can the demons be killed? Has anyone ever turned them down? Will I ever sleep again?

These creatures seem ancient, like they've been here since the dawn of time. I can't be the only person who has ever broken out of their clutches and lived. There have to be more like Mari and me. How in the world do I find people who have probably become masters of hiding in plain sight, though? My abilities are low-key. The only obvious difference about me is my eyes. What if someone had laser eyes like Cyclops, or ended up made of energy like Doctor Manhattan? Blending in might not be an option. They'd either get scooped up and experimented on, or have to go into deep hiding somewhere.

I force myself to sit down. Brushing Mari's bangs away from her face, I wonder if she'll have to go into hiding when she wakes up. What did facing Orane do to her?

The footsteps in the hall don't sound like Dana. Turning toward the door, I see K.T. and Dawn.

"She wanted to visit," K.T. says as she trails Dawn into the room.

"Brought you this, too." Dawn presses a striped stone, a large piece of tiger iron, into my hands before she leans over the bed, bending so close her nose almost brushes Mari's.

Running my thumb along the edge of the rough, circular rock, I take a breath. It's soft and barely audible, but I hear the chime of the stone's power in the back of my mind. A trickle of energy runs up my arm. As it passes through me, my muscles relax and the crick in my neck eases. It's like getting a massage from a ghost.

"Better?" Dawn asks without looking up.

"Yeah. Thanks." I roll the tiger iron between my hands, watching Dawn inspect Mariella with more attention to detail than a doctor.

After a minute she straightens, biting her lip. My grip on the stone gets tighter. I've kinda gotten used to Dawn coming up with solutions. When I saw her, I guess I expected—hoped—she'd do it again.

Forehead creased, Dawn walks toward the coffee table and runs one hand along the geodes, statues, and bowls of stone chips gathered there, almost like she's cataloging them.

"Have you heard from Horace?" K.T. asks.

Watching Dawn's inspection, I nod. "They tracked Nadette to Trenton. They think she was heading for Horace's place."

"And he wasn't there." I glance at K.T., but I can't see her face. She's sitting next to Mari, adjusting the blankets on the bed. "New Jersey is a long way to run from Florida."

"Depending on what she was running from, it might not have been far enough."

The words are out before I can catch them. K.T.'s eyes widen, and I remind myself that I've got no reason to think Nadette was running for the same reasons I did.

I grind my teeth and grip the tiger iron tighter as the tension creeps back into my body. Nadette's disappearance is one more situation I can't do shit about.

"Look, you've got to give me something to do here."

K.T. and I both look at Dawn.

"My mom has been driving me crazy, and I want to help," she says, planting her hands on her hips. "Don't tell me I'm too young to get involved because I'm already involved, so that argument won't hold water and—Gaia help me—I'll figure out something I can do without you if I have to, and I'll probably waste a whole lot of time or get myself into trouble, so you're better off giving me something to do, okay?"

"Dawn, I'd have to be stupid to say you couldn't help after everything you've *already* helped with," I tell her. "But I don't know what you can do."

A little of the determination fades, but the creases are back in her forehead.

"I mean, unless you can tell me how to open a door into the dreamworld and wipe out the demons? Or if you know how to track down other people who've lived through this, too."

She huffs, crosses her arms, and then freezes. Slowly, a smile stretches across her face and her eyes grow bright.

"I can do that."

"Do what?" K.T. asks.

"Help you look for other survivors."

Shaking my head, I ask, "How do you look for people who survived something most people don't know exists, and who probably work really hard not to be found?"

"No one can hide completely. There will be stories about people with strange abilities or *something* I'll be able to follow," Dawn says.

"Not just that."

We both look at K.T. She's smiling, focused, and nearly exuberant.

"You don't only look for the paranormal," K.T. says. "You look for the *ab*normal. Or things that are *too* normal."

Dawn seems to get it, but I'm lost. "Can something be *too* normal?"

K.T. nods. "But, to start with, we look for anomalies and outliers. That's how I found Dr. Carroll."

"She's right," Carroll says as he comes in with a fresh IV bag. "Doesn't hurt to look. At the worst, you end up in the same place you are now."

I stare at them all, one eyebrow arched. "Why do all of you seem to think I'd say no to this plan? Hell, I'll help if you tell me what I'm looking for."

Dawn grins and wraps her arms around my waist, resting her cheek against my stomach. The hug lasts for less than a second, and then she's grabbing K.T.'s shirt and pulling her out the door, pausing to warn me to watch out for an email with detailed research instructions.

Carroll smiles as he switches the IV bags. "It'll be good for them to have something to do. Especially K.T."

"No change with Emily?"

The smile drops. "No. Not that I expected there would be."

Carroll is slightly shorter than me and thin. Almost reedy. His movements, though, are swift and certain. I watch him carefully, comparing every move to the way the nurses at the hospital would perform the same task. He seems to know what he's doing.

I step back a little when Carroll moves toward one of the monitors, checking the reading on Mariella's brain waves.

"You don't trust me, do you?" Carroll asks.

Running my thumb along the piece of tiger iron in my hand, I wonder how the hell I'm supposed to answer that.

"Don't feel too bad," I say after a moment. "I don't trust most people."

He nods, pressing a button on the monitor, and then turns toward me. "It's all right. I want to make sure you know I'm going to do everything I can to get you the answers you need."

"Why?"

When he looks down at Mari, it's like he's not seeing her. It's like he's seeing someone else entirely.

"Because I've been looking for the same answers for the last twelve years, but nothing made sense until K.T. found me." Carroll stares at me, his brown eyes intense. "You don't have to trust me. *I* trust *you*."

The house has been quiet since K.T. and Dawn left a couple hours ago, so the sound of approaching footsteps pulls my attention to the door.

"I think I found a location," Carroll says as he comes into the room with a new IV bag.

"Location for what?" I keep holding Mari's hand but shift slightly for Carroll to get past.

"The clinic Horace is helping me set up."

I blink. "You're setting up a clinic?"

Carroll looks down at me, his nose wrinkled. "Well, I had to, or they would have asked a lot of questions when we bought the fMRI machine."

"We *bought* an fMRI?"

"Horace didn't tell you about this whole—" His mouth closes, and the confusion on his face clears. Shaking his head, he moves to sit on the end of Mari's bed. "Sorry. He was going to explain, but then he heard about Nadette..." Carroll trails off and shrugs.

"All right. *You* tell me."

"Ultimately, our goal is to figure out exactly how what has happened to you has affected your brain, and unlock the frequencies connecting people in comas to the dreamworld."

His eyes are bright, but it's not a happy brightness. More like the passion of a fanatic overtaking all reason. Carroll's hands fly as he talks about brain waves and electrical frequencies and research plans.

"Plus, if Dawn and K.T. are able to find other survivors and bring my study sample higher? I might actually be able to—"

"*What?!*"

Frank's shout stops Carroll midsentence. Dana comes running down the stairs as I head for Frank's office. Carroll follows.

"A *week*, Jacquelyn? A goddamn *week*?"

Frank stands behind his desk, his face bright red and his eyes bulging.

"What do you mean you *don't know*? How the hell do you not know how long your *only child* has been missing, Jacquelyn?"

Oh, hell. Foreboding crawls up my body, digging its claws in no matter how hard I try to shove it away and ignore it. Frank's mouth snaps shut as he listens to something. Whatever Jacquelyn says makes his face turn a deep red tinged with purple.

"I don't give a shit!" Frank screams. I've never seen him like this. He's so chill I never would've guessed he had this in him. "You waited a *week* to call the police. If something happens to Julian, you're fucking right it's your fault!"

Frank chucks his phone against the wall, and it falls to the floor in pieces. Dana and I stand in the doorway, not sure what to do.

"What happened to Julian?" Dana finally asks, her voice hesitant.

Frank laughs, but it's a desperate, hollow laugh. "I don't even know. Either he ran away or he's been abducted. My screw-up of a little sister *isn't sure*."

"Abducted!" Dana sways on her feet, and I reach out to steady her. Tears stream down her face, and her voice is thick and hoarse when she talks again. "Oh God, Frank. I knew we should have offered to take him the last time they were here."

Dana runs into Frank's arms, and I back off, letting them have some privacy.

Carroll's lips are pressed together, his head tilted toward Frank's office.

"Two missing kids connected to this family in a week." He takes a breath and shakes his head. "What are the chances this is a coincidence?"

I meet his eyes for a second before I pass him. "Honestly? Zilch."

Even knowing that, I also know there's nothing I can do to help them with something like this. I hope the kid is okay, but it's taking all my energy to help Carroll take care of Mariella, help Dawn and K.T. with their research, and, apparently, set up a clinic.

I can only face one fight at a time, and Mariella comes first.

Forty

Hudson

Monday, October 13 – 3:49 AM

I'm sitting in the armchair in Mariella's room when her eyes flutter open.

My heart stops as she raises her head and looks around, a smile growing on her face.

"Oh, good," she says. "I didn't miss it."

I bolt out of the chair, heart pounding and hands shaking.

It's almost four in the morning. All the light in the room is coming from the monitors Mariella is hooked to. Stepping closer, I hold my breath and watch her face for the slightest sign of life. She's perfectly still.

That wasn't a dream or wishful thinking. It felt real. It felt like the future.

I stand next to her bed for an hour. Nothing happens.

Slumping back into the armchair, I try to breathe in fours. Calm myself down.

My dreams aren't usually immediate, but they've always come true. So far.

Waiting has never been my strong suit, but I've been getting a crash course this month. Waiting for Mariella to wake up, waiting for Carroll to start his research, waiting for Dawn and K.T. to find information I can actually *use*. Even though they have a lead—some website called *The Mystical Demystifier*—they have to figure out how to get in touch with whoever runs it. Until they find a way to contact them, I can't *do* anything.

Pulling the chair closer to the bed, I take her hand and gently kiss her fingers.

"Come on, you're stronger than whatever is happening, Mari," I whisper to her. "Wake up. You have to wake up."

It's been almost a month, though. How much longer can she last like this?

How much longer can I?

Forty-One

Mariella

Wednesday, October 15 – 9:30 AM

Even with my eyes closed, I can sense everything in the room, including the furniture. The energy of the stones is like a symphony of distant wind chimes, and I sense the emotional energy of everyone in the house. Information seeps into my brain like water soaking into a dry sponge. Thoughts, emotions, memories, predictions of things that haven't happened yet. I sort through it all, trying to adjust to consciousness before anyone realizes I'm awake.

Doctor Carroll is humming show tunes as he adjusts the drip on my IV. Hudson is sitting in an armchair by the side of my bed, and my parents are both home, Mom cleaning the kitchen and Dad outside hacking apart a perfectly healthy shrub. I search their minds, looking for a date.

October 15.

It's been more than four weeks since my birthday. I have been asleep for *four* weeks.

Carroll leaves, on his way to find breakfast.

"I think she's up. Maybe?" Hudson's thoughts ring in my head as clearly as if he'd spoken aloud. Underneath the more conscious thoughts, I see the memory of a dream, one of his prophetic dreams. He's been jumping at false alarms ever since he dreamt I woke up. When he leans closer, I see my own face inside his head. Before I can open my eyes, he sighs and sits back. "Guess not."

New abilities weren't the only thing I stole from Orane. I ended up with more languages, memories, and information than I knew how to handle. It took time to sort through it all in my head, but I learned a lot about the dreamworld, a place the creatures who live there call Abivapna. Among other things, I learned that anyone who's had prolonged contact with Abivapna can hear projected thoughts. It's how the demons, the Balasura, talk to us across the dimensions.

I project my thoughts, hoping Hudson will hear me.

"You should have more faith in your instincts."

He nearly falls out of his chair, and I can't keep the smile off my face. I open my eyes as he lunges closer to the bed.

"Mari?" he whispers. His face is etched with lines that weren't there a month ago, but otherwise he looks exactly like I remember him. It felt like I spent years locked inside my own head, so long that I'd come back and everything and everyone would be different, but he's exactly like he was when I fell asleep. *I'm* the one who's different.

As much as I want to see my parents and K.T., as much as I want to reclaim my life, the draw of seeing Hudson is even stronger. The guy who went on a mission for answers and stumbled into a fight he hadn't signed up for. The guy who stepped up to help a stranger who didn't give him a single reason to stay. He stayed anyway, and I have a chance to *live* because of him.

His gaze searches my face but doesn't stray from my eyes for long. "Are you okay?"

"Be okay," he pleads in his head. "Talk to me, Mari. Be okay, please."

I picked up the ability to heal. It may feel odd to move after a month of near-stillness, like I can't quite remember what it's like to be in charge of my own arm, but I *can* move. My muscles haven't atrophied at all.

I smile, slowly reaching for him. He grips my hand tight when I slide my palm into his. There are bumps and rough patches on his skin—all his scars and callouses. Each mark on his skin is one more reason it's a miracle Hudson became the person he is now. A miracle that's staring at me with love in his dark eyes. The most wonderful part of seeing that is finally realizing what I should have known all along.

I love him, too.

"I'm fine, Hudson." My voice is low, almost a whisper, but he jumps as soon as I speak. I squeeze his hand tighter, rubbing my thumb along the back of his fingers. His eyes widen, and so does my grin. "Really. I'm okay."

Relief flows through his body, a wave of warmth that almost makes him collapse and leaves me smiling even wider. I feel his emotional shifts and hear his thoughts, my telepathic and empathic powers linking us together.

Glancing at the door to check for my parents, he whispers, "Did you—I mean, when you first woke up, did I hear you talking in my head?"

I grin. "Yes."

"Oh." He swallows. "If you can—well, can you *rea* thoughts, too?"

"Please say no," he adds in his head, a subconscious thought, quieter than others but definitely there.

My smile fades a little. I nod, and he looks down at my hand in his. Face flushing in a flash, Hudson's thoughts spin into a knot.

"Shit. She can hear—but what has she heard? What did I think? Could she hear me while she was asleep? How the hell can I stop thinking? Can she hear this?"

"Hudson, I'm sorry." Closing my eyes for a second, I imagine the power as a ball of white light. Taking that light, I shove it into a box and lock the stupid thing shut. Orane used these abilities to manipulate his victims, the thousands of children he's destroyed over the centuries. The last thing I want is to fall into the habit of using them the same way. Swallowing, I look up at Hudson and try to smile. "I'm sorry. I can stop. I stopped."

"It's okay." He smiles, and it looks a little forced, but only a little. "You already know my darkest, craziest secrets. What do I have to hide?"

All the things you don't know how to say out loud to me yet, I want to tell him.

Before I can open my mouth, there are footsteps on the stairs. I can sense Mom getting closer, walking down the steps and through the hall, hoping that what she'll find when she reaches my room will somehow be different.

Hudson pulls away, standing up and striding toward the doorway. When he appears, Mom stops moving. He smiles, and her pace nearly becomes a sprint as she screams for my dad.

I hold my breath as Mom runs into the room, her ponytail flying out behind her. It's weird; I almost forgot how alike we look.

"Mari?"

I grin. "Hi, Mommy."

Mom collapses onto the bed, wrapping her arms around my neck and squeezing me tight, laughing and crying at the same time.

The contact with her skin intensifies the emotions rolling off of her, blurring the line between where my emotions end and hers begin. Several other abilities activate—I hear the thoughts spinning through her head, get flashes of her past, and see images from her possible futures.

I don't have time to collect myself and shut them off before Dad runs into the room, catching the doorframe to spin himself in the right direction. Dr. Carroll is a second behind him.

"I'm not dreaming, am I?" Dad asks, his voice thick and his eyes gleaming. "Because I think I've had this dream before."

"Not dreaming," I tell him over Mom's shoulder as I stroke her back, smiling through the tears falling from my eyes, wrung from me by the crush of emotions that aren't even mine. It's hard to breathe, but everyone thinks my slight gasps are because of the tears. "Not this time."

A second later, Dad joins us, wrapping his arms around both Mom and me and crying.

Relief, joy, worry, love—their emotions all crash against me at once, muddling together until I don't know what I'm feeling. I see their first date, when Dad took Mom all the way to New York City to see a symphony. I shudder as chills wrack my body, a blast of icy energy coming from somewhere in the house.

The weight of it all is too intense. It's like someone has changed the pressure in the room until it's so heavy I'm being crushed underneath nothing but air. Pushing back all of the abilities at once doesn't work. They slip past me. Even one at a time, I can't get them all to shut down. I have to pick one to keep. Fast. It's only been a few seconds, but the longer I struggle with this, the more my grip on everything else slips.

Glancing at Hudson, I lock everything but telepathy away.

The thoughts of everyone in the room are almost weightless after the press of emotions and visions that assaulted me. At least until I hear Hudson's thoughts.

"—and you really think it'd be any different now? Bullshit. Even on their good days it was never like this. No way in any level of hell were they going to let you stay after what happened to J.R." He looks away from us and stares through the window into the backyard. "Horace would've wanted to be here for this. The old man better be okay."

He pulls out his phone and sends a text to Horace, actively forcing his mind away from memories of his own family. My chest aches for him, and I close my eyes, relaxing into my parents' tight embrace, letting their arms and their meaningless, reassuring words surround me and wanting so badly to walk across the room and do the same thing for Hudson.

My stomach grumbles so loud everyone hears.

"Oh!" Mom pulls away, a huge grin on her face. "Oh, you must be *starving*! What would you like? I can make you that salmon pasta you always loved when you were little? Or we can order in?"

I wipe my eyes and rub my stomach. "At this point, even a jar of peanut butter and a spoon sounds delicious."

"Here, let me get these out of your arm." Carroll bends down and gently peels off the tape holding my IV in place. "You're going to be a little weak. It'll probably be a few days before you can—"

I smile as his eyes widen. One drop of blood escaped before the hole the needle made in my arm was gone. Healed as though it was never there. A second later, even the slight bruise surrounding the injection site fades.

"Never mind." Carroll grins. "You might be up and about a *bit* sooner."

A slow smile curves across Hudson's lips, making my heart beat faster.

"If they're impressed by that, wait till they see what else she can do."

In his mind, I see the moments he noticed strange things happening—when I heated up in the hospital, when everything in the room suddenly tilted toward me, when the room started warping in front of his eyes. He's guessing at what those moments mean, but his guesses are pretty damn close. Pyrokinesis, telekinesis, and illusions.

"Well," Mom says, laughing a little. "I can't say I'm disappointed *that's* something you came back with."

Carroll quickly unhooks me from a few tubes I really don't want to think about. Then, Mom snaps her fingers and chases the guys from the room so she can help me get dressed. She talks the whole time. It's strange to hear her reference the power of the stones and Hudson's different abilities like they're commonplace, but I guess she's had a month to adapt to the idea.

We move into the kitchen, and I sit next to Hudson, moving my chair as close to him as I can. He smiles, but he doesn't say anything. He wouldn't. Not now, when my parents could hear him. I stay close to him for the rest of the day, trying to show him without words that he has nothing to be scared of.

Later in the afternoon, Mom mentions calling the rest of the family, sharing the good news of my recovery. Dad's thoughts cloud over in an instant, his mind traveling to his sister Jacquelyn and my cousin Julian.

He's still missing. All anyone has been able to figure out so far is that he wasn't abducted. They finally found him on several traffic cameras walking away from the house with a backpack and a duffle bag almost as big as his entire body. If he was kidnapped, it wasn't until after he left on his own.

Focusing on Julian, his quick smile and his intelligence and his inexhaustible optimism, I grasp for an ability that might help me track him down. Or at least tell me if he's all right. Despite the combined abilities of several moderately talented prophets, it's as if a dense fog surrounds Julian. I get the sense that he's alive and safe, but I have no idea where he's hiding. He could be in Vegas or Venice for all I know.

Taking a chance, I think about Horace's missing granddaughter, Nadette. It's harder to get as much as I sensed about Julian, maybe because I've never met her. I don't even know what she looks like. All I have is the vague picture Hudson has of her—a sixteen-year-old redhead. I can see Horace, the circles under his eyes and the weariness hanging around him as the search for Nadette drags into the fourth week. From what I can tell, she's alive, but that isn't much to go on. It's not worth mentioning. I don't have *anything* except a feeling I don't understand.

I try to focus on my parents, on how thrilled they are to have me back. To hear me speaking. The whole night, though, there's something splitting my attention away from Hudson and my parents. On top of the physical pressure of their attention—like layers and layers of thick blankets being thrown over my head—the energy upstairs pulls at me. The strange chill I felt when my parents' sudden contact overwhelmed me. Whatever is upstairs is sharp and cold and insistent, a gravity well that keeps trying to suck me in. Hudson and my family help keep me anchored, but I can't ignore it forever.

Sooner rather than later, Hudson and I are going to have to face whatever is waiting up there.

It's almost midnight and my parents are exhausted, but they fight it off, swallowing their yawns and shaking themselves awake every time they start to drift. Carroll gave up the fight an hour ago—after I promised to give him a more detailed description of what I experienced during my coma—but my parents will need to be nudged.

After a second of searching, I find the ability I need and turn it on. I glance at Hudson, remembering his reaction when he realized I could hear his thoughts and wondering how much worse it would be if he knew what I was about to do. But I don't like the chill I'm getting from upstairs, and I don't want anyone else getting involved in this.

Reaching out for my parents' minds and upstairs for Dr. Carroll's, I plant a suggestion. A couple of them, really. The idea that they should go to bed because they're so tired and then stay there until morning.

"Sleep. Rest." When they hear it, they'll think the whisper is coming from their own mind. "Everything will be fine until morning. Mariella will be fine."

It takes a few minutes for the suggestion to take root, but eventually Mom's eyes droop shut and stay shut for a few seconds. Dad smiles and nudges her awake. "I think it's time for us to go to sleep."

Mom looks around and nods. "You'll come get us if you need anything, Mari? Please?"

I lean closer to her and press a kiss to her cheek. "Promise."

I wait, holding out until they drift off to sleep before I tell Hudson, "There's something upstairs we need to take care of."

He tilts his head toward my bedroom. "The trinkets the demon left for you?"

"Yeah." We're a floor away from that drawer of glass, yet it feels like I'm standing next to an open industrial freezer. For Hudson, it's simply a reminder of what almost happened that night and the month-long recovery period after. There's nothing tangible about it to him.

We head upstairs, both of us holding our breath as we step inside my room.

The cold gets worse, but Hudson doesn't notice. I know he sensed it before the fight with Orane, but he doesn't anymore. It's like it's tied directly to me. He's aware of what's in the drawer, but he approaches it the same way he would a box of rattlesnakes rather than a dark, yawning force. Whatever those glass trinkets have transformed into tugs at the center of my chest and tries to pull me forward. It's like a black hole sucking in everything. I shudder and stop walking, letting him take the last few steps alone.

I heighten my sense of awareness, trying to pinpoint what this is. All I can tell is that the energy doesn't go through Hudson. It's going *aroun•* him. Those trinkets were never linked to Hudson, but they know me. Whatever they've become is looking for *me*.

Hudson crouches next to the drawer and glances at me as though asking for permission. I nod, even though I want to evacuate the house and condemn it so no one will ever come in contact with whatever is inside that drawer.

With a slow, deep breath, Hudson opens the drawer carefully.

When I see what's inside, I blink. The drawer of tainted trinkets is nothing but broken bits of glass. *What?*

"Huh." Hudson leans over the drawer. To him, it's a little anticlimactic. Then again, he doesn't sense the cold, dark energy pulsing out of that drawer. I want to yank him back, but it'll scare him. And it's not after him.

"Hey, be grateful for what we get." I force myself to smile and nudge him gently with my foot. "Would you rather have had smoke and fireworks?"

Hudson shudders, his mind replaying the destruction of Orane's world. "No. I've had enough of that to last a while."

He flicks through his vision filters, searching for any lingering energy, but none of these fragments show even a glimmer of light. Whatever this is, Hudson can't see or sense it at all. He's not stupid, though. He knows that the dreamworld—that Abivapna—is far more complex than he thought—and he knows that underestimating what the Balasura can do is dangerous.

"Are you picking anything up?" he asks me.

My entire body shudders, and I clench my hands, forcing myself to step a little closer to the drawer. Closing my eyes, I feel the room. The dresser, the nightstand, Hudson—everything in this room has a presence. I can see its shape and its energy in incredible detail inside my head. Everything except what's in that drawer. In my mental map of the room, that drawer is an empty black space.

"It's like there's nothing there," I finally tell him.

Hudson relaxes a little. "Well, that's good, right?"

"No." I look around the room and shake my head, trying to find the words to explain. "I can feel everything in this room. I could walk around blindfolded and not run into anything, even if you moved it all around. But this is *nothing*. Like it doesn't exist in our world."

"Creepy," he thinks. As though my description of what is inside that drawer made him more aware of it, he shivers and tightens his grip, holding himself in place by willpower alone. "So we probably shouldn't touch it."

My voice barely stays level when I answer. "I wouldn't recommend it."

"Good to know."

Carefully removing the stones lining the edges, Hudson dumps the whole drawer into a garbage bag I pull out of the bathroom.

"We'll drive out past the edge of town and burn it all. Melt it down," he thinks.

Will that work?

Sometimes if I ask a question, the answer will kind of appear—the combined powers of a couple of fortune tellers Orane destroyed—but this time I don't see anything. That in itself makes me nervous.

"And then what are you going to do with it?" I ask silently. He jumps a little, but otherwise he's perfectly accepting of the fact that I've invaded his head again. "If you think the bits have power left, how do you know fire is going to get rid of it?"

"Damnit," he groans silently, his mind already whirring as he tries to come up with a new solution. After a few seconds, he looks up at me. "Okay, well, we'll collect the ashes, lock them into a crystal-lined container, and bury the whole thing. If we ever find a way to get rid of it for good, we can come back and collect it."

I hesitate, but I can't think of anything better. Or even see what might happen if we follow through with this plan. The future is fuzzy, a hazy field of vague possibilities that all seem equally impossible.

"Yeah, sure," I finally say. "As long as this stuff is well out of our reach. Out of *everybody's* reach."

Forty-Two

Hudson

Thursday, October 16 – 12:52 AM

Mari and I sneak out of the house. Inside the plastic storage container I'm carrying are the bag of broken glass and a bunch of crystals and gemstones. Both of us are silent until we get into the Camaro, the box locked away in the trunk.

"How much trouble do you think we'll be in if they wake up and we're not there?" I ask, looking back at her house as I pull away.

"They won't."

There's no hesitation in her answer. My future dreams are vague and full of symbols. Whatever sense Mariella gets must be a lot more concrete.

"It's hard to explain," she says, answering the question I didn't ask. Swallowing, I lock my thoughts on the here and now. "Sometimes, when I think about a question I…know. But that's not…that's not how I know they won't check on me, though."

I crank the engine and head toward the Adirondack Park. "How did you know?"

Mari bites her lip and looks away. "Because I planted the idea in their heads that they didn't need to."

My chest and neck prickle. She planted ideas in their heads? My hands tighten on the wheel and I try to keep my head clear, but it's impossible. She's already *messing* with her parents' minds. That's way too close to something the demons would do.

"I know. Hudson, I *know,* but we needed to do this tonight, to get that stuff out of the house." She turns toward me in the seat, her lips pursed. "You couldn't feel it, but those bits of glass were sucking in energy and warmth like a black hole. It was awful. I had to get that out of the house, and I knew my parents would freak if they woke up and we weren't there."

I saw for myself the power she had before she woke up, before she even could process everything that was happening to her. What if all that changed her? Her reasons make sense, but most people can rationalize their mistakes. All the way until their mistakes have turned them into villains in their own lives.

Mari sighs, and I cringe, knowing she's following my train of thought.

"I tried to turn it off," she whispers. "I did. But there are too many things in my head. Keeping them *all* off takes too much energy out of me. I had to reactivate something, and the telepathy was the easiest to handle."

"It's fine." Not being able to privately process my own thoughts is going to take some getting used to, though. That's for damn sure.

She huffs. "It's *not* fine, but I appreciate the lie. Kind of."

Rolling my shoulders, I keep my eyes locked on the dark, empty road ahead of us. "Okay. It's weird, but I don't care about that as much as what you did to your parents."

Mari is silent. I glance at her.

"I don't even know what you're capable of, Mariella, but you picked up a lot of abilities that could turn you into someone I don't think you'd like much. And if you start using those powers like the demons do..." I take a breath and shake my head. "They'll have won anyway, because you'll end up just like them."

This time there's a slight pause before she clears her throat. Even with my eyes on the road, I feel her shift, feel the warmth of her getting closer.

"That's why I need your help. I need you to keep me grounded and help me figure out what to do with everything. It's too much for me to deal with alone."

My chest clenches. "Basically, you want me to call you on your bullshit?"

I can handle being used like a walking conscience, I guess, but it's not what I hoped...Whatever. It doesn't matter.

"Yeah. Bullshit meter, walking conscience, all of that, but..." Mari's hand rests on my elbow, gently pulling my hand off the wheel until she can thread her fingers through mine. "But not just that. You could never *just* be that."

My heart starts pounding, and I press on the brake, exceedingly glad no one else is driving on this road. We glide to a stop, and I stare at her hand in mine, my throat dry and my thoughts such a mess I doubt either of us can make sense of them.

"You don't..." The words disappear. I swallow and try again. "You don't have to say that. I'd be here to help you if you needed it without...anything. You don't have to—"

She shifts, pulling her legs underneath her on the seat and placing one hand on my cheek, tilting my head until I'm looking into her warm eyes.

"You're right. I don't *have* to do anything." She smiles and runs her hand over my hair, lingering on the scar by my temple and the one hidden on the side of my head. "I'm done doing things because I have to or because someone else wants me to. I've lived my entire life like that. Now I can finally choose."

The pressure she exerts is nothing, less than a breeze, but I don't have the power to resist even that. I don't want to.

Mari pulls me in, closing the few inches between us until my lips meet hers.

Sparks—actual, tiny sparks of electricity—flare between us, making my skin tingle and my hair stand on end. She sighs, pressing closer, practically climbing onto the console between us and releasing my hand. Wrapping both arms around my neck, she tightens her grip and deepens the kiss, running her tongue along my lip and sending shivers across my skin.

My entire body is overheating, and my thoughts aren't spinning—they're gone, my mind wiped clean by the shock of Mariella's lips moving against mine. The kiss releases a month of stress and worry and all of the emotions I've kept bottled up since before we walked into the dreamworld to face Orane. Even if I hadn't already been there, this kiss would've done it. This kiss would have been all it took for her to stake her claim on my heart.

Too soon, she pulls back, her hands coming to rest on my cheeks. She smiles against my lips, but I can't make my eyes open yet.

"Sorry," she whispers, her voice a little lower than it was a minute ago and her fingers tracing the planes of my face. "I've been wanting to do that since I woke up this morning."

"Yeah. No, it's okay." I swallow and finally open my eyes. "Works for me."

I take a breath and clear my throat, wishing it was as easy to clear the fog that kiss left me in. Blissed out by a kiss or not, there's still a conversation we need to finish.

"You shouldn't have done that to your parents. They could've handled the truth."

"Yeah. And then they would have insisted on coming with us." Mari's smile fades, but she doesn't pull away from me. Her fingers run back and forth over my close-cropped hair as she talks. "I don't know what we're dealing with, and I don't know what's going to happen. Putting us in front of it is one thing because we're going to be a lot harder to hurt than anyone else. After everything I've already put my parents through, how could I let them walk into something I wasn't sure I'd be able to protect them from?"

Looking away, I stare at the still-empty road and try to wrap my head around it all. Wanting to protect someone you love—I get that. I really do. I wanted to keep Horace the hell away from this mess, but I couldn't force him out. I always told him what could happen, the danger he put himself in by staying, and let him make his own choices. It's too easy to use the reasoning that you're protecting someone to justify going too far and taking away someone's right to put themselves in danger for a cause they believe in. Life happens. Things go wrong. You can't save everyone.

"You have to promise not to do that to me, Mariella. Not ever. Even if you think you're protecting me."

Turning to her, I wait. She meets my eyes, but she's biting her lip again. She looks troubled.

"I can't promise that. Not if it could save your life. You can't ask me to promise that."

"Mari, you can't choose—"

"Could *you*?" She sits up, her eyebrows sitting low across her eyes and giving her face a more determined expression than I've ever seen on it. "Could you promise me that you won't ever, *ever* try to leave me behind if you thought letting me choose for myself might kill me?"

My entire body tenses. Even thinking about it shoves all of my protective instincts into overdrive.

Mari's expression softens, and she puts a hand on my arm.

"I *can* promise that I'd never pull a trick on you that you wouldn't try to pull on me."

Exhaling a breath I didn't realize I was holding, I reach out and brush her long bangs behind her ear. Mari turns her face into the touch, pressing her cheek against my fingers and lightly kissing the palm of my hand.

I smile and give in. Like I'm sure she knew I would.

"Fine. But you also can't get mad at me for things I don't say out loud."

Her eyes narrow and her nose wrinkles. Leaning forward, she presses a soft kiss to my lips before sliding back into her seat. "I'll try. And that's the best I can do."

Nodding my agreement, I push the gas to get us moving again. Both of us are silent until we pass the edge of the park and she asks, "Do you know where you're going?"

I don't want to admit it, but no. Not really. I just know I need a place far from civilization where we can set a bonfire and not draw attention. I'm working off a vague idea that I'll know it when I get there.

"There" ends up being a lonely spot on an out-of-the-way road somewhere in the Adirondacks, standing over a metal trashcan filled with all the signs of Mari's previous life, which are doused in three bottles of lighter fluid. My life is insane.

"Here goes nothing," Mari mutters.

I take a deep breath and light a match. When I drop it into the trashcan, Mari tenses beside me, pulling me back in time to keep my eyebrows from getting singed off my face.

A roaring column of flames leaps into the sky, the bright white fire shot through with the sickening orange of the dreamworld.

"The dreamworld? It's called Abivapna," Mariella says, her eyes locked on the column of fire. "And the things that live there are the Balasura."

"Sounds too pretty for what they are. I think 'demons' fits better," I mutter as I wad up the garbage bag and throw it into the flames. It melts and disappears before I can blink. Still the fire rages. The sound is more like a forge and bellows, not a bonfire, and the height and heat of the column is crazy. This is no natural fire. It's feeding on far from ordinary fuel.

Mari and I sit at the edge of the clearing, waiting and watching and hoping no one will see the light and investigate. My instincts guided me well. We're miles from humanity.

As abruptly as the fire engulfed the night, it stops. The light and the heat cave in on themselves, folding in faster and faster until they disappear.

"Um, okay." I blink in the sudden darkness, trying to refocus. "*That* was interesting…"

We approach the trashcan slowly, not sure what to expect. Will the fire leap up again? I probably won't be able to touch it for a while because of the heat, but curiosity overwhelms caution and I slowly lean over the top.

How in the hell…?

A black box sits at the center of the can, shiny and apparently solid, and the entire bottom of the trashcan has been eaten away. I step back, flashing through vision filters to make sure I haven't turned one dangerous form of magic into another. None of the filters show anything except a heat-wave-like aura coming off the box. The can itself doesn't register as warm. No heat waves emanating, no steam rising, nothing.

"Mari, do you sense anything?"

"Actually, no." She peers into the trashcan and smiles. "Aren't you going to get it? I mean, who are we to shy away from weird?"

I smile, slowly reach down, and pick up the box, only mildly surprised to find it cold. I switch to a filter that gives me better night vision and investigate the case.

It's about the same size as a ream of paper and made of hard, shiny black plastic. Or something plastic-like. Bits of metal line the side where the case would open, and a solid piece slightly larger than the pad of my thumb is set in place of a latch. A latch that doesn't move.

"It's like what we wanted shaped what actually happened." I pass the box to Mari. "We wanted the fire contained, we wanted the ash sealed away, we wanted to make sure no bit of anything was left on the can itself. Mission accomplished, apparently."

"I was hoping it would work." Mari shrugs, inspecting the box. "Didn't say anything because I wasn't sure. All this stuff is kinda hit or miss with me."

Hit or miss? She can read minds with scary accuracy, plant suggestions in people's heads, and magically create a black box out of a trash can, a plastic bag, and fire. I'd call that impressive on any level. But we're always our own worst critics, I guess. Then again, she's been in conscious control of her powers for less than a day. I've had mine for almost six months, and I don't even know what half of my powers *are*.

I grab a shovel out of my trunk and place the black box inside the stone-lined plastic storage container I brought with me. I choose a distinctive rock feature and walk ten steps to the west before I begin to dig. I have no idea why we'll ever want to see this again, but just in case, we need to know where to find it.

"That went pretty well," Mari says when we're back in the car and headed home. "No portals of doom, no park rangers yelling about forest fires, no explosions. I'd call that a success."

I laugh. "Were you *expecting* a portal of doom?"

"You should always be prepared for everything," she says, nodding with mock seriousness.

Her hand slides down my neck, traces the line of my arm—lingering for a moment on the tattoo on my wrist—and then she twines her fingers through mine. I lift her hand to my lips and kiss her soft, unscarred skin before letting our hands rest on her thigh.

Neither of us says anything for the rest of the drive, but it's the kind of silence that speaks volumes.

Forty-Four

Mariella

Thursday, October 16 – 3:59 AM

Since neither of us was going to sleep anyway, I spent the rest of the night sitting on the couch with Hudson, teaching him how to keep people—me, specifically—out of his head. By the time my parents and Carroll come downstairs around eight, he's almost mastered it.

"I must have been more tired than I realized," Mom says over breakfast. "I don't think I moved once the entire night."

Hudson glances at me and then away, the slightest tinge of concern lingering in his thoughts.

"Sudden relief of a chronic stressor can release a flood of chemicals in your brain that help you sleep," Carroll says between massive bites of pancake. "I didn't move last night either."

His frown getting a tiny bit deeper, Hudson shifts his food around his plate with his fork. I put my hand on his back, but before I can repeat my promise not to use my powers for evil, I hear new minds on the edge of my awareness. People I recognize.

I look toward the front door, mentally tracking their progress up the street. "K.T. and Dawn are almost here."

Dad laughs. "I'm surprised they stayed away as long as they did. They said they wanted to give us some time to catch up when we called them yesterday, but it sounded more like they were in the middle of a project they didn't want to drop."

Definitely the second one. I can hear it in their thoughts, the excitement that they finally figured out how to track down DreamWeaver, the webmaster of Dawn's favorite New Age blog, *The Mystical Demystifie*•. That's what they were working on yesterday, and that's why they didn't burst through the door as soon as they heard I'd opened my eyes.

I get up to wait for them by the front door and Hudson follows, his hand finding mine. Smiling, I lead him onto the porch and lean against his chest, pulling his arms over my shoulders. He hums quietly, the sound low and almost like a purr as he leans down and kisses the top of my head.

K.T. pulls to a stop in front of the house and waves at us, a huge grin splitting across her face. She points in our direction, and Dawn waves, too, the motion so furious she almost knocks her own glasses off.

"Don't get mad, but I had to pull in outside help," K.T. says as she runs up the yard, a backpack of crystals on her back and her arms held out for a hug.

In her thoughts, I see Danny hunched over a laptop, his attention locked on the screen and K.T.'s attention locked on him.

"It's fine, K." I smile and hug the only friend who held onto the memories I'd forgotten. Pulling back a little, I meet her eyes. "As long as you didn't tell Danny *why* he was helping."

K.T.'s forehead wrinkles, and her cheeks flush a little. "How'd you know it was Danny?"

Hudson steps up behind me and taps the top of my head with one finger. "Telepath."

"Seriously?" Dawn laughs. "I am *so* glad Hudson walked into my store. You people are *awesome*!"

"Telepath?" K.T. thinks. "For real? Supercali—"

"—*fragilistic*expialidocious," I finish for her.

She laughs, only a tinge of nervousness in the sound. "Wow. *That's* going to take some getting used to."

"So Danny found DreamWeaver?" Hudson asks.

"Yeah. He's always been a computer genius. I told him I needed a no-questions-asked favor, and he said yes. I asked him *after* I tried, though. We couldn't figure out how to find more than an email address."

One word is ricocheting around her head. A place, actually. Alaster.

"Where is Alaster?" I ask.

"Eastern side of the state," Dawn says, grinning and bouncing slightly. She's so excited her words almost run in time with her thoughts. "In between Albany and New York. And DreamWeaver isn't the only person who might be there."

My heart skips a beat. "Survivors? You think you found other people who survived the Balasura?"

K.T.'s head tilts. "The what?"

Hudson explains the new vocabulary I discovered, but my vision loses focus as something else appears before me. Some*where* else.

Nestled in the foothills of the Adirondacks, the town is small enough to call itself a village. Mostly residential, Alaster has a single business center with some shops and a diner. One of those shops is a New Age store where a girl with blue hair and dark eyes is waiting. For what, I don't know, but she's waiting.

Taking a deep breath, I refocus on my surroundings in time to hear Dawn explain the oddities of Alaster.

"And then we found out that this place has had a crime rate of zero for the past decade." Dawn shakes her head.

"*Zero*. I mean, come on! For ten years? Even the nicest of small towns has something. Sometimes just people getting drunk and stupid, but still. Something! Alaster has no theft, no murders, no vandalism, no social service cases—nothing. And weirder, no one else has noticed that this place is, like, perfect."

That little bit of information is plenty for Hudson. He's already intrigued. He's remembering J.R. and his fight with Calease, ignoring his disappointment that I didn't come back from my own battle with the answers he came to Swallow's Grove looking for, and hoping that Alaster might give him another lead. Or at least one more piece to this impossible puzzle.

Even before I ask the question, I think I know the answer.

I raise an eyebrow and smile at Hudson. "So...road trip?"

His thoughts are spinning, but an answering smile creeps across his face.

"Hell, yes. Road trip."

Acknowledgments

It takes an entire cast to write a novel, so, in order of appearance, my thanks are as follows:

First to my mom, Corey, for never letting me give up on anything, even if it seemed impossible sometimes. I love you, Mom. Thank you for absolutely everything.

To my dad, David, who developed my love of fantasy at an early age. I love you!

To my sister, Haley, who's always one of my first readers and helps me push through by asking for more. I know you've read this already, love—probably a hundred times by now—but it's officially a book! Read it again!

To my sister, Colleen, who promised to put aside her general dislike of books long enough to read mine. I love you, baby girl!

To my dear friend Lani Woodland who asked me one day, "Do you have a short story you can submit to an anthology I'm putting together?" and, when I told her no, said, "Well, can you write one?" Without you, this particular book would not have been born. Thank you for being so supportive. It's hard not to smile when I talk to you!

A thank you in three parts: To Kate Nash and her song "Mariella" from the album Made of Bricks, to Silversun Pickups and their song "Creation Lake" from the album Pikul, and last, but possibly most important, to shuffle on my iPod for putting these two songs back-to-back at 7:30 AM while I was still half-asleep. Who can explain the spark that lights an imaginary fire? However it happened, these three combined provided the fuel.

To Rita J. Webb who accepted Lani's anthology, but said to me, "I think this story might work better as a novel." Thank you, Rita, for pushing me in the right direction.

To the staff at my Starbucks, especially Claudio, Matt, Matt, and Prescilla. You guys kept me well caffeinated and entertained during my marathon editing sessions! And you were all appropriately impressed when you found out why I was camped out in the corner of the café every single night.

To my friends and colleagues who tossed in their two cents when I went begging for edits: Lani Woodland, Taylor Thompson, Patrick Shawn Rowell, Asja Parrish, and Mary Gray.

To the Washington, D.C. chapter of RWA who awarded me the 2012 Marlene Award for SSN and gave me the confidence to send my story into the world.

To my wonderful editresses Patricia Riley and Danielle Ellison who heard the pitch for my story on a rooftop in New York and looked at each other and said, "Oh my God" and "I know, right?!" I think I knew at that moment I wanted to work with you both. Since then, nothing has changed my mind. Thank you for your support, your insight, your Skype calls, and for just being you.

To the entire Spencer Hill family, including but not limited to Kate Kaynak, Rich Storrs, Cindy Thomas, Britta Gigliotti, Briana Dyrness, Anna Masrud, and everyone I haven't yet had the chance to meet. You guys rock!

To Michael Stearns who gave me a chance and introduced me to my wonderful agent, Danielle Chiotti. And to Danielle, thank you for keeping me calm and on track. Thank you for your faith and your passion and your awesomeness. Most of all, thank you for looking at my incredibly weird situation and seeing the potential instead of the complications. I hope I continue to impress you.

Thank you to my cover designer Jeremy West whose talent is kind of insane. I'm excited to see where the next few years take you, Mr. West!

Last but definitely not least, thank you to everyone who picks up this book and gives it a chance. I haven't met you and I might not ever, but you're making it possible for me to do what I love. Thank you.

About the Author

Erica Cameron knew that writing was her passion when she turned a picture book into a mystery novella as a teen. That piece wasn't her best work, but it got her an A. After college, she used her degree in Psychology and Creative Writing to shape a story about a dreamworld. Then a chance encounter at a rooftop party in Tribeca made her dream career a reality. *Sing Sweet Nightingale* is her first novel.

25674507R10214

Made in the USA
Charleston, SC
11 January 2014